# SPIRIT OF
# THE BAYONET

Martha,
   So Glad we are Neighbors!
Wishing you all the Best! Come
Up for Wine Anytime!

Ted R

THE 'OKAMI FORWARD' TRILOGY
Book 1
[+]

# SPIRIT OF THE BAYONET

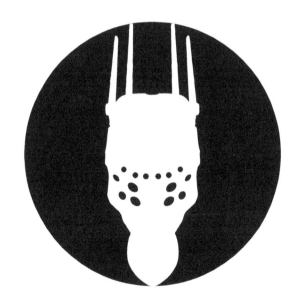

# TED RUSS

Published by Chinook Publishing LLC.

ISBN: 978-1-7343925-0-0

Author photograph: Raymond McCrae Jones

Cover design, illustration & interior formatting:
Mark Thomas / Coverness.com

*This one is for Henry.*
*My buddy. My comrade.*

# Chapter One

*Mission Cycle 383*

*Earth Year 2062*

*286,281,216 Kilometers from Earth*

C aptain Nathan Drake's station on the bridge was a testament to the engineering efforts that had kept the *Odysseus* running to and from the asteroid belt for almost thirty years. Decades-old equipment, still doing its job, sat next to state-of-the-art technology in a large horseshoe-shaped console that surrounded the command chair. The setting appealed to Paul. It was good to know that he was not the only subject of multiple retrofits.

"Sir, all cycle inspections for the week completed," Paul said as he floated up onto the bridge. "No discrepancies noted."

Drake hovered before the large forward window, his back to the command station, the infinite void to his front. He wore his navy-blue dress uniform, the rank of merchant marine captain on his shoulders. More than a year into their voyage, and it was still the only thing Paul had ever seen him wear. But the gold buttons and piping, like many things about the captain, had grown on Paul.

Captain Drake stretched one magnetized boot down to the floor to gain purchase and turned his thin body from the window. Decades in space had wrecked him. He was as skinny as a skeleton and paler than a cadaver.

"Anything interesting this week?" the captain asked, taking the inspection sheet from Paul.

"Actually, yes," Paul said. "One of the closets on the bottom level of the utility module contained a couple dozen pairs of leather combat boots."

"Leather combat boots?" Drake asked.

"Yes, sir. And ten boxes of black shoe polish."

"Only the military," Drake said with disgust.

Paul nodded in agreement.

"Seriously, Prisoner Owens," Drake said. "Who the hell brings useless leather combat boots on board a space freighter? They would do no good on Mars or anywhere else. They are purely ceremonial."

Drake shook his head.

"And I can just picture those dumb bastards shining their useless boots for months. Please tell me you didn't do that shit."

"I only did as I was told, sir," Paul said with a shrug.

"See that the boots are destroyed."

"I will, sir."

"I suppose you've earned your ration, Prisoner," Drake said, pushing off from the floor toward a locked utility closet on the far side of the bridge.

The bridge was part of the command-and-control module, or CnC, that sat on top of a narrow superstructure that rose fifty meters from the top center of the *Odysseus*'s hull. The teardrop-shaped module enclosed two levels, offering two thousand square feet of weightless, pressurized crew area. The bridge took up the top level of the CnC, and it was from there that Drake commanded his ship. The bottom level of the CnC held a small medical bay with one of the ship's two medpods, the captain's private quarters, a galley kitchen, and a storage area.

Captain Drake returned to Paul with a large silver flask and a smile visible beneath his dark beard. He kept it neatly trimmed. The black hair contrasted starkly with his pale-white skin.

Paul smiled back to conceal his unease. The captain had started sharing his personal store of bourbon with Paul almost fifty cycles ago. At first, it was novel and fun. And Paul liked bourbon. The shots mellowed Drake out, and he would start talking about his decades underway. Once the old man got going, he could talk about spacefaring for hours. Paul would float there next to the captain, sipping on bourbon and only half listening as he gazed out of the forward window at the void.

Now Paul thought the old man drank too much.

*Does it really matter?* Paul thought. *Doesn't the executive officer run everything at this point?*

Paul still loved that forward window, though. The wide, curving floor-to-ceiling glass presented a 180-degree field of view in the direction of flight. The top of the *Odysseus*'s forward hull stretched out below for more than a kilometer. The habitat and utility modules spun around like they were attached to opposite tips of a large propeller fixed to the nose of the ship.

The stars were legion, but there was no visual reference close enough to indicate that they were hurtling toward the asteroid belt at over thirty thousand kilometers per hour. Looking out the window, it seemed to Paul that the *Odysseus* was caught in the doldrums of space. Derelict, lonely, and beautiful.

"You know they laid this old girl's keel in 2038?" the captain said, gesturing out of the large window at the ship. "Almost thirty years ago."

Paul did know. He had heard it at least a hundred times.

"She was built, like the rest of her line, in high lunar orbit but has spent most of her time out here, running to the asteroid belt and back," Drake said. "She was the second M Class freighter to be commissioned, and now that the *Perseus* has officially been declared lost, she is the longest serving of her line. They brought her executive officer on line in 2040, and she was underway to the belt for the first time late that year."

The captain gestured at the great window.

"You know, if she had been built just a few years later, we'd be floating here looking at a bullshit multimode display system instead of out into all of that."

Drake held his flask in front of his face and opened it. He jerked it forward and back quickly, ejecting a small blob of golden-hued bourbon. It quivered and flexed for a few seconds before stabilizing into a perfect sphere spinning inches in front of Captain Drake's head.

Captain Drake leaned forward and sucked the floating orb of bourbon between his teeth into his mouth and then exhaled with a satisfied, "Aaahhhhhhh…"

The captain looked at Paul. "Give me a window any day," he said. "I hate to think of looking at some damn machine's interpretation of all that, rather than the real thing."

The captain handed the flask to Paul with a wink.

"Thank you, sir."

Paul ejected a large shot of bourbon out of the flask. He looked at his distorted reflection in the liquid and then swallowed it, enjoying the sugary burn as it went down. He handed the flask back to the captain.

They floated in front of the window, alternating shots of bourbon.

"Do you know the last time I walked on solid ground?" Drake asked.

"No, sir."

"Guess."

"Ten years?"

"Twenty."

Paul looked at the captain with raised eyebrows.

The captain nodded proudly. "Not Earth or Mars or even an asteroid in over twenty years."

"Where was it?"

"What?"

"Your last solid footstep."

"Earth. Back in '42."

"Do you miss it?"

"Miss what?"

"Earth."

"Not really. There are some people I miss. But I don't miss that nasty planet."

"That's a long time," was all Paul could think to say.

"There was a time when NASA thought spending that length of time in space wasn't possible. They thought that men and women would go crazy." Drake handed Paul the flask and looked out of the window. "But me and my generation of spacefarers proved them wrong. Sure, we got skinny, worried constantly about cancer, and turned as pale as ghosts. But we didn't care. We lived among the stars in a stark, apolitical, and beautiful universe that was trying to kill us. And we loved it."

The captain sounded more morose than usual to Paul.

"I know you think I'm a fool," Drake said. "That I'm weird. Well, you're fucking right. I'm a goddamn spacefarer. I've had comets fly within one kilometer of my ship. I've hauled asteroids that were so dense it took all engines at max burn a week to get us moving at a detectable velocity. I spent three days drifting in space, tethered to my ship, when an EVA went pear shaped. Fires. Reactor leaks. Decompression incidents. And, in the last few years, goddamn pirate attacks. Shit that would make an Earthsider piss their pants. But I loved it all. And I don't care that I look like an emaciated walking corpse now. Small sacrifice."

The captain looked from the window.

"Don't act like you don't know what I'm talking about, son! Look at you, for Chrissake!" he said. "Look what you let them do so you could serve. I mean, they reversed some of it, of course. But…"

The captain got quiet, sensing that he had gone too far.

But Paul was long past caring about his augmentation scars. The incision where they'd peeled back his scalp and put the brain interface cap in place was now a thin, hairless scar that encircled his head above his ears like a crown. The gap left by the removal of the rectangular data-communication module at the base of his skull had healed, but hair would never grow back there either. Paul did not try to conceal the scars. He kept his hair closely cropped so the marks were always visible. The battle-suit chassis attachment points at his major joints had done more damage. But those scars were usually covered by his clothes.

It was the absence of feeling that still bothered Paul. The expansive, multispectral, high-velocity feeling of belonging was gone forever now. And it was an absence that he knew the captain would not understand. So, he would smile and shake his head in an it's-OK gesture at the captain.

Paul knew it was coming then. The captain asked him to tell his stories.

"Come on, son," Drake said. "I know it was a world of shit for you. Just tell me a little. It's only out of respect that I ask."

Paul declined, as he did every time, but not without a twinge of guilt. He felt indebted to Captain Drake. The Fly It Off program was only open to prisoners convicted of nonviolent crimes. Paul had been an exception. Drake could have denied his assignment. Ultimately, crew composition was up to a ship's captain. But the old man had let Paul aboard.

Even so, Paul shook his head and said, "I'm sorry, sir."

Paul had sought out duty on the old freighter to isolate himself as much as possible, to be alone, to forget. Paul thought the four-year journey to the belt and back would be good for that. The triple credit for time against his sentence was a good thing too.

Paul's melancholy face, staring at the stars through the large window, pained the captain, and he gave up quickly. "At least we each served, son," Drake said, holding a hand over his heart. "Me in space, you in the mud… But we each served."

Paul usually left about then, and the captain would drink alone on the bridge afterward. Paul, back in his room, would meditate before going to bed to stave off the nightmares. So far, despite the captain's bullheaded insistence on bringing the old shit up, Paul had not had a single nightmare since he'd boarded the *Odysseus* more than a year ago.

"I love it out here," the captain said before Paul could turn to leave. "But it's different now. It's perverted. By those damn things."

Drake gestured angrily at one of the patrolling inspection-and-repair bots passing slowly from right to left about twenty-five meters in front of the window. It was one of the midsize units, twenty meters in length. It had the egg-like appearance of most of the IR bots: sensory equipment on the forward, thicker end of the asymmetric oval and main propulsion on the more tapered aft section. Two utility arms were folded against its belly, like the talons of a bird in flight. The unit used its maneuvering thrusters to keep itself pointed directly at the bridge's window as it slid slowly by. It was scanning the structure for integrity and wear and tear using ultraviolet and infrared spectrums. It was the kind of thing that always made Paul smile, reminding him of his unit and the amazing things they had done together. But as the bot passed the middle apex of the large window, the captain raised both hands, middle fingers extended, and said, "Fuck you!"

Paul chuckled. He looked down and past the offending IR bot, at the long forward length of the *Odysseus*. A handful of other IR bots were going about their patrols, looking for trouble. Their small size and quick movements further emphasized the *Odysseus*'s seeming lethargy.

"You know, the son of a bitch never asks my permission for any of this activity," the captain said angrily. "Every cycle, I watch swarms of those sneaky weasels prowling up and down my ship. I don't get so much as a 'how do you fucking do' from the executive officer. I hate it."

Paul knew Captain Drake was getting worked up when he referred to the XO by his full title. Drake said "executive officer" in a voice that dripped with sarcasm and anger. On any other ship, a captain's executive officer was his right-hand man, trusted above all others. Not on the *Odysseus*.

"You get the inspection logs, though, right?" asked Paul.

"Of course. But what else do you think they are doing?" the captain asked ominously. "They're damn sure not telling me the whole story."

Paul shook his head and rolled his eyes as he handed the flask of bourbon to the captain.

The captain's face was dark as he took the flask. "Fuck you, son. Used to be that spacefaring was a brotherhood of adventurers. We were crafty survivors facing long odds in an empty universe. I didn't care that no one on Earth, the Moon or Mars gave a shit. I knew they just wanted the commerce to flow, their cargo to show up on time. Didn't bother me. I knew where I fit in. Knew my part. Knew my role. Had authority. Now, though…" Drake took another large shot and swallowed hard. He rubbed his eyes and then looked at Paul.

Paul could see that the captain was getting worked up.

"I felt something off about this ship the moment I came aboard, you know," the captain told Paul.

"I know, sir."

"It was only about a month before you prisoners showed up," the captain continued. "The Company called me in and asked me to take command of the *Odysseus*, to take her to the belt and back. I was serving orbital dry-dock duty, waiting to command the next Romeo Class freighter, the *Satulah Prince*, on her maiden voyage. She had been promised to me."

Drake shook his head and then took another big swig of bourbon. He handed Paul the flask.

"But the *Odysseus*'s captain had fallen ill," Drake continued. "Hit with the cancer. It was a sudden thing, and the Company didn't want to miss the departure window. They didn't have anyone else. They tried to pump my ass full of sunshine and compliments, but I wasn't going for it. I told them no. 'You take the *Satulah Prince* away from me, and I'm done, goddamn it!' I yelled. I was so loud, I bet they heard me down on Earth."

Drake chuckled at the memory.

"After the meeting, though," he continued, his smile fading, "a friend of mine working in flight scheduling told me that there were no other belt-and-back command billets slotted to open up for at least two years. I was in a precarious position. If they decided to truly fuck me, I would have been stuck on that stinking orbital facility or, worse, Earth." Drake looked at Paul to make sure he was getting the severity of the situation.

Paul nodded.

"So, I swallowed my pride," Drake said, looking back to the window. "I ate my words, apologized, and took command of the *Odysseus*. I loved spacefaring too much to give it up, despite my chapped ass."

Paul resigned himself to staying a little longer, even though he had heard this part of Drake's story many times. He ejected another swallow of bourbon from the flask. It hung in front of the window like a small golden planet. The captain had always been good to Paul, and Paul had heard horror stories about the treatment of prisoners on other ships. Letting the captain vent background chatter for Paul's contemplations of the void through the glorious forward window was a small price to pay.

"And you know what?" the captain said, staring at the stars and not expecting an answer. "When Captain Drake takes command of a ship, it's a sacred goddamn thing. She's my ship now. I love her, and I'll get her and my crew to the asteroid belt and back safely, on time, and at a profit."

"I'm counting on it, sir," Paul said.

"The *Odysseus* is a strange old girl, though," the captain said with a rueful laugh. "In so many ways. The damn XO, for starters."

Paul stared out of the window, trying to ignore the captain.

"Look, Prisoner," the captain said, undaunted. "No one is going to make it to the belt and back without a powerful artificial intelligence continuously monitoring and controlling a ship's systems. And I have worked with some good ones in my time, AIs I considered shipmates.

"But I knew this one was a little off the first time I talked with him," the captain continued. "I knew his software had just been updated, so I tried not to dwell on it. Sometimes it takes a few cycles for those changes to get digested and smoothed out. But after our preflight planning meetings, I was convinced he was different, a little strange. So, I called a buddy.

"He's one of the best maintenance engineers in the fleet. He tore the CnC apart." Drake looked around in satisfaction. "Took out every communication and monitoring device from here down to the tube bulkhead." Drake pointed down through the floor at the main body of the *Odysseus*, a sly smile widening on his face. "Before anyone knew it, he had ripped out the XO's eyes and ears up here and installed a few good, old-fashioned, un-hackable mechanical switches." The captain pointed at his command chair, where he had shown Paul, maybe a dozen times, the switch that enabled the speakerphone and videoconferencing camera.

"Most everywhere else on the *Odysseus*, except some parts of power and propulsion, the XO can listen in and often see everything. Not so on my bridge," Drake said, nodding with satisfaction. "The XO can't hear or see shit in here unless I key the mic."

But the satisfaction faded, and Drake's face clouded with doubt.

"But sometimes I wonder," he whispered, his eyes darting nervously around the bridge.

Paul had had enough.

"Well, sir," Paul said, reaching a foot to the floor. "I'm going to hit the rack. Been a long cycle. I appreciate the bourbon, sir."

The captain nodded but grabbed Paul's shoulder to stop him. He gestured with his eyes and head toward the IR bot that was still in view. It was passing right to left now and almost to the edge of the window.

When it finally slid out of view, the captain reached into his tunic and pulled out a folded piece of paper. He thrust it into Paul's hand. Drake held a finger over his closed mouth to make sure Paul knew not to talk.

Paul nodded and pushed off the floor to leave.

Back in his quarters, Paul shook his head, remembering the captain's nervous look. He read the captain's note.

---

*They are out to get me. They are out to get all of us. We are trapped on this space freighter with a diabolical threat. I do not intend to go easily. I am very close to having what I need. But I sense that we are in more danger than ever. If I am killed before I can prove what he is plotting, you must know that it was the executive officer and his minions. You must avenge me and protect the crew!*

---

Paul walked over to his bureau and pulled open the top drawer. He lifted a stack of folded T-shirts and grimaced. Dozens of paranoid notes that Captain Drake had given him over the past cycles lay in a pile.

*This is why they should limit a person's time in space,* Paul thought.

He threw the latest note onto the pile and put the T-shirts back on top.

Paul closed the drawer and thought, *Crazy old man.*

# Chapter Two

*Mission Cycle 384*

*Earth Year 2062*

*286,654,464 Kilometers from Earth*

Paul woke the next cycle two hours before the all-hands meeting, as he always did. He rose, showered, and sat for his morning meditation before making himself a pot of coffee. He stood for a few moments holding a cup of the warm beverage, staring at the leather-bound book on his desk like a man sizing up a wrestling opponent.

The book lay in the center of an old wooden military field desk. Faded olive green with metal fittings, the sturdy rectangular table stood on four folding legs under the one small window in Paul's quarters. A simple metal chair was pushed under the center of the table, in front of the leather-bound book. The chair was also olive green, or was, decades ago. Now, dull aluminum showed through numerous dents and scrapes.

Paul pulled out the chair and sat down.

The stars pinwheeled slowly on the other side of the window as the habitat module corkscrewed through space. This was his favorite place to be on the *Odysseus*. In his chair, at his desk, in his quarters. Alone.

The habitat and utility modules were added to the *Odysseus* after she'd returned from her maiden belt-and-back voyage late in 2045. The Battle of Santiago had taken place earlier that year, and tensions with China were high despite the lull in earthly hostilities. It seemed the contest of superpowers, both military and commercial, was about to extend out into the solar system.

The Pentagon wanted the ability to put troops on Mars and gave Space Command the mission of getting them there. The soldiers had to be able to fight upon arrival. They couldn't be soft and gooey from nine months or more of zero gravity, so Space Command ordered the retrofit of all merchant space freighters with troop-carrying habitats. The large M class ships, like the Odysseus, got the biggest modifications.

The habitat and utility modules were pressurized to one atmosphere and spun around a center hub gear, providing one G. The long truss structure that spun them around contained an enclosed and pressurized passageway with a ladder, called "the traverse."

By 2050, during the height of the misguided preparations for war on Mars, each M Class freighter had up to ten of these rotating habitat assemblies stacked on its nose. That war never happened. The bloody stalemates on the African and South American continents were costly enough in lives and treasure that both China and the US lost their appetites for direct conflict in space.

Rather than a battlefield, Mars turned instead into a nearly lawless commercial boom planet for the countries, corporations, and privateers able to get there and to the asteroid belt beyond it. As a result, most ships were transitioned back to just one assembly like the Odysseus. The spinner offered much more space than needed for a freighter crew, but pressurized compartments with induced gravity were so valuable that the Company had left it in place. Besides, it would have been expensive to remove, and the Company was sometimes able to charge for passage to or from the belt.

Both the hab and the utility module had three levels. The bottom level of the hab housed a medical bay with the ship's second medpod, as well as crew quarters and a small mess facility. Paul lived on the bottom level with the rest of the prisoner crew members. They each had private quarters that were palatial relative to a military prison.

Crew quarters filled the second level of the hab, which also had its own small mess facility. The regular crew members lived on the second level.

The utility module, over two hundred meters away on the opposite end of the traverse, was designed to store weapons and military gear. Now it was used for food, spare parts, medical supplies, and other gear the crew wanted to have nearby. It was a much more convenient location than a kilometer or more away down the tube in a beat-up container clamped to the ship's hull. But at least half of the UM was still full of abandoned and unknown junk, accumulated over decades. That was where Paul had found his desk and chair, in a storage section full of map stands, filing cabinets, old field tables, and metal chairs.

Paul looked down from the window and took another sip of coffee, trying to get his mind ready.

In addition to the leather-bound copy of *Utsu* in front of him, there were two small stacks of books on each side of the desk. To the left, three large Japanese-to-English translation volumes sat beneath a Japanese grammar text. Several large leather-bound journals were stacked to the right. Their pages were full of his scribbled translation efforts.

Paul was working his way through *Utsu*, word by handwritten word. He had thought the four years there and back would be plenty of time.

More than a year in, he was not so sure.

Paul set down his coffee and got to work.

After an hour of translating, Paul changed into his duty uniform and reported to the all-hands meeting.

*

The captain convened an all-hands meeting on the top level of the hab at the beginning of each duty cycle.

The top level was divided into two sections. The forward section was the largest. In it, two swiveling command chairs faced a large floor-to-ceiling multifunctional display. It was possible to command the entire ship from this forward command section if control was given over from the captain's bridge. It was an impressive facility, and Paul hated it. He preferred the bridge, with its rambling landscape of old and new equipment and large window.

The aft section of the top floor was a large meeting space. A conference table surrounded by a dozen chairs sat in the middle of a windowless room. There were a couple of multifunctional displays on three of the walls. The fourth wall was adorned with a map of the solar system. It was a simple map but provided Paul with something to consider when the all-hands meetings got boring, which was most of the time.

Paul entered the meeting room and took a seat that afforded him a view of the map of the universe.

Drummond was already seated, sifting through files on his tablet computer. Drummond did not acknowledge Paul's entry and continued to ignore him after he sat at the table.

That was fine with Paul.

Mathew Drummond was the ship's CFO and second-highest-ranking officer on board. He was charged with making the voyage as profitable as possible for the Company. Drummond looked much older than his early thirties. His brow was always furrowed with concern and his face pinched with anxiety. Balding and slight with a small paunch, he looked like a waif next to the military convicts.

Paul did not understand why Drummond was so stressed out. He never had to participate in any of the maintenance or inspections, and he certainly never had to do any of the more dangerous tasks, such as extravehicular jobs.

But the man walked around like he was being stalked by something. Any time Paul saw Drummond, he was glued to his tablet display, monitoring the Bloomberg Belt Market feed and running cargo, factory, and negotiation scenarios.

"Top of the morning, bean counter!" Regas said as he stepped into the room. McNeeley and Hahn, laughing, were right behind him.

"I've told you several times not to call me that, Prisoner," Drummond said, not looking up from his tablet.

"I know. I'm sorry," Regas said. "I'm just kidding. I'm just kidding."

Belen Regas was a former Combat Corps corporal serving twenty years for desertion, theft, and drunk and disorderly conduct. A veteran of two deployments with an exoskeleton battalion, he had been awarded the Purple Heart and a Silver Star for valor. His parents had immigrated to America from Athens, and he was the first generation of his family born in America. Tall, muscular, and handsome, he was the epitome of masculine Greek beauty and a tragic disappointment to his parents.

He was also petty, hypercompetitive, easily offended, and drove Paul crazy.

Regas looked at McNeeley and Hahn. They tried to swallow their snickering.

McNeeley was a short, fat slug of a man. He was so out of shape that even on the *Odysseus*, where the blistering chill of the void kept the old girl cold at all times, he was always sweating. His brow, armpits, and the fold between the bottom of his man breasts and the top of his belly were always wet. He was the kind of specimen that Paul could never believe had made it into the military, much less thrived for a few years. McNeeley was not a Combat Corps veteran, of course. He had been part of the big administrative beast, working as an armorer, taking care of weapons and equipment.

The problem for McNeeley was he didn't take great care of the weapons and equipment. He was serving fifteen years for selling army equipment on the black market. With the Fly It Off program, he would be a free man when they landed back at Earth.

Hahn was a wiry kid from Kentucky who wore an outdoorsman's full beard. He was tall, though not as tall as Regas. Hahn exuded the quick and assured demeanor of a country boy. Paul could picture him shooting squirrels, jumping from rock to rock, and driving too fast in an old pickup truck. Paul had the sense that Hahn would have made an excellent infantryman had events played out differently in his life. As it was, though, he was serving seventeen years for dealing drugs in the barracks.

They had all been strangers when the *Odysseus* had left high lunar orbit. Now, though, Paul could see that McNeeley and Hahn belonged to Regas. They followed him around like puppies.

Regas looked at Paul. "Good morning, Captain Jigsaw," he said with false regard and cheerfulness as he sat down.

In a former life, Paul would have sprung across the table at the word "jigsaw."

But that part of him seemed a million years away. Regas had called him that since their first day on board, trying to offend. Paul never objected. He didn't care about those things anymore. And, even if he did, Regas did not matter enough to him to register.

"Hello, Regas," Paul said.

Althea walked in.

All eyes, other than Drummond's, locked on and followed her.

Dressed in her customary baggy utility uniform with multiple pockets, she succeeded in obscuring most features of her five-foot-five frame. But enough swells and curves made it through the camouflage to excite. And she was unable to hide her beautiful face. Ink-black hair cut in a swooping asymmetrical bob framed large, expressive eyes and full lips. She never wore lipstick, but it was easy to imagine.

An advanced melding of organic, mechanical, and electronic systems, Althea was the ship's administration and counseling officer. Her role was twofold. First, she assisted the executive officer in the administration of shipboard operations and served as the XO's embodied representative when the *Odysseus* was in port or docked with another ship. Her second but most important role was to serve as counselor to the small crew.

Althea's programming was optimized around behavioral observation and therapeutic communication. Years of deep space travel was hard on humans, and the shipping companies had learned the value of conversation and counseling over the course of so long and isolated a journey as a belt-and-back, even when the muse was a machine. And particularly when the crew included military inmates. The counseling initiative was, therefore, accelerated when the military's Fly It Off program started.

Paul looked across the table at Regas, who made no effort to hide his lust. He worked his lips and craned his neck to get as much of Althea as he could.

Paul wondered for the hundredth time about the wisdom of putting so attractive a synthetic on board a long space voyage. Althea was indistinguishable from a human woman. He had been around high-fidelity synthetics often in the military, so he appreciated their utility. *But why make all her organic stuff so damn good looking?* he thought. *Only an engineer who had never deployed into the real world, or real space, would do such a thing.*

Cooley walked in and scanned the table.

As boatswain, Floyd Cooley was in charge of all nonrated crew member activity, discipline, and training. It was his job to turn the four inexperienced prisoner crew members on their first space voyage into capable stevedores before they docked at the belt. It took a little over a year and a half to get to the belt. Plenty of time, he hoped.

This was Cooley's second belt-and-back voyage and his first serving as boatswain. He looked the part. Cooley kept his sandy-blond hair cut short and his goatee neatly trimmed. Six years of spacefaring had thinned him out some, but he was religious about his exercise regimen and stayed in the gravity of the hab as much as possible. He was not muscular like Paul and the other prisoners, who were little more than a year off of Earth. But Cooley looked like an Olympic athlete next to the captain.

Cooley nodded to Althea before passing his eyes over Drummond, who did not look up. He then looked from Regas to McNeeley and then Hahn, daring them to crack wise. Satisfied, Cooley looked at Paul and put his notebook down. He checked his watch: 0759 hours.

Rather than sit, he stood as he waited for the captain.

He didn't have to wait long.

"Attention!" commanded Cooley as Captain Drake entered the room at 0800 hours.

Everyone at the table sprang to their feet. Cooley stood at attention as well.

Drake took his time. When he got to his chair at the head of the table, he looked at each crew member in turn.

"Prisoner Regas," Drake said, staring at the tall military convict.

"Yes, sir," Regas said, head snapping toward the captain.

"What have I told you about uniform discipline?"

"Sir, the discipline one attends to their uniform is the same discipline one attends to their ship."

There was no edge, irony, or rebellion in Regas's voice. Regas knew that the captain was not a man he could fuck with, that he and his petty minions Hahn and McNeeley were nothing in Drake's world. Less than nothing. The captain could, here, now, at this table, order Regas jettisoned into the void. It would be done, and no one would question it.

That enraged Regas.

But he didn't show it.

Regas had been stupid in the past. That was why he was standing on the *Odysseus*, millions of kilometers from Earth, flying off a conviction for being stupid. He had promised himself he would never be stupid again.

"Check your uniform, Prisoner," the captain said as he sat down.

The room stood at attention while Regas checked his uniform. The left breast zipper of his utility suit was unzipped.

Drake shot Cooley a disappointed glance.

"Sir, may I make the correction?" Regas asked Drake.

Drake waited a heartbeat before saying, "Do so."

Regas zipped up the pocket and returned to the position of attention.

"Sorry, sir," Regas said.

McNeeley and Hahn shifted on their feet slightly, nervous for their alpha.

The captain shook his head and shifted his eyes from Regas back to Cooley.

Cooley nodded slightly to say, *I'll deal with it, sir.*

Drake looked unconvinced.

"Take your seats," the captain said.

Everyone sat down.

The leadership sat in the same seats, every time. The captain at the head of the long oval table. Drummond to the captain's left. Cooley to the right. Althea sat next to Cooley.

The prisoner crew members filled in the other seats.

"XO, we'll begin," Captain Drake said.

"Very good, sir," the XO's voice came over the speakers. "The all-hands meeting is now in session for this, the three hundred and eighty-fifth mission cycle, and is being recorded into the ship's log."

"OK, Mr. Drummond," the captain said. "Go ahead."

"Thank you, sir," Drummond said, still not looking up from his tablet. "All economic work streams are green for this cycle. Voyage forecasts remain yellow. Belt negotiation simulations and factory-planning scenarios place belt departure forecasts all between ninety-seven-point-eight and ninety-eight-point-six percent of revenue plan, and between ninety-six-point-eight and ninety-seven-point-nine percent of profit plan."

Out of the corner of his eye, Paul could see the captain's face darken.

"Unfortunately, factory output dropped to eighty-six-point-three percent for three hours during the previous cycle," Drummond continued.

"What happened?" the captain asked. "A five percent swing in factory output is a big hit."

"We would have hit ninety-plus percent had the appropriate materials made it to the mouth in time," Drummond said, looking down at his hands.

Paul thought Cooley was going to reach across the table and punch the CFO. The boatswain's face reddened, but the XO chimed in before he could speak.

"With respect, Mr. Drummond," the XO said. "Mr. Cooley and I were quite clear that a major payload transfer operation takes a minimum of five hours' notice to be conducted safely."

"How much notice did you give them, Mr. Drummond?" the captain asked.

"Two hours," Cooley answered, daring the CFO to contradict him.

Drummond looked up. "Mr. Cooley is correct, sir," he said.

Drake waited for him to continue.

"I was trying to take advantage of a surprising level of heavy metals and rare elements detected in an asteroid as it was processed by the factory. My forecasting algorithms suggest that there will be higher-than-average demand for precision drilling equipment at the belt when we arrive."

"We've been through this before, Mr. Drummond," Captain Drake said, weariness in his voice. "There are many moving pieces to this ship and her operations. She and the crew cannot turn on a dime just because your spreadsheet asks them to. The *Odysseus* is not a damn day-trading platform!"

"Yes, sir," Drummond said.

The captain leaned forward in his chair and turned his head toward the CFO.

"I remained concerned, Mr. Drummond," the captain said, "that financial performance is still forecasted below one hundred percent, and I see no evidence to suggest you have a plan to get us back in the green."

The captain glared at Drummond, who nodded nervously.

The lack of response angered Drake.

"You do realize, don't you, Mr. Drummond, that you have a very narrow reason for existence on my ship?"

Drake did not wait for Drummond to respond.

"Your only reason for being is to maximize the Company's financial return on this voyage," the captain continued. "To achieve that purpose, you have only four basic inputs you need worry about."

Drake held out his hand and counted each point with a bony finger as he walked through them, the edge in his voice increasing with each point.

"What to transport from Earth to the belt, what to produce in the ship's factory on the way to the belt, what cargo to select and bring back to Earth from the belt, and what to make in the factory on the long voyage back to Earth from the belt."

The captain let his four fingers hang in the air in front of Drummond for a moment before continuing.

"You get two bites at the goddamn apple," Drake said, volume rising. "When the *Odysseus* docks at the belt, and when the ship arrives back in high lunar orbit. The only thing left to be done at those two points in time is unload the old girl, sell what she's got, and tally the final number!"

The captain was yelling now. Everyone looked down at the table, scared to make eye contact with the enraged officer.

"Any voyage that does not score at least a hundred percent to financial plan is a failure! It is a failure for the Company, and a failure for the crew! Small to no financial share after five years in space is a hard goddamn blow, I can assure you! But it is nothing compared to the indelible tarnish that stains each crew member's career and reputation!"

The captain pointed at Drummond, who was shaking in his chair.

"Get your act together, Drummond!" the captain yelled. "I want a green forecast within seven cycles, or I will arrange for your replacement at the belt! Do you understand me?"

"Aye, sir," Drummond said.

The captain stared at the CFO as he leaned back in his chair.

"Very well," Drake said, his voice returning to normal. "Thank you, Mr. Drummond."

The captain looked around the table as if remembering there were people other than he and Drummond in the room.

"Mr. Cooley?" the captain said.

"No maintenance or inspection anomalies to report," Cooley began. "In terms of training, we've just completed the extravehicular activity module, which puts us slightly ahead of syllabus. Anticipate no issues having Owens, Regas, and Hahn fully trained by the time we get to the void. They are green across the board. McNeeley failed his second attempt at the EVA practical exercise."

McNeeley swallowed hard and looked at his hands, which were folded on the table. More sweat than usual beaded on his brow beneath his bald head.

Drake sighed. "Prisoner McNeeley," he said with disgust. "By my count, this is the third module you have required multiple attempts to satisfactorily test out of and advance."

McNeeley wiped the sweat from his forehead but did not raise his eyes to meet Drake's gaze. Hahn and Regas looked straight ahead.

Paul shared a furtive, *what-a-piece-of-shit* glance with Cooley.

"Prisoner McNeeley," the captain said in a low voice.

McNeeley's eyes jerked up.

"Yes, sir?" he said.

"My patience with you is exhausted. If you don't pass the EVA practical within the next three cycles, you're done. I will not approve your Fly It Off credit, and you will forfeit your one-tenth share. Do you know what that means, Prisoner?"

"Yes, sir."

Everyone knew what it meant.

McNeeley would get no credit or pay for his four-year tour of service on the *Odysseus*. He would land back Earthside and go back to serving his time, which would not have decreased a single day since his departure.

"I'll take this time to remind all of our prisoner crew members," Drake said, swiveling his head back and forth as he spoke, looking each of the prisoners in the eye. "The captain of a space freighter is the final approval authority for all Fly It Off program participants. My approval is not, and will never be, a rubber stamp. Is that clear?"

"Aye, sir," the four prisoner crew members said in unison.

"Good," Drake said before turning to Cooley. "See that it happens, Mr. Cooley. If Prisoner McNeeley does not pass the EVA practical, it will be reflected on your voyage efficiency report."

"Aye, sir," Cooley said, staring at McNeeley. "Consider it done, sir."

Paul felt sorry for Cooley. A boatswain's voyage efficiency report was all-important. A good one meant a larger share and career advancement that made the long years in space worth it. A poor or even average rating meant career stagnation and a reduced share.

For Cooley to be put at financial and professional risk because the Fly It Off program had saddled him with McNeeley was some real shit luck. McNeeley was undisciplined, weak, of low intelligence and even lower morals and motivation.

And extravehicular activity was for real.

Paul had been through the most demanding training the military had to throw at a person. He had seen some of the worst combat situations in the past ten years. Still, being outside of the *Odysseus* with just a pressure suit between him and the insatiable void was unnerving. There were so many ways to die. Quick ways. Slow ways. Painful ways. And some ways a person would never even see coming. Add a few complex maintenance or other tasks, and EVAs were the thing that everyone on board dreaded the most.

So, Paul couldn't blame McNeeley for being scared. But he still didn't like the fat asshole.

"XO?" the captain said, moving on. "Anything to report?"

"No, Captain Drake. All monitored systems nominal."

Drake nodded and glanced at Paul.

Paul looked down at his hands.

"Miss Althea," the captain said, not even trying to conceal the loathing in his voice. He looked down at his notes as she spoke.

"Crew health remains strong, Captain," she said. "No concerns at this time."

"Thank you," Drake said.

The captain looked around the table.

"I'll open the meeting up to anyone at this point. Any concerns or issues we need to discuss as a crew?" The captain waited for a moment before saying, "Very well. XO, this all-hands meeting is concluded."

"Noted, sir," the XO said. "Transcription ended."

"Attention!" Cooley said. Everyone sprang to their feet as the captain stood up.

Drake pushed his chair back into place and said, "I appreciate everything everyone is doing to keep us safe and underway. Be careful during this cycle. Carry on!"

The crew stood at ease as the captain left. As soon as the door closed behind Drake, Regas said, "Hey, Mr. Drummond. If we catch up to the revenue plan, can we discuss increasing prisoner shares?"

Drummond ignored Regas. He gathered his tablet and papers.

"Hey," Regas said, a slight edge creeping into his voice. "Did you hear me, Drummond?"

"That's enough, Regas!" Cooley said sharply.

"Whoa! Hey," Regas said, raising his hands in a friendly surrender gesture. "I'm just kidding. He knows I'm just kidding. Right, Mr. Drummond?"

Drummond exited the room without acknowledging Regas.

"At ease, Regas!" Cooley said.

Regas saw the anger in Cooley's glaring face. He nodded at the boatswain and shut his mouth.

"McNeeley," Cooley said between his gritted teeth. "Come over here, you fat, useless slob."

Paul walked out of the room, fleeing the irritating antics and attitudes of his fellow prisoners. He was ready to immerse himself back in the *Odysseus*'s solitude.

Captain Drake was waiting for him.

"Prisoner Owens!" Drake yelled as Paul walked toward the aft ladder.

"Yes, sir?" Paul answered, coming to a halt.

Hahn and Regas, stepping out of the meeting room, sped by and down the aft ladder to begin their cycles. They wanted distance between themselves and the captain's ire.

"I noted a discrepancy on your last inspection report," the captain said in a gruff voice as he stepped in front of Paul. "What have I told you about inspection reports?"

Paul was puzzled but popped off with the first thing that came to him. "Sir, an inspection is not complete until the report is rendered."

"Exactly!" the captain said, raising his voice as he poked Paul in the chest with his bony index finger. "So why the hell am I still dealing with incomplete paperwork from you?"

Confused, Paul stayed silent.

"Damn it, Prisoner!" Drake said, frustration welling up. "The *Odysseus* has been ridden hard for a long time. She's ferried troops, done a few belt-and-backs, and hauled cargo to Mars. And I think every crew that she took on board left some of their shit behind. She is a mess!"

Drake poked Paul in the chest again as he spoke. Paul stood at attention, wondering how many times he had heard this speech before, and why the captain was so worked up.

"Well, the old girl is ours now," Drake continued. "We're going to take care of her, and part of that is inventorying her burden."

On the next poke, Drake unzipped Paul's left breast pocket.

"Do you understand me?" Drake demanded.

Paul looked down, puzzled.

"Answer me, Prisoner!" the captain said sharply.

Paul looked up. "Sir, I don't know what you are talking about," he said.

"That's your damn problem, Owens," Drake said, poking Paul again in the chest. "You don't know what I am talking about."

On the last poke, the captain shoved a note into the pocket and made a show to Paul of looking at the zipper.

*This is ridiculous*, Paul thought, realizing what was going on.

"Do you understand me, Prisoner?" Drake said, taking a step back.

"Yes, sir," Paul responded. "It won't happen again."

"It better not."

Paul nodded.

"You are dismissed, Prisoner," Drake said.

# Chapter Three

*Mission Cycle 384*

*Earth Year 2062*

*286,803,763 Kilometers from Earth*

*Paul, something is very wrong. I suspect that there has been a deviation in our course and that the XO is responsible. How? For what purpose? I do not know. I should have my calculations completed in a day or so, and then you and I should meet to discuss. Please trust me this time when I say that something is very wrong. Meet me in power and propulsion, section ten, transfer room 105, in two cycles. 2430 hours.*

Paul tried not to scream as he stood in his quarters. He held the captain's note in one hand and his forehead in the other.

*Maybe it's time for me to tell someone about all this,* Paul thought as he walked over to his bureau. He opened the top drawer and placed the note in the growing stack under his T-shirts.

*But who?*

He walked over to his utility closet and pulled out his pressure suit. He was going to knock out his inspection first thing this cycle. He mulled the situation over as he donned his suit.

*I guess I tell Drummond?* he thought. *He is second in command, after all.*

Paul stood up straight in disgust at the thought.

*No way. That guy is an idiot.*

He grabbed his helmet and headed for the aft ladder.

Paul's inspection assignment for this cycle was a shipping container on the aft end of the ship almost two kilometers away, near power and propulsion. It would be a long float through the tube. *Perfect,* he thought. *I could use a little time to think.*

Seen without cargo, the *Odysseus*'s two-kilometer-long hull looked like a bony, disembodied spine, and her cargo rigging system, which ran along the bottom of her hull, looked like a series of stunted ribs. These ribs were as effective as they were strange-looking, though, and could secure any type of modular container as well as secure entire asteroids.

A maintenance and cargo access passageway, called "the tube," ran the length of the ship on top of her skinny hull, giving the crew access to the numerous compartments as well as the cargo and rigging systems. The tube was twenty meters in diameter. A ladder ran along the top of it, and a utility tram, used for hauling loads, ran its length along the starboard side. At regular intervals along the bottom of the tube, hatches gave access to cargo rigged to the ship.

The tube was not pressurized and required a full suit. Even so, Paul liked to go there and drift aft, snooping around the cargo. Open one bulkhead, and he'd see a stained and ugly container that had traveled to and from the belt with the *Odysseus* for decades. Open another, and he'd gaze on a gleaming thousand-ton asteroid full of rare-earth metals. From the outside, when fully laden with a cargo of odd-sized containers and massive asteroids, the *Odysseus* looked more like a collection of drifting space junk than a spacecraft.

Paul made his way up the aft ladder to the first level of the hab and then walked to the middle bulkhead to access the traverse. He twisted his helmet on before starting his climb. The traverse was pressurized, but it was easier to climb the 120-meter ladder wearing his helmet rather than holding it.

Paul's weight reduced as he climbed until he kicked off of the ladder and floated up into the center chamber called "the hub." He paused there.

He liked to float in the zero gravity of the hub and listen to the low-frequency thrum of the massive gears driving the two arms of the spinner. Most of the *Odysseus* was silent, doused in vacuum. But in the hub, Paul could hear the old girl working. He liked it.

Paul activated the air lock and worked his way into the tube.

He had learned that with a firm kick and one or two strong arm pulls on the ladder along the way, he could float from one end of the tube to the other in about twenty minutes. It was a relaxing and contemplative way to move through the tube.

*If I tell anyone, it will be Cooley,* Paul thought as he floated aft.

Cooley reminded Paul of the good noncommissioned officers he had known in the Combat Corps, each a unique but familiar cocktail of coach, disciplinarian, dictator, and older sibling. They were the glue of every good unit. Cooley was the *Odysseus's* glue.

*Why does it even matter, though?* Paul thought. *So what if the captain is a paranoid drunk? The XO runs everything anyway. He's not going to let anything bad happen to the ship or us.*

Paul reached the center of the ship and passed beneath the CnC bulkhead as he debated the situation.

*Crazy old man.*

By the time Paul reached his destination, he knew what he was going to do.

*Nothing,* he thought with a nod. *I'm not going to do a damn thing. I didn't come here to join a crew or be part of any drama. It's not my problem.*

Paul opened the bulkhead to access the container. Empty.

He shook his head at the sight and chuckled to himself. Early in the voyage, this would have sent Paul into an impotent rage: suiting up and shagging his ass two kilometers through the tube to confirm a shipping container was empty. Now it seemed like a good way to start the cycle.

Paul closed the bulkhead and started back to his quarters to complete the paperwork.

*

Later that cycle, at the end of Paul's duty period, he walked toward Althea's quarters on the middle floor of the hab. It was time for his mandatory counseling session.

Paul gritted his teeth as he walked. The sessions always came at the most inconvenient time of cycle: either at the beginning, when he did his best translating, or at the end, when he was tired and just wanted to hit the rack. This cycle, it was the latter.

Paul had met Althea for the first time on the top level of the hab the day he and the rest of the prisoner crew members had reported to the *Odysseus*. She'd briefed them on her role and capabilities in a matter-of-fact stream of high-tech psychobabble. Paul was confident that, given his background and all that had happened, someone at the Company or Space Command had routed Althea, the latest-model counseling synthetic in the fleet, to the *Odysseus*. The last thing anyone needed was another high-visibility incident involving Paul Owens.

He didn't care. He had earned the reputation and precautions. So, as Althea had run down a list of her own abilities like someone describing the features of a car, the only thing Paul was thinking was that she was beautiful.

She was short, coming up to about Paul's chin. Though he knew her flesh had been grown in a lab before encasing her mechanical parts, her skin exuded warmth and looked inviting to the touch. The oversized and pocketed utility suit she wore allowed only hints of her true shape. But, for a group of convicts who had been locked up for years, a hint was all that was required. Hahn and McNeeley grinned like schoolboys as Althea spoke. Regas leered at her. At one point, he'd even licked his lips, causing Paul to roll his eyes.

*This must be a mistake,* Paul thought at that first meeting. *Somewhere in the fleet, a brothel ship is puzzling over a homely, professorial, middle-aged male companion, and we've got this lap dancer trying to navigate four crazy, horny, convicted fiends. Another bang-up job by personnel command.*

A couple of his army buddies had been fans of synthetics as temporary companions. Paul wasn't, though he did see the practical advantage for soldiers who spent most of their lives in war zones. And the stories he heard left no doubt that the synthetics performed at a high level of sexual expertise. It wasn't that he didn't desire sexual release; synthetics just didn't do it for him.

Nothing did it for him anymore.

He wanted nothing to do with Althea. He wanted nothing to do with anyone on the *Odysseus* beyond what his duties mandated.

So, he was disappointed to learn that all crew members had to sit for a counseling session with Althea at least once every ten cycles. That was the minimum. Crew members could do more.

Paul made it clear to Althea from the beginning and on every subsequent interaction: he would attend the sessions, but he had no intention of ever participating.

Paul sighed with resignation as he reached her door. He adjusted the small satchel on his shoulder and stood up straight, squaring his shoulders as if preparing to take a punch. Then he knocked.

Althea greeted him with a smile.

"Hello, Paul," she said, stepping aside to let him in.

The door to Althea's quarters opened into a small sitting room. It was furnished with a large, comfortable sofa that sat against the wall and faced the only window. Two chairs sat opposite the sofa on the other side of a small coffee table beneath the window.

Paul walked in without greeting her. He sat down on the sofa and pulled the leather-bound book and his translation journal out of the satchel.

Althea sat in one of the chairs.

Paul checked his watch and then opened the leather-bound book.

"Remind me what your book is about, Paul," Althea said in her most inviting voice.

Paul answered but did not look up. He had learned that Althea's price for leaving him alone was a few minutes of friendly chatting.

Well, chatting, at least.

"It's an old text," he said, not looking up from its pages. "Written by a rōnin, a masterless samurai, sometime in the early 1500s, during the Sengoku period when the fighting was really bad. It was only recently discovered in 2059, during the excavation of a newly discovered Sengoku-period military compound in Japan."

"What is it about?"

"The leader of a fighting school and his students."

"What happens to them?"

Paul looked up from the book. His face was tight with irritation. He glared at Althea to make it obvious that this was the end of the friendly chat.

"I don't know. I haven't finished it yet."

Althea nodded.

Paul returned to the book.

He studied the pages and tuned her out, pausing now and again to write himself a note in the margin.

Althea sat in silence and watched him as he worked.

Forty minutes later, he stood up and left without saying goodbye.

Every session was the same. Paul entered the room without greeting Althea. He sat on the sofa and tolerated several minutes of talk before descending into silence and working on his translation. Althea would fold her hands in her lap and sit quietly, watching him work. At the end of the session, she would wish him well as he walked out the door without comment.

They were not very far from Earth when Paul heard that Regas had been reduced to one session every thirty cycles. Paul was jealous.

"How do I get on that schedule?" he'd asked the boatswain as they prepared for an EVA training task.

"Fucking Neanderthal won't stop asking her for sex or trying to masturbate during his sessions," Cooley had said with frustration. "After a few sessions, she got justifiably concerned he was going to force himself on her. She appealed to the captain and, even worse, included it in her weekly report to the Company. So, her exposure to him was reduced to monthly. Worst part is that now I have to monitor their sessions."

"What does that mean?" Paul asked.

"I have to sit in there with him and make sure he doesn't get creepy with her."

"For the whole session?"

Cooley nodded his head.

Paul chuckled. "I guess I have it better than I realized."

"Don't get me wrong," Cooley said. "She's hot. I think about it every time I see her also. But, shit. The guy has no throttle, control, or self-discipline. I really wonder what genius thought he would be a good fit for a belt-and-back."

After his session with Althea, Paul climbed down the aft ladder to the third level. He was tired and ready to quit for the cycle. He walked through the crew galley on the way to his quarters. Regas was holding court.

"Now listen to how I wrap it up, guys," Regas said with excitement.

Hahn and McNeeley listened to Regas as he worked through a document. He was standing at the end of the table, reading in a proud and sure voice.

"We, the prisoner crew members, do, therefore, request our pay be increased to a full share in recognition of our outstanding and worthy service."

"So good," McNeeley said.

"I know, right?" Regas said.

Paul filled his water bottle. All of their heads turned toward him.

"You should get in on this, Owens," McNeeley said, his belly straining his sweaty T-shirt.

Paul ignored him.

"Seriously, Owens," Hahn said, stroking his beard. "You should get in on this. At least sign it so the captain knows it is unanimous."

"Come on, Jigsaw," Regas said. "How about a little crew unity out of you for once?"

Paul turned around like a tired parent.

"What are you idiots up to now?" he asked.

"We're demanding a full share," McNeeley said.

"That's right." Hahn emphasized his words with a cocky nod of the head.

Regas smiled and crossed his arms. "Who is the idiot now?" he said, nodding slowly.

Paul belly laughed.

Hahn and McNeeley sagged. Regas glared.

"Fuck you, then, Jigsaw," Regas said. "You'll be sorry." Regas turned back to face the table. "He'll be sorry, guys."

"Do you guys really think you are getting screwed?" Paul asked in a patient voice.

"Hell yes," Regas said, spinning around to face Paul. "We are being exploited. You are just too stupid to see it."

"That right?" Paul said. "Who held a gun to your head and made you sign up for the Fly It Off program?"

"That's not the point!" Regas said, raising his voice. "You know as well as I do there is a freighter crew shortage. Command can't fill the billets without us. And if they can't crew the ships and man the belt operations, the Chinese will have dibs."

"Exactly!" Hahn said, snapping his fingers. "Chinese don't play. They just press poor bastards into service over there. They got no problem crewing their damn fleet!"

"And if Command does not crew its fleet, the Chinese will dominate the asteroid belt and get all of the energy resources, precious metals, and exotic materials."

"You've been studying hard, I see," Paul said with an insincere smile. "I'm impressed."

"It's the truth!" Hahn said. "No one in their right mind would sign up for this if they didn't have to. Four years on this piece of shit? It sucks!"

"And it's dangerous," McNeeley said. "There are a thousand ways to get killed on this death trap."

"Yeah," Hahn said with an emphatic nod. "Killed, lost, or taken by pirates. Look at the *Perseus*! Gone forever. We could be next."

"And for what?" Regas asked.

"For your freedom, you idiots," Paul reminded them. "Three years of credit for every one year of duty. I don't know about you, but I jumped at it."

They looked at him, unable to argue the point.

"You're doing fifteen, right, McNeeley?" Paul asked.

McNeeley nodded.

"How many you got left?"

"Twelve," McNeeley said softly.

Paul shook his head.

"You'll be a free man when we get back. Don't let him screw this up for you," Paul said with a nod toward Regas. "I don't see this bullshit playing well with Drake. The cranky old man might get pissed and kick you out of the program, give you zero credit. Then what?"

McNeeley looked from Paul to Regas and then back to Paul.

Regas saw the doubt welling in McNeeley's eyes.

"You wanna be a rich free man?" Regas asked McNeeley. "Or a poor free man?"

"Rich," McNeeley said.

"That's right," Hahn said.

Paul shrugged and said, "Good luck with that."

"Don't listen to this stuck-up jigsaw," Regas said, turning back to the table. "He don't know shit."

Paul turned to leave.

"You sure you don't want to sign?" McNeeley asked Paul, leaning to his side so he could see around Regas.

"I never trust a barracks lawyer," Paul said as he walked toward the door.

"What if he can get us a better deal, though?" McNeeley asked, gesturing at Regas.

"Then he wouldn't be on this ship with us."

# Chapter Four

*Utsu Book One*

*Circa 1510*

*Translated from the Japanese*

My name is Manji Saito, student of School Hiroaki, friend of Hiroaki Ashikaga himself, and the only survivor of the Battle of the Covered Bridge.

I apologize to the reader. I am a warrior. I am not a writer.

I wandered as a rōnin, a masterless samurai, for many years, fighting in many battles for different sides. I was wounded badly in the Siege of the Seven Swans. I would have been killed had it not been for the bravery and skill of an older rōnin named Kusunoki. He saved me and was wounded in the process. We both lay bleeding as the siege concluded. Both in pain. Both happy to be alive.

Our side was victorious. Kusunoki and I were taken to a small village to heal. It took me many months to recover. During this time, Kusunoki's stories were my only diversion. He was a master storyteller. He told them well and for many hours at a time. I lay on my bed and looked at the ceiling listening to them.

Kusonoki spun tales about School Hiroaki. In those days, it was heard of only in whispered rumors. A school of the famous general and sword-fighting master, Hiroaki Ashikaga. Kusunoki claimed to be a member of the school. He claimed to know Hiroaki himself. Kusunoki claimed that he was not really a rōnin. Instead, Hiroaki and the practice were his master.

Sadly, Kusunoki's wounds were grave. He descended into fever. His stories became more fantastical. Then he stopped speaking. Eventually succumbed. In his last lucid moment before dying, Kusunoki asked me to carry his body back to Hiroaki's school so that he could be buried with his brothers. I still did not believe his stories. But Kusunoki saved my life in battle. I was honor bound to try.

I spent a week trying to remember every detail that Kusunoki had told me. I wrote my notes in a small journal so that I would not forget. I also drew a map that resembled, as closely as I could manage, the route into the hills that Kusunoki had described.

I wrapped Kusunoki's body and rigged it on two long poles. One end rested on my shoulders, the other dragged on the ground. I put Kusunoki's katana and a note he asked me to give Hiroaki into my sack and set out on my journey.

# Chapter Five

*Mission Cycle 385*

*Earth Year 2062*

*287,400,960 Kilometers from Earth*

Paul sat down at his desk at the beginning of the cycle. He felt good. It had been a good meditation, and he was ready to translate.

He opened *Utsu* and took a deep breath at the sight of the dense Japanese text. Such a long way to go on it.

The loud shriek of the ship's decompression alarm startled Paul.

Paul jumped from his seat toward his utility closet.

A rapid succession of jolts ran through the floor, accompanied by strange banging sounds. Both stopped as quickly as they began.

"Attention on board, there has been a decompression event on the command-and-control module," said the XO in his ever-unperturbed voice.

Paul yanked his pressure suit out of the closet.

"The hab and utility modules do not share life-support systems with that section of the ship and have not been compromised, so I have terminated the alarm," the XO announced.

"What is the status of the captain?" Paul yelled as he continued to don his pressure suit.

"I am trying to determine the captain's status. But at this time, the bridge has lost all atmospheric pressure. I have dispatched IR bots. They will be on station in three minutes."

"Damn it," Paul muttered.

He pulled on his helmet and activated the seal. Paul then turned and headed for the middle ladder.

Drummond and Althea stood gawking as Paul climbed through the second level.

"What are you doing, Paul?" Althea asked.

He ignored her and kept climbing.

Cooley, almost two kilometers aft in the tube, transmitted on the ship's intercom as Paul worked his way to the hub.

"Captain Drake, can you give us your status?" Cooley transmitted.

"Paul. What are your intentions?" the XO's voice asked over the intercom in Paul's suit.

"I'm going to the bridge," Paul said angrily.

"I don't think that is advisable," chimed the XO. "My IR bots will be there in ninety seconds. Shouldn't you wait for Mr. Cooley's instructions?"

"Fuck you. I am headed that way." Paul pulled hand over hand on the traverse's ladder. His weight decreased, and he sailed upward as he neared the center of the hub.

Paul flew into the center hub and activated the airlock. Once in the tube, he grabbed the ladder and yanked repeatedly, increasing his speed. He barreled through the tube toward the CnC.

"Captain Drake, this is Prisoner Owens," Paul transmitted. "Can you give us your status, please?"

No response.

"Owens, where are you?" Cooley called on the radio.

"In the tube. Headed for the bridge," Paul responded.

"Roger," Cooley said. "Me too. I'm coming from PPM. Meet you at the bulkhead. All other crew members stay put. I repeat. All other crew member stay put. XO, any clarity on the captain's status?"

"Negative, Mr. Cooley," the XO responded. "As you know, I am unable to monitor the CnC. Furthermore, he was not wearing a bio-monitor when the incident occurred, so I am getting no information from him."

"I want a report as soon as your IR bots are on-site," Cooley demanded.

"Of course."

Paul and Cooley were in sight of each other now and closing in fast. Paul reached up to the ladder rungs on the roof of the tube to slow himself. Cooley did the same.

They met under the CnC bulkhead. Cooley gestured that he would go first. Paul gave him a thumbs-up. They opened the bulkhead and started climbing the ladder that ran up the superstructure.

They were almost to the CnC air lock when the XO spoke up again.

"Damage report follows, Mr. Cooley. Extensive damage to the bridge. Total loss of atmosphere. Captain Drake is dead."

# Chapter Six

*Mission Cycle 385*

*Earth Year 2062*

*287,483,285 Kilometers from Earth*

Captain Drake floated in the middle of the bridge. Most of his head was missing, as well as his left arm, which was severed cleanly just above the elbow. Bits of blood and fleshy debris orbited the captain in a cloud of frozen gore.

"Oh God," Cooley said.

Paul closed his eyes and shook his head. "Damn it," he mumbled from behind Cooley.

"Oh, Captain…" Cooley's voice was choked with emotion.

"Any idea what happened, XO?" Paul asked. He touched the toe of his right mag boot to the floor for traction and eased next to Cooley, who floated motionless, staring at the captain's disfigured body.

As Paul passed the boatswain, he put a hand on Cooley's shoulder and got his attention. He and Paul locked eyes.

Tears floated in Cooley's helmet, smearing his visor. But he gave Paul a thumbs-up.

"I'm good," Cooley said.

Paul nodded and turned back toward the captain. He dropped a mag boot to the floor and pushed off.

"It appears that we were struck by a group of meteoroids," the XO said. "In addition to the bridge, we have sustained damage to multiple hull sections and cargo containers. The factory was damaged as well. No indications of fire at this time."

"That's good," Paul said.

Fire on a spacecraft was a death sentence.

"Inspections are still underway," the XO continued. "But we have counted over two dozen hull perforations so far. Aside from the bridge, however, no other pressurized sections have been compromised."

Paul approached the captain's body. It floated upside down relative to him and Cooley and rotated slowly. More than half of the captain's head was gone. Only his right cheek and ear remained.

Paul reached out and grabbed the captain by the shoulders. He pulled Drake toward the port-side wall and turned the body right side up as he pushed it against the wall. Paul let go of the captain for a moment and grabbed a cargo strap from a nearby utility closet. He secured the body to the wall so that it would not continue to float around the bridge while they made a plan.

The action snapped Cooley back into mode, and he helped Paul. Then they both inspected the damage.

Paul tried to ignore his quickening pulse and clammy hands.

The port side of the bridge looked like it had been shot open by a machine gun. There was a gaping, ragged hole large enough for a person to pass through, surrounded by numerous smaller holes. The penetrations radiated out from the large hole, pockmarking the entire port side with small glimpses of the void. Paul gave up counting. There must have been over a hundred holes.

He and Cooley turned to look at the starboard wall of the bridge. The holes were mirrored on that side. The mighty *Odysseus's* armored body had not slowed the galactic projectiles at all. They had passed through her, and the captain, in an instant, and had kept going. Forever.

Paul and Cooley locked eyes again and shared rueful shakes of the head.

"Damn," Cooley said, looking back at the captain.

*At least he died instantly,* Paul thought. *Brain vaporized before it could register pain or fear.*

A flash of light outside the pierced hull caught Paul's eye. The inspection-and-repair bots were getting started.

"Mr. Cooley, I estimate that repairs to the bridge will take several cycles," the XO said.

"Got it," Cooley said. "Proceed, and we will take care of the captain."

"That's really not necessary," the XO said. "I can have the body transferred to storage and—"

"I'm not debating this with you," Cooley interrupted.

"You know that is not what the captain would have wanted, XO," Paul added. Cooley nodded.

The XO hesitated for a moment and then said, "You are right, of course. As you wish."

"We will need some towels and a body bag," Paul said. "It's going to get messy when he starts to thaw out."

"I will have Althea bring you the necessary supplies," the XO said. "May I ask your intentions for the captain?"

"What does his file say?" Cooley asked, though he knew the answer.

Every spacefarer was required to fill out a last will and testament before leaving Earth. This file included disposition of remains, if there were any.

"Burial in space," the XO answered.

"Then those are our intentions," Cooley said. "Please notify Drummond."

"Aye, Mr. Cooley."

Paul and Cooley floated in the depressurized command-and-control module with the captain, waiting for Althea to show up with cleaning materials and a body bag. They stared in silence at the captain. It seemed to Paul like a long time since he had been that close to a dead body. To a fallen comrade. Unfortunately, he had been close to many. Both human and robotic. He felt the familiar discomfort and sadness begin to creep into the edge of his mind. The anxiety was there too. He did not want to remember.

The air lock opened down on the CnC's first level, startling Paul and Cooley. Althea glided up through the passageway onto the bridge, two large utility bags in her hands.

"You guys OK?" she asked.

"Fine," Cooley said.

"Can I help you with this?" she asked as she handed Cooley one of the large utility bags and pushed the other toward Paul.

"No."

"I'd really like to help." She looked at Paul, the concern on her face obvious, even from within a pressure-suit helmet.

Paul ignored her.

Althea floated nearby, observing as Cooley opened the utility bags. The IR bots worked silently just outside of the module, sparks erupting from their efforts on the *Odysseus*'s hull.

Paul was motionless as he looked at the captain's bloody fragment of a head. Memories exploded in his mind. The blood. The torn flesh. The pain and fear. The cries for help.

"Paul?"

Althea's hand on Paul's shoulder startled him. He realized he had been staring at the captain. He was shaking. Paul turned and looked at Althea floating next to him in her pressure suit.

"What do you want?" He was irritated now.

"I want to help you," Althea answered. "Let me help you guys with this."

"We'd rather take care of it ourselves," Cooley said.

"Are you sure? I think—"

"Althea, please!"

Paul realized he was shouting at her. Embarrassment flushed his face.

Cooley gave him a look as if to say, *I just got my shit back together. Don't lose yours.*

"I'm sorry," Paul said, shaking his head.

"Althea, I really appreciate you bringing the stuff," Cooley said. "But I need you to leave. Now."

Althea looked at Cooley. Then back to Paul, who was now unzipping one of the utility bags.

"Yes, sir," she said.

But she did not leave right away. She floated motionless, still looking at Paul.

He tried to ignore her. Then he glared at her through his helmet visor and pointed at the passageway.

She nodded. "Call if you need anything," she said as she turned and left.

Paul and Cooley got to work. Cooley went first to the storage unit down on the first level and retrieved a pressure-suit repair gun. Back at the captain's body, he sprayed the remains of the captain's head while Paul held the body steady.

The aerosol-propelled fiber-and-adhesive compound bound itself to Drake's flesh, sealing the gaping bloody cavity. It was not a technique one would ever use on a live person's wound, given its toxicity. But since it was designed to instantly restore integrity to a damaged pressure suit, Paul figured it would contain the captain's lifeless blood for the next few hours until they set the old man on his final journey.

"Go to his quarters and get a new uniform," Cooley told Paul.

"Aye, sir."

Paul touched a mag boot to the floor and pushed off toward the passageway down to the first level.

He went to the captain's closet and retrieved a new dress uniform. He also grabbed the captain's saber and formal hat.

Cooley had cut off the captain's tattered clothes by the time Paul returned to the bridge.

They put Drake in the new uniform, being careful not to allow any of the suspended frozen blood drops to cling to the new outfit. They pinned the left sleeve back on itself beneath the severed arm's stump. Then they gently pulled the black body bag over the captain and zipped it up.

"Mr. Cooley," Drummond called on the intercom. "Can you, um, give me a, um, status, please?"

Cooley made eye contact with Paul. But to Cooley's credit, he didn't break. He didn't say, "Now I've got to report to that asshole." He didn't make a face or even roll his eyes slightly. In that glance, Paul could see Cooley make the reluctant transition to a new captain. One who was unsuited for the task.

"Aye, sir," Cooley said, looking away from Paul. "Prisoner Owens and I have secured Captain Drake's body and prepared it for burial. We were going to make our way back to the hab with it."

"You are bringing it here?" Drummond asked.

"Yes," Cooley answered. "I assumed we'd do the ceremony from the air lock there. Did you have something else in mind, sir?"

The lowest level of the hab, the floor where Paul and the other prisoner crew members' quarters were, was equipped with an air lock located in its forward-most section. It was useful as an on- and off-loading access point when the *Odysseus* was docked. But underway, with the spinner rotating, it wasn't very useful for anything other than emergency egress. It would be perfect for the captain's burial.

Cooley waited for the CFO's response. Nothing.

"I figured, that way, we wouldn't have to suit up and you could easily say a few words to the crew, sir," Cooley said after a moment, hoping to unstick Drummond.

Silence.

"In a brief ceremony, sir," Cooley added.

"Yes," Drummond responded. "Um…I concur. Proceed."

"We're on the way now, sir. Probably need about half an hour to get through the tube and get Captain Drake's body into position." When it became clear that Drummond was not going to acknowledge his last transmission, Cooley said, "XO, let me know when the bridge repairs are complete."

"Of course, Mr. Cooley," the XO responded.

Paul and Cooley floated through the tube, pushing Captain Drake's body in front of them.

\*

"Ding-dong the son of a bitch is dead, eh, fellas?" Regas said with a chuckle.

"Stow that shit, Regas," Cooley said with a glare in Regas's direction. He and Paul had just finished setting the captain's casket down in the hab air lock.

"Hey," Regas said with a friendly shrug. "I'm just kidding. I'm just kidding. He was a nice guy." Regas winked at Hahn and McNeeley, who chuckled.

Paul couldn't tell if they were amused or embarrassed by Regas's behavior. Either way, Cooley was pissed. Paul would not have been surprised if Cooley spaced Regas along with the captain. Paul would not have been opposed.

Paul and Cooley stepped out of the air lock and took their positions with the rest of the crew. Paul activated the bulkhead, sealing the living area off from the air lock.

Drummond shuffled his feet and adjusted his glasses. He was in agony. Paul had seen this before. Someone thrust by death into a role they were not up to. They knew it. Their unit knew it.

Regas, Hahn, and McNeeley stood on one side of the narrow passageway facing Paul, Cooley, and Althea on the other. Drummond stood at the end of their small formation, in the middle of the passageway, facing the air lock. Through the glass, they could all see the captain's casket sitting on the floor of the air lock.

Everyone waited for Drummond.

The pause was awkward.

Regas smiled. He stared at Drummond the way a schoolyard bully stares at his next victim. Hahn and McNeeley alternated their eyes between Regas and the CFO. They were nervous.

Cooley's hand rested on the handle of the large utility knife on his hip, the one he had used to cut the captain's bloody uniform off. Cooley glared at Regas, daring him to say or do something stupid.

Regas moved his eyes to Althea. They roved over her, head to toe and back and then down again.

Paul felt the slightest shift in Althea's posture. She stiffened in resistance to Regas's assaulting gaze while putting on a show of ignoring him.

Cooley couldn't take it anymore. He looked at Drummond and said, "You can begin now, sir."

Drummond coughed. "Y-yes," he stammered. "Um...of course."

He pulled a piece of paper out of his flight-suit breast pocket and unfolded it slowly.

"We are gathered here on this cycle to bid farewell to Captain Nathan Drake," Drummond said. "Born on Earth in 2012. Killed in the line of duty on this cycle, in the year 2062. We, um, thank him for his service."

Drummond folded the paper and placed it back into his pocket.

He looked at Paul and said, "OK, Prisoner Owens."

Paul looked at Drummond and then to Cooley to be sure.

Cooley looked at Drummond and then back to Paul. His face was a mask of sadness and disgust as he nodded at Paul.

Paul pulled the lever, activating the air lock. The lights on the other side of the bulkhead flashed red for ten seconds in a countdown before the outer doors opened. When they did, the violent rush of escaping air launched the captain's coffin. It leapt out of the air lock and tumbled into the void.

Paul watched it for as long as he could. It was gone in seconds, impossible to discern among the stars.

# Chapter Seven

*1420 Hours, 21 July 2037*
*Reinholds, Pennsylvania*

Belen Regas laughed as he skinned the frog alive. He was twelve years old at summer camp. He had led a small group away from the campsite during lunch and caught the little dark-green frog by the pond.

"Oh my God! So gross!" a girl screamed as he pulled on the dark, rubbery skin. Pink and white flesh resisted the separation.

He held the frog's skinless rear legs in one hand as he tried to pull its skin off over its head like a sweater with the other. He grunted with effort.

The two girls ran away from the scene.

Three boys his age stood around him. They squinted, horrified but unable to look away, knowing it was wrong but not knowing what to do.

"Belen," one of the boys said, almost in a whisper. "Stop it."

"Shut up, Carlos!" Regas yelled, furious at the challenge.

He let go of the frog's skin with one hand, maintaining his grip on the tortured amphibian's legs with his other, and lunged at Carlos.

"If you love frogs so much, why don't you kiss it?" he said as he slapped Carlos in the face with the dying frog.

Carlos yelped as the other two boys turned to run. Carlos ran after them, crying as he wiped frog bits from his mouth.

Mr. Watson, a camp counselor, heard the commotion. He saw Regas standing by the pond and shook his head. *Crazy, that kid,* he thought to himself as he walked toward the cruel boy.

Regas saw him coming. "You're lucky, you little bitch," he whispered to the frog as he tossed it into the pond.

"Belen!" Mr. Watson said. "What was that?"

"Nothin'," Regas said.

Mr. Watson looked at the disturbed water where the frog had landed in the pond and sunk out of sight. He shook his head at the young boy. "Belen..." he started to say. Then he stopped. The kid looked back at him, hands in pockets, unafraid. Almost taunting.

Mr. Watson turned and walked away. He was tired of dealing with Belen Regas. *No wonder his parents signed him up for eight weeks of summer camp,* he thought. *I wouldn't want that little shit around either.*

*

Corporal Regas woke up in the aid station. He was thirty-three years old on his second combat deployment. He couldn't see anything.

"I'm blind!" he yelled. "I'm blind! I'm fucking blind!"

"No, Corporal!" a voice said as he felt hands restrain him. "Corporal Regas, listen to me! Your eyes are fine. We bandaged them for your comfort. They were full of sand when they brought you in," she said.

"Sand?" Regas asked, lying back down.

His mind was fuzzy. Blurry thoughts passed by, just out of reach. Gradually, he remembered where he was. He was a squad leader. There had been a firefight. Had they won?

"Your helmet was destroyed in the blast. It's a miracle you survived."

"Fuck!" Regas shivered as blinding pain cleaved his forehead. He gripped the rails of the bed.

"Easy," the voice said. "Your brain has sustained a terrible concussion. You need to rest."

"How long was I out?" Regas whispered through the pain.

"Two weeks," she said. "The last week of it was induced, though. We had to keep you sedated because of all of the brain swelling. You're a strong man, Belen. You took…"

Her voice faded away. Thankfully, so did the pain.

*

A month later, Corporal Regas walked into his company commander's office and saluted.

"There he is!" the captain said, returning the salute. "Regas the killing machine." The captain grinned and gestured at the pair of chairs. They both sat. "How do you feel?"

"Good," Regas said. "Thank you, sir."

"No more headaches?"

"Not nearly as many, sir," Regas said, nodding.

"Good," the captain said, smiling. "You're a lucky soldier. When that vehicle went up, I thought we'd be scraping you off the roof. I still don't know how you survived."

"Me either, sir," Regas said.

"And, my God, son," the captain said, shaking his head. "The way you attacked them. I've never seen anything like it."

Regas just nodded. The truth was he had enjoyed it. But he knew that he wasn't supposed to admit that.

"How is the lieutenant?" Regas asked, to change the subject.

"Oh," the captain said, his face darkening. "He is going to make it. But it's going to be a long road back for him."

The captain paused.

"You saved his life, you know," the captain said. "I'm putting you in for a Silver Star."

"Thank you, sir," Regas said, meeting the captain's gaze.

The captain nodded and looked at Regas for a long moment.

"Look, Corporal," the captain said, knowing there was no good time to tell him. "I'm sure you're wondering. We got the results back."

Regas said nothing. He could tell where this was going.

"You didn't get picked up for the Centaur Corps. I'm sorry. I know you really wanted it."

Regas resisted the urge to yell at the captain, to tell him he didn't know shit, to tell him that it was a fucking crime the Centaur Corps was not taking him. What a bunch of fucking idiots.

But, truthfully, Regas had expected it. It was just like the Academy. He never really had a chance. They tolerated his application and then denied it with pleasure. They couldn't deny his enlistment, though. And they couldn't deny he was the best killer in his unit. He loved it. He was good at it. He should have been welcomed into the Centaur Corps with wide-open arms. But they were just like the rest. Idiots.

"Any feedback as to why, sir?" was all Regas said.

"No, son, they generally don't give out that kind of information. It's a simple yes or no."

"I understand, sir," Regas said.

The captain looked at the crestfallen soldier. "Look, Corporal Regas," he said. "You know you're in the running for squad leader when we rotate back. I know the lieutenant feels strongly about it. That would be another stripe. You'd be a sergeant, with a bright career in front of you."

Regas nodded. That was something. But it did not take away the sting.

"Am I dismissed, sir?" he asked.

"Sure, son," the captain said.

Regas stood up and saluted. The captain stood and returned the salute. He watched as the corporal left his office.

To join the Centaur Corps, an enlisted soldier had to serve a successful combat tour and then pass the rigorous assessment process. A tortuous one-month endurance test that ended in an extensive psych eval for those who made it that far.

Centaurs were augmented human soldiers. Not only was each centaur a $100 million investment by the military, it was a considerable physical upgrade to the human. Not the kind of upgrade you wanted to make to a person of unstable or otherwise undesirable mental makeup. The conditions and situations that Centaurs were exposed to were excruciating for even the strongest of constitution. And the damage they could do if they went haywire was extensive.

The captain walked back to his desk, sat down, and leaned back in his chair.

On his desk sat a file with Regas's name on it. The captain closed his eyes, remembering what it said.

---

*CLASSIFIED—Though physically and tactically well qualified, psychological evaluations of Corporal Belen Regas reveal a lack of stability, a quickness of temper, and a tendency toward antisocial behavior. This combination of factors calls into question his ability to be loyal to his comrades, unit, or chain of command. This deficiency is exacerbated by his underdeveloped conscience and strong ego. Corporal Belen Regas is not fit for duty in the Centaur Corps.—CLASSIFIED*

---

The captain remembered Regas fighting his way through the ambush to get to the lieutenant, who had been riding in the lead vehicle. When Regas charged forward, there was a moment of hesitation by the rest of the unit. It was chaos. Multiple vehicles had been hit, and there were so many enemy.

But Regas cut through everything in his way.

At the time, it had thrilled the captain. The courage. The will to win.

In retrospect, he wondered if he had seen some of what Regas's psych eval had described. He remembered looking for Regas when it was over. The medevac drones were cycling the wounded back to base, and the captain was not sure if Regas had been hurt or not. He had found the corporal near the prisoners.

There were half a dozen enemy that had survived the skirmish and been captured. They had been stripped of their exoskeletons and armor and sat on the ground, arms bound behind their backs inside a hastily assembled concertina-wire perimeter. Two soldiers stood guard over them.

The captain found Regas circling the POWs like a shark. He walked slowly around the captives, just outside the wire that encircled them. He held his bayonet in his right hand.

"Corporal Regas," the captain said, approaching. "Any injuries you need to have checked out?"

No response.

The captain stepped in front of Regas, who stared at the POWs as he walked. "Corporal!"

Regas stopped and slowly swiveled his head to the captain.

"Sir?"

"You OK, son?"

"Yes, sir," Regas said, turning his head back toward the prisoners. "I'm fine."

"What are you doing?"

"Was just thinking, sir."

"About what?"

"Old pictures I've seen from the Vietnam War. You know they used to cut the ears off the enemy and make necklaces out of 'em?"

"Uh-huh..." The captain looked from Regas to the POWs and then back. "Well, we're not going to do that today, Corporal. If you are not hurt, I need you back on convoy security. We've got to get to the outpost before dark."

Regas's vehicle struck a land mine on the way back, killing everyone inside but him.

At the time, the captain had not thought much about Regas's comments. People said all kinds of weird shit in combat.

Now, he wasn't so sure.

Regas seethed as he left the captain's office.

The Combat Corps was the elite fighting force of the US military. Formed after the disaster in Santiago, it was the unified fighting force that took the place of the fragmented special-operations community. Taking only the best, the Combat Corps was the most important and most honored branch of the modern military. The Combat Corps was made up of Centaurs and infantry, and they were not created equal. The Centaurs were the elite. They were meldings of man and machine that could rain down death and destruction on an astounding scale. The Centaurs were the ones that counted. Wherever they went, they were in command. They were the real show.

Rather than full augmentation, the infantry component of the Combat Corps received epidermal electronic implants that were not much more than tattoos that sensed vitals and conveyed information to the exoskeletons they wore and fought in. In addition to working for the Centaurs, they did the shit details. The MPs, the transportation, convoy security, etc. These were important jobs. But still shit details.

Regas hated taking off his exoskeleton and armor at the end of a mission. He was back to being human. He knew that his destiny was to be a Centaur. He had waited as long as he could before applying.

Less than 5 percent of applicants made it through the assessment. Less than 5 percent of those ultimately made it through the training and augmentation process to become true Centaurs. Nonetheless, Belen Regas had been certain he was going to make it. He deserved it. His family had not had the money to send him to college, and he had not been able to get into the Academy. That was the first time the military had failed to recognize his greatness, and he never forgave that first offense. But the prospect of joining the Centaurs had helped him to move forward.

He realized now he had been a fool. It was rigged. Always would be.

He did not know what to do. That made him angrier.

*

Two weeks later, Regas was on a security patrol with his squad. It was their final mission. The next day, they would start the process of rotating back to the States. As they walked through the dusty streets, Regas spotted an open door. Usually, when they patrolled through a place, it was locked up tight. No one wanted any trouble with the American infantry.

Regas peered inside the open door. He thought he heard a noise inside, the shuffling of feet, perhaps. He turned sideways and crept with bent knees in order to get the bulk of his armored exoskeleton through the doorway. When he straightened up and turned into the room, a frightened male teenager looked back at him.

Regas leaned his rifle against the wall and pulled out his bayonet.

*

Four months later, Corporal Regas was drunk at the NCO club back at Camp Lejeune. He sat at his stool, ordering beer after beer. The waitress felt increasingly uncomfortable serving him. But she could tell he was one of those guys. A little crazy from what he had seen and what had happened to him, and not one who walked away politely after being cut off. It was easier to just keep serving him and call the MPs when he wasn't looking. They would be here soon.

Regas guzzled beers but was unable to swallow what had happened earlier that day. He sat hunched over at the bar, sagging under the weight of his indignation. He got madder and madder as he replayed the day's events over and over in his head. He punctuated each insulting memory with a large swallow of beer.

He remembered waiting in the battalion orderly room. He was so excited, it was hard to sit still, so he'd stood in the corner.

"Corporal Regas!" the major had called from his office.

The captain was a major now. He'd been promoted a month after they got back. Everyone was getting promoted. Today was supposed to be Regas's turn.

He snapped to attention and entered the major's office. Regas walked up to the major's desk and saluted.

"Sir, Corporal Belen Regas reports as ordered."

The major was sitting at his desk. The sergeant major and new lieutenant were seated in chairs just to the left of the major's desk. Regas had heard his old lieutenant was still in the hospital. He should be released soon but would never be back on combat duty.

"At ease, Corporal," the major said, returning Regas's salute.

Regas felt fantastic. He knew his uniform looked perfect and he had nailed the interviews earlier in the week. Now, finally, was his moment.

"Corporal," the major began. "We want to thank you for stepping up and applying for the squad leader position for third squad. It's the charge-the-hill attitude we've come to expect and rely on from you."

The major smiled nervously and glanced at the sergeant major.

That's when Regas knew. Fucked again.

"But the truth is, son, we are going to go in a different direction with third squad. You have demonstrated…"

Regas's mind went blank with rage. His head sagged and his arms went limp by his sides, leaving the position of at ease. He couldn't hear a word the major was saying.

"Fuck!" Regas heard himself say loudly.

"At ease, Corporal!" the sergeant major said, flying out of his chair. He was a salty old enlisted man, someone whom Regas actually respected. "You will maintain your military bearing, soldier!" the sergeant major yelled at Regas, closing the distance between them in an instant. Regas could smell the sergeant major's breath.

The new lieutenant sat stunned, eyes wide, in his chair.

The sergeant major's anger bumped Regas back from the edge. Just barely. He stammered as he tried to say his piece.

"I just don't get it, sir," Regas said. "I am the best soldier in this company. Period. You know that. I fucking saved my lieutenant's life when no one else would leave cover. What else do I need to do?"

Regas's voice was pleading. He heard it himself. He was ashamed.

The major gestured at the sergeant major to back off a little. The old NCO took half a step back but maintained a glaring overwatch of Regas.

"Son," the major said. "I'm going to be as honest with you as I know how to be. You deserve that."

The major stood up and walked around in front of Regas. He leaned back against his desk and crossed his arms.

"You are a good soldier, Regas," the major began. "But you are damaged, son. And not just from the combat. That leaves a mark on all of us. And we're all filthy from it. But you…"

The major paused, deciding if he should measure his words or not.

"Look, we've heard about the ears, the questionable battlefield killings, the way you bully other soldiers. We've never investigated, son, because we need you out there, outside of the wire with us. Every unit needs a crazy-ass killer like you. And I'm damn glad you're ours. And you did save the lieutenant. I don't forget shit like that. None of us do."

The major looked around the room. The lieutenant nodded. The sergeant major just stared at Regas.

The major uncrossed his arms and sighed. "But there is a difference between a good killer and a good leader. And stripes are for leaders, son. Not murderers. There is no way I'm giving you sergeant's stripes. Ever."

It was the finality in the major's voice that enraged Regas now as he sat drunk on a stool at the bar in the NCO club. The major's voice, more than his words, told Regas that his dreams were dead, that he didn't have a purpose anymore, that he wasn't good enough.

"Can I get another goddamn beer, please?" Regas yelled. The waitress looked at him from the other side of the bar.

Regas felt a hand on his shoulder.

"Evening, Corporal," said the MP. "Why don't we call it a night?"

Regas turned around on his stool to face two military policemen. They each smiled at Regas with hey-we've-all-been-there grins meant to lower the tension. They were relaxed, not expecting a confrontation.

Big mistake.

Regas's beer mug shattered on the face of the nearest MP, shredding the flesh of the young man's cheek and knocking him unconscious.

In the next heartbeat, Regas kicked the other in the groin. Hard.

As the shocked MP bent over in pain, Belen broke his nose with a punch to the face. He fell backward, blood spraying on the floor.

"What the hell are you doing?" the waitress yelled at Regas.

He glanced at her and then scanned the NCO club. The small crowd was stunned by the sudden violence. No one was making a move for him yet.

Regas bolted for the door.

"Someone stop him!" he heard the waitress yell.

But no one followed him.

*

Regas ran. He knew he was done.

He snuck off post that night, avoiding the gate guards, and then bought a bus ticket. He didn't go home. That was the first place the MPs would be looking for an AWOL soldier.

It was an overnight bus to Baton Rouge. Regas did not sleep at all, kept awake as his mind lurched from anger to shame to sadness and back to anger. The shame faded first. Then the sadness. All he had left when he got off the bus in Louisiana was anger.

Two months later, he was still on the run. Regas was living in a South Texas town, trying to figure out how to cross the border without getting picked up, when the MPs caught up with him. A few days earlier, he'd gotten in a fight in front of a convenience store where he had been hanging out, being rude and confrontational while he mulled over his plan. A hapless smart-ass teenager had drawn his ire with loud music and a sneer. Regas beat him, would have killed him had two truckers not intervened.

It got him noticed.

Getting noticed got him caught.

"You dumb fucking son of a bitch," the major said to Regas when the MPs returned the disgraced corporal in handcuffs.

Regas just stared back at him from behind the bars of his prison cell. He imagined himself on the other side of the bars, pounding the smug officer into a bloody pulp. Then he would step on the unconscious man's head and grind it into the concrete floor. Then—

"Are you even listening to me?" the major asked.

Belen's eyes came back into focus and swiveled to meet the major's.

"You were AWOL for longer than thirty days. We're still at war, so that is called desertion. It's punishable by death."

No reaction from Regas. He would not give the major that satisfaction.

The major, who had been called into the brig to sign paperwork after Regas's return, was flabbergasted. Sadness came over his face. He shook his head, turned, and left without saying goodbye. It was useless.

The court-martial took half a day. Regas got twenty years for desertion, theft, and drunk and disorderly conduct. He sat in his cell afterward, not fully understanding what had just happened. He knew he had been charged with multiple counts of aggravated assault. But he had declined court-appointed counsel, so he hadn't really followed why those charges seemed to have gone away. He knew enough to know that he had gotten lucky, though. Those crimes carried decades more time in jail. As it stood, he'd still be a little over fifty when he got out.

The night before they shipped him to Leavenworth, he found out the source of his good luck.

"You're a lucky prisoner," a guard told him, delivering his dinner.

"Doesn't feel like it to me, sir," Regas said, taking the tray of slop and returning to the corner of his small cell.

"Shit," the guard said, shaking his head. "If that lieutenant of yours had not appealed to the judge, you'd have gotten about a hundred years for all those violent-assault charges."

Regas looked up from his slop.

"I guess you guys served together?" the guard asked.

"Yes, sir."

"I read the account of that day," the guard said, shaking his head slowly and raising his eyebrows. "Sounds like it was some serious shit."

Regas nodded, recalling. It seemed like a million years ago. Was that his best day ever? Would he ever feel like that again?

"Your old LT appealed to the judge. Made a case on your behalf. You know, all the damage you got up here." The guard pointed at his head. "Gave a long speech about how he lost his legs, but you lost your way."

Regas looked at the guard, wishing he would shut up, and then went back to eating his slop.

The guard chuckled. "Shit worked, I guess."

Two days later, Private Belen Regas was processed into the United States Disciplinary Barracks at Fort Leavenworth. Less than a year later, he applied to the Fly It Off program and was accepted due to the nonviolent nature of his convictions.

# Chapter Eight

P aul woke up screaming. He tried to jump out of bed, believing it to be a pile of bodies. He had thrashed in his sleep, though, and tangled his legs in the sheets. He fell heavily to the floor, which helped clear his head. It was the metal floor of the hab module spinning on the front of the *Odysseus*, not that dusty village square. He lay on the cool floor for a few minutes, drenched in sweat and panting as he calibrated to his surroundings.

"I'm on the *Odysseus*," he said quietly to himself.

"Everything OK, Paul?" said the XO over the intercom.

"Yeah. I'm fine." Paul rubbed his eyes.

"You sounded very alarmed. I hope you understand I don't eavesdrop, but if certain parameters are exceeded, I do check in just to ensure that—"

"I'm fine, XO. Just please let me wake up in peace." Paul stood up and walked to his bathroom.

"As you wish, Paul. My apologies."

"I'm definitely on the *Odysseus*," Paul grumbled to himself as he stepped into the shower.

Paul let the warm water run over him as he stood motionless. *Haven't had that dream in a while,* he thought. He looked at his hands. They were trembling. He began to get angry. His mind raced.

*I can't fucking believe this. I left Earth on this voyage to isolate myself from the triggers. To get the fuck away from anything that would remind me. I've worked so hard to get my shit together. I get out here, and a man gets his head taken off and I'm picking brains out of my clothing. Are you fucking kidding me!*

"Paul. Are you OK?" It was the XO. Paul realized he had been screaming in the shower.

"Um…yeah… Thanks. I'm good."

"Very well. Please let me know if you need anything."

"I need you to leave me the fuck alone."

Paul sat down in the shower. He closed his eyes and did his breathing exercises as the warm water ran over his body.

By the time he'd left the shower, toweled off, and gotten dressed, Paul had de-escalated himself from enraged down through panicky to just anxious. He dove into his daily ritual, sitting for a longer-than-usual meditation before making himself a pot of coffee. He sat at his desk with a cup.

His watch alarm clock chimed.

"Fuck!" Paul muttered. *I just sat down to translate.*

But when Paul looked at his cup of coffee, no steam rose. Hadn't he just poured it? He grabbed the cup. It wasn't warm. He dipped his finger into the coffee. It was cold. He looked at his watch.

It had been forty-five minutes. He had ten minutes until the meeting Drummond had scheduled.

"Shit," he muttered.

*

"Attention!" Cooley said as he entered the room ahead of Drummond.

The room sprang to attention.

Cooley walked to his seat. Drummond walked to his and sat down.

Cooley cleared his throat. Drummond looked at him.

"Oh," Drummond said. "Yes. Please be seated."

Regas glanced at McNeeley and Hahn, who just managed to hide their snickering. Cooley glared.

"Mr. Cooley," Drummond said, glancing quickly around the room. "You may conduct this meeting, if you will."

"Aye, Captain," Cooley said.

"Congratulations," Regas said before Cooley could continue. Regas wore his most friendly smile to disguise his act of disrespect.

"Excuse me, Prisoner?" Cooley said.

"I'm sorry, Mr. Cooley," Regas said, still wearing the bullshit smile. "Just seems like we should acknowledge Mr. Drummond's—I mean, Captain Drummond's—promotion, shouldn't we?"

Paul looked at Cooley, wondering if he would explode. Then he looked at Regas. Paul noticed that Regas's left breast pocket was unzipped, just like last time. Paul knew it was not a coincidence.

"Prisoner Regas—" Cooley began.

"It's OK, Mr. Cooley," Drummond interrupted him. "Let's just get on with it. We've got less than six months to the belt. When we get there, we'll let the Company know what has happened, and they will have resources, including people, that I am sure will be very helpful."

It was clear to everyone that Drummond was hoping that a new captain would come aboard at that time. Space Command always had experienced senior officers posted at Belt Station for contingencies like this one.

But his comment did raise another question.

"Has the Company not already been informed of the incident, sir?" Paul asked Drummond.

Drummond glanced at Cooley and then looked down as he said, "No, Prisoner Owens. They have not."

The crew exchanged looks.

"XO," Cooley said, "please review the damage report for the crew."

"Yes, sir," the XO responded. A schematic of the *Odysseus* sprang to life on the table's display. Red highlights blinked in dozens of areas, including the bridge.

"The *Odysseus* was struck by a total of one hundred and seventy-one meteoroids across her entire length. There were two main clusters, however, that caused most of the damage. One was concentrated aft of the hangar, below the tube."

Red circles appeared around two areas on the *Odysseus*'s floating image as the XO outlined them.

"And the other was concentrated on the bridge. This is the meteoroid cluster that killed Captain Drake, of course."

"At what angle did the meteoroids strike us?" Paul asked.

"The meteoroids struck the *Odysseus* at eighty-seven degrees off of flight path." As the XO spoke, red lines traced the meteoroids' paths passing through the *Odysseus* on the table displays.

"Damn near a perfect broadside," said Paul.

"We'd have been fucked if anything had hit the spinner," Regas said.

"Indeed, Prisoner Regas," the XO said. "A large enough strike to any part of the spinner would have created a severe out-of-balance situation that I would not have been able to control. It would have torn itself apart. We'd have lost both the hab and the utility module and likely suffered severe damage to other parts of the *Odysseus*."

"Please continue with the report, XO," Cooley said with some irritation in his voice.

"Full atmosphere and environmentals have been restored to the bridge, but most of its command-and-control capabilities remain offline. Twenty-seven percent of hull perforations have already been repaired, and I estimate we will be at one hundred percent in less than five cycles."

As the XO talked, the 3D *Odysseus* schematic image rolled and expanded to show the precise impact areas.

"Cargo damage assessment is not yet complete but so far looks limited primarily to raw materials. The factory was only slightly damaged and is fully operational again. Communications systems, however, were heavily damaged, given their location aft and below the tube."

"That's not good," Paul said.

"You're right," responded the XO as the image zoomed in. "This is the main communications antennae array site. Five small meteoroids impacted this area, damaging our ship-to-ship communications antennae and destroying our long-range antennae array. The ship-to-ship antennae can likely be repaired, and we should be able to achieve seventy-five percent capacity."

"That's great, XO," Regas said. "Especially since we are at least fifty million kilometers from the nearest ship, and the range of that antennae is, what? A couple million kilometers?"

"You are correct, Prisoner Regas."

"What about the long-range antennae?" Paul asked.

"The long-range antennae array was damaged beyond repair," Cooley said.

The crew sat silent for a moment, staring at the image of the *Odysseus* floating over the large table.

The long-range antennae array served two purposes. First, it allowed the *Odysseus* to communicate with the Company back on Earth and in the belt whenever there was a need. This included the Bloomberg Belt Market feed. Drummond had nearly cried when Cooley had explained this to him.

Second, it transmitted the *Odysseus*'s location and other data on a regular schedule. This data provided the Company with situational awareness that enabled it to effect rescue if possible, warn of hazards and known pirate activity, and de-conflict flight paths. Without this communication link, the *Odysseus* was on its own in the void until it made it to the asteroid belt.

The *Odysseus* suddenly felt much more remote.

"Any other good news, XO?" Regas asked.

"No. That is it. As tragic and irritating as this situation is, it could have been much worse."

"I thought these shipping lanes were constantly reviewed for foreign object violations like this," Paul said, turning his head toward Cooley.

"They are," the XO said. "Command takes care to plot courses that are out of the way of all known meteoroids and other hazards."

"Fuck load of good it did us," Regas said.

"The void is infinite," Cooley said with a shrug. "It is too big. There's too much stuff out there. And, unfortunately, the usual method of discovery is a collision like this."

"I have recorded the meteoroid cluster," the XO said, "as well as calculated its new trajectory as a result of the collision with the *Odysseus*, and will upload it to command as soon as I am able."

"You mean when we dock at the belt?" Paul said.

"Unfortunately, yes."

"OK," Cooley said. "So, as we discussed, Mr. Drummond is serving as captain. I will be adjusting our training and maintenance schedule in coordination with the XO as he completes the damage assessment. The old girl is going to need a lot of repairs, and we are going to have to pitch in. The new cycle watch and duty schedule will be posted in a few hours."

Cooley looked around the room and then at Drummond, who was looking at his tablet computer.

"Sir?" Cooley said.

"Yes, Mr. Cooley?"

"Will that be all, sir?"

"Oh," Drummond said. "Yes. I think so."

"Then are we dismissed, sir?" Cooley asked when it was obvious Drummond still didn't get it.

"Yes," Drummond said, looking back down at his tablet. "You are dismissed."

The crew stood up and began to leave. Drummond stayed in his seat.

"So, no other promotions, then?" Regas said to no one in particular. "Damn."

McNeeley and Hahn snickered.

Althea and Paul were the last to filter out of the room. As they neared the door, Paul gestured to Althea to go ahead of him.

"Paul," she said instead, "how are you feeling?"

"Fine," Paul said.

"Are you sure? The XO told me you have had a rough time sleeping."

"I'm fine, Althea," Paul said with some irritation. "I promise. Just leave me alone."

He pushed ahead of her and walked out.

\*

Later that cycle, after his duties were complete, Paul went to the fitness room. Located across the hub on the top floor of the utility module, it was an old facility that was part of the original retrofit of the spinner. "The military doesn't go anywhere without a weight room, beer, and porn," Captain Drake had said about the facility. It had clearly gotten a lot of use by previous crew members. It was one of the grungiest rooms on the *Odysseus*. It smelled worse than a locker room. Despite years of cleaning by sanitation bots, the smell of sweaty soldiers persisted.

Paul visited the fitness facility every second or third cycle. Occasionally, he would get on one of the old-style treadmills, but usually he lifted weights.

He did both that cycle, hoping a good workout would help him sleep.

Paul woke up screaming anyway.

He thrashed himself awake but managed to not fall out of the bed. But he was stuck. He lay in sweaty sheets, unable to move. He could not speak. Could not break his gaze at the ceiling. Brains floating in the bridge, entrails dragging through the dirt, aircraft falling in flames from the sky, a pile of dead foot soldiers, a bayonet slicing, rockets flying, bullets impacting. Kill after kill. His brain cycled from image to image to image as he relived it all... He started to tremble. He was being swallowed by it.

"Paul," he heard a voice say from the void.

He couldn't find it.

"Paul," Althea repeated.

He felt a hand on his shoulder.

"Paul," Althea said tenderly, but with some force to get through to him. His head swiveled quickly, and she met his gaze.

She was sitting on the edge of his bed.

His eyes were wide and darting back and forth. His breathing was rapid.

Althea noted his pulse rising.

"Paul, you are in your quarters on the *Odysseus*, and I am here with you," she said.

She maintained eye contact, beckoning him back.

"You're safe, Paul."

His wide eyes narrowed slightly. His breathing slowed. He recognized her.

She gave him a few minutes to breathe before whispering, "It's OK."

"I can't believe it," he said. "I thought I had gotten far enough away from it," he said. Tears began to run down his face. His voice quivered with pain. "How fucking far do I have to go to get away? They are all around me again."

His microexpressions trended negatively again. His face flushed and his heart rate spiked. His eyes broke their lock with hers and lurched left and right.

Althea grabbed his other shoulder and gently turned him to face her squarely.

"No!" she said. "I know it feels that way. But it's just you and me here. In your room. On the *Odysseus*. Together."

Paul looked around nervously. "I know. I know. I just…" he stammered. Then he locked eyes with Althea.

Althea nodded. "I won't let you get lost again, Paul. I promise. I've got you. But you've got to meet me halfway."

Paul nodded. Then he sobbed.

Althea sat next to him, hand on his shoulder, for the next hour. When Paul was spent and had fallen asleep, she stood up carefully and left.

She closed Paul's door. When she turned to go back to her quarters, Regas startled her.

She stopped herself just before running into him.

"Can I get some room service also?" Regas said, taking a step closer, one foot almost between her legs. He towered over her, head angled down, eyes running over her body.

"Have a good evening, Prisoner," Althea said sharply, moving to step around him.

Regas matched her step to the side, blocking her path.

"Come on," he said. "It ain't fair. Why does the jigsaw get special favors?" Regas stared at Althea's breasts and rubbed his chin.

"If there are issues you need my assistance with, you may schedule a time through Mr. Cooley," Althea said without emotion. "That is the policy."

Regas dropped his hand from his chin and adjusted his crotch.

"I ever tell you how much you remind me of someone I knew?" he said. "It was my first deployment, I think."

Althea stayed silent, not taking the bait.

"Some*thing*, actually," Regas continued. "Something I knew. A synthetic. My squad and I found her when we were patrolling behind a jigsaw unit that had carried out a major raid the night before. Who knows? Maybe it was Captain Jigsaw's unit?"

Regas gestured past Althea at Paul's door.

"Those guys were always in and out without coordinating with anyone, so how would I know?" Regas said with a shrug. "All I know is they killed a lot of people. The little town was all shot up. It was a mess. One of the other guys heard her. She was inside a bombed-out building, kneeling over a wounded civilian, administering aid. The four of us snuck up on her."

Regas chuckled at the memory.

"She looked kind of like you," he said. "Black hair. Skin work wasn't as good as yours by a long shot. But nice titties. She was missing a hand and about half that forearm. A couple of wires dangled out of her stump. But, other than that, she was good to go. You guys don't really bleed as much as we do, you know."

An ugly smile spread across Regas's face.

"I went first," he said. "Then I went again when the others were done. We tied it up and hid it in a closet in that shot-up house," he continued. "I mean, we couldn't tell anyone else in the unit about it. They would have worn it out in a day. We kept it a secret. Just our squad."

Regas paused, as if recalling one of his fondest memories.

"The fellas got mad at me, because within a few days, I had broken her up pretty bad. I didn't care, though. In fact, I liked it better that way. I didn't care that she didn't have a head anymore. Or that the one leg bent the wrong way."

Regas's eyes roved all over Althea as he spoke.

"It got to be ridiculous. I mean, it was really broken. I didn't care. But that's when the rest of the unit found out about it. You know what my commander did when he heard?"

Althea kept her face placid, knowing that he would feed off any reaction.

"He laughed," Regas said. "Thought it was hilarious."

Althea looked down.

"I bet your jigsaw captain would have laughed too," Regas said in a mocking whisper. "So, you see," he said, hand reaching out to her. "I've got stuff I need to talk about too," he said.

"Prisoner!" Althea said, slapping his hand and stepping back. "Let me pass or I will report this incident."

"Incident?" Regas said, raising his voice. "What incident? I haven't gotten shit. It's the jigsaw who you've been fucking." Regas pointed at Paul's room with growing anger. "You're the one who should be reported!"

Althea squared her stance, readying herself for violence.

"That will be enough, Prisoner Regas," the XO said over the hallway speakers, startling Regas. "I asked Althea to visit Prisoner Owens's quarters for medical reasons."

Regas looked at the speaker in the ceiling and then back to Althea.

"Return to your quarters this instant, and I will not report this incident to Mr. Cooley and Captain Drummond," the XO said.

Regas stared at Althea, who met his gaze with disgust.

"No problem, XO," Regas said, letting his eyes rove over Althea one more time before he slowly backed down the hallway. "Nice talking to you, Althea."

# Chapter Nine

*Utsu Book One*

*Circa 1510*

*Translated from the Japanese*

I dragged the body of Kusunoki for many weeks. I walked through the hills and small villages following the map I had drawn from Kusunoki's fantastic stories. Along the way, I asked those I came across if they knew of the school.

Those I asked denied any knowledge of such a school. They laughed at me. It was a common delusion, they said. They offered to let me bury Kusunoki in their village graveyard. It had been almost a full year since the Siege of the Seven Swans, and the battle was now well known across the land. It had brought a measure of peace. They would be honored to have his body rest with them.

I refused. I continued to walk.

After forty days, fatigue made a coward of me. I wanted to stop. I felt foolish. I was dragging the body of Kusunoki down a narrow road in the woods many miles from the nearest village. It would have been easy to bury Kusunoki in those woods. To give him a peaceful grave many would have been grateful for.

I stood still for many minutes, staring into the woods and trying to convince myself it would be OK. There was not, after all, a School Hiroaki. So, in fact, I could not fulfill my vow. Therefore, it was no dishonor to break it.

"So it is true!" a voice called from behind me.

A man approached on the road. He walked with a horse. He was an older man, I thought. In his fifties perhaps. He wore simple clothes and a single katana on his waist.

"I heard about a crazy rōnin dragging a body from village to village and through the hills," he said. "But I did not believe it."

He walked up and stood next to me, taking my measure. He chuckled at what he saw.

"I seek School Hiroaki," I said. "Do you know it?"

"There is no such thing," the man said. "It is a myth."

I nodded in exhaustion.

"Why do you drag that body behind you?" he asked me.

"It is the body of my friend Kusunoki. A hero of the Siege of the Seven Swans. I owe my life to him. His last wish was to be buried at School Hiroaki, where he studied. I promised to fulfill this wish."

"Then he has bound you to folly," the man said with a chuckle.

This angered me. But I had no strength left.

"Nonetheless," the man said. "I would not see a traveler burdened in this way and not help. I appear to be going in your direction. We could put your friend's body on my horse until the next village. Then we must part ways."

I nodded my assent. "I am grateful," I told him.

We walked in silence for a few miles before the man asked me, "What will you do if you cannot find the school?"

"I do not know," I answered.

"What will you do if you find it?"

"I will bury my friend," I said. "And I will give Hiroaki my friend's katana and a note meant for him."

"And then?"

"I do not know."

"You are rōnin, are you not?"

"I am."

"Would you tell me about the Siege of the Seven Swans?" the man asked me. "Tell me how your friend saved you."

Happy to be free of the weight of Kusunoki's body, I did not mind telling the man the story. For the next few miles, I described the siege to him. I described all of our preparations and all of the violence. I described the moment when Kusunoki saved me. I described our wounds and convalescence in the village. I told him of Kusunoki's crazy stories and of my vow and, finally, of his death.

The man listened closely. When I finished, he nodded.

"Thank you for telling me," he said.

We walked in silence for a long time after that. The man was lost in thought, and I was no longer in the mood to talk. Remembering Kusunoki had saddened me. I did not know what I would do when I reached the next village.

"Stop," the man said.

We came to a halt at a remote spot on the narrow road.

I looked at the man to ask what the problem was, but he gestured at me not to speak. He whistled the call of the kingfisher and waited. From the woods came the call of the snipe.

The man smiled at me and whistled the call of the kingfisher again.

Four armed horsemen stepped out of the woods, guiding a riderless horse behind them.

I reached for my katana, but the man put his hand on my shoulder.

"Relax, friend," he said. "These are my students."

"Who are you?" I asked, hand still on my sword.

"My name is Hiroaki."

# Chapter Ten

*Mission Cycle 387*

*Earth Year 2062*

*288,893,952 Kilometers from Earth*

Paul sighed heavily as he stepped in front of the door to Althea's quarters. It was late in the cycle, and he was showing up for a counseling session. He wasn't scheduled to see her for another six cycles. But Althea had told him, and he agreed, that he needed it. The captain's death had unearthed a lot of things he had worked hard to bury.

Despite Paul's certainty, he fidgeted at the door and thought about leaving, about walking away quickly before she knew he was there.

He looked at his watch. It was time. He hesitated.

Althea opened her door suddenly.

Paul looked at her, trying to mask his resignation with a smile.

"Oh my," Althea said, regarding him. "You look like a man about to walk the plank."

"Feels a little that way," Paul said.

"This will be a good thing, Paul," she said, taking his hand and pulling him gently behind her into her quarters. "I promise."

They stopped next to the coffee table, between the sofa and two chairs.

Althea wore an oversized white sweater and white leggings. It was the first time Paul had ever seen her out of her flight suit.

"I made you some tea," Althea said, gesturing to the pot and cup on the table.

"Thanks," Paul said. "Maybe in a bit."

Althea nodded and walked to one of the chairs.

Paul sat down on the sofa. As he did so, he noticed an object in the corner of the small room.

"Is that a yoga mat?" he asked Althea as she sat down.

"Yes," she said.

"What is it for?"

"What is a yoga mat for?"

"Yeah," Paul said.

"It is for yoga."

"You do yoga?"

"Yes."

"Like, real yoga?"

"Yes," she answered with a patient smile. "Is that so weird?"

"No. I just didn't know you…guys did yoga," he said.

"Well, some of us do." She crossed her arms.

"Interesting," Paul said. "I do too, you know."

"I didn't know that," she said. "Tell me about it."

"I like it." Paul shrugged. "They taught us yoga when they taught us the meditation techniques to deal with our augmentations. I've tried to maintain my practice since then. I haven't been that regular. But, through all the deployments, the court-martial, my imprisonment, and even now on the *Odysseus*, I've managed to stick with it somewhat. I felt like it helped with the nightmares," Paul said. "Until now."

"I think that is great," Althea said. "It is so good for you."

"Why do you do it?" Paul asked.

"It helps to keep my biomechanics limber and in sync," Althea said. "My chassis is an advanced polymer, a lot harder than your bones. But my musculature is frailer than yours, more prone to degrade. Something about the way they grow it. In any case, if I don't stretch every day and consume the correct balance of nutrients, my mobility quickly degrades. If I took, say, a week or two off, I'd get very sore and tight."

"Does it have to be yoga?" he asked.

"No. Any kind of stretching is fine," she said.

"So, why yoga?"

"I just like yoga," she said. "I like the way it makes me feel. Good for my chakras."

Paul nodded.

Althea observed him for a moment before asking, "You don't doubt I have chakras?"

Paul shrugged.

"Usually, that kind of comment gets a ridiculing reaction from humans," Althea said.

"A long time ago, I would have laughed at the notion," Paul said, nodding. "But…" His voice drifted off.

"But what?" she prompted him.

"I learned not to underestimate."

Althea smiled.

"Perhaps we could practice together sometime," she said.

Paul shook his head. "The last thing you need on board this ship is to be caught out there in a yoga outfit by one of those idiots." Paul gestured at the door.

Althea's eyes narrowed.

"I'm sorry," Paul said. "I just—"

"No," she interrupted. "It's OK. You are right, unfortunately."

Paul nodded.

"But enough about my exercise routine," Althea said, shifting in her chair. "Are you ready to begin?"

Paul sighed and looked out the window at the endless void.

Althea waited.

Just when she thought Paul had decided against it, he began to speak. Paul kept his gaze out the window as he told Althea about his first days in the military.

# Chapter Eleven

*1712 Hours, 27 June 2051*
*Fort Benning, Georgia*

Paul walked down the barracks hallway, one large duffel bag on his back, another in each hand. Sweat darkened his gray T-shirt and ran down his head in tickling, itching rivulets that made him want to rub his face.

But his hands were full.

The barracks seemed ancient. Constructed out of cinder block almost a hundred years ago, just before the Vietnam War. Beads of water oozing out of the humid Georgia summer air clung to the painted walls.

Each barracks room doorway was full of a couple of brand-new lieutenants hanging out, half paying attention to each other's listen-to-what-I-did-on-leave stories. They all kept one eye on the newcomers stumbling out of the stairwell and walking down the hall looking for their assigned barracks room.

The more alpha among them sized up each passerby like wolves examining a new pack member. *Can I take him?* they thought to themselves. *Where will they rank in the hierarchy? Will she be one of the ones who makes it through? Will I?*

Paul ignored the silent assessments and walked into his room. He dropped his bags just inside the doorway and worked his fingers to regain circulation. Then he grabbed the biting shoulder straps that held the last overstuffed duffel on his back and slid them off.

The bag made a loud thud, and he exhaled, trying to ratchet down the tension in his back.

"Who the hell are you?" said a female voice.

Startled, Paul's head jerked to his right.

A female lieutenant, wearing only a towel, stared at him.

"Uh…" Paul stammered. "What room am I in?"

"Mine," she answered.

"So, not 312?"

"310."

"Ah," Paul said. "Shit."

The female lieutenant shook her head and put her hands on her hips. Paul noted her triceps muscle. She had the physique of a professional tennis player. Her black hair was like his, shorn down to an even, skull-covering stubble. High cheekbones. Hazel eyes.

*She looks like one of the ones who will make it through,* he thought to himself. *Will I?*

"Room 312 is next door to the left," she said, pointing past Paul into the hallway. "You will recognize it because it has the number '312' on the door."

"Thanks for the tip," Paul said. He gave an embarrassed grin, hoping to tap into a little empathy before he left.

He got nothing.

She crossed her arms and glared.

*Fuck you,* he thought as he bent over to pick up his bags again.

Paul left without saying goodbye.

She slammed the door behind him.

The hallway seemed livelier to Paul now, even though only a few minutes had passed. Lieutenants walked back and forth from the latrines. Some in towels. Some partly in uniform.

Dress blues. As ordered.

*I am running late,* Paul thought, stepping into his room and closing the door. *Quick shower for me.*

Seventeen minutes later, just before 1800 hours, Paul entered the auditorium in his dress blues along with more than a thousand of the military's newest second lieutenants. Paul stepped into a row of seats, not realizing until it was too late that he was standing next to the inhospitable female lieutenant from earlier.

She noticed him and frowned.

"Give me a fucking break," she said under her breath, but loud enough for Paul to hear.

Paul tried to reverse course, but the file of lieutenants close behind him prevented it.

He turned back to face the front of the auditorium as Colonel Filson, the commandant of the Officer Assessment and Training Course, walked onto the stage in the old auditorium.

"Look at that scar," the female lieutenant whispered to Paul. "Did you know he was one of the first Centaurs?"

Paul leaned away from her. He didn't know why she was talking to him, and he did not want to get caught talking in formation. Particularly not to her.

And, of course, he knew Filson was a Centaur. They all did.

Filson was part of the army's first generation of Centaurs, augmented combat soldiers implanted with electronics that enabled them to command and control drone weapon systems via brain-to-machine interface. They had read about his exploits at the Academy. His actions at the Battle of Santiago were the subject of an entire semester of modern strategy and tactics classes. And if someone didn't know the colonel's record, the large scar that circled his head just above his ears was a giveaway.

Colonel Filson was also a legendary hard-ass.

He wore his hair skintight on the sides. Above his augmentation scar, gray hairs gave his flattop a weathered look, and deep crow's feet ran from the sides of his eyes into his temples.

But as tired as his face appeared, his six-foot body radiated energy and seemed to want to break into a sprint as he walked across the stage. There was something lupine about the old colonel. He stepped up to the podium and surveyed the room from what seemed like more of a fighting stance than a speaker's posture.

"Take your seats," Filson commanded.

Over a thousand second lieutenants sank into their seats. A few of them muttered to each other as they did so.

"It doesn't take any fucking talking!" the colonel yelled. "I said sit. Not speak." A jarring squelch of feedback spilled out of the speakers as Filson's rage overwhelmed it.

The class was startled into silence by his ferocity. He was living up to his reputation already.

"Welcome to the Officers Assessment and Training Course," the colonel said without warmth. "I am Colonel Filson, commandant of this school. It is my duty to prepare each of you for service as officers in the United States military. I want to congratulate each of you for successfully earning your commissions as second lieutenants. And I want you to know that your commissions don't mean shit to me."

Filson swiveled his head from left to right in silence, taking in the auditorium full of brand-new officers.

"I am talking to all of you. All the valedictorians, all the sports stars, all the class presidents, all the fraternity rush chairmen and sorority big sisters, and especially all the goddamn debate captains. You have done nothing. None of you. Your road to becoming an officer starts here!"

He jabbed his finger on the podium.

"Tonight!"

Another swift jab.

"And does not end for the next one hundred and eighty days unless you quit, or fail out."

A final solid jab of his finger landed on the podium like a bayonet driving into a block of wood.

"And, please, those of you who know you are going to quit, do so now and save my cadre the hassle." He paused, letting the thought sink in. "Come on. I know you're out there. It will be over in a moment. Sergeant Major McGowan is here and can process you out before the mess hall closes."

A tall, muscular soldier stepped out of the shadows at the front corner of the auditorium beneath the stage. He also bore the augmentation scars of a Centaur, and his left arm was an advanced prosthetic. He walked to the center of the stage beneath the podium and smiled as he held up a stack of paper in one hand and pens in the other.

The colonel and his sergeant major looked around the auditorium. And waited.

And looked.

And waited.

Paul thought they were belaboring their point until he heard a shuffling noise to his right.

Every head in the auditorium swiveled to see a lieutenant stand up. He made his way to the aisle and then kept his eyes on the floor as he walked down to the sergeant major.

Several other students stood up and worked their way to the front as the first, sad lieutenant took a piece of paper and pen from the sergeant major.

"No fucking way," someone near Paul whispered.

The colonel waited as four officers signed their resignation papers in front of the entire class.

A staff sergeant walked out and corralled the four shamed junior officers and led them away.

"Any more takers?" Colonel Filson said to the room. "The dropout rate for O.A.T is twenty-five percent," the colonel finally continued. "That's right. One-quarter of you will quit before the course is over. Might as well get it over with."

The colonel looked around until he was satisfied that no one else was going to make the walk of shame. He nodded to the sergeant major, who turned and walked back to the side of the auditorium.

"At least another twenty-five percent of you are going to fail," he continued. "Look around this room. Less than half of you will graduate in six months."

The colonel paused again to let the number sink in. As he did so, Paul thought he heard a noise behind him, past the closed auditorium doors. He looked around at the lieutenants next to him. No one seemed to notice anything.

"A less-than-fifty percent graduation rate!" he yelled. "It's a ridiculous number, for which I take shit from the Pentagon every cycle. 'How in the world can you fail fifty percent of the officers that we have just commissioned?' they ask me.

"I'll tell you the same thing I tell them. Because they are commissioning weak, spineless, and cowardly men and women."

The colonel glared at the auditorium for a long moment.

"Helluva motivational speaker, huh?" the female lieutenant whispered in Paul's direction.

Paul shrugged her off, not inclined to be her friend and terrified of drawing attention.

Again, Paul thought he heard something. A noise from the lobby. A few others must have also, as their heads swiveled around, looking to the rear.

"I regard it as my solemn duty to root out as many of you as I can, to not allow you to get out into my military and fuck it up. I have seen what happens when just one weakling slips through the cracks. Soldiers die. I will never allow that to happen on my watch."

Colonel Filson crossed his arms, his chin jutted forward in determination.

"The purpose of this course is threefold," Filson said. "And I just told you the first purpose."

He uncrossed his arms and held up two fingers.

"Second," he continued, "this course is designed to give every commissioned officer a common foundation that grounds them in what the military is for. And that is, fighting wars."

Now Paul was sure. A crowd was building just outside of the auditorium. It sounded boisterous. Several lieutenants around Paul heard it too. They shared what-the-hell faces before swiveling back toward the colonel, who seemed oblivious to the growing noise.

"Third!" Filson said loudly, holding up three fingers. "This course thoroughly tests and assesses newly commissioned officers to find those candidates best suited for the Combat Corps. The first and second goals will be achieved. No doubt. I am going to root out the unworthy among you. And those of you who graduate, no matter which candy-ass corner of the military you go on to serve in, you will goddamn know, for fucking certain, what being a real officer is all about. No matter what cushy REMF assignment you serve in, you will know, deep down in your bones, what the real, war-fighting soldiers are doing. And you will be able to draw a straight fucking line from what you are doing at that moment, no matter how clean and shiny, to what the real war fighters need. And you will fucking do it for them. On time. Every time."

The colonel paused again and looked at the crowd. He crossed his arms as his eyes swept slowly over the class from left to right. He was in no hurry. Paul's back stiffened as Filson's eyes passed over him.

The female lieutenant next to him sat straighter as well.

The noise from the lobby was getting louder. *How many people are out there?* Paul wondered. *How is that not pissing off Colonel Filson? And what is about to happen?*

"The third goal?" the colonel said, almost to himself. "Well, with you lot, I don't hold out much hope for the third goal. We'll address that later if we need to."

Now there was shouting outside of the auditorium. Hundreds of closely shaven lieutenant heads looked around nervously.

Colonel Filson was notorious for beginning each Officer Assessment and Training Course differently. He knew that junior officers were a chatty, secret-sharing bunch, and he was determined that everyone would face a terrible surprise on their first night. After a week or so, the course settled into its grinding, predictable rhythm, and that was fine. It didn't matter at that point. It was going to suck, and there was no way around it. It was designed to test wills and to teach.

But the first night, and the following couple of days, were designed to terrorize. To frighten. To test one's ability to deal with uncertainty and the unknown, as well as the uncomfortable and hostile.

"I wish you all good luck," the colonel said as he stepped back from the podium. "Sergeant Major! Take command of the class."

The sergeant major walked back out to the center front of the auditorium, under the podium. He saluted the colonel and then turned to face the class.

There was banging on the auditorium doors now. Frightened faces looked over their shoulders back toward the noise.

"On your feet!" the sergeant major yelled.

The class jumped out of their chairs to the position of attention.

*Here we go*, Paul thought.

"On the command of fall out," the sergeant major began, "you will exit this auditorium and take direction from your training cadre."

The sergeant major paused to let the roar outside of the auditorium take full effect. It sounded like a pirate ship had disembarked just outside of the doors. It sounded angry. It sounded violent. It sounded hungry.

"Fall out!" the sergeant major yelled.

The class surged for the exits. Paul and the female lieutenant ran side by side through the doors with their classmates.

They were knocked to the ground by blows to the head as they stepped through.

Paul saw stars. His first thought was, *Shit, I just lost my hat.* But then he blinked and looked up at the scene.

Hundreds of cadre in black riot gear were beating the shit out of the candidates.

The cadre wore padded gloves and boots, but the blows still hurt. Noses were breaking. Eyes were blackening. And guts were being punched.

Paul gaped at the surreal brawl. The candidates in their dress blues looked ridiculous next to the black-clad cadre. Their formal uniforms were not designed for fighting. Seams were ripping. Buttons were flying. Dress jackets were splitting open.

The cadre, veterans of close-quarters combat, overwhelmed the candidates despite being outnumbered at least ten to one. The candidates were not all handling it well.

The instant transition from civilized lecture to physical threat was too sudden. Candidates who could not make the mental turn either froze or wept. They would be processed out of the class that night. The first washouts.

"It's road march time, candidates!" a cadre member yelled on a megaphone. "Your rucksacks are waiting for you just outside the building. You will grab a rucksack and follow the route! Those of you who are first out of the building can pick a light one! Those of you who are later can have the heavy ones!"

A new urgency surged through the class. Candidates redoubled their efforts to get through the cadre. But not with any better luck. The blows came hard and fast. More candidates fell to the ground.

Bodies were piling up just past the auditorium doors. Paul was stuck under a couple of flailing candidates.

"Come on!" the female lieutenant yelled as she grabbed Paul's wrist. "Get the fuck up!"

She yanked him up, and they both charged forward.

"Together!" Paul yelled.

"Roger that!" she answered.

"Him!" Paul pointed at one of the black riot suits absorbed in pummeling an unfortunate candidate.

They hit him at once. Paul took another punch to the head, but they overwhelmed him for an instant.

It was enough.

Paul fell forward.

The cadre member kicked the female lieutenant in the back in retribution as she slid by. She fell hard.

The cadre turned back to face the surge of other candidates trying to get out.

Paul leapt to his feet. They were now less than twenty feet from the exit. He could see the pile of rucksacks just outside. He pulled the female lieutenant off the ground.

"You good?" Paul asked, shoving her forward.

Wincing, she pointed at the door without answering him.

Paul pushed her forward, and they sprinted out.

"Candidates, halt!" yelled a voice as they got outside.

Paul and the female lieutenant skidded to a stop and came to the position of attention, both panting.

"Names?" asked the cadre member, looking at his clipboard rather than them. They were both relieved to see that he was wearing the olive-drab flight suit of a battle-suit driver, not a riot suit. The sounds of the melee roared behind them.

"Kata Vukovic," she said.

"Paul Owens," he said.

The cadre member scanned his list. He nodded to himself as he put a check mark next to each of their names.

"Grab a ruck and get moving," he said, gesturing over his shoulder at the pile.

"Halt!" the cadre member yelled as another cluster of candidates stumbled out of the auditorium. He turned from Paul and Kata and walked briskly away.

"Names?" they heard him ask the newcomers.

Paul and Kata jogged over to the pile.

There were hundreds of rucksacks in a mound that loomed over their heads. They scanned the various sizes of rucks. Most seemed moderately full. But there were many that were overstuffed and several that were obviously empty.

Paul leaned over to test one of the overstuffed ones.

"Shit!" Paul said. "Has to weigh a hundred pounds."

Kata grabbed a medium, and he did the same. It didn't feel right to grab one of the empties.

Kata adjusted the shoulder straps and then set her rucksack on the ground. She took off her battered dress blue jacket and threw it aside.

"It's hot as balls out here," Kata said. "And it's trashed anyway."

Paul yanked his jacket off. He shook his head at the sight of it. One sleeve was nearly pulled off, and none of the buttons remained. One of the side seams had burst open.

"Fuck it," Paul said, yanking off his starched white dress shirt. His undershirt was already drenched with sweat.

"Good idea," Kata said, taking off her dress shirt.

They slung their packs onto their backs and then acknowledged each other with a shake of their heads. Their sweaty white T-shirts, accented by the olive-green rucksack shoulder straps, looked ridiculous over their dress blue pants.

Paul chuckled.

"What?" Kata asked.

"Your dress pants have holes in both knees," he said.

"Yeah?" Kata said. "I tore them saving your ass. So, you owe me."

A cadre's voice interrupted them. "Candidates, halt!"

They crouched as they scanned the area, fearing the return of the black-suited aggressors. But the voice had come from back toward the building. More candidates were emerging, and cadre members with clipboards were all over them.

"Let's keep moving," Kata said.

A green chem stick glowed in the middle of the parking lot to their front, fifty meters from the pile of rucksacks. Another burned in the distance in the middle of the road that stretched away and up a steep rise. At the top of the rise, over half a mile away, lay another dim green light, just before the road dipped down the other side of the hill and into the darkness.

"I guess that's the route," Paul said. "Let's go."

They walked as fast as they could. Not knowing how far they had to go, they were reluctant to jog. Who knew how much energy they would need tonight? They crested the small rise and went over the other side, the noise of the chaos behind them fading.

Soon, they were in marching mode. Their strides in sync, their breathing measured, they tried not to wonder how far they had to go.

Kata broke the silence.

"So, did I hear right?" she asked in a transactional tone. "It's Paul?"

"Yeah," he said.

They walked a few more minutes in silence before Paul asked, "What kind of name is Vukovic, anyway?"

"Croatian. Grandparents on my dad's side came over back in the nineties during the war."

They walked along, both wondering about the other. Kata finally came out and asked, "So, are you going for Combat Corps?"

"Yes," he said. "I want to be a soldier. Not a REMF."

Kata nodded at the answer.

"You?" he asked.

"Same."

They walked in silence for a long time, both wondering how many Combat Corps slots their class would have and knowing that it was usually just one.

Paul stopped dwelling on it first. His dress shoes, which he had purchased a week ago and were not yet broken in, had been biting into his heel and the top of his toes for miles.

He kicked them off.

"What are you doing?" Kata asked him.

"I don't know how long this road march is going to last," he said. "But my guess is that it is going to be much longer than I want to walk in those damn things. I figure, this way, I am fucked the least."

Kata kicked her dress shoes off as well.

They walked farther into the darkness, their socked feet a final blow to their dignity.

"I think it's going to be a long night," Kata said.

It was.

# Chapter Twelve

---

*Mission Cycle 387*

*Earth Year 2062*

*288,968,603 Kilometers from Earth*

---

P aul finished talking and took a slow sip of tea.

Althea still sat in one of the chairs facing him. The black of space spread out behind her, beyond the window over her shoulder. The stars cascaded endlessly in the distance as the habitat traced its circle around the hub.

Paul leaned forward and put his tea down on the table between them. He rested his elbows on his knees and sighed as if weary from a heavy task.

"Oh please," Althea said. "It was not that bad."

"We haven't gotten to the bad parts yet."

"Nonetheless, you have begun," Althea said. "And even just this beginning will help. You'll see." She smiled.

"What?" he asked.

"I am happy for you," she said. "And, I hope you will allow me to say, I am proud of you."

"I'll allow it."

Paul leaned back in his chair, looking out of the window behind Althea. She read layers of nostalgia on his face and let him ride the emotions in silence.

His face soon clouded, though.

"What is it, Paul?" Althea asked.

He looked at her for a moment and then leaned forward to grab his tea. He took another sip and said, "Fiona Malloy."

"Who?"

"Are you familiar with the name?"

"No."

"Well," Paul said, "about the time that Kata and I were trying to survive O.A.T., Fiona Malloy was plotting her own entry into the military."

"Was she an officer?"

Paul laughed.

"No," he said.

"OK," Althea said. "Who is she, then?"

"She is the person I am going to kill when I get back Earthside," Paul said evenly.

Althea folded her arms in her lap. He looked serious to her.

"Why are you going to kill her?" Althea asked. "Was she an enemy of yours?"

"No," he said. "Not really."

Althea sat silently and waited for him to continue.

"More like, we were the ship at sea, and she was the hurricane." Paul's voice was distant and sad. "She didn't know we existed."

# Chapter Thirteen

*1515 Hours, 12 October 2040*
*White Plains, New York*

Fiona's mother sobbed next to her in the front row. Her younger brother, Eugene, cried quietly on her other side. Fiona reached out and took her brother's hand without taking her eyes off her father's casket.

Members of their extended family filed by, offering condolences, some placing flowers on the casket.

Fiona took inventory of her family. She was only fifteen but had learned well the signs of alcoholism, drug addiction, and depression. She kept a running total of each affliction as Malloys stopped to lean over and console her, her mom, and Eugene.

*Not a lot of happy Malloys,* she thought.

She looked across her father's casket at the reason.

Her grandfather.

Robert Malloy II looked bored, sitting aloof, legs crossed, in a black suit and tie. Had Fiona not known it was his son's funeral, she would have thought he was enduring a tedious business meeting.

But it was his son's funeral. And her father's.

Fiona thought about the moment, three days ago, when she'd heard her mother moan in despair. Fiona was upstairs in her room. Her mother was in the living room on the first floor.

Fiona's uncle, her father's brother, had shown up for a surprise visit a few minutes earlier.

"Roberta," he said, calling Fiona by her first name. "I have something to discuss with your mother."

"Go on upstairs, darling," her mother said with a weary smile. Fiona went upstairs without protest or delay. She was used to the request. In the Malloy family, there was always some drama, grievance, or disappointment to discuss.

A few minutes later, her mother was sobbing.

Fiona ran to her brother's room.

He looked at her with wide eyes when she threw open his door and rushed to him.

"What is it?" he asked, tears beginning to run down his face. "What is wrong with Mother?"

"I don't know," she said, hugging Eugene. "I don't know."

Fiona fought off her own tears. Anxiety welled in her gut.

Minutes later, her uncle appeared in the doorway. They could still hear their mother crying downstairs.

Fiona looked at her uncle's face, and she knew.

Her father was dead.

"Died suddenly on his trip," was all her uncle would tell them.

No one told her the truth, but over the next three days, Fiona had listened closely to the adults around her and pieced together what had happened. Her father, supposedly on a duck-hunting trip with friends, had gone alone to one of their family's lodges and killed himself with a shotgun blast to the head. His body had been discovered by one of the staff.

No one, not even Fiona, was surprised. Her father had been depressed for her whole life. He was a sad, sensitive man. Fiona loved her father. She loved his softness and sensitivity. She basked in it when they were together. But she knew it made him fragile.

She knew she had to be careful with her father, and she knew why.

The day before the funeral, she'd overheard her mother telling Fiona's aunt, "He went his whole life without ever hearing the words 'I love you' or 'I'm proud of you' from the one person he needed to hear it from the most."

Now, Fiona stared across the casket at her grandfather. She hated him.

After her father's casket had been lowered, Fiona helped her mother get up, and they walked toward their car.

"Candice," her grandfather called to her mother.

Her mother squeezed Fiona's hand tighter as she stopped and turned to face Robert Malloy II.

"I'm sorry, Candice," he said, stepping closer. "He was a disappointment. But I know that you loved him. I am sorry." Her grandfather noticed Fiona crying. He looked down at her and said, "Stop crying, child. Everything is going to be fine."

But they were tears of anger. That was the day she decided she would never answer to the name Roberta.

*

Fiona sat in the back of a chauffeured town car on her eighteenth birthday as it worked its way through the clogged streets of New York City.

Fiona's phone vibrated. She reached into her coat pocket to retrieve it.

*I love you, Fi,* read the text from Eugene. *Don't let the bastard get you down.*

*Thx. I won't,* she responded. *How is Italy?*

*Bella.*

*Good. Call you after.*

Fiona put the phone back in her coat pocket as they pulled up to the building. A doorman opened her door the instant the car pulled to a stop.

The elevator opened on the seventy-ninth floor, which entirely dedicated to the Malloy Family Foundation and Malloy Family Investments.

It was an austere reception area with a single desk.

The lone receptionist recognized Fiona Malloy immediately and gave her a quick nod, which relaxed the security guard. The large, suited man stepped back from the elevator and spoke discreetly into his earpiece.

"Good morning," the receptionist said, approaching Fiona with an appropriate mixture of respect and indifference. "Right this way, if you will."

The receptionist led Fiona down a short hallway into a small meeting room.

"Mr. Malloy will join you in just a few minutes," the receptionist said before returning to her desk.

The meeting room was small. An oval, dark wood table surrounded by eight chairs sat in the middle of the room. One of the chairs, at one end of the table, was much larger than the others and had arms and brass nailheads. One wall was entirely floor-to-ceiling windows looking north toward the green expanse of Central Park.

Fiona walked to the window. From where she stood, almost a thousand feet above the avenues and cross streets, the expansive green park stretching north, the view conveyed a sense of order. Fiona tried to plug into the fact that none of the thousands of humans her eyes could see cared about her family.

"Hello, Fiona," her grandfather said as he entered the room. "Thank you for making the trip."

He was spry for seventy-three. Slightly taller than Fiona, at just under six feet, with a back that was unbent. He had a rangy build like a mountain climber and eyes that were quick and clear.

"Of course, Grandfather. I appreciate your time."

"You are looking good!" her grandfather said as they shook hands. He squeezed Fiona's shoulders. "Indeed! I've seen videos of you on the lacrosse field. You're a bruiser! It's made you strong."

Her grandfather returned his arms to his sides and smiled.

"And congratulations on Yale," he added, his smile widening.

Fiona smiled back, hating that he could kindle feelings of pride within her. She stepped on the feelings and dissolved her smile.

"And how is your mother?" he asked.

"She's fine," Fiona said. But really, she didn't know for sure. She had only received superficial check-ins from her mother for a while now. Her mother had remarried a little more than a year after Fiona's father died. She'd put Fiona and Eugene into boarding school and moved out West with her new husband.

Fiona understood not wanting to be reminded. She understood the desire to escape. But it still hurt.

Her grandfather let the moment linger too long before saying, "Let's have a seat and talk."

He sat in the large chair at the head of the table.

Fiona sat next to him.

"So, I am sure your cousins have told you what this meeting is all about?" her grandfather asked.

"Sort of."

Her grandfather nodded.

When Malloys turned eighteen, they were summoned to meet with their grandfather. Momentous and terrifying events for the grandchildren, the meetings were the stuff of whispers and anxiety across the family.

"My father started Malloy Markets in 1970," her grandfather began. "He worked himself to the bone. Died of a stroke at age sixty-one in 2007. I was at his side when it happened. I had been working by his side at that point for almost twenty years. I was the eldest of three children. My father split the business equally between us, but left control solely to me. Because he knew I was the only one worth a damn.

"We buried Father the day after he died. The next day, I went back to work while my brother and sister contested the will. They did not want me in control of the business because they wanted to sell it. They wanted to cash out and walk away from my father's legacy.

"I was in the middle of executing my strategy to take Malloy Markets online, you see," he continued, looking out the window at Central Park. Fiona had the sense he was recalling the story for himself, not for her. "It was something Father believed in wholly. And something that my brother and sister regarded as foolhardy and expensive. They had no understanding of the endeavor and no stomach for the effort involved. So, they fought me.

"They failed, of course," he said, swinging his head back to Fiona. "And afterward attempted to mend fences and pitch in. An effort they stayed committed to for about a week. They soon lost interest when it became clear that the company was going to thrive under my leadership. They reverted back to being worthless."

Her grandfather spoke slowly, daring Fiona to react or object to anything he said.

Fiona knew better. Besides, she had heard this version of the family history before. She sat still and met her grandfather's gaze as the monologue filled the room.

"By the time I was sixty-one like my father, the business was fifty times bigger than when I'd taken the helm. My siblings and their offspring, and mine, were all very wealthy. Because of me."

Her grandfather pointed at himself with his thumb and then placed his fist on the table.

"Me. Alone. I ran the business while my brother and sister fucked off. I ran the business while our families grew and the subsequent generation proceeded to fuck off. Your father, his brother and sister, and all of their cousins, the third generation of wealthy Malloys, have done nothing but fuck off their whole lives. The greatest measure of exertion demanded of them is a walk to the mailbox to get their check.

"Now comes your generation. Fifteen of you. Each of which I expect to do fuck all. To earn fuck all. To accomplish fuck all."

A side door opened, and the receptionist stepped into the room, a leather folio in her hand. The old man kept talking as the receptionist reached across the table and placed the folio in front of Fiona.

"As I'm sure you know by now, when a Malloy turns eighteen, they are given access to a twenty-five-million-dollar trust fund. It's their money, no strings attached, to do with as they wish. I do this for every Malloy. Even the ones who choose to go by their middle name, rather than carry forward the name of my father."

Her grandfather paused.

He stared at Fiona.

Fiona looked back at him, wondering if they were going to have that argument again.

But, the slight recorded, her grandfather continued after a few heartbeats. "And I will also do it for little gay boys who prefer Italy to our own country." Again, he paused, making sure his grievance was noted.

Fiona looked back at him. She pictured herself caving in the old man's head with her lacrosse stick and smiled.

Her grandfather reached across the table and opened the leather folio between them.

"I've been sued by members of my own family six times. I won each time. But it cost me time. Time is the most precious thing in the world to me. This document gives you total, unilateral, unfettered control of your trust. But it also writes you out of any more of the Malloy family fortune. Irrevocably."

Her grandfather leaned back in his chair.

"In exchange for a sizable fortune, which is more money than your great-grandfather and I had to our names when we were your age"—the old man gestured at the document in the folio—"you are forfeiting your right to scheme, connive, lie, and steal any more. Because that is what the people in this family invariably try to do."

Fiona looked down at the document. She estimated it to be about ten densely printed pages.

"You can leave the money with the Malloy Investment Fund to be managed by us, or you can do something else with it. Do with it what you will, frankly. I don't care."

Fiona placed her hand on the document and ran her finger along the edge, letting the top-right corner of each page hang on her fingertip before falling to the table.

"You don't have to sign, of course," her grandfather said. "You can choose not to. Then you can wait until I die to confirm that I have written you out of my will already."

Fiona was tempted. She hesitated. *Oh…to be free of this monstrous family.* She chuckled at herself.

*Who are you kidding, Fiona?* she thought. *You're going to turn down twenty-five million dollars to spite the old man and your family? No. You're not an idiot. You're going to do something much better than that.*

"What in the world is going through that head of yours, child?" her grandfather said.

Fiona looked up.

He stared at her.

"You are a curious one, Roberta," he said with a different smile than she had ever seen. "Curious indeed."

Fiona picked up the pen in the center of the folio and signed the document. She was ready to be out of there.

"Thank you, young lady," her grandfather said, standing up.

Fiona stood up also. The receptionist opened the door and stepped into the room.

"We're done here, Ms. Frank," Fiona's grandfather said.

"Very good, sir," she answered.

Her grandfather extended his hand to Fiona and said, "Happy birthday."

Fiona shook her grandfather's hand. "Thank you," she said.

But her grandfather held on when Fiona tried to release her grip.

"Twenty-five million dollars," the old man said, pulling her slightly closer. "No strings attached. And no fucking safety net. That's it. You understand me?"

"Yes, sir."

Her grandfather released her hand, smiled, and left the room.

# Chapter Fourteen

*Utsu Book One*

*Circa 1510*

*Translated from the Japanese*

Hiroaki was grateful that I had returned Kusunoki's body to him and told me that I was welcome to remain at his school. I intended to stay only until I had recovered from my long walk, finished healing, and figured out which lord to sell my services to next.

I stayed at the school for three years.

In that time, I learned a lot about Hiroaki Ashikaga.

Hiroaki was the son of a samurai. His grandfather had also been a samurai. Service was an important tradition in his family. Hiroaki wanted to serve his lord as a samurai, like his father had. But he did not want to benefit from the favor his father and grandfather had won from Clan Shingen.

So, Hiroaki left home at the age of thirteen. He spent the next decade wandering, learning, and perfecting his fighting technique. When he returned, he was a master swordsman. He had fought many a duel with junior samurai and rōnin seeking to make their name by besting the next of the Ashikaga line. None was successful. Lord Shingen took notice.

Hiroaki was soon serving Lord Shingen as a samurai and fought in many campaigns for the clan. Over time, Hiroaki became a military leader in Clan Shingen. In many campaigns, it was Hiroaki's strategies that won the day. Lord Shingen came to regard Hiroaki as his greatest general.

But after the Campaign of Many Rivers, Hiroaki desired to retire. He still loved his clan and Lord Shingen. But Hiroaki looked at the endless and innumerable campaigns and mourned his comrades. He realized that the conflict between clans, which had raged for almost a hundred years, would last for at least another thousand.

Hiroaki gave up his office as Lord Shingen's general. He left everything behind, including the Ashikaga wealth and status, and walked out of Shingen's fortress on bare feet. Shingen cried when he left. But allowed him to go.

Hiroaki spent the next seven years wandering. He thought deeply about his years of combat. About the comrades he had known. About the mistakes he had made. And tried to keep to himself.

But as he wandered, he was sought out by many. Again, as in his earlier years, samurai and rōnin challenged him to duels. They sought to make their name by slaying the most famous of the Ashikaga line and Lord Shingen's favorite general.

They never did.

He was also sought out by those seeking advice and instruction. And by those like himself, who had seen many battles, and sought perspective and understanding.

After seven years, a dozen men wandered with Hiroaki. They prevented the senseless duels and cleared the way for their master. Kusunoki was one of these men. Eventually, the group left the villages and roads, seeking solace and anonymity in the forest.

Hiroaki was tired of wandering and had accepted his fate. He accepted that he could no more stop war than he could stop the rivers, and that he could no more abandon his brothers than he could abandon his own breath. Pinned between those two truths, he chose the only path he could conceive of. He would teach and mentor, but never again command.

In the early years, School Hiroaki was not much. Other than the core dozen, on any day, it was only a few wandering rōnin and those visitors who had fought for Hiroaki when he was a general and sought out his company, conversation, and advice. It was a place where samurai, rōnin, and common soldiers could rest, practice, and study without clans, politics, or indebtedness.

Over time, word of the school spread. First the rōnin class, seeking new skills to enhance their value. Then young ones without lineage, seeking a path to samurai. After a few years, alumni of the school could be found in the ranks of all of the clans. Hiroaki's school was loyal to the warrior's ethic, avoiding matters of clan.

When I was there, a hundred students lived and studied at the school. There is no count of graduates and students who had come and gone. But it was many.

And for good reason.

Hiroaki's practice went beyond the sword. It encompassed also the long spear, the bow, the horse, and cannon. All working as one. His years as Lord Shingen's general taught Hiroaki to think this way. His students, therefore, studied all disciplines and were required to master each individual skill.

Hiroaki's method was simple and excruciating. Students trained at the fundamentals until they demonstrated mastery. Then conditions were made more challenging. Then the students were made to do more than one discipline at once. It was a simple but challenging progression that most did not have the patience to endure.

Those who did endure were trained also in command. Coordination, communication, and timing became their focus. They studied every battlefield task from this new perspective. Their minds were recalibrated to function like timepieces. "You can always get more men, horses, arrows, or cannon," Hiroaki told them. "Time, however, is the one thing a commander cannot regenerate."

Though a veteran rōnin of many campaigns, I went through the training as well. After eighteen months, my skills were greatly improved.

Most students left the school after two years, returning to the world and its conflicts as better soldiers. I chose to stay. Hiroaki began to assign administrative tasks to me. I accepted these tasks as the honor that they were. The master held me in his trust. This was my happiest time.

# Chapter Fifteen

*0029 Hours, 20 August 2051*
*West Virginia*

P aul was wet, filthy, and exhausted.

It was the last night of phase one. The class was on a seven-day field exercise that pulled together everything they had been taught to that point: land navigation, survival, marksmanship, close-quarters combat, first aid, etc. Six days ago, the cadre had put each trainee alone in the mountains of West Virginia with a map, a compass, two canteens of water, and a week's ration of food. No GPS. No radios. No drones. No nothing. So not only had the class been dropped into the empty, mountainous armpit of West Virginia, they had been dropped over a hundred years back in time.

"This is some real bullshit," Kata said to no one, holding up her magnetic compass as they walked to the drone copters.

Paul and several other heavily laden candidates in the file nodded in exhausted agreement.

"It's like we're training to be doughboys," Kata added, shaking her head.

"Huh?" a candidate next to her said.

"Doughboys," Kata repeated.

The candidate looked back at her.

"You know," she said, looking around at the group like an impatient schoolteacher. "World War I soldiers."

Paul avoided eye contact with her. *So arrogant,* he thought.

*Idiots,* Kata said to herself with disbelief as they filed into the idling aircraft.

It was nighttime, with only a sliver of the moon providing illumination. The drone flew with its doors open. Some grumbled, sure that Filson had arranged it to do so. The blustery combination of rotor wash and night air tugged and pulled through the cabin, wrapping everyone in a chill despite it being August.

Paul looked around. There were two dozen candidates on board, including him and Kata. Most looked miserable. But a handful wore the same intense face Paul did. Class standings were well known at that point, and Paul was in the running for the one Combat Corps slot. So was Kata. And so were about twenty other candidates. So, the phase-one results were important.

After twenty minutes of flight, the drone's nose rose slightly, and it began to shed airspeed and descend.

Sixty seconds later, the aircraft's four large turbofan thrusters swiveled and howled as it came to a hover. The small red light over the door changed to green, and the lone cadre on board kicked the coiled fast rope out the door. He turned and pointed at the first candidate, yelling, "Move!"

The candidate stood up and headed for the door. He wobbled for a few steps under the weight of his pack. The shifting floor of the aircraft did not help. It was windy.

He gave the cadre a thumbs-up, grabbed the fast rope, swung out into the darkness, and slid out of sight.

The cadre leaned out to observe. Satisfied the candidate had not killed himself, the cadre hauled in the fast rope. He coiled it neatly on the aircraft floor in smooth, efficient motions borne of long experience.

Then the cadre took his seat next to the door. The engines whined louder, and the drone's nose dipped slightly as it accelerated and climbed away.

Paul noted the augmentation scar visible just below the cadre's black knit skullcap. He was a Centaur, and there was no need for him to speak to command the drone. Verbal communication was only required with the soft meat of the candidates.

An hour later there were only a few candidates left on board.

At the next insertion point, the cadre pointed at Kata and said, "Move!"

She popped up and walked to the door.

The aircraft swayed in its final deceleration, but Kata was unperturbed. She did not even reach up for one of the handgrabs.

The light changed to green.

The cadre gave a thumbs-up.

Kata vanished down the rope.

The test was simple; the trainees had to locate themselves on the map and make their way to the extraction point, eighty miles away, in seven days. Along the way, there were testing stations, which they had to navigate to and arrive at within one minute of an assigned "time on target."

If a trainee missed a TOT, they were done. A drone copter arrived within five minutes to yank them off the mountain. When they arrived back at Fort Benning, they were given the option of resigning their commission or recycling back to the first day of phase one.

Most resigned rather than start over.

At one station, they had to field strip and reassemble a weapon within two minutes and then progress through a firing range. At another, they had to correctly assess and render first aid to several types of injuries. There were about five stations a day, and trainees had one chance at each. If they failed a station, they were done. The drone copter was on the way.

So, each day and most of each night consisted of hours of trekking up and down mountains, punctuated by high-stakes military skills tests.

It was raining on the last night, and Paul was sheltering under a small rock overhang. After studying the map, he calculated he had about two hours before he needed to start humping again. He had just taken off his waterlogged boots and was trying to dry out his socks in front of a tiny fire he had built when Colonel Filson appeared.

The colonel seemed to materialize at the edge of the dim firelight. Paul was startled. He hadn't heard an aircraft or Filson approach and could not conceive of how the colonel had found him. But Filson could do that. He did it to Paul more than once during O.A.T. He would step out of the darkness during the dirtiest, wettest, most lost and isolated moments of the training.

Paul fumbled around on the ground trying to get to a position of attention, but before he could stand up, Filson said, "As you were, Owens. Don't get up."

"Yes, sir."

The colonel sat down across the fire from Paul and leaned in to warm his hands. Paul noticed Filson was soaking wet.

"Good fire, son," Filson said. He looked around. "Good hide-site selection also. Your fire is concealed, and you have good cover. Nice."

"Thank you, sir."

"Most of your class is worthless. But you and a couple others have potential. Particularly Vukovic."

Paul just nodded and stared at the fire. *Damn it*, he thought. *I knew that she was doing well.*

"What do you think of O.A.T so far?" Filson asked, pulling a plastic bag out of the breast pocket of his field jacket.

"It's pretty tough, sir," he said as he shifted his weight and thought, *Terrific, there goes my plan to get some sleep.*

"It was a lot different before I got here, you know," the colonel said as he pulled a cigar out of the plastic bag. He returned the bag to his pocket and bit off one end of the cigar, spitting it into the fire. "It was a joke. Two weeks of bullshit they called 'fieldcraft,' which wasn't much more than roasting marshmallows and playing grab ass in the woods."

Filson leaned forward until one end of the cigar touched the small fire. The red glow of the flames lit his face from below, highlighting his augmentation scar. The sharp horizontal shadow across his forehead looked like a seam that suggested you could lift open the cap of his skull. Which, of course, they had, over fifteen years ago.

"You know, when they first asked me to be the commandant of O.A.T, I told 'em no. When they asked again, I said, 'Fuck no.' I was stationed out West at the time. I had just gotten back to my unit after healing up. I was ready to get back into the fight. They asked a third time, and I just ignored it. So I was surprised when the supreme commander, General Tom Havron, showed up. In fucking person."

Filson made a wide-eyed, mock-surprised face to emphasize the point. It was the most human thing Paul had seen him do yet, and it almost made him laugh out loud.

"It was late afternoon," Filson continued. "I had just gotten in from working out with a combined-arms drone team on the maneuver range. The general was waiting for me at the armory. 'Get the fuck out of that exo and meet me in my office, Filson!' he yelled.

"Tom didn't have an office there, of course. It was my office. I could tell he was pissed, so I jumped out of the exoskeleton and double-timed to meet him. One of my platoon sergeants walked my equipment back to the armory.

"'What's your goddamn problem, Don?' he asked from behind my desk as soon as I shut the door.

"'I don't understand, sir?' I responded.

"'Why are you fighting me on this assignment?' he asked me.

"'What do you mean fighting you, sir? I've just been back and forth with personnel. I didn't know...' I started to say.

"'I'm the supreme fucking commander of the US military, you moron!' he yelled at me. 'You fight with personnel, you are fighting with me!'

"Now, you have to understand," Filson said to Paul with resignation. "I would have then, and still would now, do anything the old man asked me to. Anything. But...I really didn't want this assignment."

Filson stared at Paul until he was certain Paul understood. Then he continued.

"'So, it was your stupid idea to put me out to pasture as the commandant at Fort Benning, sir?' I said to the general, getting mad. 'I thought I was just dealing with the faceless bureaucratic stupidity of the institution! But now that I know it is your specific brand of stupid, you better believe I'm gonna fight it!'

"That made General Havron chuckle. He smiled and nodded. 'Don,' he said to me. 'What have you been bitching about for years now?'"

The colonel took a long drag from his cigar and then leaned into the fire and looked at Paul.

"You have to understand, Owens," Filson said. "I was one of his company commanders when we fielded the first real ground drone and Centaur units, and he was just a maverick lieutenant colonel. We co-developed a lot of the first organizational and tactical principles for employing the increasingly complex units the US Army was fielding. We saw a lot of shit together. He had asked for me and my battalion, by name, when he was scraping together a force to go south and kick the Chinese out of Santiago. And along the way, we had grown more and more dismayed together."

Filson paused, staring into the small fire.

Paul grew uncomfortable as the silence extended. He tried to stare into the fire also.

"You see, son," Filson finally continued. "For as long as there have been soldiers, they have lived on one side or the other of an ancient schism."

Filson outstretched both arms to emphasize his point.

"And I'm not talking about the divide between the soldier and society. I'm talking about the schism between the soldier and the REMF. For as long as there have been armies, the warriors have despised the logisticians and administrators, the 'Rear Echelon Motherfuckers,' sitting far back from the fighting, safe with their clean sheets, warm showers, and hot meals.

"And the REMFs," Filson continued, "have despised the warriors right back, looking down on the knuckle-dragging brutes with their colorful medals, bullshit stories, and hulking egos. The REMFs were fine letting the warriors get all the glory because they thought they were smarter than us. You heard that bullshit that 'amateurs study tactics, while professionals study logistics'?"

Paul nodded.

The colonel spat into the fire.

"Nonetheless, for millennia, a grudging truce and understanding persisted. The system worked. But over the past twenty years, the ancient system has slowly been turned upside down by all the goddamn technology we've been fielding. Most of which, by the way, has benefitted only the defense industry. It's been almost a hundred years since Eisenhower warned us about the military-industrial complex, and I'm telling you, Owens, it's never been stronger. Those bloodsucking profiteers have accelerated the widening of the schism, dazzling the REMFs with shiny objects, overly complex systems with no soul and often no fighting ability."

The colonel rubbed his eyes.

"Some days," he said, "I think we really are just cannon fodder, and the military-industrial complex is eternal, the one part of this story that will never, ever change."

Colonel Filson shook his head in disgust at his own statement.

"Over the course of our careers," he continued, "General Havron and I watched as the number of fighting robots increased every year, while the number of fighting men and women decreased. I remember taking command of my first company and being shocked to learn I had more robots assigned to me than human soldiers. Then, when I was a battalion commander, I actually commanded fewer men and women than when I commanded a company!

"And don't think the military has gotten any smaller as this has gone on," the colonel said, shaking his head. "Quite the fucking opposite. When I was commissioned in 2029, the active-duty military was about one-point-two million strong, and less than three hundred thousand of those were real combat forces. The military you were just commissioned into is one-point-three million strong, and less than twenty thousand of us are combat soldiers."

Filson's eyes got big and he arched his eyebrows for emphasis.

The colonel stared at Paul for a moment, and then said softly, "Think about that, son. Less than one percent of the population serves in the military. And little more than one percent of the military actually fights."

The colonel shook his head.

"Ever since the French Revolution and Napoleon's Grande Armée almost two hundred and fifty years ago, the percentage of society's population that serves in the military has been steadily decreasing. And in the past few decades, the percentage of the military that actually fights has fallen off an even steeper cliff.

"General Havron and I bitched to each other often about the direction of things as we slogged through some of the world's garden spots. The ancient schism was out of whack. Permanently. It was never going to be right. The REMFs run things now. Always will. The problem for over a decade was, they had no idea how to run it. That's how Santiago happened.

"But when the general sat behind my desk that day in my office and asked me what we'd been bitching about for twenty years, I just looked back at him like an idiot. Not sure what he was saying.

"'Don, I want you to go to Benning and fix the officer course,' he said to me.

"'Sir, you won't like what I do with the place,' I told him.

"'Yes, I will,' he said, without blinking.

"'It won't work unless I have total, unfettered authority to do what needs to be done,' I demanded, looking for him to waver.

"'You will,' he told me.

"I thought about it for a minute and then said, 'If you're serious, sir, I'll do it. But I'm going to quit the first time I encounter bullshit.'

"'It's a deal, Don,' General Havron said, smiling with excitement. 'I've got your back.'

"And, son of a bitch, he sure did. I wrecked the place," Colonel Filson said with satisfaction. "Got rid of all of the instructors and replaced them with real warriors I had served with. I established the course structure you're going through. Sixty days of intense individual instruction, followed by sixty days of small-unit leadership, followed by sixty days of combined-arms training and assessments.

"Then, after the first iteration, when I failed over half of the class, the chief of military personnel, a four-star REMF general at the Pentagon, called me. Left a long voice mail about what an arrogant idiot I was and told me to pack my bags because he was sending a new commandant the next day."

The colonel took another tug from his cigar.

"I forwarded the voice mail to General Havron with a message from me that said, 'Your pick. Me or the REMF. No hard feelings either way, sir.' The next day, I got up early, packed my bags, and waited for the aircraft with my replacement to arrive. Around lunchtime, though, I saw the announcement of the military's chief of personnel's sudden retirement on the *Military Times* website."

The colonel chuckled at the memory.

Paul smiled at Filson from across the fire, trying to picture the surprised four-star general when he was relieved by the army chief of staff for crossing a lowly colonel.

Filson caught Paul smiling and nodded back at him.

"After graduation, ninety-nine percent of your class will never have mud on their boots again," Filson said. "But I goddamn guarantee you they will understand what it means to be a soldier. And those REMFs will support you better because of it."

Filson stood up and stretched his back. He took one last tug on his cigar and then threw the rest of it into Paul's small fire.

"You understand, son?"

"Yes, sir," Paul said, lying.

"Good. Don't miss your TOT tomorrow, or I'll fail your ass."

"Yes, sir," Paul said. But the colonel had already disappeared into the shadows.

# Chapter Sixteen

*Mission Cycle 389*

*Earth Year 2062*

*290,386,944 Kilometers from Earth*

"Attention!" Cooley said, entering the meeting room.

Drummond followed close behind him. As soon as Drummond sat down, the rest of the room did as well.

"Mr. Cooley, please begin," Drummond said.

"Aye, sir. Priority for this cycle remains cleanup and repair after the incident," Cooley said, throwing the assignments from his tablet to one of the monitors on the wall behind him. Cooley gave the group a moment to read the assignments. There were a few winces and groans as crew members matched their names to undesirable tasks.

Cooley ignored them.

"XO, repair status update, please?"

"Yes, Mr. Cooley. Repairs are going well. Full atmosphere and life support have been restored to the CnC. We are now shifting priority to hull repairs. I estimate that we will have finished everything that we are able to do within ten cycles. The rest will have to be done when we get to the belt."

"Very good," Cooley said before turning his head toward Paul. "Prisoner

Owens. Inspection assignments, please?"

"Yes, sir." Paul leaned forward and slid Regas, Hahn, and McNeeley each a printed inspection sheet. "Pretty standard stuff. Return your inspection sheets to me when complete, as usual."

Regas made sure Paul saw him roll his eyes. Paul smiled at him.

"OK," Cooley said. "That's all I've got. I want to keep these meetings short so we can get back to taking care of the *Odysseus*. We've got a lot of training left to do before we get to the belt. Any comments from you, sir?" Cooley looked at Drummond.

"No."

"Very good, sir. Then let's all—"

"I've got a point of order," Regas said, leaning forward in his seat. Hahn and McNeeley exchanged excited glances.

Cooley regarded Regas for a moment. Paul tried to imagine what was going through Cooley's head.

*Should I just kill him now?* he must be thinking.

"What is it, Prisoner?" Cooley said.

Regas nodded to Cooley in exaggerated thanks for yielding the floor. "I'd like to propose an increase in prisoner shares," he said.

Drummond's head snapped up at that. "A what?" he asked.

Regas turned his head to meet Drummond's surprised gaze. "An increase in prisoner shares," he said slowly.

Paul noted the lack of "sir" and that no one corrected him.

"I have prepared a detailed letter outlining our position," Regas said, unfolding papers he took from his flight-suit breast pocket. "Our intention was to submit this request to Captain Drake. But we now submit, herewith, to the current holder of that, um, office. Shall I read our letter into the record?"

The disbelief on Cooley's face almost made Paul chuckle.

"That is ridiculous," Drummond said, interrupting Paul's humor with the most force he had ever seen from the man.

"Oh really?" Regas said, leaning back in his chair. "You were promoted. Seems like we're all going to be shouldering more responsibility and an extra load as a result of the incident. And"—Regas held up a finger as if he were onto a brilliant idea—"with the captain dead, the Company won't have to pay him at all. Seems like there will be more to go around. Am I right?"

Regas looked to Hahn and McNeeley, who both nodded in agreement.

"Prisoner Regas," Cooley began in a tired voice. But Drummond cut him off.

"That is the most ridiculous thing I have ever heard!" He pointed at Regas, raising his voice to a near shout as he went on. "Totally ignorant of how such things are actually structured!"

"Sir," Cooley tried to interject and get Drummond back under control. The rest of the room was transfixed by the outburst from the normally muted CFO.

Regas nodded his head slowly as Drummond continued to yell.

"Ignorant also of the intricate financial considerations at play on such a complex endeavor as a long-haul space voyage!"

"Sir," Cooley tried again.

"I will not stand for such outrageous demands from a mere prisoner crew member. This is not a negotiation!"

"Sir, I think—"

"You are not a signatory of any contract. Our obligation is with the United States military, which has granted us you as a resource for this voyage. You are nothing to me!"

"Sir!" Cooley yelled, slapping his hand on the table.

Drummond looked at him, eyes bulging.

Regas's smile had dissolved. He stared at Drummond and smoldered.

"Sir, I think you have made your position clear," Cooley said in his most calming voice. "I recommend we conclude this meeting."

Drummond blinked, then nodded. He stood up and left the room.

Cooley looked at Regas. "Prisoner Regas, you will leave this room and report to your quarters for five cycles of confinement."

Regas looked back at Cooley. He stood up without speaking and then pushed his chair back into its place at the table.

"Aye, Mr. Cooley," Regas said.

After Regas had left the room, Cooley said, "XO, once Prisoner Regas has returned to his quarters, you will lock him in for five cycles. No visitors authorized except by me."

"Yes, Mr. Cooley."

The rest of the room sat still for a moment, digesting the confrontation.

"Althea and Prisoner Owens," Cooley said, rubbing his eyes, "please give me the room. I need to have a conversation with Prisoners Hahn and McNeeley."

Paul and Althea stood up and left.

Paul was glad to get out of there. He could see what Regas was doing and was happy that it was not his responsibility to keep the troublemaker in line.

Althea cast Paul a worried glance as they walked down the hall toward the center ladder.

"It's going to be fine," Paul said to her. "Regas will get tired of it after a few confinements, and we'll be back to our boring normality."

"I hope so," she said, unconvinced.

"Trust me."

"I do," she said. "Are we still on for another session at the end of this cycle?"

"Sure," Paul said. "I guess."

"Come on, Paul. I think the first few sessions have been really good for you."

"We haven't gotten to any of the bad parts yet, Althea," Paul said. He had continued to meet with Althea over the past few cycles, telling his story in small pieces. They weren't very far into it yet.

Paul stepped out onto the center ladder and began to climb down toward the second level.

"I know," she said. "But it all counts."

"I hope so," he said as he descended out of view.

# Chapter Seventeen

*2115 hours, 5 May 2049*
*Cambridge, Massachusetts*

Fiona managed her time at Yale and then Harvard Business School like an architect, building the structure of skills she would need later. It was surprising to most how hard this attractive trust-fund baby applied herself.

She met Martin Pruden the day she started at Harvard Business School.

The two were a mismatch: a guy from a tight-knit working-class New Jersey family who had slaved for four years as an analyst for a bottom-tier investment bank before somehow making it into HBS, and a girl from a dysfunctional, ultrawealthy bloodline, straight out of undergrad with no work experience, who gained easy access to Harvard because of her family name.

In addition to being four years older, Pruden, at six feet, was also four inches taller than Fiona. Somehow, though, he came across as slighter than she. His short blond hair, pleasing smile, and unimposing body cloaked him in a blandness that obscured his acute intelligence and relentless logic.

While Pruden's appearance made no impression at all, Fiona looked like she could step back onto her college lacrosse team and still deal out serious punishment. She'd discovered CrossFit early in college and had not slowed down at it. She wore her hair in a tight athlete's ponytail all the time and was often seen wrapping up her day just before midnight with a jog through campus.

They didn't seek each other out. Their work ethics and class loads synchronized them. They were assigned to the same core curriculum classes in their first semester. Soon, they started pairing up regularly when small teamwork projects were assigned. Within a few months, whether it was in the business-school study rooms, the library, or just venting at the pub, they were spending the majority of their time together. They chose all the same electives their final year.

The rumors that they were sleeping together began immediately. They were not, but Fiona and Pruden exerted no effort to dispel them. They were uninterested in the social scene and focused on their studies.

Entering their last semester, they were close. Their classmates were surprised whenever they were seen apart. But they were not friends, more like soldiers who had shared the same foxhole for a long time. They were intimately familiar with the other's habits and thought processes. But that was it. When the war was over, they would part ways forever.

As they neared graduation from business school, though, Pruden was offered a job at Goldman Sachs. He was excited as he told Fiona about it over beers in a booth at their favorite pub in Harvard Square.

"No," Fiona responded, surprising herself as well as Pruden.

"What do you mean, no?" Pruden asked. "I wasn't asking you a question. I'm telling you about my great opportunity."

Pruden's parents worked at the local high school, back home in New Jersey. His dad taught math and coached the basketball team. His mom was a career counselor. Goldman was offering Pruden a starting salary that was more than his parents made, put together, in five years.

"You're not going to waste your time with that crap. You're going to come work with me, and, I promise you, you are going to be happy you did. What did they offer you?"

Pruden was quiet.

"I'll double it," Fiona said. "Whatever it is. And give you an equity stake in everything we do."

Pruden hesitated as he grappled with the interaction. He had always known they were from different worlds. But this was the first time since meeting Fiona that he'd felt the yawning socioeconomic chasm that separated them.

It didn't feel good.

"Are you serious?" was all Pruden could get out of his mouth.

"A hundred percent," Fiona said, feeling her commitment well within her as she spoke. She wanted Pruden to come with her.

It was a great offer. But what exactly were they going to be doing? Pruden wondered. And if it failed, how would it translate to another potential employer?

"Pruden," Fiona said, seeing the raging risk assessment play out on his face. "Do you want to be part of a big, safe, slow-moving machine, or do you want to take a shot at building something?"

Pruden leaned back in his chair, put off by her reaction to his good news.

"Hey," Fiona said. "No hard feelings either way. All I will say is that the big, safe jobs will always be there. There will always be room for another sheep at the trough."

"Learned that from your billionaire's vantage point, did you?" Pruden said.

"Touché," Fiona answered, smiling at the barb.

Pruden didn't throw many brushback pitches, but when he did, they had heat on them. Fiona liked that. Fiona liked a lot about Pruden. She wanted him on board. She was going to need his help.

"Let me start over," Fiona said, leaning forward toward Pruden. "Goldman is a great outfit. You should be proud. Shit, I'm proud of you. You've busted your ass to get to this point. I know we've got different backgrounds. Nonetheless, the last two years proves we work well together, and I respect your judgment, intelligence, and work ethic. I need your help. And I'm willing to pay for it."

"Why?" Pruden said. "Working on what? I don't even know what you are trying to do. This is the first time in two years you've talked about what happens for you after graduation. To be honest, I assumed you'd go back to your family office to help manage activities and investments. Like, part time."

Fiona leaned back in the booth.

Pruden waited for her to speak.

"I would rather die than do that," Fiona said.

"OK," Pruden said, mocking her melodrama with a shrug. "So, what are you going to do?"

"Free myself. And my brother."

# Chapter Eighteen

*0055 Hours, 19 October 2051*
*Fort Carson, Colorado*

Paul trudged up the mountainside just a few steps behind the Geek, another O.A.T candidate. It was almost one in the morning, and their platoon had been moving up the steep incline, in full unaugmented combat gear, for more than three hours.

Kata, who had been marching behind Paul, took a few quick, long strides to catch up to him.

"He's not going to make it," she whispered, gesturing with her weapon at the Geek, whose wobbly and uncertain legs threatened to collapse at each step.

"Shut up," Paul hissed. "He's going to make it."

Paul sped up to separate himself from Kata and bumped into the Geek from behind.

The Geek, unable to take a hit at this point, lost his balance.

"Shit," Paul said, grabbing the stumbling candidate by his rucksack shoulder strap to steady him.

"Sorry, Geek," Paul said. "My bad."

The Geek nodded, not able to spare the breath to speak.

"Just think of that photo," Paul whispered to him. "And keep going."

After a few seconds rest with Paul's steadying grip on his rucksack, the Geek turned back uphill.

Paul gave him a moment to get some separation between them. Kata stepped up and next to Paul, glared at him, and threw one hand up in the air.

"Fuck you," Paul muttered before turning uphill.

Paul and the Geek, Wallace Bandy, had become friends over the past months of Filson's crucible. There was no pair of candidates more dissimilar. Paul seemed born for a life of military service. Bandy seemed destined to be cast from it.

Wallace stood only about five and a half feet tall. He wasn't fat, exactly. But he was chunky and a weakling. He was also the smartest candidate in the class. Wallace had graduated from Georgia Tech with a double major in nuclear engineering and robotics.

Wallace was also self-aware. He knew he was not well suited to Filson's gauntlet. He also knew that none of his fellow trainees thought he would make it through O.A.T. But Wallace was resolved to try.

Wallace did not hide his geekiness. It would have been impossible to do so. And within a day of the start of O.A.T, everyone referred to him as "that fucking geek."

Wallace took no offense. He embraced it and kept his head down. By the time he shocked everyone, especially Colonel Filson, by making it through phase one, the jeer had been transformed into a nickname.

Paul respected the Geek's intellect, but he was intrigued by the Geek's spirit. He never quit. Ever. Paul had recognized that fire within Kata the moment he'd met her. That's why he regarded her as competition for the Combat Corps slot. But it took him a while to see it in the Geek.

He sought to understand it weeks earlier, one night in the high desert west of Kirtland Air Force Base near Albuquerque. They sat on the cold ground and leaned against each other's backs, unable to sleep as they tried to stay warm.

"Why do you want this so badly?" Paul asked the Geek.

"I am a fourth-generation officer," the Geek answered. "A fourth-generation Georgia Tech to military commission, as a matter of fact. There are photos of my father, my grandfather, and my great-grandfather on the wall of my ROTC battalion's headquarters in Atlanta."

Paul waited as the Geek paused for a moment. He pulled his Mylar thermal blanket tighter.

"I should have said, I *want* to be a fourth-generation officer. I want to continue the tradition," the Geek continued. He looked at Paul with a weary smile. "I am not one yet. And it's clear that Filson doesn't want me to be one."

Paul looked at the Geek and nodded slightly. It was true. Filson despised the Geek.

The class was well into phase two now. Most of Filson's technology prohibitions still applied as they roved from base to base across the country. They trained in mountain, swamp, desert, and urban conditions as each candidate rotated through positions of leadership from squad to platoon leader. In a system modeled after the army's old Ranger School program, each candidate's turn in a leadership role was graded by both instructors and peers. They got very little sleep, lived on one meal a day, and never came out of the field or showered.

Filson was ahead of his normal pace for O.A.T and had already run out over a third of the class. Now, in the thick of phase two, he was failing candidates at a rate of almost one a day. He was determined to get the Geek and made no secret of it. But, somehow, the Geek kept soldiering on.

"How do you keep going?" Paul asked him.

"You mean, despite my unsuitability?" the Geek responded.

"Um…no," Paul said. "That is not what I meant. I just…"

The Geek smiled as wide as Paul had ever seen. "It's OK, Paul," he said. "Sincerely, it's OK. I'm playing with you."

The Geek chuckled as Paul shifted in his thermal blanket.

"It's true, after all. I am poorly suited to all this." The Geek looked around at their austere surroundings. A dozen other exhausted candidates, huddled in pairs and wrapped in thermal blankets, were dispersed around them. All there trying to force themselves to sleep. They would be on the move again before daybreak.

"But you know the REMFs that Filson scorns? The ones he rails against? Well, I can do that job. The military needs REMFs, after all. And, if I make it through this, I think I'll be a really good one."

"There is no doubt in my mind about that, Wallace," Paul said.

The Geek smiled at the comment from his friend.

"I know you want to make it into the Combat Corps, Paul," the Geek said. "And I hope you do. Me? I just want to serve in uniform like my family has for generations. That's what keeps me going. You know those three photographs I told you about? In my most lonely, droning, and zombie-like moments, I picture my photo on the wall next to them, and I just keep walking toward it. And I won't stop until my heart stops, or Filson tells me to go home."

Paul nodded, his intrigue with the Geek becoming awe. Paul and Kata were doing well at O.A.T. They were in the running for the one Combat Corps slot. Their wills were fierce, their bodies strong, and Filson curious to see who would win. The Geek, though? His body was weak. Filson wanted him out. All he had was his spirit.

*Could I make it if I were him?* Paul wondered.

As they slogged up the mountainside, Paul thought about that conversation in the desert. Then he thought about the colonel.

Earlier that day, as Filson was assigning the Geek platoon-leader duties for that night's mission—an assault on a mountaintop position that would require them to hike all night—Paul and Kata made eye contact. They both thought that Filson was stacking the deck against the Geek.

The Geek collapsed, falling face-first on the rocky slope.

Paul jumped to the Geek's side and started pulling his rucksack off. Kata walked up quickly and leaned over the Geek.

"What the hell do you want?" Paul asked her.

"Give me his pack," she said.

Paul regarded her for a moment. "No," he said. "We'll split it."

They emptied the Geek's rucksack and divided the load. A couple of other platoon mates followed. One took the Geek's weapon, and another grabbed his ammo.

"What are you guys doing?" protested a nearby candidate who stood watching. "He's not going to make it. He's failing."

Paul lunged at him.

"Yeah. He is failing," Paul said, grabbing the candidate by the collar. "But he's not quitting."

"Easy, Paul!" Kata shouted, stepping between them and breaking Paul's grip. "We've got a lot more to do tonight. We all need our energy."

Paul shook his head in disgust and turned back to the Geek.

The candidate nodded in agreement with Kata, as if she had taken his side. She shoved him hard. He stumbled back a few meters.

"What the hell?" he said, taking two aggressive steps forward before stopping at the sight of Kata in a ready position.

"What is wrong with you two?" he said.

"The Geek is doing his best," Kata said. "If he weren't trying so hard, I'd say, fuck him also. But he fell on his face moving forward up the hill. He never sat down. Never complained. Never quit." Kata paused to make sure the candidate understood her when she said, "So he is coming with us. Every step of the way. You got it?"

The candidate sneered and looked around for support. But the other platoon members stared back, hands on their hips, and nodded.

"Yeah," he said. "I got it."

Kata returned to the Geek's side.

"Thought we were saving our energy?" Paul said.

"Fuck you," Kata answered.

They had to clean blood off of the Geek's face. He had busted his lip and nose open in the fall. Then they propped him up and shoved him up the rest of the mountain.

The assault was successful.

Paul and Kata had made sure that everyone in the platoon marked the Geek's performance as a success when it was time to turn in peer ratings. Most were happy to do so. No one thought the Geek was actually going to make it through and graduate from O.A.T. But it felt good to foil Colonel

Filson in some small, temporary way.

The respite was short-lived.

Swamp training was the most hated part of phase two. They trained for three weeks in a nasty part of northern Florida and were in at least ankle-high water the entire time. The heat and humidity were oppressive. It felt like breathing through a dirty, wet sock. Every candidate got rashes and skin infections, and by the third week, their skin would slough off at any rough contact. It had lost all its strength. Their knees, elbows, and backs were raw.

By the end of swamp training, Paul's platoon was down to twenty-four candidates, and it was the Geek's turn again to lead the mission. And, again, the colonel circled like a hungry buzzard. The whole platoon knew that if they did not succeed at the night's assault, the Geek was done.

They groaned when they got the mission. It was a direct assault on a machine-gun nest dug into a small rise in front of which lay a putrid stretch of chest-deep water thick with mangroves and leeches. It had been raining for over a week, and the water was high. So high, in fact, that the cadre gave them four rubber rafts to assault in. Colonel Filson was sufficiently worried that, in their exhausted state, some of the weaker candidates would drown.

"Well," the Geek said in an insincere voice, "the man does have a heart."

Paul shook his head.

"What?" the Geek asked.

"We're fucked," Kata said. "Notice how they did not give us any paddles? We're going to have to drive those pieces of shit with our rifle butts. We won't be able to steer, and we're going to be moving slow."

"And we have only one very obvious avenue of approach to the objective," the Geek said.

"And they know it," Kata said.

"And we're going to be noisy," Paul said, standing up.

The platoon watched as he walked over and climbed into one of the black inflatable boats. Squeaky rubber barking noises marked his slightest movements. He sat in the boat in silence for a few seconds before climbing back out. The symphony of chirps and squeaks began again.

"Each boat holds six," Paul said, walking back. "So, we're going to make so much noise the enemy will hear us coming long before we can get to the beach and begin the assault."

The dejected platoon huddled and tried to come up with a plan. They were exhausted, so they sat cross-legged in the shallow, fetid water that came up to their navels. They were miserable.

"I think this is it for me," the Geek said. "Just want you to know it has been my honor to work with all of you." He spoke to the platoon, but his eyes rested on Paul and Kata.

"Bullshit!" Kata said. "We can do this!"

The Geek shook his head. "I appreciate your enthusiasm, Kata. But I don't see a way to successfully pull it off in these boats." He gestured at the cluster of boats tied to a mangrove behind him. They made loud squeaking noises as they jostled together.

Paul remembered how Filson had smiled when the cadre had given them the boats.

"What if we don't use them?" Paul mumbled to the group.

Kata looked at Paul and smiled, getting his meaning instantly.

The Geek looked at Paul. "The colonel said we had to use them," he said. "For safety."

"Oh, we'll use them," Paul said.

Kata belly-laughed.

The Geek looked at Kata. Then back at Paul. Then smiled as he looked back at Kata. By the time he looked back to Paul, the Geek was also laughing.

"I don't have the slightest idea what you have in mind," the Geek said to Paul, breathless from laughter and fatigue. "But it must be better than what I was thinking."

Half the platoon rolled in the water, laughing. Kata was slapping platoon mates on the back and punching them in the shoulder. They winced as they felt their skin slough off and went right back to laughing.

The rising morale spread through the platoon like a tonic. By the time Paul had finished briefing them on his idea, they all felt like they had just taken a shower. They felt refreshed and alert in a way they had not in months, excited to try to pull one over on the colonel.

Paul knew that the cadre would be expecting them to assault in the boats as they had been told to. So he divided the platoon into two teams of ten and one team of four. Paul and Kata each took a ten-man team and stripped down to their basic uniforms. They put their packs and gear into the boats but kept their weapons on them.

Then the team of four—the Geek and three others—each got into one of the boats. The four of them started paddling up the lone route to the objective.

Paul took his team wide to the left of the main assault. Kata took hers to the right. Unburdened from the seventy-five pounds of equipment they carried everywhere, they were able to swim and bound quickly in the water without making a sound.

The boats were so slow that Paul and Kata had their teams in perfect position on the flanks of the enemy position by the time the Geek was able to begin his assault.

The rubber boats had been so loud, the cadre had not suspected any other threat.

Paul and Kata waited for the cadre to engage the Geek's force, then attacked on the flanks.

It was a total surprise and a perfect envelopment. They captured the enemy position in just a few minutes and took no casualties.

Colonel Filson seethed. Paul could tell later, during the debrief, that the colonel wanted to explode. But he allowed the victory to stand. The Geek recorded a successful assault.

The colonel did exact a price out of them, though. The whole platoon was punished for "employing unsafe tactics." They were given extra duty for the next week.

But their morale was so high, they didn't care. They felt not only like they had gotten one over on the colonel but that they had also saved a buddy.

# Chapter Nineteen

*Mission Cycle 389*

*Earth Year 2062*

*290,610,893 Kilometers from Earth*

L ater in the cycle, after Paul completed his training academics, he changed into his pressure suit and set off to conduct his inspection. He had smiled when he'd read the inspection sheet: "Factory. Section Seven. Level Two. Utility Closet B658." It was a random corner of the old girl, over a kilometer away, past the CnC bulkhead. A real pain in the ass to get to.

Before the old man had been killed, this would have set Paul off. From the beginning, Paul had thought it was ridiculous that the captain's inspection cycle bounced unpredictably all over the *Odysseus*. He'd told Drake so during one of their clandestine bourbon sessions on the bridge.

"Captain, what is the deal with this inspection regime?" Paul said, floating in front of the big window. He maintained his gaze at the stars, not wanting Drake to see the smirk on his face.

Drake didn't turn from the window either, not allowing Paul to see he was amused rather than irritated. "We've covered this, son."

"I'm not arguing. I'm with the program and am going to do them. I just don't understand why you have structured them as a random-assed Easter egg hunt."

Drake took a shot of bourbon.

"Usually, there is a logic to inspection regimes," Paul said. "Front to back, top to bottom, by department, or whatever. But this is a random walk through the endless nooks and crannies of the *Odysseus*."

"Because it's my fucking inspection regime, that's why," the captain said in a curiously low voice. Drake turned to Paul and winked.

Paul shook his head.

Later, as Paul was leaving, Drake motioned at him to wait a moment while he wrote a note.

"Thank you, Prisoner Owens," the captain said, handing him the note. "You are dismissed."

Paul left and read the note as he floated through the tube toward the spinner and his quarters.

---

*I use a random inspection regime to keep the fucking XO guessing. That is why I've given it to you in paper form, which I printed back on the station before we got underway. I have the only other copy. Only you and I know the schedule. It's one of the few checks we have on the son of a bitch.*

---

Paul shook his head now, remembering that classic Drake interaction as he floated aft through the tube. *Can't believe I already miss the old man,* he thought to himself as he started climbing the traverse.

The factory was located topside, midway between the command-and control superstructure and power and propulsion. It was a large three-level facility that extended for over three hundred meters along the top of the *Odysseus*'s hull, designed to ingest asteroids, scrap metal, and other debris on one end and produce finished equipment, parts, and material on the other end. Drake referred to the factory as "the indispensable facility on the *Odysseus*." Drummond called it "the only reason there is an *Odysseus*."

The factory was divided into seven sections. Section one's official name was "material intake," but Drake referred to it as "the mouth," a term that better matched its appearance. The mouth was a large, imposing orifice in which one could see grinders and laser turrets before the shadows got too dark. The mouth's role was to pulverize whatever the tug drones pushed into it.

Section two, analysis, was called "the lab" in Drake-speak. As base element powders emerged from the mouth's processes, the lab identified them before they passed into section three, segregation, where they were separated into different raw-material containers before being placed in section four, storage.

Section five, printing, was where the magic happened. There were a dozen industrial-grade, zero-gravity 3D printers into which the raw material was fed, based on what the factory was tasked to produce. The printing section was equally adept at printing massive components or tiny objects. All of which were then transferred to section six.

Assembly and programming had multiple separate lines that could be configured for any type of system assembly. There were two dedicated circuit-board assembly lines that could manufacture the electronics components. At the end of section six, a large programming-and-upload module stood ready to program the brains of the factory's creations. The factory had several program-generation modules that could compose mission-based software for just about any bot or equipment profile, or it could load software put in storage by the Company before they'd left high lunar orbit.

Finally, section seven, "the hold," as the captain called it, was a large warehouse area where finished systems and components were held until they were deployed to their destinations throughout the *Odysseus* or sold upon arrival at the belt or high lunar orbit.

The factory was fully automated and run by the XO. Sections six and seven were the only sections human crew members could get into. The others were not configured in a way that made them accessible. Which was fine with Paul.

The factory was a fascinating place to Paul, and he looked forward to this visit. It was not a place he went to be contemplative, like the hangar or the bridge, but he enjoyed looking at all the interesting, high-tech manufacturing robots. They reminded him of the maintenance bots in his last unit. And it was always interesting to see the random things waiting to be transferred out of the hold.

A large hatch in the top of the tube provided crew access to the factory. Paul opened it and then pulled himself up the hand ladder through the passageway.

Paul emerged on level one of the hold. The ladder continued up to levels two and three, but Paul stopped climbing when he spotted the cargo-handling system in motion. The robotic arm held a metal spar in its grip as it propelled itself along the ceiling-mounted track up the aisle toward Paul.

Shelving and closet-like containers rose from floor to ceiling in the hold and extended in long rows the entire length of the massive space. There were twenty-four storage rows whose containers grew from small to large as Paul looked left to right. The leftmost containers were about the size of a golf ball, while the rows of shelving and containers to his far right were large enough to accept a school bus.

On the ceiling, the tracks of the cargo-handling system ran above the aisles between the storage containers. The arm stopped near the end of one of the storage rows to Paul's front. A long, skinny locker popped open, and the arm extended and swiveled, placing the shiny new spar into its temporary home.

The arm then retracted. The door snapped shut, and the cargo-handling system sped away on its tracks, down the aisle back toward assembly and programming.

Paul shook his head in wonder as he looked at the large volume of storage and realized that there were two more levels of storage above him.

"Damn, XO," he said. "How do you keep track of all this shit?"

"I'm a computer, remember?" the XO responded in his headset. "I don't forget things."

"Seems like you have enough room here to build another *Odysseus* if you wanted."

"Not quite. But maybe a smaller version."

"All this capability, and you can't make us a new long-range communications antenna?"

"It's a good question, Paul," the XO responded.

*Did the XO hesitate?* Paul asked himself.

"But, unfortunately, I am at the mercy of my onboard ingredients, so to speak," the XO continued. "The range and sensitivity we require demand particularly pure samples of very rare metals. Rest assured, I'm searching and analyzing everything I can get my hands on. Hopefully we'll get lucky and I'll be able to get us back on online with command."

"Yes," Paul said. "I hope so."

Each locker had a small LED light on the top center of its door. It glowed green when it was storing something, red when empty. Paul noted that most of the storage units on level one had a soft green glow.

"Seems like you're nearly full down here," Paul said as he started climbing to level two.

"Yes," the XO responded. "We're only about half a year out from the belt. I've got a big list of orders to produce before we arrive, and Drummond is quite insistent I get it all done."

"I bet he is," Paul said.

Paul climbed up to level two. Two small utility closets were attached to the wall, on opposite sides of the crew ladder. Paul opened the one marked "B658."

Empty.

Paul smiled and nodded. "Fuck you, sir," he said softly to himself.

"What's that, Paul?" the XO said.

"Nothing," Paul answered, embarrassed. "That was directed at Captain Drake. Another inspection of an empty place on the *Odysseus*."

"I understand."

Paul made the notation on his inspection sheet and started the journey back to the hab.

When Paul passed through the factory passageway and entered the tube, he looked aft toward the rear of the *Odysseus*.

The power-and-propulsion bulkhead loomed, over five hundred meters away at the end of the tube. Paul remembered the captain's note. He thought about going there now but decided against it. He wanted to shower and was done for the cycle.

*Soon, sir,* Paul promised Drake. *Next time I am back here. I promise.*

Paul turned toward the front of the *Odysseus* and started back to the hab.

"Paul," the XO called on the radio. "May I make a statement?"

Paul rolled his eyes at the overly polite XO.

"Sure."

"Althea told me about your sessions together," the XO said. "I think it is very constructive that you have agreed to participate in those. I commend you. I hope you don't mind I sent her to your room when you were having your troubles."

"No," Paul said. "I think that was probably a good move."

Paul knew that the XO could listen in to most sections of the *Odysseus*, including personal quarters and even his sessions with Althea, but he tried not to think about it. He didn't know if the XO was reminding him of this to fuck with him, or because the XO was really just a geeky and awkward program. Paul reminded himself that the XO had bigger things to worry about, like navigating the *Odysseus* and not blowing up one of the nuclear reactors. Nonetheless, Paul hated that the XO got to hear his sob story.

"I'm also quite glad that Captain Drake's inspection regime seems to have survived his passing."

"You are?" Paul said. "I figured you thought this kind of thing is stupid."

"On the contrary. A ship as complex as the *Odysseus* can only benefit from multiple inspection regimes," the XO said. "There are several areas of the ship where I have no direct sensing available. It is good to have a human crew member periodically check these areas. The bots are not always as adept. And, as I am sure you know, our service has been long and varied. We've served under many fine captains, worked with many fine crews, and safely conveyed thousands of passengers. I've been honored to do so. But two decades of service have left us with a lot of abandoned, derelict, and—in some cases, I am sure— dangerous material on board that I am not aware of."

"You mean to say," Paul said, floating forward with a smile. "People left a lot of shit on board."

"Indeed," the XO said. "You could say that. And I appreciate that you and your prisoner colleagues are getting the situation sorted."

"I hate to tell you, but I think the old man would have been disappointed to hear you say that."

"I am sure you are right, Paul," the XO said happily. "I think he preferred to think of it as a way to keep me in check. To block my nefarious plans."

Paul laughed at that. "That he did. Just so we're clear, though. I don't give a shit about your nefarious plans. Just get me to the belt and back and leave me alone, and you and I are going to be fine."

"It's a deal, Paul."

"Good."

The AI hesitated a moment before continuing. "I wish Prisoner Regas shared your peaceful outlook."

"Me too," Paul said. "You got that crazy asshole locked up?"

"Yes," the XO said. "I've got half a mind to cause a tragic loss of atmosphere. But that would not be consistent with my core mission of protecting life."

"Well, I don't think he would be missed."

"I think you are right," the XO said. "He worries me, Paul."

"You and Althea," Paul said with a chuckle. "Don't worry. Cooley has his number. Besides, guys like Regas wear out quickly."

"I hope so," the XO said. "Have a good evening."

# Chapter Twenty

*Utsu Book One*

*Circa 1510*

*Translated from the Japanese*

One day, in the beginning of my third year with Hiroaki, Lord Shingen visited the school.

Hiroaki welcomed his lord with much joy. They embraced as old friends, and Hiroaki showed him around the school grounds.

The lord asked for a demonstration, which Hiroaki was hesitant to give. But there was no polite way to refuse. So, his students showed Shingen what they were capable of. The lord was pleased.

Later, I sat next to Hiroaki as Lord Shingen made his request.

"I am mightily impressed," Shingen said. "What you have accomplished here should give you great pride, my former general."

"I thank you, my lord."

"I am sorry, my friend," Lord Shingen said. "But I must ask something of you."

"Do not hesitate, my lord," Hiroaki said. "How may I be of service?"

"This is a time of great risk and opportunity for Clan Shingen," the lord said. "We are not at our strongest. Tax monies have decreased. The endless wars have weakened the people and the land and their ability to support our armies. But we have managed to pin our dread enemy Lord Hayato and his clan inside their last fortress. We have the opportunity to finally defeat them and end our long conflict."

Hiroaki listened intently.

"The fortress is protected by the Hayato Clan's Elite Guard, commanded by Anotsu Hayato, Lord Hayato's son. We have made six attacks, and they have repelled us each time. On the final attack, they killed my last general."

Lord Shingen paused, sadness gripping him. "I can promote more generals, of course," he finally continued. "But they are not ready. I can feel the opportunity slipping away, Hiroaki. But if you will command our next attack and add your forces to our number, we can win."

Hiroaki sat in silence, considering Shingen's words. I knew how this weighed on my master. He loved his clan and felt a duty to his lord. But he also loved his students, and he had sworn to never lead men into battle again.

"Without you, Hiroaki, the clan is lost," Lord Shingen said, sensing the debate within his old general.

I have thought about this moment many times since. What if Hiroaki had said no?

But he did not.

"The honor is to serve, my lord," Hiroaki said. "We shall do our best."

Lord Shingen smiled in relief. "I am most happy, my friend." He stood up to leave. "I shall expect you at my castle tomorrow."

"I shall be there, my lord."

That evening, Hiroaki gathered his students. "Our greatest challenge is upon us," he said. "I would not have committed us to this fight if I did not believe it was worthy. It is our opportunity to win a measure of peace. But those who do not wish to fight can leave with my blessing. You will always be students in good standing."

Hiroaki looked around slowly, making eye contact with as many of his students as he could.

"Those who remain will fight with me."

Every student stayed.

# Chapter Twenty-One

*0345 Hours, 9 December 2051*
*New York City*

"**A**re you absolutely sure about this, Fiona?" Pruden asked.

Fiona looked up from her computer. Pruden, bleary eyed from lack of sleep, stood across from her on the other side of her desk. The sleeves of his customary blue button-up shirt were rolled up to his elbows, and his khakis showed the stained wear and tear of a string of late nights.

Fiona stood up and stretched.

She scanned the room as she reset her long brown hair into a tighter ponytail. The room was a mess. Pizza boxes, dirty dishes, beer cans, and empty water bottles were scattered about the large office she was renting in Midtown Manhattan. The leather sofa, where Fiona had been sleeping for weeks, was also serving as her clothing storage area and was obscured by dirty clothes and a single uncovered pillow. Thick white notebooks were strewn about the hardwood floor like misguided steppingstones. Two printers and a couple of reams of paper sat in one corner against the floor-to-ceiling window, next to large, plastic trash bags of shredded paper.

Fiona smiled at the mess. It made her feel good. Evidence of homework done, preparedness.

Their two analysts had left about an hour ago. Faithful Pruden had stayed, of course. It was crunch time. Fiona had until nine a.m. to accept the last and final offer from Spitting Metal, a promising but deeply indebted AI weapon systems designer and manufacturer.

"Yeah," Fiona said, turning her gaze to Pruden. "I am sure about it. We've been over the numbers a hundred times. I think they work."

He nodded, unconvinced.

"Pruden," Fiona said, sensing his anxiety. "How long have we been at this?"

Pruden looked at his watch, but Fiona shook her head.

"Not tonight," she said. "I mean on our strategy. Our plan."

"Oh," he said, scratching his head. "Two years, I guess?"

"More like two and a half," Fiona said.

Pruden shook his head in weary disbelief.

Fiona and Pruden had set up shop in New York City after business school. It was irritating for Fiona to be close to her family. But it was where her network was strongest and where her name would be taken the most seriously. People would not realize she was going rogue.

They had spent six months flying in the top thought leaders in the world: economists, technologists, anthropologists, historians, philosophers, anyone who struck them as a potential source of information and insight. They did not claim their activities were related to the Malloy Family Investments, but they did not say they weren't.

At the end of these sessions, they made their decision.

"Artificial intelligence," Fiona had said to Pruden across a pizza box after midnight, surrounded by their laptops and notebooks. "That is where we focus."

"Military applications," Pruden added with a nod. "They still haven't figured out a good answer to the kill chain problem that both works well and complies with the Tokyo Accords," he said.

"They are going to be the biggest customer for AI solutions for decades," Fiona said. "And after the big Department of Defense reorganization a few years ago, their buying behavior is even more concentrated."

"That's right," Pruden agreed.

After the Santiago debacle in 2045, Congress had restructured the armed forces. The images of the US military running into the ocean begging for sealift had embarrassed and enraged the country. Americans don't like to lose.

A handful of military veterans in Congress had led the crusade for reform, spurred on by an irate electorate and a vocal veteran community. Skeptical of the Pentagon's ability to transform itself, they'd forced change by defunding the Joint Chiefs and making the majority of the bloated general officer corps retire.

Then they'd tapped a young, visionary field commander to lead the transformation. They had named General Tom Havron, the man who had led the liberation of Santiago, the supreme commander of US military forces.

He'd walked into the Pentagon and torn the place apart.

Havron had demolished as much of the old bureaucracy as he could. In Havron's eyes, you either fought or you supported those who fought. The old concepts of the army, navy, air force, and marines were no longer valid to him or anyone else who understood the changes technology had wrought upon warfare. He'd gotten rid of the separate military branches and anything else he viewed as bureaucratic artifice. When Havron was done, the military chain of command was flatter, more streamlined, and more focused.

In Fiona's and Pruden's eyes, a more concentrated and rational customer had been created. In addition to the chain of command, buying power had been focused and streamlined.

Fiona's decision to invest in military AI had launched another deep dive. That one had lasted a year. They'd learned the market, the players, the technologists, and mastered the entire landscape.

Fiona had enjoyed scheduling meetings with artificial-intelligence companies under the guise of due diligence for Malloy Family Investments. The cash-starved start-ups or debt-ridden mature players would tell her everything as she'd pretend to get excited about their robotics, algorithms, or whatever their secret sauce was. Fiona and Pruden would suck their brains dry and then break their hearts. They never invested.

By the summer of 2051, they had narrowed their focus to three target companies. The first was a group headquartered in Silicon Valley called Spitting Metal. They were scary, driven only by hard-core killing efficiency at scale. They wanted their robots to be the deadliest ever, and to be global. Their vision was big: battleships, nuclear submarines, aircraft squadrons, and orbital platforms.

They frightened Pruden. He called their vision "apocalyptic."

Fiona loved them, especially their "driver in a box" architecture. But they were a long way from profitability, and their grand vision had a price tag. Hundreds of millions of dollars and a few lucky breaks. Pruden worried it would be a black hole, sucking Fiona's money into oblivion.

And Pruden valued Fiona's money.

The second was a DARPA spin-off. A group of MIT robotics experts that was more focused on solving extreme mobility challenges like, "How can we get our robot to climb a wall of wet ice in a hailstorm?" or "How do you intercept a hypersonic aircraft while pulling as few Gs as possible?" They didn't directly address the kill chain problem, but their mobility solutions were the best in the world. Fiona loved them for that reason, and because their management team was easy to manipulate. Best of all, they had numerous patents and didn't cost much to operate. Fiona called them the DARPA Boys.

Then there was a man named Dr. Musashi.

Musashi ran a small company of robiticists. They didn't focus on mobility questions, like the DARPA Boys. And their goal was not maximizing destruction, like Spitting Metal. They were trying to create reliable soldiers that could be led by and counted on by human small-unit leaders who would command the robots and provide kill chain compliance. They were on the verge of what they believed would be a breakthrough but needed a quick infusion of capital to make it happen.

After initial enthusiasm, Fiona decided she didn't like them very much. "They don't think big enough," she'd told Pruden.

"But the Combat Corps loves them," Pruden had countered. "Of all the companies we have evaluated, they have the most current revenue and surest path to profitability."

Fiona had nodded. Pruden knew that, in Fiona's world, revenue and profits won every argument.

Fiona had acquired a controlling interest in Dr. Musashi's company and the DARPA Boys and put both in a holding company named, Determined End States. She avoided associating her name with the holding company and the two subsidiaries. Fiona never wanted her grandfather to discover her connection to them.

Now, almost two and a half years since starting their business endeavor together, they were poised to do the same with Spitting Metal. The problem was that it required Fiona to borrow a large amount of money.

"It's two hundred and fifty million dollars that you have to personally guarantee, Fiona," Pruden said as Fiona walked away from the desk toward the windows. "You will owe two hundred and fifty million dollars whether Spiting Metal comes through or not. It would bankrupt you."

"If they come through, we'll make billions," Fiona said.

*You will make billions*, Pruden thought.

Fiona stared out of the window at the lights of Manhattan.

Pruden decided he would make one final run at it. "It's a ton of money, Fiona. A lot more than you have. And it's too risky. Even the best scenarios we've modeled show these guys are going to need hundreds of millions of dollars to get to the finish line. I'm worried you will regret this one day, Fiona."

"Always the downside with you," Fiona said.

"You hired me to help you. That is what I am trying to do."

"I know," Fiona said. "But you're not looking at it the right way. Spitting Metal rounds out our portfolio."

Pruden sighed and leaned back in his chair.

"Think it through with me," Fiona said. "What do you like about Musashi?"

Pruden looked at his watch. He was tired.

"Please," Fiona asked him.

"Fine," Pruden said. "But then I'm going to bed."

"Deal," Fiona said.

"I think Musashi's vision is ambitious and unique," Pruden said. "He has spent decades trying to develop dependable, even noble, AI soldierbots. Then he bonds those soldierbots to a human leader who is on the battlefield with them. Then, through data links and enhanced situational awareness, he enables that human to authorize or deny kill permissions.

"Musashi's architecture does put a huge burden on the humans who are forward with the soldierbots," Pruden continued. "Mentally, conceptually, and emotionally. But he believes that is where the burden is best shouldered… forward, where the reality is. And I agree."

Fiona nodded and then said, "And the Spitting Metal architecture harks back to the early drone-control days during the turn of the century. Human controllers monitoring and controlling their units from high-tech command-and-control nodes back in the US. Any kill is authorized and enabled by the officers 'back in the box.' I'm no Clausewitz, but why put a human in harm's way if you don't have to?"

Fiona paused, but Pruden did not rise to the argument. He just shrugged.

"Truthfully," Fiona said, "I don't care which solution wins, as long as it is one of ours. And that is the beauty of what we're going to do. We'll have two different solutions to the kill chain problem. One ancient in inspiration. The other an updated, battle-proven architecture. The DARPA Boys will provide both with robotics and mobility solutions. That's a winning and diversified portfolio. Without Spitting Metal," Fiona concluded, "we're half a loaf."

Pruden chuckled.

"What?" Fiona asked, deflated at the reaction.

"Only you would try to spin taking on two hundred and fifty million dollars of debt to acquire a risky start-up venture as a risk-mitigation action."

Pruden and Fiona stared at each other for a moment, both exhausted.

"Fiona," Pruden finally said, "I think it's a mistake. I'm worried about you. But I'll do whatever I can to make it successful."

"With us working together"—Fiona smiled—"what could possibly go wrong?"

# Chapter Twenty-Two

*Mission Cycle 396*

*Earth Year 2062*

*295,612,670 Kilometers from Earth*

It had been a good cycle. Paul rose early, meditated, worked on his translation, got some exercise in, and then completed his training academics. All he had left was his cycle inspection, and then he would have a few hours of spare time. And he knew exactly what he was going to do with them.

He was climbing up the hab's center crew ladder when he ran into Althea.

"Hi there," she said to him on the first level as he emerged from the second.

"Hello," he said, noting she was wearing her standard utilitarian flight-suit uniform. He preferred the leggings and sweater.

"What are you up to?" Althea asked.

"Inspection time," Paul said, still hanging on the ladder.

"And what exotic corner of the *Odysseus* are you bound for?" she asked.

"Power and propulsion," Paul said, stepping off the ladder onto the floor of the first level.

"Oh my," Althea said, widening her eyes in feigned enthusiasm. "I wish I could go with you."

Paul laughed, marveling at the detail in her facial expressions. He caught himself having a crazy thought.

"What is it?" Althea asked.

"Oh, uh," Paul stammered, embarrassed she'd caught him. "Nothing."

"Tell me," she said in a playful voice. "Please, Paul. I thought we were a team?"

*Fuck it,* he thought.

"Well, the truth is, lately, sometimes, at the end of a cycle, I'll go up to the bridge and…hang out and enjoy the view."

Althea nodded. "It doesn't bother you to be there, where it happened?"

"No," Paul said. "It doesn't. In a weird way, it feels nice. No one else ever goes up there, since everything is still offline."

Paul fidgeted as he spoke and looked at his feet. The flood of nonverbal and microexpressions flooded Althea. It was a new signal. One she had not gotten from Paul before.

"Well…" She stalled as she tried to make sense of it. "I think it's great you have found a place on the *Odysseus* you can spend time like that. In solitude."

"Yeah," Paul said, looking up from his feet. "Do you want to join me sometime? Maybe at the end of this cycle?"

Paul felt a sudden warmth on his cheeks.

*I'm fucking blushing,* he thought, astounded at himself. *Real smooth.*

"I'd like that very much, Paul," Althea said.

"Great," said Paul, a big smile breaking across his face.

Althea smiled also.

Paul thought for a moment.

Althea read the concern on his face and thought he was about to take the invitation back.

But then he leaned in and said, "We probably shouldn't leave together. So, let's shoot for around 2030 hours. Meet you there, on the bridge."

Althea looked at her watch. That was in an hour and a half.

"I'll be there," she said.

"But it's not a session," Paul said, climbing back onto the ladder. He pointed a serious finger at Althea. "You come at me with any analysis bullshit, and you're uninvited, understood?"

"Understood," Althea said, stifling a chuckle.

"Good."

⋆

The aft end of the tube terminated in a large bulkhead that led to level one of power and propulsion, the largest module, by far, of the *Odysseus.*

The power-and-propulsion module, or PPM, was organized like a twelve-story building laid on its side, parallel to the ship's direction of flight, with the twelfth story being farthest aft. Only the five middle compartments, sections four through eight, were pressurized. The rest were primarily storage and left in freezing vacuum. All the sections were connected by a large, central freight elevator that was designed to move massive, ultradense reactor parts from section to section if needed, and by two outboard crew ladder tubes on the port and starboard sides. The PPM was completely automated, enabling the XO to manage the maintenance, fueling, and operation of the three reactors.

Paul was always amazed when he visited the PPM. He thought about the XO simultaneously overseeing the ship's navigation, life-support systems, maintenance fleet, everything. As well as splitting atoms in three live nuclear reactors.

*And while XO's hyperintelligent brain managed all that, the cranky old man thought he was pulling one over on XO by making me conduct random inspections laid out in a secret spiral-bound notebook,* thought Paul as he opened the bulkhead. *Ridiculous.*

Paul pulled himself into section one of power and propulsion, and the bulkhead slid shut behind him. He moved to the starboard crew ladder tube, gave a yank on the farthest rung, and coasted through section two. He arrested his flight with a quick grab of the ladder in section three and made his way to the designated storage room.

Along the way, Paul marveled at the cleanliness of the PPM. Every surface was pristine white, a glaring contrast from the grubby, nasty-as-a-subway environment of the tube, which was just on the other side of the bulkhead.

It was no coincidence that the PPM was the cleanest module of the *Odysseus*. Everyone on board, from the captain down to the dumbest robot, treated the place like a church, like a holy chamber in which lived a fiery beast whose energy kept the deadly void from overtaking the *Odysseus*. It kept them all alive. If there was a hiccup in the reactors, they were dead. All of them.

There was an unspoken sense that: *Hey, we can jerry-rig anything else we need out here, but if we lose the power plant, we're fucked.*

And it was true. Everything on board needed power to survive. So, it was kept in the most revered state a thing can be kept in on a ship at sea or in space or anywhere else.

It was kept clean.

Paul almost started to cry when the door opened and he looked in the small room. A single rack of packaged cleaning rags was fastened to the far wall. The ridiculousness of the one-hour dick dance of donning a pressure suit, climbing up the traverse, pulling himself two kilometers through the tube, and then up to section three of the PPM should have sent him into a rage. Instead, a sense of nostalgia and the loss of Captain Drake washed over him.

*Fuck me,* Paul thought. *I'm getting to be one oversentimental son of a bitch.*

He held it together, though, only because he knew from experience how much crying in a pressure suit sucked. There was no way to wipe your eyes, and the tears floated around in the helmet, screwing up your visor. Paul hated that.

After he noted his findings in his inspection notebook, Paul made his way back to the tube bulkhead to start back. But he hesitated at the bulkhead, halted by a strange thought.

*Section ten, transfer room 105,* he thought. *That's where Drake wanted me to meet him. I'm already all the way out here on the ass end of the ship.*

Paul floated in the open bulkhead. He looked down the two-kilometer tube. Halfway down the long structure was the CnC bulkhead he would take to the bridge to meet Althea.

He looked back into the now-dark PPM toward the room where the captain was supposedly going to unveil evidence of the XO's conspiracy. Paul checked his watch: plenty of time until he was meeting Althea.

*Fine,* Paul thought, pushing back into the PPM. *Your goddamned Easter egg hunt put me back here, so I might as well prove to myself how stupid this is.*

He noted each section as he floated aft. At section ten, he grabbed the ladder to arrest his glide and opened the bulkhead.

"Transfer room 105" was designated the fifth transfer room in the tenth section. The rooms were numbered from inboard to outboard, so room five was midway through the passageway toward the center section of PPM. Paul floated outside of the room for a moment, readying himself to be surprised by what he would find. As he did so, he remembered the captain's foul mood and urgency the last time they had spoken.

*All right, you weird old man,* thought Paul as he activated the door. *Whatcha got for me?*

The light in the small room came on automatically. Paul eased himself in. The room was empty except for a small device fastened to the middle of the floor. The black metallic device was about the size of a small shoebox. There were several blinking lights and a digital display of the date and time. But other than that, there were no obvious clues to suggest the device's purpose.

Paul floated closer to the object and touched his toe to the floor to pull himself down. Mag boots secured to the floor, he bent over and examined the mysterious metal square. He noted some writing on the top of the device: "IMU-M151-47."

It seemed like a familiar designation to Paul. Like something from his time in the military. But he couldn't quite place it.

There were a few unused data input/output connections on each side. Paul reached into his utility pocket and pulled out a standard data storage stick. He fiddled with the stick and device, trying each of the I/O connections until he found one that fit. The stick slid into place with a click.

The unit beeped, and the date/time display changed to read: "Download Course Data?"

*Oh yeah.* Paul thought to himself. *It's an inertial measurement unit. A self-contained system that measures linear and angular motion.*

Paul examined the simple interface and decided on the green "OK" button.

He pressed it, and the display said: "Downloading to Memory Device."

Paul stood up straight as the IMU loaded whatever data it had onto his memory stick. He remembered the captain's note saying he had discovered that the XO had changed their course and he could prove it.

*When the hell did you put an inertial measurement unit on board?* Paul thought, wishing he could ask the captain.

Paul figured Drake must have brought it on board back in high lunar orbit, when he'd taken command and started getting paranoid about the XO. A freighter in LOE was a frenetic and chaotic scene as the ship was upgraded, refitted, and provisioned in a mad rush to make a launch window. No one would have noticed the captain putting this thing in such a remote corner of the *Odysseus*.

And the old man had put it back here, where the XO could not directly monitor or detect it. An IMU didn't emit any energy or signals in any case, so the XO would never have known it was here.

*But why would the XO have cared?* Paul thought. *Seems like he, for the most part, didn't give a shit what the captain was up to.*

Paul shook his head. He suddenly felt uneasy. The device at his feet chirped, and the display read: "Data Transfer Successful."

Paul grabbed the memory stick and placed it in his cargo pocket. He worked his way forward to the bridge to meet up with Althea. The prospect of spending time with her was a much nicer thought than Drake's obsessions. He would deal with this later.

# Chapter Twenty-Three

*0930 Hours, 5 January 2052*
*Fort Benning, Georgia*

C olonel Filson changed the suck for phase three. For those candidates who graduated, phase three would be their last and only exposure to "real military missions." So, the colonel's goal was to expose them to as many mission profiles as possible. The curriculum called for ten missions over the sixty days of phase three. Mission cycles lasted about six days. They kicked off with a mission briefing in the auditorium where high-level tasks and unit assignments were given. Then two days for planning, three for execution, and one for recovery.

The good thing was the mission cycle meant the candidates got to sleep in their bunks in the barracks at least two nights a week. But it was an exhausting grind.

Like the rest of the candidates, Paul and Kata noticed that the cadre's tone changed. It was as if Filson, after running out over half of the candidates, was satisfied he had whittled the group down to its core. There was less yelling, more instruction. The cadence of candidates dropping from the course and being flown out on the morning drone was down to one every couple of days. And generally, those were for injuries, not failures.

There was also a rising atmosphere of competition among those who believed they were in the running for a Combat Corps slot. Most candidates, like the Geek, were happy to have survived this far and were starting to allow themselves to believe that they were going to graduate. They were counting the minutes.

Filson was silent on the matter, giving no clue as to class standings or how many slots were actually available.

But the class knew. For the past few weeks, a group of nine real contenders had emerged. Paul and Kata were among them.

Now, with one week left before graduation, the class entered the final mission cycle. After the initial mission briefing, the class left the auditorium buzzing. Filson had orchestrated a complex and exciting combined-arms extravaganza for their capstone mission.

This one had everything: long-range drone insertions, armored blitzkrieg raids, combat engineering tasks, and even several unaided nighttime river crossings. The final objective was a wooded mountaintop fortress that would be assaulted by four infantry platoons in exoskeletons after midnight. It was the kind of military experience the REMFs would talk about for the rest of their lives.

But it was also obvious that Filson had set up the capstone mission as a winner-take-all competition. Leadership of the four infantry platoons was not yet designated. During the mission brief, the colonel said simply, "Leadership of the four assaulting infantry platoons will be assigned based on the tactical situation and unit strengths."

"Bullshit," Kata said to Paul later.

Paul nodded and said, "It will be assigned based on who is still in the running for the Combat Corps. Anyone that is not a platoon leader on this one is out of it."

"Yep," she said. "And whoever does best on the assault will get the slot."

Paul and Kata shrugged and followed the rest of the class to the mess hall for breakfast before joining their assigned units and diving into the mission planning.

Five days later, they both led a platoon of candidates in exoskeletons up the hill toward the objective, along with two other rival platoon leaders.

The exoskeletons were nothing special. They were underpowered and saddled with multiple governor settings to prevent candidates from hurting themselves. While they did succeed in giving REMF-bound candidates an augmented infantry experience, they were terrible assaulting platforms.

"Move!" Paul yelled at his platoon over the radio. He was frustrated by their progress.

Pyrotechnics exploded all around them as they slogged forward. Drone gunships, which were supporting their assault, shrieked by at treetop altitude.

Paul's platoon was tired. Fifty-six hours into the operation, all they wanted was to be done, to get a shower, and to graduate.

But Paul was still gunning for the Combat Corps slot.

"Come on, damn it!" he yelled again.

Paul checked his map display. One kilometer to go. He wondered if any of the other platoons were ahead of him.

Filson had warned them during that night's mission brief that "enemy jamming will prevent the transmission of friendly unit positions." The colonel had smiled as he'd continued. "So, unfortunately, the four assaulting platoons will not be able to coordinate their attack."

Paul was getting anxious.

"Come on, Second Platoon!" he yelled. "We can do this!"

Gunfire erupted all around them.

"Get down!" Paul yelled.

They had walked into an ambush.

Buzzers began sounding off around Paul. "Shit!" he said to himself.

When simulation tracking and command determined that a candidate had been killed or wounded, they rendered that candidate's exoskeleton inert. The suit emitted a loud buzzer sound for three seconds before immobilizing so that the wearer could get into as comfortable a position as possible. Sometimes it was hours before they were repowered. A second loud buzz accompanied the loss of power.

"We've got to get out of this kill box!" Paul transmitted to his platoon. "Everyone who is still able to fight, follow me!"

Paul jumped up and sprinted up hill.

Alone.

He covered about fifty meters before something charged out of the shadows and knocked him over.

He tumbled across the ground.

An enemy exoskeleton towered over him.

Paul tried to stand up, but his exo's right leg had been damaged. He was able to get to a kneeling position just before the enemy ran into him again.

Paul was splayed onto the ground. Hydraulic fluid leaked from multiple joints. Red indicator lights flashed in his helmet.

His suit was faltering.

Paul rose again and reached for his pistol.

But the enemy was on him again, pinning him down. Paul fought. But it was over. His suit had lost all mobility and power.

The enemy exo ripped Paul's helmet off as a half dozen soldiers in black riot suits surrounded Paul.

They tore him out of the rest of his exo and put a black hood on his head. Paul cursed as they bound his hands.

It was over.

Someone grabbed him roughly by his bound hands and dragged him uphill. After five minutes, Paul was winded and stumbling. He had not slept in four days, and his captor was charging up the hill on fresh exo-aided legs.

*Fuck you,* Paul thought.

Suddenly the ground was level. It felt to Paul like they were on a dirt road. He heard the rumble of a diesel engine and the slam of what sounded like a large tailgate being dropped open.

The hands that had dragged him raised his bound arms until his palms touched metal.

"Get in the truck," the voice said.

Paul fumbled his way into what felt like an old cargo truck. Once he hoisted himself into the back, he felt for the bench seats and sat down.

A feeling of utter defeat washed over him.

# Chapter Twenty-Four

"**I** can't believe how fast these guys go through money," Fiona said, standing up. She dropped the Spitting Metal financial statements on her desk and rubbed her neck. It was late. They had been at it for hours.

"Really?" Pruden asked, sitting at his own desk. "Their cash burn is exactly what we forecasted during due diligence."

Fiona's face hardened. She forced herself to smile at the comment.

Pruden looked away from her thin-lipped grimace.

Fiona sighed heavily and walked toward the windows of her office.

"What about the Talisman option?" Fiona said, not turning away from the window.

It was Pruden who sighed this time. He looked at the large white binder on the corner of his desk.

"What?" Fiona asked, walking over to Pruden and grabbing the binder. "We never really walked away."

"No," Pruden said, standing up and stretching. "But we haven't spoken with them in over a month."

Talisman Partners LLC was a hedge fund. Pruden had been trying to arrange a line of credit with them to help fund Spitting Metal's ravenous need for cash. The conversation with Talisman was the result of an extensive due diligence process involving Fiona, Pruden, a team of researchers, and Fiona's favorite private detective. The diligence objective was to optimize on a single attribute, absence of connection to the Malloy family.

Fiona wanted a lender that had no association to her grandfather. She could not risk him finding out about her activities. He was a notorious and vindictive meddler. She was going to be operating too close to catastrophe for too long to risk Robert Malloy II gaining line of sight.

"Can you get us a meeting with them tomorrow?" Fiona asked.

"I don't see why not."

"Good," Fiona said. "Do it."

Pruden looked at Fiona with concern.

"We won't need them very long," she said. "But we really need them at the moment."

"What are you going to do?" Pruden asked.

"Sweeten the deal," she said. "See if I can get them over the hump of that NDA."

Pruden looked at Fiona.

She smiled. Without the thin lips this time.

"I won't do anything crazy," she said.

"I know," Pruden said. "Because I am going with you."

*

The next morning around ten a.m., Fiona stood at the front of a conference room facing the six partners of Talisman. They had taken places on each side of a long conference table. The senior partner, Buck Dorrity, sat with his arms crossed at the head of the table.

The table had room for twelve, which left a couple of empty chairs between Fiona and them. Pruden sat to the side of Fiona as she concluded her pitch. She had been presenting thier case for over an hour.

Pruden smiled as Fiona wrapped up. He loved to watch Fiona pitch a deal. She was a natural.

"I appreciate the opportunity to present Spitting Metal's strategy, financial forecast, and capital requirements to you this morning. We are very proud and excited about where we are."

Fiona looked around the room, making eye contact with each partner. Then she glanced at Pruden, who nodded.

"I'd like to end with a bit of historical context, if you don't mind."

The high-definition display behind Fiona, which for over an hour had been showing graphs and spreadsheets, went black.

"As I am sure you all remember, in January of 2042, Russia moved to end their Ukrainian dispute once and for all," Fiona said. "They sent two battalions of autonomous robots into the country and conducted a raid into Kiev, the capital."

Behind Fiona, pictures of the carnage in Ukraine flashed onto the large display. Now-infamous photos of destroyed buildings, mangled bodies, and lethal robots clicked by in rapid succession.

"These AI-enabled war machines were given a mission to accomplish on their own, without human intervention. They invaded Ukraine in the middle of the night, and by the time the robots marched back across the border into Russia, they had killed over twenty thousand people, including civilians and children. It was murder. The world recoiled from the vision of autonomous robots killing humans. It struck a core nerve. A fear of the future was finally realized."

Fiona paused for effect.

"Then, three months later, in April of 2042, world leaders met in Tokyo," she continued. "And on the fourteenth of April, the International Agreement Regarding the Prohibition of Machine-Based Killing Decisions was signed by every country with a functioning government."

A picture of the massive signing ceremony appeared behind Fiona. Formally dressed dignitaries assembled on a large outdoor staircase lined by blooming cherry trees.

"The agreement mandated that a human be involved in and approve every decision to kill another human. Known as the Tokyo Accords, it codified the requirement for a human-anchored kill chain and ushered a new level of complexity into warfare."

The display behind Fiona faded to black.

"Complexity due not only to the moral and legal risks of kill chain compliance, but also because of the effectiveness of machines in combat. Because, the fact is, strategists who were able to look at Ukraine dispassionately realized the Russians were on to something. The machines fought well and accomplished their mission. Repulsive or not, the strategy had worked.

Dorrity nodded. Fiona took a step forward, closer to the table.

"The politicians of the world want to be able to fight with machines. Their constituents are much happier when robots are sacrificed for their country instead of humans. Generals would rather fight with machines also. Machines don't get bored, scared, or forgetful."

Fiona looked directly at Dorrity.

"But no one wants to be charged as a war criminal."

Fiona chuckled.

"The Russian general that conceived of and commanded the operation in Ukraine can't leave Moscow for the rest of his life. If he does, he's going to find himself sitting behind bars in The Hague being prosecuted."

Fiona paused, acknowledging the nodding heads around the table.

"We want machines to do the fighting for us," Fiona continued. "And the brave men and women of our military deserve the best AI-augmented fighting robots in the world. We have seen what happens when we don't equip our military properly and give them the means to win."

A picture of Santiago appeared behind Fiona. Smoke rose from the besieged city. Fiona paused as the image changed to the well-known photos of panicked US military personnel scrambling into the Pacific Ocean and climbing into boats fleeing the Chinese army.

"They also deserve a kill-chain-compliant architecture that doesn't leave them wondering if they are going to be prosecuted for war crimes. Because, ultimately, the essential character of this shitty world's conflicts has not changed. Humans will, at some point, have to be killed if we are going to win our nation's wars."

The photos behind Fiona dissolved, and the image of a waving American flag took their place.

"That is Spitting Metal's value proposition, gentlemen. Victory," Fiona said. "Efficient, kill-chain-compliant victory. Whether it be air, land, or sea."

The flag behind Fiona faded away and was replaced by the Spitting Metal logo, a coiled robotic cobra with bullets and missiles spraying from its fangs.

"Thank you for your time," Fiona concluded.

Dorrity uncrossed his arms and looked around at his partners.

"Are there any questions for Miss Malloy?" he asked the table.

No one spoke up. Their poker faces were strapped on tightly.

"OK, then," Dorrity said, standing up. "Miss Malloy, if you'd give us just a few minutes to confer in private, I would appreciate it."

"Of course, Buck," Fiona said, grabbing her bag.

Pruden stood up, and they all shook hands.

Pruden and Fiona each took a seat in the luxurious, cushioned velour chairs in Talisman Partners LLC's lobby.

"Well, what do you think?" Fiona asked Pruden as they watched the doors to the meeting room close.

"They'll sign it," he said.

Fiona nodded in agreement as she looked at her phone.

"I mean, why wouldn't they?" Pruden continued. "You are offering them double the going rate on a line of credit as well as five percent in the company. It's a rich deal, and they know it."

Fiona looked up from her phone. "What's bothering you?" she asked Pruden. "You think it's too rich?"

"It's definitely too rich," he said.

"I told you not to worry," Fiona said. "We're going to rotate out of this piece-of-shit LOC in twelve months. Don't worry about it." She looked back at her phone.

"It's not the richness of the deal that bothers me," he said. "It's the punitive measures if we fall behind on payments. They could end up owning a lot more than five percent if we can't—"

"This is my brother," Fiona interrupted, getting up from her chair and pointing at her phone. "Grab me when they are ready."

Fiona turned toward the far corner of the lobby and walked away as she answered the call.

"Hey, Eugene," Fiona said. "Where did you decide on? The Dolomites? How is the snow?"

# Chapter Twenty-Five

*Mission Cycle 396*

*Earth Year 2062*

*295,687,066 Kilometers from Earth*

Paul and Althea floated in silence in the bridge facing the big window. The *Odysseus*'s hull, long and slender, stretched away for over a kilometer in front of them. The hab and utility module alternated into view on the ends of the spinner. They seemed tiny at this distance, two ridiculously small volumes of life-sustaining pressure and oxygen spiraling in the vastness of cold vacuum.

Inspection-and-repair bots worked over the ship. Paul was always surprised by the amount of activity. Two IR bots passed beneath the bridge. They were moving fast relative to the old girl, headed toward her front.

A glare of fire caught their eyes. Paul and Althea looked to its source. Fifty meters starboard, at about the same level as the bridge, a tug drone pushed a large piece of metal aft. Paul studied it as it moved out of sight behind them.

Paul pulled a bottle of bourbon out of his backpack.

"I see it's not all about solitude and reflection up here," Althea said.

Paul smiled.

"It was a gift from the captain," Paul said, holding the bottle up and staring at it as he recalled the old man. "He and I used to spend time up here. He's got a stash of the stuff somewhere on board, and he would share with me from time to time. He gave me this bottle at the end of a long cycle. I've been rationing it ever since." Paul looked at Althea. "I hate to admit it, but it does help me relax," he said.

"If you ask me," she said with a smile, "you've earned anything that helps you relax."

Paul opened the bottle and jerked it up and down to free a swallow of bourbon. Paul looked at Althea and winked as he leaned forward to capture the floating golden liquid blob with his lips.

Althea giggled.

"What?" he asked.

"It looks like you are kissing the bourbon," she said. "And kissing it well. It's cute."

Paul looked at her sideways.

"It's true," she said with a shrug.

"How would you know what a good kiss looks like?"

"I know plenty of things like that," Althea answered.

"Let me guess," Paul said. "Kissing releases endorphins and has many physiological benefits and blah blah blah."

Paul stopped talking when he saw the look of hurt on Althea's face. He wasn't sure what to say.

"That wasn't very nice," she said.

"Uh…"

Althea smiled to let him off the hook.

"Shit," Paul said. "Thought I really stepped in it there."

"You did," she said. "Lucky for you, my expectations for old soldier boys like yourself are low. Very low."

Paul nodded. "You are wise beyond your years," he said as he ejected another shot of bourbon in front of his face. When it stabilized into a spinning sphere, he leaned forward and sipped it from the air.

"Is it because I am attractive?" Althea asked.

"Huh?"

"I know that I am very attractive," she said in a troubled tone of voice Paul had never heard from her. "I had nothing to do with that, though. I was just designed this way. Is that why I seem so artificial to you? Is that why you don't take me seriously?"

"I take you seriously, Althea," was all Paul could think to say. "I'm not inviting anyone else up here to spend time with, am I?"

Althea let a weary smile spread across her face. "And I appreciate it, Paul. Very much."

They both turned back to the window. They floated in silence for a long time. Paul occasionally sipped on floating orbs of bourbon he set free from his bottle, Althea sneaking glances each time and smiling.

"May I ask you a question?" Althea said quietly.

"Is it therapeutically loaded?" Paul asked with narrow eyes.

"No."

"Then yes."

"Why do you come up here and do this. Stare out of the window?"

Paul looked at Althea, close to objecting to the question.

"I promise it's not loaded," she said. "I'm just curious."

"What do your algorithms tell you?"

Althea frowned. "Always about the algorithms with you," she said, letting irritation tinge her voice. "You have a lot more faith in my algorithms than I do."

She shook her head at him and looked out the window.

"I like the way staring out at the void makes me feel," Paul said. "Makes me feel small. Makes my problems seem small. My sadness seems small. Easier to bear."

Althea turned her head to look at him.

"Besides," Paul said, "it's also really beautiful out there."

Althea nodded in agreement, and they floated in front of the window for a few minutes in silence. She looked over at Paul for a moment and tracked the microexpressions on his face signifying deep thought. She stayed quiet and turned back to the window.

Paul was right. It was beautiful.

Paul, maintaining his gaze out of the window, reached for her hand.

She smiled and took it.

# Chapter Twenty-Six

P aul heard the truck slip into gear. It lurched a few times before surging forward and cruising down the mountain. Someone grabbed his hands and cut away his binding.

"Take your hoods off," Colonel Filson said.

Paul pulled the black hood off.

The colonel sat across from him, swaying with the jolts and leans of the old truck.

Kata sat next to Paul.

Their eyes met, and they saw defeated reflections of themselves. Kata shook her head slightly as if to say, *This sucks.*

The roar of several assault drones passed overhead, shaking the canvas covering the back of the truck.

"Final wave of the assault," the colonel said, pointing an unlit cigar at the overhead sound. "Two platoons are still in the fight. They are doing well."

Paul wanted to punch him.

"Hey," the colonel said, feeling the disappointment radiating off of the two exhausted candidates. "You guys did your best. You have nothing to be ashamed of. You should both hold your heads very high."

Paul and Kata were too heartbroken to talk.

The colonel shrugged and lit his cigar. The flares from his igniting breaths cast a glow throughout the back of the vehicle. After a dozen puffs, Filson leaned back and inhaled deeply.

"When were you born, Owens?" he asked.

"Sir, I was born in 2029."

"Christ on a cracker," Filson muttered. "You?" he asked Kata.

"Same, sir."

The colonel cocked his head to one side in disbelief and then let out a long, exhausted sigh. "That is the year I was commissioned," he said.

Paul and Kata were silent, not in the mood for Filson's story time. But they were trapped.

"The whole military was going through a transformation back then. I didn't realize it at the time, because I was downrange for about ten years straight. First few years on the tail end of that fucked-up Global War on Terror and then whipsawing around the world when we finally woke up and started reacting to the Chinese," the colonel said, shaking his head.

"More automation. More AI," the colonel continued. "More and more technical shit. I remember when I was a new Special Forces captain commanding an A-team in Pakistan, they gave us a suitcase full of small, helicopter-like drones. They could fit in the palm of your hand. I thought it was the coolest shit I had ever seen."

Filson chuckled.

"What I didn't realize, and I don't think anyone did, was that human combat skills and stamina were being de-emphasized. I mean, me and the rest of the tough guys in Special Operations Command were still out there doing our thing. And getting all of the press coverage, by the way. So, it seemed like the military was still doing its job. But, high level, the dial was turning toward technicians, administrators, and analysts…away from the warriors. Not intentionally, maybe. But it happened."

Filson put away the combat knife he'd used to cut off their bindings.

"I wasn't following any of this shit at the time," Filson said. "I was a dumbass new major, staring down at least a decade of staff weenie assignments before getting a crack at battalion command. It looked to me like the new soldier-augmentation program was where the action was. So, I wanted in.

"The augmentation protocol sucked, of course," he continued. "But it was exciting, cutting-edge stuff. So many things were changing so fast in the army then. I remember when they discontinued Ranger School. A bunch of us wondered what the hell was going on. Ranger School was the soul of the army. How could they cancel it? Something about budgets and relevance and roles and missions."

Filson shrugged.

"It was going to be a brave new world," he said.

Filson put his cigar in his mouth and pulled the long combat knife back out from his utility belt. He crossed his right leg over his left, leaned forward, and grabbed his boot. The cigar illuminated the colonel's face as he carved a large piece of dried mud off the bottom of his boot with the blade. It fell to the floor of the rambling truck.

Filson smiled and leaned back. He sheathed the blade and took the cigar from his mouth.

"Couple years later," the colonel continued in a low voice. "In 2045. Santiago."

The colonel stared at the chunk of mud he had dislodged. It slid toward the rear of the truck in spurts as the truck bounced and vibrated along.

Paul and Kata did the same, waiting for him to continue and wondering when they would finally be alone so they could process their failure.

"You guys study Santiago in school?" the colonel finally asked, not taking his eyes off the chunk of mud.

"Yes, sir," they both said.

The colonel looked up at Paul. "Tell me what you know about it," he said.

"Um..." Paul stammered. He knew Filson had been there. "I guess the consensus is they caught us napping."

"Ha!" the colonel burst out, startling Paul. "We were worse than napping, Owens. We were weak. They kicked our ass almost all the way out of Chile and into the sea. If they had succeeded, the red flag of China would be flying over that whole continent, as it does in Caracas tonight."

The colonel glared out of the back of the truck. Paul was uneasy.

"Our generation's Task Force Smith," the colonel said in a more reasonable tone. "The Chinese, of course, had some grotesque shit. Their equivalent of our augmentation program was over the top. Still is. I'll never forget some of the Centaur horror I saw down there.

"But our problem was we had evolved into a soft, overly technical force," the colonel continued, settling into one of his long stories. "Great tech, but no spine. And not just the army, by the way. Air force, navy, and marines—all weak. By then we were more of a logistics and administrative outfit. No one knew how to fight without a joystick anymore.

"When Santiago fell, the Joint Chiefs shit their pants. They had no idea what to do. Luckily, one of them was familiar with a little-known one-star general named Havron.

"Commissioned infantry. Havron made the Green Berets as a lieutenant in the middle of the Global War on Terror. Saw some real shit. Tough bastard. A smart one too. When he got his star, he was put in charge of the soldier-augmentation program. He spent two years trying to push the military forward, writing think pieces on hybrid man-and-machine units, Centaur theory, and tactics. Shit that no one else had the balls or foresight to write about. Hell, he was the first one to even use the term 'Centaur.'

"He had been so insistent about his ideas, they told him to put together a test unit to demonstrate the potential of all of the hybrid man-and-machine units about a year before Santiago.

"When Santiago fell, they asked him if his new unit was ready.

"Havron said they were not. But he pulled together all the combat veterans he could find across the army. It was not enough. So, he sent word to every Ranger School graduate, every Special Forces vet, every SEAL graduate, every marine infantry or special warfare graduate, asking for volunteers. And they came. Everyone. You should have seen some of those scrappy old fuckers," Filson said, laughing. "But, holy hell, could they fight…"

The colonel's eyes drifted back toward the rear of the truck.

"It was a crazy idea. Not only a man-and-machine hybrid unit. But also a cross-branch hybrid. Army, navy, air force, and marines all fighting side by side under a streamlined, unified command."

Filson looked at Kata.

"Then, you know what the old man did?" the colonel asked her.

She did not know what to say, thinking maybe it was a rhetorical question. It was.

"He led us back to Santiago and kicked ass. By the end of that fight, we were pulling the enemy out of foxholes and bayonetting them," the colonel said with pride. "It got pretty old-school."

Paul and Kata nodded. They were familiar with what the colonel was talking about. As legend, though. As mythology.

"When we got back, all hell broke loose. Congress, the president, and the American people were pissed. That's when the Joint Chiefs realized they'd fucked up. They had created a monster. Havron was a hero."

Filson took a long tug on his cigar.

"Congress fired the Joint Chiefs and restructured the whole shop. They gave Havron the keys to the Pentagon, and the old man formed the Combat Corps," Filson said in a reverent voice. "The mission of which is to select, augment, and train human soldiers to fight our nation's enemies in direct combat. The Corps absorbed the Special Operations Command as well as the last remaining and scattered combat commands across the military, including the army combat divisions and marine divisions and expeditionary units. The Corps also absorbed a few high-speed supporting units as well. If you fought, you were in the Combat Corps."

They all leaned forward as the truck decelerated. The vehicle hesitated and coughed as it changed gears before making a turn.

"By 2047, it was all over. General Havron had reorganized the whole fucking show. For good. That was the year he asked me to take over O.A.T."

The colonel looked at his cigar and took a long last pull. He released the fragrant smoke slowly. It wafted through the back of the truck before being sucked out of the gaps in the canvas.

Paul watched the tendrils of smoke disappear like his dreams of joining the Combat Corps. He felt the truck decelerate and turn. It straightened out but did not speed up. It seemed like they were close to their destination.

"The Combat Corps does more than just complete the kill chain," the colonel said, snuffing his cigar out on the bottom of his boot. "We are the small group of real soldiers in a big military. We are its diamond-hard center."

Paul had heard enough. "We're familiar with the history, sir," he said, nodding toward Kata. "It's one of the reasons we both had hoped to make it."

"Well, Lieutenant," the colonel said. "Like I said, you both did your best."

The truck finally came to a stop. Paul and Kata wanted off. Now.

Filson sensed their urgency.

"Give me a minute, candidates," he said, pulling the canvas to one side and hopping out.

They sat alone in the truck. After a minute, Paul turned and looked at Kata. She looked at him and shrugged. There was nothing to say.

"Owens and Vukovic!" the colonel hollered. "Dismount!"

Kata looked at Paul with a face that said, *I am so fucking over this.*

Paul just nodded. He pulled aside the canvas, and they climbed out of the truck.

Colonel Filson stood a few feet from the truck, smiling.

A walkway extended behind him for 150 feet, leading to a wide three-story building. The middle of the structure was dominated by a large cupola sitting on top of six tall columns. Two building wings extended left and right.

But it was the cupola structure that demanded their attention. A spotlight shone from its ceiling onto a large statue that stood over twenty feet tall. An infantryman, from a lost time almost a hundred years ago, charged forward, calling to his soldiers to follow him.

Paul realized they were back on Fort Benning, in front of the Infantry Museum.

Dim lights embedded in the walkway lit the path from where they stood between the two center columns to the base of the statue, where a lone person stood. As their eyes adjusted, Paul and Kata started to make out the outline of a crowd on either side of the walkway, which was lit by the soft glow of the pathway lights.

It was their O.A.T class, standing at ease, hands behind their backs, looking at them. Paul spotted the Geek. He was smiling in excitement.

"Sir?" Kata said, unable to put it all together.

"What is going on?" Paul echoed her confusion.

"Let's go," the colonel said. "The old man is waiting."

He turned and took a few steps. Noticing that the two exhausted junior officers had still not figured it out, he resorted to commands.

"Owens! Vukovic!" he said forcefully. "On me!"

That worked.

They walked quickly to catch up to him. Then the three of them walked, side by side, down the path.

Members of their class, fresh off the mountain and still in their filthy combat uniforms, nodded at them respectfully as they passed.

Soon they were walking by the cadre, who also looked at them with approval.

Halfway down the path, though, strangers stood in formation on each side. They were Centaurs. Some wore obvious prosthetics. Some faces were old. Older than the colonel's.

"Who are these people, sir?" Kata whispered.

"Every Combat Corps personnel who could make it," the colonel answered in a normal voice. "There aren't many of us, and this doesn't happen very often. You'd be surprised how far they travel for this when we put the word out."

"Word out about what?" Paul asked.

"For Chrissake," the colonel said, stopping. "I know you guys are tired, but you're going to have to be quicker than this going forward."

"But, sir, we failed the last mission," Kata said, hope building within her.

"Do you really think, after six months, decisions like this are made based on one mission?" Filson asked.

Paul and Kata gaped at the colonel mutely.

168

The colonel let a smile spread across his face and said, "And what makes you think that last mission even counted?"

Kata and Paul looked at each other, then the colonel, then around, and then at the lone figure at the base of the statue in a combat flight suit.

"Is that—" Paul began.

"General Havron," Filson said. "Supreme commander of the US military. Liberator of Santiago. Founder of the Combat Corps. Not a man to keep waiting."

The colonel turned and continued down the path. Paul and Kata followed, passing between the columns. The statue of Iron Mike loomed above them. His shouting face and upheld right hand called unseen comrades forward. His left hand held his rifle, bayonet fixed on the end of its barrel.

Colonel Filson and his two exhausted charges came to a stop in front of General Havron under the statue.

Filson saluted and said, "Sir, this is Lieutenant Paul Owens and Lieutenant Kata Vukovic."

General Havron returned the salute, and Filson took several steps back.

Paul and Kata stood at attention.

"At ease," the general said.

Paul and Kata adjusted their feet to a shoulder-width stance, hands clasped behind their backs, as Havron looked them over.

Paul and Kata could not help looking him over as well.

His olive-drab flight suit was old. Not the new, starched uniform with colorful patches most flag officers usually went around in. He wore a battle-suit driver's utility belt. A bayonet hung on his left hip.

Despite his broad shoulders, the general had a wiry air about him, the hint of a hidden quickness. His gray hair was closely cropped and contrasted with the dark pupils in his tired face.

The general smiled and said, "I've heard good things about you two."

"Thank you, sir," they said in unison.

"How was O.A.T?" he asked with a smile.

"Sucked, sir," Kata said.

Havron smiled broadly at the comment and nodded. "Good," he said. "Good." He shot Colonel Filson an approving look. "Do you know what they're all here for?" The general gestured over their shoulders toward the gathered crowd that had turned to face them.

Paul and Kata turned to look. The darkness lent the crowd an endless quality, faces extending out of the glow from the cupula and off into the eternal distance.

"There are less than five hundred ground combat officers in the US military," the general continued. "Four hundred and eighty-nine, to be exact. Our full authorization is five hundred and twelve. But I can't seem to keep us at that level. After tonight, there will be four hundred and ninety-one."

The general let the comment hang for a moment.

"I usually only let Colonel Filson pick one per class," he continued. "But he was insistent about you two. Said you were a team. Said it would be a damn shame." The general's voice feigned irritation and got louder as he went on, to be sure Filson could hear him. "Said I would be an idiot not to take you both. Said a bunch of other disrespectful shit about me."

There were a few chuckles from the crowd.

The general leaned in toward Paul and Kata. "He is a stubborn old bastard," he said in a voice only they could hear. "But he was right," Havron said, straightening back up.

The general gestured to an aide standing a few paces to his left. The lieutenant colonel stepped forward and held out the large wooden box in his white-gloved hands.

"Do you know the spirit of the bayonet?"

"To kill, sir," they both said as the general opened the box. Two large bayonets lay at rest on the felt box liner.

"Yeah," the general said, turning back to them. "That's what we train you to say. That's what it meant for a long time. For centuries, when it boiled down to fix bayonets, it was the last round of the fight. The situation was shit, and it was time to do or die. Chamberlain at Little Round Top. Cole at Carentan. Millet at Hill 180." General Havron looked at Colonel Filson.

"That old bastard in Santiago," he said.

"But that's not all of it. Not anymore. The question is no longer: Can you stick this thing in the enemy's heart? I think most would at least try to do that in the right circumstances."

The general patted the bayonet on his hip.

"In this dark age," he continued, "the curse and blessing is that our bayonets are too powerful. They reach across the globe, into space, under the sea. They walk around, fly, swim, and talk. They are colossal. And they are microscopic. It's never been easier to kill. And it has never been harder to fight.

"The spirit of the bayonet is now about leadership. It's the sacred duty the military honors and burdens you with when you join the Combat Leadership Corps. You train, care for, and lead those who carry the bayonet. You decide how your nation applies the bayonet. Who we kill. Who we spare. You are the human being, the American human being, in our nation's killing machine. You are asked to be both the tactical mind and the value system. Sparta and Athens. And we ask you to be this philosopher-warrior downrange. Alone. In the worst possible circumstances."

Havron stepped closer.

"You see, guys, you are the spirit of the bayonet now."

The general paused. Paul realized that a loudspeaker had been pushing Havron's words to the assembled crowd.

"The insignia of the Combat Leadership Corps is crossed bayonets," Havron said as he turned and took one of the bayonets from the box, "symbolizing the leadership, toughness, and courage it takes to lead our forces in combat."

The general unsheathed the bayonet and held it up so that Paul and Kata could see it. The number "2476" was engraved in a large font on the blade.

"Contrary to what many believe, it is not a symbol of guts-in-your-teeth bloodlust and thirst for battle. Rather, it is an acknowledgment of the solitude we in the Combat Corps face. The load we carry." He returned the bayonet to its scabbard and snapped it onto Kata's utility belt. "No one else in the entire US military is authorized to carry a bayonet."

Kata felt the heft of the blade on her left hip and could not stop herself from smiling.

The general put his hand on her shoulder and nodded. Then he turned and grabbed the second bayonet from the box.

"These bayonets are symbols of your belonging to the small and elite core of the US Army," Havron said as he unsheathed the second bayonet and held it up. It bore the number "2477."

"And they are a reminder that it will, someday, for all of us, boil down to a singular killing thrust."

Havron fastened the bayonet onto Paul's utility belt and then stepped back. He looked around past the small group under Iron Mike and out at the crowd assembled in the night.

"Which officer vouches for these two?" he asked loudly, directing his question to the assembled crowd.

"I do, sir," Colonel Filson said, straightening up to attention.

Havron nodded.

"Which enlisted soldier vouches for these two?"

"I do, sir," Sergeant Major McGowan said, snapping to attention.

The general nodded.

"Which peer will vouch for these two?"

The Geek came to attention as he said, "I do, sir!" Paul and Kata had not seen him join the small group under Iron Mike. The Geek smiled and fidgeted with excitement.

General Havron turned back to Paul and Kata.

"Lieutenant Vukovic, do you accept this nomination into the Combat Leadership Corps and the burdens that accompany it?"

"I do, sir."

"Lieutenant Owens, do you accept this nomination into the Combat Leadership Corps and the burdens that accompany it?"

"I do, sir."

"Very well," General Havron said.

He pulled a three-by-five card out of his flight suit's left breast pocket.

He always read the orders, even though he had them memorized. It was too important, too sacred of a thing to fuck up.

"Attention to orders!" Havron commanded. Hundreds of heels scuffed and knocked as soldiers, officers, and civilians snapped to attention. "The president of the United States, acting upon the request of the secretary of defense, who, having heard the affirmation of the superior officers, enlisted soldiers, and peers that these two officers serve with, has placed special trust and confidence in the patriotism, integrity, and abilities of Second Lieutenant Kata Vukovic and Second Lieutenant Paul Owens. In view of these special qualities, their demonstrated potential, and desire to serve, Second Lieutenant Vukovic and Second Lieutenant Owens are accepted into the Combat Corps. Effective this twelfth day of January, 2042, by order of the secretary of defense, they are the two thousand four hundred and seventy-sixth and two thousand four hundred and seventy-seventh officers of the line."

# Chapter Twenty-Seven

*Utsu Book One*

*Circa 1510*

*Translated from the Japanese*

Hiroaki took me with him to Shingen's castle. There we met with Lord Shingen and his war council. Then we traveled with them to the besieged Clan Hayato fortress.

The castle was impressive and lay on good and defensible ground. The north of the castle was covered by difficult and mountainous terrain. The south of the castle was protected by a wide and fast-flowing river that offered only three crossings: a shallow place to the west, a rocky place to the east, and a large covered bridge to the castle's front.

Hayato's Elite Guard formed an impenetrable wall of samurai around the castle so that none could approach. The bodies of Clan Shingen samurai, killed in failed attacks, lay in piles on the ground.

"What do you think, General?" Shingen asked Hiroaki. "Can it be done?"

"It shall be done, my lord," Hiroaki said. "I will return in four weeks with my students."

I returned to the school with Hiroaki. He rode in silence for the entire seven-day journey, devising his plan.

We arrived back at the school late in the day. That evening, Hiroaki called every student, even the young ones, to a meeting.

"Tomorrow, we begin training," he said. "Ensure that you are rested."

We practiced Hiroaki's plan several times a day, every day, for twenty-one days, until Hiroaki was satisfied that every student knew the plan by heart.

The night before we marched on Clan Hayato, Hiroaki instructed the school cooks to empty the stores and send hunters into the woods. They prepared a great feast. Hiroaki walked among the students as they filled their bellies. He spent time with each one, assuring them they would be brave and would fight well. He spent time with the older veterans, thanking them for their leadership in the coming battle. Then he retired to his quarters.

The next morning, we began our march toward Clan Hayato's castle.

# Chapter Twenty-Eight

*Mission Cycle 399*

*Earth Year 2062*

*297,859,914 Kilometers from Earth*

P aul closed the *Utsu* text and pushed back from his desk.

He found that when he followed his ritual, the words flowed. The sleep, meditation, yoga, and exercise pattern built a momentum within him that rolled over the anxiousness, memories, pain, and anger that simmered, always, beneath his surface. After nearly a year of following this practice in the solitude of the *Odysseus*, it was bulletproof, putting him in a zone, every time, that he would have paid money for back on Earth. Particularly during his imprisonment and court-martial.

But not this morning.

He had only translated a short section before his wandering mind forced him to quit.

He knew the culprit.

Paul reached into the breast pocket of his flight suit and pulled out the memory stick. He turned it over in his hands several times. He shook his head, returned the stick to his breast pocket, and pushed away from the desk.

*Fine,* he thought. *I'll go for a walk instead.* Paul suited up and moved through the traverse toward the hub.

As a military officer, Paul had walked a lot. He'd had a reputation for preferring walking meetings over sitting in a tent or conference room, and he'd conducted as many of his staff meetings as possible that way. He also liked to walk alone. He could work things out better once his body settled into a comfortable stride. He came up with his best tactical plans on his solo walks.

But often when he walked, his mind was blank. His body moved, and his brain rested. Recharged. He was notorious for circling the perimeter or fence line of whatever remote outpost he was based at. During their deployment to South America, Kata had gotten so frustrated and concerned about Paul's walks, she had ordered Paul's first sergeant to assign a drone guard whenever Paul left his hooch.

Walking on the *Odysseus* was a different thing, though. It meant passing through various states of atmosphere, gravity, and temperature. Sometimes rapidly. It required getting into and getting out of pressure suits, mag boots, thermals. So, rather than just setting off on a walk and seeing where you ended up, as one did on Earth, on the *Odysseus*, you had to decide where you were going first.

Paul liked his shipborne walks, nonetheless. What they lacked in spontaneity, they made up for in setting.

This time, Paul headed for one of his favorite places to sit and think: the drone hangar.

Like many of her facilities, the hangar was a retrofit added at the request of the military during the *Odysseus's* troop transport days. The military needed a hangar facility for their landing and tender vehicles.

From a distance, the hangar looked like a large shoebox fastened to the belly of the long ship. At two hundred meters long and fifty meters wide and deep, the facility provided half a million square feet of protected hangar space for the military vehicles. The Company had complained loudly at the time about the loss of over two hundred meters of the *Odysseus's* cargo rigging, but when the crisis had dissipated, they'd seen the virtue of the hangar. Until then, the *Odysseus's* small complement of inspection-and-repair bots fastened themselves to the side of the ship like sucker fish. With the hangar, the *Odysseus* was able to upgrade to a larger squadron of XO-controlled IR bots. The Company was pleased, envisioning the *Odysseus* under way for another century or more under the constant inspection-and-repair protocols of her expanded complement of shipmates.

The hangar had no bottom to it. The structure was entirely open to the void so that military transports and drop ships could come and go on their missions easily. That was one of the things that made it one of Paul's favorite contemplative spots on the ship. A ten-meter-long oval-shaped blister of glass, reminiscent of a World War II aircraft machine gun turret, protruded from the belly of the *Odysseus,* which was the top of the hangar. This was the observation-and-control facility from which an officer could direct troop loading and receiving in the hangar during military operations. Now, with no military activities to control, the module was only good for observation.

But it was really good for that.

The military had, of course, overengineered the chair. A big, ballsy metal-and-leather commander's chair hung from an articulating arm in the middle of the glass blister. A joystick on the left-hand armrest allowed Paul to angle and swivel the chair as he pleased. The chair in the observation-and-control facility was a favorite spot of Paul's. He considered its view to be second only to the captain's window on the bridge.

While the CnC offered an expansive view of the void spreading out in front of the good ship, sitting in the hangar commander's chair felt like sticking your head into an aquarium full of fish. Inspection-and-repair bots came and went as they finished and began their patrols. Others were docked against the walls or from power cables that extended from the ceiling. Most of the IR bots used a compressed-gas propulsion system that enabled them to maneuver around the *Odysseus.* The puffs of expelled gas flared randomly as the school of IR bots jockeyed in the massive but busy space.

Paul still had the heart and eyes of a drone pilot, and he loved the purposeful shapes of the IR bots. There were many different configurations. Egg shaped.

Cigar shaped. Jellyfish-like. One version that reminded Paul of a manta ray. Some had arms. Some had large sensor arrays. All were purpose-built, like the soldiers he had served with.

His favorites, though, were the tugs. There were four large tug bots used to haul large loads. They were squatty and muscular and looked vaguely like their earthbound ancestors. They had soft rubber bumpers fastened to their noses and sides that allowed them to nudge into and drive things without damage. The bumpers were circular in shape and evoked visions of bearded crew members throwing roped tires onto the sides of tugboats. Paul wondered if nostalgia was at play at all for the Earthside engineers who'd designed them, or if the tire-like shapes actually were the best solution. Some things didn't need to be improved on very much.

Like all the other IR bots, the tugs used compressed gas for maneuvering but also had powerful onboard rocket engines that enabled them to tug or push heavy loads.

Paul had been awed only a few cycles into the voyage by a display of their power. He stood on the bridge with Cooley and Captain Drake and watched as one of the tug bots moved a massive payload to a new position farther forward. Paul gaped at the enormous asteroid. The tug looked like a minnow pushing a basketball.

"Wow," he mumbled as they watched.

"You're damn right, son," Drake responded. "We don't have to worry about losing the main engines as long as we have those bastards around!" He chuckled, slapping Paul on the back.

In addition to their raw power, Paul appreciated the tugs' scratches and dents. It was rare that an IR bot would actually touch something with anything other than its robotic arms and hands. As a result, they always had a pristine, fresh-from-the-factory look about them. The tugs, though, were made to push, pull, bump, and nudge things, and they looked like it. They were weary and beat-up, like Paul.

Paul turned the memory stick over in his fingers as he watched one of the tugs push a welding bot to its mooring spot. The endless void spread out beneath him, outside of the hangar.

He watched the tug work and thought about the XO and Captain Drake. The tug, the welder bot, all the bots inside and outside of the hangar, were like everything else on the *Odysseus*, networked to and controlled by the XO. And that was fine with Paul.

But now, with a mysterious data set on a memory stick that he wanted to analyze in private without the XO knowing, he was stymied. Worse, he was forced to think like Drake. And not like the parts of Drake that Paul admired. Rather, the darker, paranoid parts he did not.

*Fucking crazy, mean old man*, Paul thought to himself.

Paul ran a mental inventory of the analysis tools he could think of. They all seemed like dead ends. Ideal, of course, would be the 3D displays on the first level of the hab. But the XO was integrally connected to all of that.

Everything Paul could think of had the same issue. The XO would not only get access to the data but would also know that Paul was analyzing the data. Paul did not expect to find anything important, but he did want to be able to digest it on his own before sharing it with the XO.

He was stuck.

Rapid-fire puffs of gas erupted along the tug's long and short axis as it swiveled around to aim at the bottom of the hangar and the void beyond. It was finished with the welder bot and was preparing to resume its post just below the hangar opening.

"Hello, Paul. You are on the move early this cycle. How are you?" the XO's voice came over the speakers in the OC.

Paul put the memory stick back into his breast pocket as he responded. "Hello, XO. Doing well. You?"

"I am fine, thanks. All systems nominal. Should be another uneventful cycle for all of us."

"That's the way I like 'em," Paul said.

"Me too."

The tug's small-maneuver thrusters fired for a two count, and the large drone moved slowly down. When it had cleared the hangar, a different combination of thrusters fired. The tug swiveled into an overwatching position just to port side and below the hangar opening, facing forward in the *Odysseus*'s direction of flight.

"Paul," the XO said. "I'd like to ask your point of view, if I may?"

"Sure."

"How do you think the crew is getting along?"

Paul smiled and shook his head. Regas had been let out of confinement a few cycles ago. He was cordial enough with Drummond and Mr. Cooley, but the simmering anger beneath the surface was clear for everyone to see. There was unease on board.

"Not great," Paul said. "But I have seen worse."

"Have you faced such disunity in units you have commanded in the past?"

"Not like this. And, honestly, not from a position like this," Paul answered.

"A position like what?"

"Powerless," Paul answered. "I'm just a cog in the *Odysseus*'s machine, XO."

"That may be so, Paul," the XO said, "but I find leadership roles to be confounding at times and thought your perspective would be valuable."

*That's an odd comment,* Paul thought.

"How are the sessions with Althea going?" the XO asked before Paul could probe what he was talking about. "Is it OK that I asked?" the XO said, responding to Paul's hesitation.

"Of course," Paul said. "It's fine. I mean, there really can't be many secrets between us out here, can there?"

"No," the XO said. "Not very many."

"And I know you've noticed when I've had…difficulties on board…" Paul said.

"I have."

"How much do you know about what happened?" Paul asked.

"More than I am supposed to," the XO said. "Most of it is classified, as you know. But, Paul, you mustn't think worse of yourself. What you've been through is just terrible. I think you've shown great strength and resilience. More than most would have."

"Did you have any reservations about letting me on board?"

"No. I had no reservations, and neither did Mr. Cooley or Captain Drake. The captain, in particular, felt a great respect and affection for you, Paul. I am sure you could sense that."

Paul smiled at the memory of Captain Drake. "Yeah. I did. I miss the old man."

The XO waited half a beat before prodding Paul, "So the sessions are going well, then?"

"Yes," Paul said. "They are."

"Good."

Paul smiled at himself. He knew the sessions with Althea were helping him. But he was surprised that he was starting to value her companionship. For the first year of their journey, she had been no factor. He wasn't rude to her the way the captain was. And he didn't leer at her body the way Regas did. But he did not spend any more time with her than he had to. He had come aboard to be as alone as he could. And she was not part of that formula.

Now, though? He had to admit that he liked being around her.

"And Althea?" the XO asked.

"Huh?" said Paul. "What about her?"

"You two seem to be getting along well."

"Sure. We are," Paul answered. "Why?"

"Just because we have so much longer to go," the XO said. "It would be a shame if you did not enjoy each other's company. And I am certain that she enjoys yours."

"She told you that?" Paul asked, immediately regretting it.

"Not in so many words," the XO said. "But I can tell."

Paul felt a spark from the XO's comment. He drowned it quickly, though. *Of course she enjoys my company,* he thought, scolding himself. *Her job is to spend time with me and the rest of the crew.*

"That's good, I guess," Paul said, looking at his watch.

"Well," the XO said. "Thank you for indulging me. I won't bother you any more. Enjoy the rest of your cycle, Paul."

"I will. Thanks."

Paul, unsettled, sat in the OC chair for another half hour. Something about his conversation with the XO troubled him. But he wasn't sure what.

That was when he realized: *The captain would not have a rogue inertial measurement unit on board without having his own discrete, unmonitored way to analyze it.*

Paul pushed out of the command chair and headed for the CnC.

Arriving, he left his helmet in the air lock but did not remove his pressure suit. Paul floated into the spotless facility and looked around. The cleaning bots still visited the CnC every other day despite the fact that no one occupied it anymore. The patches in the hull were the only reminder of the captain's astronomically bad luck. They had been painted to match the interior, but the slightly raised welding beads that encircled them were still visible, like Paul's puffy scar tissue. The *Odysseus's* repairs were now part of her long tale of service.

Paul smiled as he envisioned crew members decades in the future gawking at the repaired hull breaches and marveling at the cosmic violence dealt to the good ship and her captain. It was the kind of thing that gave ships reputations of bad luck and being jinxed.

Paul's smile faded. *Am I the jinx?* he wondered.

He shrugged his shoulders to shake off the thought and searched the bridge. He found nothing and moved down to the lower level and entered the captain's quarters.

Paul floated in the middle of the wood-paneled room for about fifteen minutes. It felt creepy. Everything was in its place, undisturbed by the captain's death. The bed, a cacoon-like sleeping bag tethered to the wall, was still ready and waiting for the old man.

He pushed off the floor to get a slow rotation going to his right and tried to refocus. He forced himself to take in every detail of the room.

*Where would I hide an unmonitored bootleg computer if I were a crusty old captain?* Paul thought to himself.

He completed three full revolutions. The third time the old man's desk came into view, Paul laughed at himself.

*I wouldn't hide it at all if it were my fucking ship.*

He pushed off the ceiling, bouncing himself to the floor, where he crouched and then shoved himself off toward the desk. He floated smoothly and caught himself against the zero G chair.

Paul opened the lap drawer. *Bingo*, he thought as he reached in and grabbed the tablet computer. He turned it over in his hands and pressed the on button. The screen glowed and asked for the password.

Paul shoved the tablet into a small utility bag and pressed a foot to the floor to turn for the door.

An idea struck him.

He started searching the captain's quarters. It didn't take long to find it.

*Yes!* Paul thought, a grin spreading across his face. He looked with appreciation at part of the captain's bourbon stash. He knew the bulk of Drake's contraband was stored somewhere else on the *Odysseus*. That fact alone was reason enough to continue the cycle inspections. Paul hoped to be able to find it at some point over the next year or so.

The bottle the captain had given him was almost empty, so the eight bottles Paul stared at were enough to significantly raise his morale. They sat snuggly in a small, cube-shaped wall storage unit. Paul entertained the thought of taking one with him back to his quarters but decided against it. The last thing he wanted was to somehow be found out and forced to share precious bourbon with anyone.

No. The stash would stay here. Hidden. His secret.

After he took just one swig, of course.

"Here's to you, Captain."

# Chapter Twenty-Nine

P aul's Officer Assessment and Training Course started with 1,134 students. Six months later, on January 19, 2052, 498 graduated. The rest failed out, quit, or were recycled.

The graduation ceremony was held on the parade field in the shadow of the Infantry Museum, where Paul and Kata had been accepted into the Combat Corps. It was well attended by military and civilian officials and also by family members. Paul's and Kata's parents beamed and swelled with pride all day.

Later that evening, most of the class spent a few hours at the officers' club after the graduation ceremony, saying their goodbyes. Their class was dispersing the next day, headed for assignments all over the world.

Paul and Kata sat at the bar and watched the revelry. Their minds had already turned toward their next challenge. They shipped off for duty with an exoskeleton battalion in the morning and would likely be in combat in a few months.

"There they are!" they heard the Geek say over their shoulders. "Paul. Kata. I've been looking for you!"

The Geek stepped through the crowded o'club floor. A girl's hand in his, and an older man just behind him.

The older man's resemblance to the Geek was clear, but Paul and Kata were more surprised by the girl. Shorter by an inch or two than the Geek, she was a pretty blond.

Kata's eyebrow arched as she and Paul shared glances.

"Paul, Kata, I'd like you to meet my father."

The Geek's father smiled and offered his hand. "Congratulations to you two!" he said with enthusiasm. "Combat Corps! Just incredible! And Wallace has told me all about you both. Thank you for being such a good friend to my son. He told me he never would have made it without your help."

"That's bullshit," Paul said.

The Geek's father was startled by the force of Paul's voice.

"Yeah," Kata said, just as loudly. "Without this guy, I don't think I would have made it through."

The Geek's father straightened, trying to assess Paul and Kata.

"Toughest son of a bitch in the class, right here, sir," Paul said, pointing at the Geek. "We were lucky he was in our class."

"You going to introduce us, Wallace?" Kata said, glancing at the Geek and then the blond girl.

"Oh. Yes. This is Susan," the Geek said.

"Nice to meet you," Kata said, extending her hand. "Kata Vukovic."

"Thank you," Susan said. "The pleasure is mine."

Paul leaned forward from his stool so that his arm would reach. "Susan, I'm Paul."

Susan nodded as she shook Paul's hand.

"Yes," she said. "I have heard of you both. So nice to meet you."

"One hell of a man you've got there," Paul said, making eye contact with the Geek. "I'm going to miss him."

The Geek looked down at his shoes.

"He got the prime assignment of our whole class, you know," Kata said.

Susan looked at the Geek. "He told me what he would be doing. I didn't realize it was…"

"Those high lunar orbit jobs with Space Command are the toughest to get. Period," Paul said.

"Probably the most important, too," Kata added. "The way the Chineese are militarizing space so quickly, we need officers with balls up there."

Kata gestured at the ceiling to make it clear she meant the moon and Mars and beyond, unaware her reference to male anatomy made Susan blush and the Geek's father smile.

"And they asked for Wallace by name," Paul added, to move the conversation along.

The Geek's father and Susan both looked at him, pride and adoration in their eyes.

"That's enough," the Geek said, making a waving motion with his hands. "I really just wanted to be sure you all met."

"Yes," his father said, turning back to Paul and Kata. "Congratulations again."

"I've got to get them back to the hotel," the Geek said. "We leave early in the morning for Houston."

"Roger that," Kata said.

The Geek gave Paul and Kata each a quick hug and then led Susan and his father out of the o'club.

# Chapter Thirty

---

*Mission Cycle 401*

*Earth Year 2062*

*299,344,896 Kilometers from Earth*

---

"That seems like such a sudden goodbye after all you went through together," Althea said, having just heard the latest installment of Paul's story from their now-frequent informal counseling sessions.

Paul nodded in agreement from the sofa in her quarters. "It was," he said. "It was a busy time. A real blur. And we didn't realize at the time that most of us would never see each other again."

"Really?"

"Filson tried to warn us. But the military complex is just so big," Paul said. "We all got lost in it the next day."

"And what exactly did the Geek do after graduation?"

"He reported for astronaught training and about a year later he was in space." Paul said, smiling at the thought of his old friend the Geek. "Kata was right. Remember, this was almost ten years ago when China and the US were both rapidly building up their military presence in space. Those high lunar orbit assignments were as important and high visibility as they got. It was already obvious to anyone paying attention, even at graduation, that he was destined to really be a big deal."

"You and Kata too."

"Huh?"

"You and Kata were obviously destined for great things also!" Althea argued. "You both had been selected for the Combat Corps, after all."

Paul chuckled. "Yes, but our selection was not viewed with the same awe as the Geek's or some of the other REMF assignments."

"Well, that is crazy."

"Not really. The REMF roles are excellent preparation to become captains of industry. The span of control given to guys like the Geek is very large. In just a few years, they have thousands of people working for them, hundreds of millions of dollars' worth of equipment under their management, and are pursuing endeavors that only the largest companies in the world can undertake, like deep-space logistics and orbital capital projects. Just a couple years later, as a young captain, the Geek was responsible for more people and a larger budget than a civilian executive could hope to amass in a thirty-year career. Compare that to Kata and me, who shipped off for exo duty the next day."

"What is 'exo duty'?" Althea asked.

"Your first assignment with the Combat Corps is always with one of the exoskeleton battalions," Paul said. "Descended from the old US Marine battalions and Army infantry divisions, these are the scrub units of the Combat Corps."

"Scrub?" Althea asked.

"Bottom rung," Paul said. "The shit detail."

"That's not very nice," Althea said.

"It's not," Paul agreed. "But it's true. And it's important. The missions the exo battalions take on are critical. Mostly military police and combat support missions for the Centaur units. The essential, non-sexy mission components that make Centaurs successful and give Combat Corps command the chance to observe new soldiers and officers in action before investing billions of dollars in them to turn them into Centaurs."

Althea nodded in approval of what she was hearing.

"You're eligible to apply for the Centaur program after a minimum of twelve months of service with the exos, but there are plenty of officers and soldiers who spend their whole careers there."

Paul was quiet for a moment and then chuckled.

"What is it?" Althea asked him.

"We used to say that there are only two kinds of exo soldiers," Paul said, a thin smile on his face. "Those who are applying to the Centaur Corps, and those who have already been rejected."

Althea noted the signs of nostalgia and remembrance on his face. She waited.

"It's not true, though," he said. "There are plenty of career exos. Soldiers who want no part of augmentation. They regard it as weird, or heresy, or, worst of all, cheating."

Paul chuckled.

"What?" she asked.

"It's just funny to me now, years removed and hundreds of millions of miles away," he said.

"Go on."

"The military is the most egalitarian, merit-based organization in America. Anyone can join and compete and progress based solely on their competence," Paul said. "But the structure within the military is the pettiest caste system you can imagine. One's status is defined and limited by their unit. Even a brave group, like the exo battalions, are not immune. They are among the tiny number of Americans who actually fight for their country. They dodge bullets, take hits, bleed, and die facing a hostile enemy. And, still, within the Combat Corps, they take an ungodly amount of ridicule."

"Ridicule?" Althea said with indignation.

"Yeah," Paul said, chuckling again. "Their nickname is 'nasty legs.'"

"Nasty legs?"

"It's an old army nickname for infantry," Paul said. "Based on the unhygienic and smelly state most infantrymen live in when in combat. But over time, it morphed to signify a sweaty, unaugmented body in an exoskeleton. Command was always trying to stamp out the term. But it stuck. And they were fighting words, I can tell you. I've been called a nasty leg and have called others nasty legs, and, in every case, punches were thrown soon after."

Paul waved his hand to emphasize the end of that tangent.

"Anyway, the cannon-fodder track doesn't quite have the same commercial sex appeal as a guy responsible for the construction of a trillion-dollar space dry dock in high lunar orbit."

Althea sat with her arms crossed and a disapproving glare.

"Look," said Paul, "it just is what it is. And, at the time, Kata and I were very proud. Out of the one hundred and twenty-three graduates of our class who were medically eligible and applied for Combat Leadership, only the two of us were chosen."

"Were you excited?"

"Sure, we were. A little scared too, to be honest," Paul said. "There were several hot spots at the time, particularly the African continent. The exo battalions were, like the rest of the Combat Corps, very busy. We were anxious to get our first taste of combat and hopeful of making the Centaur program."

They were both quiet for a moment. Paul remembering. Althea thinking. She broke the silence.

"Are you still in touch with the Geek?"

"Yes."

"When was the last time you guys spoke?"

"Just before our departure burn. I called to thank him for helping me get into the Fly It Off program and on the *Odysseus*."

"What!" Althea said. "That authorization came from the commander, Space Transportation and Logistics Command."

"Yep. General Wallace Bandy," Paul said. "The highest-ranking officer from our O.A.T class. Known to his classmates as 'the Geek.' I would never have qualified for the program without his intervention. Because of—you know."

Althea waved off his negativity. She beamed at Paul like a proud mom.

Paul looked his watch.

"Yes," Althea said, noting his time check. "I think that is a great place to end for this cycle."

"That's not what I was thinking," he said.

"Oh," Althea said. "We can go longer, if you'd like."

"That's not what I was thinking either," Paul said, a smile emerging.

Althea picked up on the mischief. She smiled also.

"Join me on the bridge in an hour?" Paul asked.

"Yes," Althea said. "I'd love to."

# Chapter Thirty-One

*Utsu Book One*

*Circa 1510*

*Translated from the Japanese*

The siege of Clan Hayoto Castle was Master Hiroaki's greatest victory. Hiroaki's students were spread throughout Shingen's forces to lead the execution of the plan.

Like darting birds of prey, we struck across the river's shallow and rocky place at the same moment.

Hayato's Elite Guard countered these attacks but were then surprised by a strike from the mountains north of the castle. They had to split their forces again, and their communication and coordination became difficult.

Finally, at the critical moment, Hiroaki struck boldly across the covered bridge. The master himself led the attack.

The Elite Guard fought well but, by then, were no match for Hiroaki's expert attack. Anotsu Hayato refused Hiroaki's request of him to surrender several times. He was too proud to surrender as his father watched from the castle walls.

The battle brought Hiroaki and Anotsu together. They fought. Hiroaki cut Anotsu down with a lightning-quick killing stroke with his katana. Anotsu fell to the ground in halves.

Lord Hayato's cry at the sight from the castle wall was heartbreaking.

Hiroaki's forces took the surviving Elite Guard as prisoners and took their captured banner back to Lord Shingen.

Clan Hayato castle was now surrounded, with only its castle guard within its walls. The castle guard was thought to number between one and two thousand troops. Perhaps two hundred horses. Not enough to last.

It was all but over.

Lord Shingen sent an emissary into the castle demanding its surrender in the morning.

Lord Shingen and Hiroaki ate dinner together in the lord's tent in celebration that evening. Hiroaki asked me to join as his guest. In the middle of dinner, Lord Shingen was approached by one of his counselors. There was much whispering.

"Excuse me, please, General Hiroaki," Shingen said, rising. "I must tend to matters. Please enjoy your dinner and well-deserved rest. Tomorrow, our long war ends."

# Chapter Thirty-Two

"I thought you would be pleased about this," Pruden said.

Fiona stewed in front of one of the big windows in her office, arms crossed, shoulders sagging.

"It's your first real revenue associated with any of our deals," Pruden said, walking up next to her. "Enjoy it for a few seconds at least."

Fiona shook her head and then looked at Pruden. Half of a smile broke the surface of her face.

Pruden could tell she was fighting it. "You are ridiculous," he said.

Fiona surrendered to the grin. "You're right," she said with a chuckle. "You're absolutely right."

Fiona held out a fist. Pruden bumped it with his own.

"This calls for a toast," Fiona said, turning from the window and walking to the wet bar in the corner of the office.

"That's the spirit," Pruden said.

"Scotch, beer, or wine?" Fiona asked.

"Beer works for me."

Fiona returned. She handed Pruden a bottle of Singha and said, "To our first decent-paying contract with a real customer."

"Cheers," Pruden said, clinking Fiona's soda water and lime.

They each drank.

"It's fucking irritating, though," Fiona said before Pruden had even swallowed.

"For Chrissake," Pruden mumbled, turning away from Fiona. "Then at least let me enjoy it."

"Seriously," Fiona said, following him. "Don't you prefer the Spitting Metal architecture?"

Pruden didn't answer.

"It's so much safer for our soldiers," Fiona continued. "With Spitting Metal, they sit in air-conditioned boxes safely tucked away in the States, controlling combat robots thousands of miles away in hostile territory. Musashi wants our soldiers to walk into the breach side by side with his precious soldierbots and take the same shots they take. It's going to get people killed."

Pruden turned suddenly.

Fiona almost ran into him.

"That's a crock of shit," Pruden said without smiling.

"Crock of shit?" Fiona asked. "No. That's actually exactly how the architectures work." She crossed her arms as if transgressed.

"It's a crock of shit that that is the reason you prefer Spitting Metal," Pruden said.

Fiona put on a wounded face.

"Come on, Fiona. It's me you're talking to. You can bullshit everyone out there." Pruden swung his beer around at the wide world. "Not me, though."

Fiona smiled the smile of the guilty. "I care about our troops," she protested.

"Of course you do," Pruden said without sincerity.

"Spitting Metal is a much bigger payday, and you know it," Fiona said, pointing at Pruden.

Pruden nodded, half in agreement and half to underline that he had been right about Fiona.

"It's a much bigger play!" Fiona said. "Human operators controlling large numbers of big-time weapons systems: tanks, bombers, surface warfare ships, submarines. The big toys with big-ticket prices! These guys are building an entire remote-control army, navy, and air force. If we can sell that, it will be a massive payday."

Fiona took another swig of water. Pruden matched her with his beer.

"Musashi's end goal is much less grand, in my view," Fiona said, looking into her glass. "He's just trying to build a good soldier."

Pruden nodded.

"You like them, though, don't you?" Fiona said, catching the look on Pruden's face.

Pruden shrugged. "I do," he said.

"You and the Combat Corps," Fiona said, rolling her eyes. "I don't get it."

"That's because you don't get them," Pruden said. "The Corps is being run ragged. They're stretched paper thin all across the world, and they keep getting more and more missions piled on them. And it's the last organization where human soldiers do real, old-fashioned fighting. They 'close with and destroy the enemy,' as they put it. Even if Spitting Metal pulls it off, the Corps' mission will not change. They will still be where the pain is. They will still be where the casualties are borne. Think about it," Pruden said, looking straight at Fiona, his face tightening with emotion. "They have the most to gain by having machines bear some of the load."

"For them, maybe," Fiona stated. "Not the most to gain for us."

There was an edge to Fiona's voice.

Pruden knew the debt weighed heavily on Fiona. He couldn't blame her. Spitting Metal would need more funding soon, and the line of credit with Talisman had ballooned to more than $20 million. He estimated it would be more than two fifty before the end of first quarter 2053. The monthly interest payments were getting onerous, and the punitive covenants were always in the back of Fiona's mind.

Pruden knew that, for Fiona, this had nothing to do with which type of military architecture was best suited to the task. It was boiling down to survival for her. The bigger deal had to win. Period.

And his job was to help her get it done.

"It's a ten-million-dollar contract," Pruden said, trying to ease his boss's anxiety. "And that's just phase one."

"Tell me the deal again," Fiona said.

"Pretty simple. Phase one is soldierbot performance testing. Mobility. Basic combat skills. Connectivity and extension platform validation. Durability—"

"We'll crush that," Fiona said with a wave of her hand.

Pruden nodded. "After that, we move on to phase two. Small-unit training."

"How will that work?" Fiona asked.

"Don't know yet. Truthfully, I don't think the military knows yet. They are still trying to figure out who is going to run the program."

"Doesn't matter. We'll crush that also. That's not part of the ten million, though, right?" Fiona said, raising her eyebrows.

"No," Pruden said. "We haven't even started negotiating that yet. The ten million is just for phase one."

"Good," Fiona said. "So, give me the bad news. What will phase one cost us?"

Pruden smiled. "Dr. Musashi says no more than five million."

Fiona's grin returned. "Good," he said. "We'll use the rest to service Spitting Metal's debt."

"We can't do that," Pruden said.

Fiona looked at him.

"Why the hell not?"

"Because," Pruden said with patience, "Dr. Musashi is going to need that money to get ready for the next phase."

"All of it?"

"Yes."

"We'll see about that."

Fiona's cell phone rang. She pulled it from her pocket.

"It's Eugene," she said.

Pruden nodded. He pointed at himself and then the door.

Fiona's brother called her every day, and Fiona always took the call. There was no telling how long the two of them would talk, and Pruden was not going to hang around to find out.

"We'll continue this conversation tomorrow," Fiona said as Pruden reached the door. "Go celebrate!"

Pruden gave her a thumbs-up and closed the door behind him. He was glad Eugene's daily had interrupted the conversation. It was old ground, covered many times. And Eugene eased Fiona's anxieties in a way no one or nothing else could. Having endured their family together, there was a strong bond between Fiona and Eugene that they both drew strength and perspective from.

Pruden thought it strange to use the word "endured" to describe growing up in the wealthiest family in the world, but he knew it had been hard on them both. He did not begrudge their scars.

"Hey," Fiona answered. "How are you? How is Mio Posto?"

"It's perfect as always," Eugene said. "How are you? You sound tense."

"I'm good. It's just work. Nothing important."

"You lie," he said, sighing heavily. "Why do you put yourself through this?"

"Why do you always ask me that?"

"Truthfully, Fi, I don't know why I bother. It's fruitless. You are crazy. You are torturing yourself. Sell those stupid companies and come live with me over here."

"Someday, Eugene. But not yet."

"Then let your guy run them and come over here. The cute one. What is his name again? Poolen?"

"Pruden," she corrected.

"Yes. Him. Let him run it. Even if only for a week. Come visit me."

"I will soon, I promise."

"More lies," he said. But Fiona could hear his smile.

"So, I am really glad you called to yell at me again," Fiona said.

"I know," he said. "I'm sorry. I was really just calling to say hi."

"I'm glad you did," Fiona said. "You caught me just in time."

"What are you up to?" he asked.

"About to grab a workout."

"Shocker," Eugene said. "Go grab a drink. Grab a guy. Live a little, for crying out loud."

Fiona took another sip of water and waited him out.

"Fine," he said. "Call me later."

"I will," Fiona said.

"Love you," he said.

"You too."

Fiona hung up. She pictured Eugene on the patio of the small Italian villa he had purchased when he'd turned eighteen and gained access to his trust. Eugene had fallen in love with Italy early in his life. He'd planned his escape from the family during a semester abroad in high school and left the States the day after meeting with their grandfather. Eugene had never told Fiona what was said in the meeting. But she knew it had been more hurtful than most.

"Wow," Fiona had said the first time she'd visited him there. "When you run away, you don't mess around. This place is gorgeous."

Eugene had beamed. Hers was the only opinion in the world he cared about. Fiona smiled at his happiness.

"So, no more school, then?"

"College, you mean?" He laughed. "No thanks."

"What are you going to do?" she asked.

He rolled his eyes at her. "Are you kidding?"

"No. I am serious. What are you going to do when you get sick of Italy, art, wine, farming, and whatever else you're getting into over here?"

"If that happens, I'll figure something out," he said. "But I'm sure whatever it is will make no sense to you at all. I love you, Fi, but we're different. I just needed to escape. I don't need revenge."

"I'm not out for revenge," she said.

"Uh-huh," he said.

"I'm not," she tried again.

"So, you're getting a JD/MBA at Harvard because you love law and business sooooooo much that, even though you have probably more money than you will ever need, you just want to do more business."

Eugene looked at his sister. He'd said the word "business" like it was a derisive punch line.

"What happened to the girl who spent every car ride looking for airplanes?" he asked. "Remember how you could tell me what every plane in the sky was? You would yell out, 'Boeing!' 'Airtruck!'"

"Airbus," Fiona corrected.

"What?"

"It's 'Airbus,' not 'Airtruck.'"

"Whatever," he said. "That's not my point, Fi. Why don't you go learn how to fly planes or something?"

Fiona shrugged.

"Seriously," Eugene said, stepping closer to her and putting his hand on her shoulder. "I feel like you are binding yourself more and more tightly to Grandfather's world, when you already have the power to escape."

"I can't explain it, Eugene," she said.

"This works for you"—she gestured around at the grounds of the villa—"and I'm glad. But it won't work for me. I wish it would."

"I know this won't," he said. "I'm telling you to find what will."

"I know what will."

Eugene took his hand off her shoulder and put it on his hip in frustration.

"I want to create something," she said. "Something really fucking big."

"You mean make a lot of money," he said.

"That's how 'big' is measured."

"And then what?" he asked her.

"What do you mean?"

"You create something big. Make a lot of money. Then what? What will happen?"

"He will know."

"Who?"

"Grandfather," she said.

"Know what, Fi?"

"That he underestimated me. Should have treated me better. Should have

201

treated us all better. And damn well should have treated you better."

"We promised we would never speak of that," Eugene said, cocking his head and raising a finger.

"We're not," Fiona said. "I'm just saying. I want him to know how wrong he was."

"Even if the scales do one day fall from his eyes," Eugene said, "Grandfather will never say that."

"He'll know it. That will be enough."

"Will it?"

Eugene looked at his sister. "I worry for you," he said, shaking his head.

"Don't," she said.

"You're on a fool's quest, Fi."

"Then wish me luck."

Eugene sighed.

"Only if you promise you'll move here when your quest is over," he said.

"Deal!" she said with a smile, glad the topic was changing, and realizing she was serious. "This place really is beautiful," she said.

Eugene nodded and turned away from Fiona. He looked at the rolling green hills. He kept turning, his eyes sweeping over the olive trees, the old barn where his painting studio was set up, the stables, and then back to his sister.

"God help me," he said. "I know this is just a material thing. It's just a simple place. But I love it so."

"What did you decide to call it?" Fiona asked. "Places like this need a name."

"Mio Posto," he said with a big smile. "It means 'my place.'"

# Chapter Thirty-Three

*0843 hours, 11 March 2053*
*Fort Bragg, North Carolina*

"It feels like someone went to work on me all night with a baseball bat and an ice pick," Kata groaned as she sat down across from Paul in the hospital mess hall.

The past two months had been long for the both of them.

After a year traveling around the world getting into scraps with their exo battalion, Paul and Kata had submitted their Centaur program applications as soon as they were eligible. It surprised no one in their unit when they were accepted.

Paul and Kata reported to Fort Bragg after the new year and went right into surgery. It was not pleasant.

And it wasn't just the pain of having electronic implants attached to their skulls. They were injected with nanobots to fight disease and accelerate healing. They had hundreds of tissue samples taken to be analyzed for weaknesses and to begin growing spare vital organs. Their musculoskeletal systems were reinforced to withstand the use of military-grade exoskeletal battle suits.

"Yeah," Paul said, taking a sip of bad hospital coffee. "I'm over it." He set down his mug and ran his hand along the scar on his forehead, tracing it around behind his ears, where it got bigger.

"It will be good to get out of this place," Kata said.

Paul nodded and said, "Good to see the colonel too."

They had been stuck in Womack Army Medical Center for twelve weeks for the augmentation process. During the first few weeks, they were too sore to get out of bed. When they were ambulatory again, though, they had not had the time. The physical therapy sessions were long and tiring.

This week, though, they were feeling good.

Colonel Filson had checked in on them a few times during their augmentation. But, as he well knew, they were in no condition for visitors. The colonel would poke his head in and say hi if they were awake. If not, he'd scan their charts and check in with their doctors.

Now, though, the colonel sensed their increasing strength and resulting restlessness. He had called the day before. The plan was to pick them up and treat them to a night out of the hospital.

It was unusual for Centaurs to get a night away so early in the protocol. But Filson knew General Davidson, the director of Military Augmentation Programs, well. He'd been one of the general's first patients.

"I promise I'll bring 'em back fully operational, sir," Filson had told the director over the phone.

"Where do you want to take them, Don?" the general asked him.

"To the lake house, sir. Just for the night."

The general was quiet.

"I just want to give them one night away, sir," Filson said, sensing the general wavering. "Think about it. They signed in from a twelve-month combat tour with their exo battalion and went right under the knife. They need a chance to relax, time away from being poked and prodded by strangers in lab coats. You and I both know how aggressive the training is about to get."

"Damn it, Don," Davidson said. "I've got one mission: to deliver successfully augmented soldiers to phase-one training. You're asking me to jeopardize that mission just so—"

"Sir," Filson interjected. "With respect. That's bullshit. I don't care what your job description says. Your mission is to deliver Centaurs with the highest possible chance of graduating from the program. All of it. Not just phase one."

The colonel paused for effect before continuing.

"And I'm telling you that giving these two soldiers a night away from the goddamn flagpole is the best possible thing you can do for that mission."

Filson waited, wondering if he had pushed too hard.

"Jesus, Don," the general finally said. "I forgot what a drama queen you were."

"Is that a yes, sir?"

"No swimming, Don," General Davidson said.

"Of course not, sir."

"I'm serious. They cannot get in the water at all. Not for at least another two weeks."

"You have my word, sir."

"And no drinking."

"Of course not, sir."

"The last thing I need is one of them stumbling into a wall and setting their grafts back weeks or, God forbid, necessitating a reattachment."

"Sir, please don't worry about it," Filson said, realizing that if he did not get off the phone soon, the general would talk himself back out of it. "I really appreciate it, and they will too."

"Don't make me regret this," the general said.

But Filson had already hung up.

The colonel picked Paul and Kata up at 1700 hours. Kata hopped in shotgun, and Paul got in the back seat of the colonel's old pickup truck. He handed them each a beer as soon as they were out of sight of the hospital.

"Oh God," Kata moaned, taking the cool beverage in her hands. "Thank you, sir."

"You're welcome," Filson said. He handed Paul one also. "But I'd advise you to savor it. I'll be rationing this shit tonight. I promised the general you would be undamaged and fully operational when I return you tomorrow."

Colonel Filson swiveled his head to glare at Kata.

"I also promised him I would not allow any alcohol tonight. So, Centaur code of secrecy invoked."

"Invoked it is, sir," she said.

The colonel shifted his stern gaze to the review mirror to lock eyes with Paul.

"Invoked, sir," Paul said, popping open his beer.

Convinced their oaths were sincere, the colonel grabbed the open beer he was stabilizing between his legs and raised it toward Paul and Kata.

"To the fallen," Filson said.

"To the fallen," they echoed.

The three military officers took large swigs of beer.

The colonel secured his beer. Paul and Kata settled into their seats.

"Where are we going, sir?" Paul asked.

"Lake Harris. About an hour north."

"What's there?" Kata asked.

"My cabin."

"You've got a cabin, sir?" Paul asked.

"One of the advantageous to being stationed at Bragg for fucking ever is you get to put down more roots than most," the colonel said, gesturing at Kata to put her beer down. They eased past the Fort Bragg gate guard and rolled onto the highway heading north.

"When they airlifted me back from Santiago to Womack, I had about eighteen months' worth of salary plus combat pay that I had not been able to spend," he continued as he put his truck into autonomous cruise and turned to face Kata. Paul leaned forward. "God, that was a long deployment," Filson said with a weary face.

"Six months later, when I got out of the hospital, I had about ninety days of leave built up. I rented a cabin on Lake Harris and took forty-five days off. By the end of my leave, I had talked the owner into letting me buy it. It's been my fortress of solitude, you might say, ever since." Filson shook his head. "It's what I miss most when I am in Benning running an O.A.T cycle. God, I hate Fort Benning."

"Cheers to that, sir," Kata said.

Paul raised his beer as well.

An hour later, at the end of a dirt road, they parked in front of the small cabin, about a hundred yards from the water.

"Damn, sir," Kata said, getting out of the pickup truck. "It's perfect."

"Yep," Filson said with a smile. "It is."

The three them stood still for a moment and gazed at the small Appalachian-style cabin. The two-story board-and-batten-sided building was well maintained. A small, neat stack of wood sat on the left side of the porch, an olive-drab wooden military trunk on the right side.

The colonel led them inside. The downstairs was one big room, encompassing the kitchen and a sitting area with a stone fireplace. Upstairs, there were three small bedrooms.

Hours later, after exploring the water's edge and getting a tour of the lake in the colonel's old boat, Paul and Kata sat in large chairs on the back porch overlooking the lake. The colonel brought them each a plated hamburger, corn on the cob, and another beer.

Filson watched as they devoured the food. The sun sank below the rolling hills to the west, and shadows cast by the tall pines stretched across the lake, reaching for the cabin.

Paul burped loudly and leaned back in his cushioned chair.

Kata smiled and did the same.

The colonel chuckled and leaned against the porch railing, his back to the water, his own beer in hand.

"So how does it feel to be supersoldiers?" he asked them.

"Sore and tired," Paul said. "That's how."

"Have to tell you. I don't feel shit yet, sir," Kata said. "Other than lumpy in places I used to be smooth."

"Long as you're not smooth in places where you used to be lumpy!" the colonel said, laughing.

Paul and Kata smiled, each thinking about the relative meaning of that statement for them.

"I was the same, guys," the colonel said. "Coming out of the augmentation, you don't know shit. But you've got some monumental things coming your way. Things that will separate you from the average administrative REMF military officer for the rest of your life."

The colonel took a sip of beer while they waited for him to continue. The man knew how to use anticipation to hold his audience's attention.

"The first is when you get into an exoskeletal battle suit for the first time. I know you both have driven exoskeletons before, but a battle suit is different. In addition to being more powerful, more armored, and more lethal than an exo, it's made to integrate to you. That's why you go through the suck of the augmentation process. So that you and the battle suit can become an integrated fighting system.

"The helmet has a special visor that uses near-eye-display technology," he continued, "enabling you to see from the point of view of your drones as well as integrated situational displays. Maps. Imagery. And other stuff. All selected via mental command. The battle suit's powerful communications suite extends your ability to command and control drone assets over very long distances. Using it, you can maneuver drones and employ their weapons systems in real time. And since it's you doing or overseeing the shooting, the kill chain is perfectly compliant with the Tokyo Accords. It's slick."

The colonel paused. Paul and Kata looked at each other. Filson's enthusiasm was contagious. They wanted to climb into their battle suits right then.

"I'm not going to lie to you guys, though," the colonel said. "It is going to suck for a few weeks."

He took a long pull of beer and set his glass on the railing.

"What is, sir?" Kata asked.

"The adjustment period."

"Adjustment to what?"

"To commanding and controlling drones," the colonel said, pulling three cigars out of this shirt pocket. He gestured them toward Paul and Kata in offering.

Paul shook his head.

Kata nodded.

Colonel Filson took a step closer to her as he said, "It doesn't sound like much. But, holy hell, it sucks at first."

Kata took a cigar. Filson stepped back to the railing. In a few moments, cigar smoke wafted back and forth across the porch, pushed around by eddies of the slight evening breeze.

"You have to understand," Filson continued, "the human brain is the product of millions of years of evolution that perfected its ability to drive this thing around. The human body," he said, gesturing at himself.

"When you give it a direct feed from, say, an airborne drone system flying nap of the Earth, at an airspeed of over one hundred knots, making erratic course changes to avoid enemy anti-aircraft systems, the brain gets pissed. It compares that to the data it is getting from its actual body saying it is stationary, and the brain says, *Fuck you. This sucks for me, so I'm going to make life suck for you also.* The nausea is intense. For the first month of training, my abs were sore all the time from barfing."

Filson took a lazy sip of beer while Paul and Kata looked at each other, their excitement fading.

"Seriously," the colonel said, almost to himself. "After the first week, my battle suit reeked of vomit and piss."

"OK," Kata said, waving her cigar to dispel the mental image. "We get it, sir."

"Sorry, it's not that bad, really," Filson said without conviction.

"What is the training like, sir?" Kata asked.

"It's hard," Filson answered. "But it's also a lot of fun."

They looked at him skeptically.

"I'm serious, guys," he said. "I mean, it's going to have its shitty moments, but, for the most part, it's good training."

He could see they were not believing him.

"Remember, the drones we fight with are smart. But they don't have any real independent decision-making capabilities. They are just mobile sensor and weapons platforms that a battle-suit pilot can tap into remotely. So, the course is trying to teach you how to play chess in three dimensions, while on the run."

The colonel put placed his beer on the railing behind him.

"But to get to be that fluid with a platoon of combined-arms drones," he continued, "takes about six months. Most of it is out in the desert at Tonopah, where you can't do much damage as you learn the systems."

Filson leaned back against the railing and took a pull from his cigar.

"The training has a couple main phases. The first is battle-suit qualifications, where you'll learn how to get around in the battle suit without killing yourselves. That takes about a month. Then they put you in 'the box' for phase two."

"The box?" Kata asked.

"The simulator. Basically, an immobile battle suit in the hangar facility. That second phase is all about learning how to control drones from the suit.

"After proving you can keep drones under control from the suit, you move on to phase three, which is out on the maneuver range. There you learn to move around in a battle suit while commanding drones. That's when the nausea is the worst. Ugh." The colonel made a retching face.

"Seriously, sir," Kata said. "We get it."

"The graduation task for phase three is Dead Man's Canyon," Filson said, reaching for his beer.

"Dead Man's Canyon?" Paul said with disbelief.

"Yeah. I know. It's cheesy," the colonel said with a shrug. "I didn't name it."

"What is it?" Kata asked.

"It's a canyon near the Tonopah training site. Water beat the shit out of ancient mountains for thousands of years for the sole purpose of destroying drones. It's only about twenty miles long, but it's narrow, twisty, and very difficult to fly through. It's claimed thousands of drones, and, funny thing, they never pull out the crashed machines."

The colonel smiled and took another sip of beer.

"They let them pile up. The canyon floor is littered with them, and there are burned impact points polka-dotting the canyon walls for the entire route. It sets quite a mood."

"So, you have to fly your drone through the canyon in one piece?" Kata asked.

"Yes." The colonel nodded, putting his beer back on the railing. "But that is not all of it. While the trainee pilots their drone through the canyon, they have to simultaneously negotiate their own canyon obstacle course. Dog Hobble Canyon. It's shorter than Dead Man's. But lots of vertical drop, fast-moving water, and overhanging rock that make it really tricky for a battle suit to get through quickly."

Kata nodded.

"It is a simple task: pilot your drone and battle suit through the canyons as quickly as you can without wrecking either."

"How did you do?" Kata asked.

"I did OK. I never lost a drone or hobbled my battle suit."

The colonel raised his fist in a show of victory.

"The last three months then get increasingly tactical," the colonel continued. "Until the last month, when you're commanding not only your drones but a handful of other soldiers in battle suits controlling their own drones."

He looked at the pair of young officers.

"It's a long course, guys. But it's more than worth it," he told them.

"What did you like most?" Paul asked him.

"About what?"

"Being a Centaur."

"The sensation of flying," the colonel said without hesitation. "For me, that was the best. Those points in a mission when you truly forget you're telling a drone that is miles away from you how to zig or zag. When it feels like you are the thing that is zigging or zagging."

"That must be a crazy sensation," Paul said.

"It is." Filson nodded. "And really because there is no sensation to it at all. A Mark IV aerial attack drone can pull over twenty G's. But, strapped into your battle suit, you feel none of that. The heads-up display conveys everything about the drone and its systems, of course. Airspeed. G-forces. All of that. The thought-control architecture encodes your thoughts into maneuver commands, and the battle suit's communications suite is in continuous communication with the drone. As soon as you think it, the drone executes. But you don't feel the G's, the burning impact of enemy fire, the force and explosion of losing control and careening into the earth. That drone's data feed simply ends, and you toggle through your deployed forces to call up the next best positioned platform according to your plan."

The colonel stopped.

"Sorry," he said, shrugging. "I tend to babble on about it."

Filson took a long pull from his cigar. The end burned bright red in the fading evening light.

"You miss it?" Kata asked.

"Every damn day."

The sat quietly for a few minutes. Paul and Kata watched as the last glints of reflected light receded from the surface of the lake. The colonel looked at his cigar.

"Can I ask you a question, sir?" Paul said, breaking the silence. "It's about O.A.T."

"Ancient history?" the colonel asked.

"Seems like a zillion years ago," Kata said.

"Combat tours do that to your perception of time," Filson said. "Even if you're just a nasty leg. There's before and after, and the before always seems a long way away."

Paul and Kata nodded at the observation.

"What's on your mind, Owens?" the colonel prodded.

"Were you pissed when the Geek graduated O.A.T?"

Filson raised his eyebrows at the question and then slanted them down. Paul thought he saw a flash of anger pass across the colonel's face.

But the colonel just took a long pull on his cigar.

"I had that REMF dead to rights," Filson said with a smile. "And I was going to send him out on the morning drone."

"Then why did you let us get away with helping him?" Kata asked.

"I learned long ago not to doubt the process. No matter how mad I get or how much I disagree…I know that it is wiser than me."

Paul and Kata shared a side-eyed glance. But she couldn't hold it in.

"A classic, mystical Colonel Filson response," Kata said, shaking her head and raising her beer toward the smiling old man.

"What process is that?" Paul asked as the colonel tipped his beer toward Kata.

"What you and your class went through," he said. "The crucible."

The colonel looked at them as if his statement should have explained everything. He saw their blank faces and rolled his eyes at their lack of understanding.

"The experience rewired you guys," he said, pointing at them with the glowing red end of his cigar. "I reprogrammed you. You and the rest of your graduating class are all part of the same unit now. It's not an official unit. But you're connected, and you understand each other. Our military complex is huge now, and the REMFs run it. But, mark my words, years from now, when you are downrange for your country leading men and robots against our enemies, when you need help, the Geek and guys like him will tear the world apart to get it to you."

He caught them glancing at each other again.

"I don't give a damn if you believe me or not," he said with a shrug. "I trust the wisdom of the unit. A well-led unit will make the right decision about its comrades. Who it allows to stay. Who it eliminates. So, when the Geek made the cut in your unit's eyes, I'll admit…I did not expect it. I was surprised. I disagreed. I tested it. I subjected it to stress. I made it prove itself. But I accepted it."

"Isn't that just the rule of the mob?" Paul asked.

"I said a 'well-led' unit," the colonel answered. "Big difference. You know that. Mobs do not make it through my training."

"And how about that envelopment in the swamp phase?" Kata asked him.

The colonel shook his head and took another sip of beer before saying, "You realize your platoon is the only platoon to pass the swamp phase machine-gun nest assault?"

Paul and Kata bumped fists, smiling.

"It's true," he said. "That task is ordinarily a surefire failure for the platoon leader. I was certain I'd get rid of the Geek that night. But, damn it. Your harebrained, borderline-cheating idea to split your force worked."

"That must have really pissed you off," Paul said with a hint of taunt in his voice.

"No, son," he answered. "You're not fucking hearing me. I just about cried when you guys pulled that off. When you guys risked getting kicked out for the Geek, I knew the bond was there. So, no matter how much I personally wanted to kick that chubby egghead out of my program, I knew I'd done my job and that the process had gotten it right."

The colonel smiled as he recalled that night in the swamp.

He put his beer on the railing, leaned back and said, "As you guys know, sometimes as a leader you have to maintain your mask. Play the role. I had to be the angry superior officer on the outside. To cement it, you guys had to believe you had beaten not only the cadre, but also me."

"We did beat you, sir," Paul said.

"You did, son," he said with a gracious smile.

"And you know what?" Kata said. "Since then, the Geek has been promoted twice already. He's the highest-ranking member of our O.A.T class. Gonna be a general, no doubt."

"Fucking REMF," the colonel growled in mock disgust.

Paul and Kata smiled. They all sat in silence as the last bit of light behind the colonel faded and the surface of the lake darkened.

# Chapter Thirty-Four

*Mission Cycle 402*

*Earth Year 2062*

*300,091,392 Kilometers from Earth*

P aul rose from bed early. He meditated, exercised, and then sat down at his desk to work on the captain's tablet. He put it into administrative mode and started looking for a back door into the operating system.

An hour later, after a few unsuccessful attempts, he gained access to the tablet. He took the memory stick out of his flight-suit pocket and inserted it into the data port.

*All right, you sneaky bastard,* he thought as he clicked to open the drive, *let's see what you were up to.*

The drive had only one massive data file on it. Paul recognized it as a navigation data set. He searched the tablet's list of programs and found a navigation utility, which he used to open the file.

The tablet displayed the *Odysseus*'s measured course line all the way back to Earth. The course line was blue with about a dozen red circle icons dotting the last half of it at irregular intervals. Paul placed the cursor over one of the icons and an acceleration and time value appeared.

*Strange,* he thought.

He moved the cursor to the next red icon. Then the next.

Paul gasped when he realized what he was looking at. Each red circle highlighted an instance where the inertial measurement unit had detected acceleration and course change.

Paul leaned back in his chair and tried to get his head around the implications.

The Hohman routes to and from the belt were strictly prescribed and designed to minimize time en route, energy required, and exposure to known hazards. That was one of the things that made the meteoroid strike that had killed the captain so strange. A lot of work by a lot of smart people and AIs had gone into the effort to chart a course where that would not happen.

A ship's path to the belt should not have any midway course changes. The Hohman routes were not designed that way. There were the initial maneuvering burns to depart orbit, followed by the long primary burn, which would put the ship underway. After the primary, there could be several smaller adjustment burns to fine-tune the ship's trajectory to within Hohman-route parameters, but these would all have been completed within the first few weeks of being underway. On a normal voyage, there would be no subsequent adjustments to course until the ship began to prepare for deceleration and arrival.

But there, on the tablet display, were a dozen course deviations, starting approximately six months ago. As a result, the *Odysseus* was millions of miles off course before the meteoroid strikes.

And she was still deviating, drifting farther from her assigned course every second.

*Fuck me,* Paul thought. His head was spinning. If the *Odysseus* had executed a maneuver burn, Paul would have noticed. Everyone on board would have. When the maneuver thrusters kicked on, it jolted the whole ship. Sure, maybe he could have slept through one such burn. But the course analysis showed at least a dozen.

*Fuck me,* Paul repeated in his head.

Was it all an effort to kill the captain? Were they being hijacked? If so, who the hell was hijacking them? The XO?

*No one else could have pulled this off,* he thought.

Paul zoomed in to look at the course deviations. The first was long in duration. The off-course acceleration had lasted for almost five hours. But it was small in magnitude. It was only .33 meters per second per second; a tiny, undetectable fraction of the acceleration of gravity. But when finished, it had added a course deviation of almost 6,000 meters per second.

The other accelerations were smaller and closer together. The interval between the first and second deviation was almost a week. But the interval between the eleventh and twelfth was less than a cycle. It was as if whoever was making the course deviations was fine-tuning their work. Why? To rendezvous with the meteoroids that killed the captain?

Paul looked at the time stamp for each burn and noted they all took place late in the cycle, when it was likely most of the human crew would have been asleep.

Paul set the tablet computer down on his desk and pushed back in his chair. He leaned back and rubbed his eyes, letting the situation sink in. Then he stared out of his window.

He was startled by the chime of his watch almost twenty minutes later; he was still staring out of the window. He glanced at his watch and tapped the alarm off.

It was time for his session with Althea. He wondered if he should go. *Not in the mood to spill my guts to her right now,* he thought.

*Is she involved?*

Paul passed Althea as he climbed up the center crew ladder on his way to the traverse.

"Paul?" Althea called to him.

"Hey," he said. "What's up?"

"I thought we were talking at this time."

"I decided I'm not in the mood," Paul said. "I'm going to hit the gym instead."

"Oh," Althea said. "OK."

Paul nodded awkwardly and started to climb the ladder again.

Althea looked around to make sure there was no one in earshot of them before saying, "Meet on the bridge later, then?"

"No," Paul said. "I'm sorry, Althea. I need some alone time this cycle."

"Paul, I don't understand," Althea said.

But she was talking to an empty ladder.

*

Regas floated down the traverse toward the utility module. *Another bullshit inspection,* he thought as his weight increased. *And another day on this piece-of-shit freighter that I'll get paid one-tenth of what I should. Fucking bullshit.*

Regas grabbed the ladder as his relative weight began to increase and climbed down onto the utility module bulkhead. Before opening the bulkhead, he looked at the inspection sheet on his clipboard.

"Damn it," Regas muttered. His objective was one of the old storage units on the bottom floor of the utility module. Of all the random corners of the *Odysseus,* he hated that one the most. All the odd military equipment, despite its age and obsolescence, reminded him of what should have been, the career he was robbed of, and why he was now little more than an indentured servant on a freighter in the wasteland between Earth and the belt.

As he climbed down the central ladder, Regas heard music. He stepped off the ladder onto the second level and walked to the gym, where the music was playing. He peered through the window in the door and saw Paul working out.

"Well, good morning, Captain Jigsaw," Regas said in his most insincere voice as he swung open the door.

Paul fought the urge to tell Regas to fuck off. He didn't want to reward the simpleton with conflict.

"Hello, Regas."

"Working out?" Regas asked, walking toward Paul.

"Yep."

Regas nodded as if Paul had confirmed a super-insightful observation.

Paul ignored Regas as he went on with changing the weights on the bench press.

"You been spending a lot of time with Althea lately," Regas said. "What's up with that?"

"Nothing," Paul said, not looking at Regas.

"Talking about your feelings and shit?" Regas asked. "Is that required to get alone with her? Cuz I'll do that if that's what it takes."

"I think the only thing it takes is to not be a creep around her," Paul said, moving to the other side of the bar.

"Oh, come on, Captain Jigsaw," Regas said in a falsely wounded tone. "That ain't fair. I'm an all right guy."

Paul put another plate on the bar and moved to the bench.

"Would you talk to her for me, Owens?" Regas asked. "Tell her all I want to do is be alone with her and talk about my feelings. Bare my soul, you know?"

Paul sat down on the bench and loosened up his shoulders.

"Bare my soul along with some other things, you know what I'm saying?" Regas laughed too loud and slapped Paul on the back.

Just a little too hard.

Anger surged in Paul. Before he could stop it, he was on his feet, swiveling to face Regas.

Regas didn't flinch. The two men stared at each other for a long heartbeat, waiting to see if it was going to happen.

Regas blinked first.

He laughed, taking a small step backward from Paul. "Come on, Owens. I'm joking. I'm just joking. Sheesh, man."

Paul maintained his ready stance.

Regas smiled before saying, "I'm sorry. I was just kidding. I didn't realize you Centaurs had so many big feelings."

"Let's be honest with each other, Regas," Paul said. "You don't know shit about Centaurs. You were just a nasty fucking leg."

The smile drained from Regas.

Paul's comment crashed over him. All the rejection and disappointment and jealousy from that world they'd left millions of miles behind them rushed in and covered Regas up.

Paul smiled at the reaction. "I thought so," he said to Regas. "There are only two kinds of nasty legs. Those who got rejected by the Centaur program. And those who haven't applied yet."

Regas did not smile back.

"Did I touch a nerve, wannabe?" Paul asked him, his voice dripping with false concern.

Paul didn't wait for an answer. He sat down on the bench, lay back, and started knocking out repetitions.

Regas was enraged Paul saw that in him. He wanted to kill him.

But he hesitated.

Paul finished his set. He racked the bar and stood up.

"I'm glad we had this chat, Regas," Paul said.

Regas left the weight room.

Regas stewed as he went down to the bottom level to conduct his inspection. He was angry. Angry at Drummond. Angry at Cooley and the XO. Angry at Althea. Angry at Paul. And angry he had years left to go on this fucking voyage.

He kicked his way through some of the old junk and walked down an obscure passageway, heading toward his inspection objective: a storage unit in the far corner of the lower level of the utility module.

As Regas stepped around piles of junk, he noticed a fine layer of dust covering everything.

*It must be years since anyone has been in this forgotten corner of this godforsaken ship,* Regas thought. *What a fucking waste of time.*

Finally, he arrived. He reached out to open the storage unit, but the door wouldn't give. It had been years since it had been opened. Dust and age worked together to make it stick.

"Damn it," Regas muttered, setting down his clipboard so that he could use both hands.

He grabbed the door mechanism and pulled. Nothing.

He hit the door a few times with his fist and then grabbed the door again and shook it.

Still nothing.

"Fuck you!" Regas yelled.

He punched the door. He kicked it. He yanked on it. He pictured Paul, Drummond, and Drake and took his rage out on it.

It popped open.

Regas, panting from his tantrum, looked at the three large green wooden trunks stacked on top of each other in the storage unit.

He stepped forward and opened the top one, looking to see what it contained.

"Well, well, well…" he said with a broad smile.

# Chapter Thirty-Five

*0217 Hours, 23 June 2054*
*Twenty Thousand Feet Above the Horn of Africa*

The aircraft ramp lowered, revealing the black night sky. Paul walked aft past the soldierbots of Outlaw Platoon. Their multi-sensored heads swiveled to watch him as he walked out onto the ramp and placed the heel of his armored boot on the edge. The sparse lights of isolated villages passed twenty thousand feet below his toe.

Paul closed his eyes and let the swirl and tug of wind at the edge of the ramp beat against his face. The air was cold. It felt good.

It would be much warmer on the ground.

The air mission commander interrupted Paul's meditation. "One minute, Captain," he said over the intercom. "You gonna wear your helmet tonight?"

"Fuck you," Paul said, holding a middle finger up toward the video camera in the front of the drone's cabin without turning his head away from the night. The soldierbots looked at his finger with curiosity.

"Easy, Captain," the voice came back. "You are addressing a major."

"Uh-huh," Paul mumbled. Deployed almost a year now, he had no love or patience for the drone-flying smoothies he had to work with. He pictured the major reclining in a swivel chair, steam rising from his cup of coffee due to the overworked air-conditioning, gazing at multiple displays of imagery and data with half interest.

Paul always left his helmet off until the last possible second. Whether he was in an aircraft, in a ground vehicle, or walking, he preferred the feeling of "open air," as he'd told Kata during their training back at Bragg. She'd told him that was stupid.

Paul turned and looked forward, his back to the open ramp and night sky. Staff Sergeant Gamal and Sergeant Anton stood by their soldierbot squads, helmets on. They gave him a thumbs-up.

Paul nodded.

"Thirty seconds," the air mission commander said.

Paul pulled on his armored helmet. It clicked against his battle suit's collar fitting, and he listened to the familiar ratcheting sound as his battle suit twisted the helmet into place.

A flood of information glimmered across Paul's heads-up display. He cycled through unit, soldier, and soldierbot statuses before settling on a tactical guidance format.

Paul took a deep breath and tried to center himself before the chaos. Commanding a Centaur platoon was like being that clown in the circus that spins a dozen plates at a time above his head. He had to maneuver himself in his armored battle suit while monitoring and commanding his soldierbots via his HUD. He had to constantly cross-check his team's telemetry feed: their positions, ground speeds, directions, energy and weapons statuses. Based on the situation, he had to jack into individual soldierbots, assume their point of view, take over their guidance and weapons, and fight the enemy while confirming rules-of-engagement compliance for those soldierbots he was not actively driving. Because he was more than just the commander on the ground. He was the critical link in the kill chain. The piece that made their application of violence legal.

All that, while trying to not get killed.

He knew that once things got loud, he would be fine. The training would take over. He also knew that he was really good at this.

This mission was not going to be easy, though. A female American physician named April Sanchez had been captured eight hours earlier by a warlord whose treatment of prisoners was not nice. Intel gave her twenty-four hours to live. Tonight was their only window.

What made it a trick shot was intel's inability to nail down her location.

"She's in one of these three small villages," was the best they could do.

Paul and Kata had listened carefully just a few hours ago as the briefing officer pointed at the map display and talked through specifics of each target site. The villages were about fifteen kilometers from each other and sat in the middle of an area controlled by one of the region's most violent warlords.

The briefing officer had launched into a familiar refrain of "unconfirmed this" and "no way to definitively say that," and Paul had felt his anxiety level rise. He'd looked at Kata, the only other Centaur platoon leader in theater. She'd met his gaze, eyebrows raised in apprehension.

*Here we go again,* they'd thought in unison.

The problem was that the Chinese had equipped the warlords handsomely in exchange for money, rare-earth metals, and conflict diamonds. And the warlords didn't give a shit about the Tokyo Accords. They'd throw some wicked automated tech into the fight without any kill chain whatsoever, putting the robot on the "fuck everyone" setting and letting it go.

So, Paul and Kata never knew what they were headed into. Some villages seemed to be living in the 1800s, and they'd face off against soldiers with old bolt-action, single-shot rifles. And then, in the neighboring town, a Chinese autonomous biped tank would walk around the corner and go into murder mode, killing half of the town while trying to get at the American soldiers.

Earlier, as they had huddled around the mapping table in the small planning facility, Paul had listened to the situation report and realized that they would have to hit all three villages simultaneously. If they hit the wrong village, word would get out and they wouldn't get a shot at the other two. April Sanchez would be dead. Furthermore, given the number of enemy foot soldiers believed to be in each village, they would not be able to approach the targets on foot or by drone copter. The likelihood of detection and failure was too high. Somehow, the plan had to provide assurance for the element of surprise.

When these kinds of missions came down, the squad leaders would get the team ready while Paul and Kata made a quick plan, met with the air component, and gave their commander, Lieutenant Colonel Andrews, an overview. Once the colonel had approved, he would go to the command center to monitor the mission and get them support, should things go to shit. At this point in their tour, they could get through the planning-and-prep cycle and be wheels-up in thirty minutes.

Paul's plan was straightforward, but it had still gotten a grimace from Andrews. The colonel stood across the mapping table from Paul, his arms crossed and his face masked with skepticism as Paul outlined his plan.

"Sir, I am going put three squads out of an aircraft at twenty thousand feet," Paul had explained. The mapping table panned back from three red triangles that highlighted the three target locations. "Each squad will track toward their target village in free fall down to five thousand feet above ground level. At that point, we will deploy and proceed the rest of the way under canopy. When each squad is positioned directly above their target structures at approximately five hundred feet, I'll give the command to cut away, and we will drop onto the targets."

Colonel Andrews rubbed his chin and looked at the mapping table as green icons descended onto the target triangles. He was one of the early Centaurs, assigned to the Combat Corps immediately after it stood up. Paul took his tense silence as likely approval, so he gave the colonel a little more.

"I'm going to assign the most likely target village to Staff Sergeant Gamal and give him two squads," Paul said. The map display zoomed into target village one. "He is the best small-unit leader in the battalion and a hell of a drone driver."

"Rumor is he held the Dead Man's Canyon record for a couple of years," Kata said, trying to help Paul's case.

"I don't know if that is true or not," Paul said, nodding. "But I've seen him pull off some amazing things with his soldierbots."

The colonel remained silent. Still rubbing his chin.

"Sergeant Anton will take a squad into target village two," Paul continued. "And I'll take one into village three." The map display tracked as he talked.

"You'll be on the ground on this one?" the colonel asked.

"Yes, sir," Paul answered. "Have to. I'm still down two squad leaders."

Colonel Andrews shook his head slowly, remembering that two of Paul's squad leaders were still recovering from wounds. The operations tempo was wearing them down.

"What about your first sergeant?" Andrews asked Paul.

"He's with a squad outside the wire on a convoy escort mission."

"Continue," Andrews said with irritation.

"From there, it gets kinetic, sir," Paul said. "We'll work through the houses, swarms out and weapons up, until we find her."

"And what is your role tonight, Captain Vukovic?"

"I'll have a quick reaction force of two squads orbiting ten kilometers south," Kata said, gesturing at the map display, which panned south. Six icons representing quad copter assault drones circled clockwise in a tight formation. "The QRF will be on call in case things get sporty. If not, we'll extract Captain Owens and his platoon when they call."

Colonel Andrews stared at the map. As he did so, Paul looked at the augmentation scar that ringed the colonel's head. It passed just above his ears and across his forehead, just like Paul's. The colonel's scar was more than ten years old, though. It was instantly recognizable, of course. But it was no longer pink and puffy like Paul's or Kata's.

"There is a lot I don't like about this," Andrews said. Paul took his eyes off the augmentation scars and met the colonel's gaze. "But I don't have any better ideas."

Colonel Andrews looked at his watch.

"And none of us have any more time," he said. "Do it."

"Roger that, sir," Paul said as he and Kata turned from the table and headed for the door.

"Oh, and, Owens?" the colonel called after him as he left.

"Yes, sir?" Paul stopped and turned to face Colonel Andrews.

"You ever done a five-hundred-foot drop in a battle suit?" he asked with raised eyebrows.

"No, sir."

The colonel chuckled. "It sucks," he said.

Now, with the toe of his armored boot hanging off the edge of the aircraft's ramp, twenty thousand feet above the ground, Paul remembered Colonel Andrews' knowing chuckle.

*Maybe this is not such a great plan,* Paul thought.

"Exit! Exit! Exit!" the air mission commander said.

Paul and Outlaw Platoon ran off the aircraft ramp.

Paul held himself head down for about eight seconds to reach terminal velocity before flaring. He leveled out and assumed a tracking position. His battle suit computed the optimal canopy deployment point given the winds, their weight, and other factors and marked it as a green X thirteen thousand feet below and three miles in front of him. Paul tracked toward it and called up a tactical display to check on the rest of the platoon.

Things looked good. Staff Sergeant Gamal was tracking well toward his target, with ten soldierbots behind him. Sergeant Anton was doing the same with his five. Paul's team of five soldierbots fell with him in a loose trail formation.

*So far, so good.*

Forty-five seconds later, Paul bull's-eyed the green X and deployed his parachute.

He cycled through statuses on his HUD. Green across the board. No canopy malfunctions, and all three teams seemed assured to hit their next checkpoints, directly over the target houses.

Paul felt his pulse quicken as he monitored their altitude. He tried to slow his breathing as they descended through two thousand feet above ground level.

His HUD superimposed a vertical green column over their target that rose from the house's roof and extended seemingly to space. When Paul and his team flew into that column, they were to cut away their canopies.

The cutaway point was now about thirty seconds away.

Paul looked down and cycled his HUD through infrared to ultraviolet and back again as he scanned the target area. He counted at least a dozen enemy patrolling the outside.

Paul thought for the hundredth time that night how lucky they were there was not much of a moon.

Ten seconds to the cutaway point.

Paul checked his altitude and winced: 575 feet above ground level. He resisted the urge to try to bleed off altitude. Any maneuvers now would screw up his cutaway point.

*Three.*

*Two.*

*One.*

Paul gave the cutaway command to his battle suit and entered free fall for the second time that night.

Paul resisted the urge to flail when gravity snatched him down. That enabled his battle suit to do the work as well as it could. They were falling subterminal, with very little vertical airspeed to fly with. Paul knew that when they got close to impact, the suit would execute whatever maneuvers it could, based on their rate of fall and what it sensed below them to optimize their configuration.

Paul expected those maneuvers to be abrupt.

A battle suit equipped with a full combat load weighed about five hundred pounds. Paul was carrying extra ammo tonight, though, figuring it would be a short but intense engagement. Adding his weight, Paul had calculated during mission planning that he would tip the scale at over 750 pounds when he "landed."

Maintenance had assured him that the impact was well within the battle suit's capabilities.

Paul watched their altitude wind down to zero.

*You've got to be fucking kidding me,* he thought as his battle suit assumed a tight cannonball pose.

The initial impact as he penetrated the roof was less jarring than Paul had expected. The second even less so as he blasted through the flimsy second-level floor.

But the third, as the colonel had predicted, sucked.

Paul shook his head to clear it as he stood up.

Per the plan, he was standing on the first floor of his target house with two soldierbots from Dagger Squad. Eight shocked bandits, four of whom were suited in armored exoskeletons, looked back at them. With a thought, Paul designated them enemy combatants.

Four of them dropped to the floor in bloody heaps without getting a single shot off.

At the same time, Paul and the two soldierbots deployed their swarms.

The two dozen scout drones they each carried and controlled had limited range but were very useful as extended, multispectral eyes and ears. The swarm of marble-sized airborne sensors dispersed through the house. A complete tactical situation map began to form on Paul's HUD.

Paul noted the charging suited enemy behind him just in time.

He jumped to his left as the lumbering exoskeleton's battle-ax came down. It struck a glancing blow to his helmet.

His helmet absorbed most of the oblique impact.

But his ears rang and visuals flickered as he sank into a kneeling position. Immediately, he threw a punch at the armored enemy's chest, adding his battle suit's leg strength to the motion and extending his battle suit's forearm-housed depleted-uranium bayonet as he swung his fist.

The punch caved in the bandit's chest armor as the blade impaled him.

Paul withdrew his fist, sheathing the bayonet as he scanned the tactical situation on his HUD.

The enemy armored suit, now housing a dead man, took a few mindless steps back until it bumped into the wall.

Paul studied the other dead enemy on the floor. Four were in oversized exoskeletons. Like the one he had just killed, they seemed to be designed more for intimidating crowds and close-quarters fights than fire and maneuver work. Intel knew that the warlords had 3D printing capabilities. Seemed they remained focused on gang work over higher-level tactical applications.

*They've got fucking imaginations too,* Paul thought, looking across the room at the exo's battle-ax appendage, which reached almost to the floor. Blood ran down its chest onto the floor as it stood motionless, its back to the wall.

Paul winced, thinking about what would have happened if the ax had found its mark. And then sent the intelligence out to his platoon. It was going to be a bruising fight if they lost the advantage of their surprise. They had to move fast.

Paul put his battle suit into park-and-defend mode and relaxed his body so that the suit could make any moves it needed to. It went into a defensive crouch position with weapons at the ready.

There were two potential target buildings in Paul's assigned village. The other three soldierbots in Dagger Squad were taking down building two. Paul switched his POV to their targeting feeds. About a dozen bandits looked at Paul in disbelief via data link with Dagger Three. He counted five in exos.

The bandits scattered as Paul swiveled Three's integrated minigun toward the group. He dissected four of them while giving Dagger Four and Dagger Five the weapons-free command. Antipersonnel rounds from Dagger Five decapitated several more of the bandits.

The last bandit charged Dagger Five and pulled the pin from a hand grenade. It detonated as the bandit tackled Five. Red mist and soldierbot parts flew through the room.

Paul gave up control of Dagger Three as swarm data confirmed the rest of the building was empty.

The assault had been underway for thirty seconds, and their targets were secure. But he'd already lost one soldierbot. And no April Sanchez.

The man-down alert flashed on Paul's HUD. Staff Sergeant Gamal, commanding Saber Squad in village one, was down. His battle suit transmitted a Mayday plus vitals.

With eighteen structures and at least three dozen bandits, Paul had a hunch Sanchez would be in village three, though intel refused to make a similar bet.

Gamal had been struck by an armor-piercing RPG round, which had severed his left arm just below the shoulder. His battle suit's first-aid system and his own internal nanobots had cauterized the wound, stemming the blood loss. His vitals were strong and stable, but he was in shock and unconscious. Out of the fight.

Their kill chain was broken.

With a thought, Paul ordered Staff Sergeant Gamal's battle suit to move to the exfil site and threw Saber Squad's telemetry up on his HUD.

Their swarm data confirmed Saber was in direct contact with at least two dozen enemy. The soldierbots dodged RPGs, small-arms fire, and at least two directed energy systems while trying to shield Gamal's withdrawal. Saber One, escorting the unconscious Gamal, provided covering fire. A small swarm flew ahead of them, scouting the route to the extraction site three kilometers south of the village.

"Shit," Paul muttered to himself. Based on the well-equipped force Saber Squad was facing, he was starting to feel more confident that Sanchez was there.

Paul took over Saber Two and began to kill enemy soldiers while checking the telemetry from village two. It did not look promising, but he called Sergeant Anton, the squad leader in village two, on the radio.

"Blade Six, this is Dagger Six," Paul transmitted. "What is your status?"

"Dagger Six, Blade Six. We've got a dry hole here, sir."

Paul nodded inside his armored helmet. That confirmed it.

Sanchez was in Saber's village.

"Understood," Paul answered. "Banshee on Saber."

"Roger that. Banshee on Saber," Anton repeated, ensuring Paul knew he'd heard the code-word command. They would both converge on village one to assist Saber Squad.

And they both knew they would get there too late.

Paul focused on Saber Two's telemetry and weapons system. As it acquired targets, he confirmed the ROE compliance before authorizing kill shots.

Meanwhile, back in village three, where Paul was actually standing, his squad signaled complete. The soldierbots' facial-recognition systems had scanned and cataloged the dead enemy and had secured any potentially valuable intel. Paul signaled the copters for exfil and gave his squad the command to withdraw.

Dagger Four led them out.

Paul took a deep breath as he put his battle suit into autopilot. It was always a difficult transition when his suit started sprinting, and he was trying to stay limp, mind focused on another fight kilometers away.

The squad of five ran out of village three with Dagger Four in the lead. Paul was in the number-three position in the formation. They were out of the village four minutes and seventeen seconds after the attack had begun.

Paul focused on the fight in village one as his squad moved to their pickup zone. Fifteen kilometers away, Gamal's battle suit had gotten him to the aircraft, and he would soon be in the air. Saber One was still with them to provide security. A couple of foolish bandits had followed them and were now bleeding out on the ground.

Paul gave Saber Four and Saber Five the weapons-free command. They provided covering fire as he maneuvered Saber Two and Three around the enemy. At that point, he had five weapon bore sights up on his HUD and was working through kill shots and managing all five soldierbots. He needed help.

He called Kata.

"Raptor Zero Six, this is Dagger Zero Six, requesting driver assist."

"Dagger Six, this is Raptor. Got your back."

"Raptor, take Saber Four and Saber Five."

"Sabers Four and Five, roger. I have the controls."

Kata relaxed her shoulders and leaned back in her seat as the drone copter she rode on orbited in a long, lazy left-hand turn pattern at fifty feet above ground level, three hundred knots airspeed.

*Let's get it on,* she thought as her heads-up display flooded with high-definition video and telemetry from Sabers Four and Five.

Centaurs preferred to have the commander on the ground drive a Centaur unit in combat. It was old-school thinking that had been around since the Battle of Jericho. But it worked.

It was simple enough to throw control of a subunit to a remote commander, though. And it helped in situations like this, where the commander on the ground was close to task saturation. So, Kata, orbiting fifteen kilometers away with the quick reaction force, got into the fight and assumed part of the kill chain.

Down to fighting with two soldierbots, Paul sped up. He and Saber Three sprinted toward the last enemy building, firing as they went.

They had been on the objective for almost seven and a half minutes. Paul felt the window closing. A few swarm drones had penetrated the target house. They counted ten enemy and put together a partial floor plan before being destroyed. Paul would have preferred a more complete tactical picture. But it was now or never.

Paul and Saber Three charged the house.

As he accelerated his soldierbot, Paul switched his HUD to infrared. It was an imprecise imaging system, and the signal noise caused by all of the discharging weapons made it worse. But at least it provided some kind of check against warm bodies on the other side of the wall he was running toward.

He didn't want to kill Sanchez when they breached.

Paul hit the wall at twenty-eight miles an hour. Saber Three bested him by two miles an hour.

They burst through opposite walls.

Bricks, dust, and debris filled the air.

Violent chaos erupted inside the house.

There were times like this in every operation when, despite all of the slick technology and data, it became a close-quarters melee. Paul and Saber Three each took multiple hits as they shot, bludgeoned, and stabbed their way toward the back of the structure.

There was another ax-wielding exo in the mix.

*Are you kidding me?* Paul thought.

The bandit charged.

Paul jumped back fifteen feet, to the far side of the room.

He lost his footing, though, and fell onto his back.

The bandit ran after him, just a step behind. He raised his ax for a killing stroke, and then his upper body disintegrated.

Paul saw Saber Three across the room, its smoking minigun still pointed at the halved bandit.

Blood ran down the enemy exoskeleton's still-functioning legs as they ran into and tripped over Saber Two. They skidded into the wall, dark blood from the bandit's lower half pooling around them.

Paul quickly righted Saber Two. He and Saber Three charged forward.

The POV from Saber Two was flickering, and Paul struggled to keep the soldierbot moving forward.

Saber Three ran with a limp, hydraulic fluid streaming from its left knee.

Finally, after what seemed like forever to Paul, the two soldierbots burst into the room where Sanchez was.

A lone bandit held a pistol to her blindfolded head.

Saber Three had the better angle and clearer POV, so Paul swapped to its bore sight while commanding Saber Two to charge.

Paul squeezed off a dozen rounds from Saber Three's minigun. They stitched a line from the bandit's jaw to his pelvis. His body folded in a bloody spray and fell away from Sanchez.

She screamed, expecting to die. The warm blood of her captor sprayed on her face.

Saber Two reached her as she fell. It caught Sanchez and cradled her in its metal and ceramic arms. The battered soldierbot straightened up, lifting Sanchez off of her feet and into its chest. Paul swapped back to Saber Two's POV and transmitted his voice through it as he used its hand to gently pull the blindfold from her eyes.

"April Sanchez?" he asked softly, from the quad copter flying in her direction at three hundred knots ground speed.

"Yes," she whispered, confirming what Saber Two's facial recognition routines were saying.

"You're safe now," Paul said.

"Who are you?" April asked in a cracked and weak voice.

"I'm Captain Paul Owens, of the United States military."

# Chapter Thirty-Six

*1326 Hours, 29 June 2054*
*Italy*

"I'm so happy you're here!" Eugene said, running toward his sister.

Fiona stepped out of the driverless car and met her brother's charge with a hug.

"I can't believe you finally came," he said, releasing her and grabbing one of her bags. "How long has it been?"

"I was wondering about that on the flight," Fiona said as they walked to the main house. *When I wasn't wondering how to tell you what I need to tell you,* she thought. *How to ask what I need to ask.*

"Five years?" she guessed.

"Way too long!" Eugene declared as they walked through the large wooden doors into the main house.

Built of wood and stone over three hundred years ago, the kitchen flowed into the dining area, which spilled out onto a large stone patio. Massive beams ran the width of the ceiling, holding up the wooden upper floor and its four small bedrooms. The sand-colored walls were made of local stone, and despite their variation in size and color shade, each stone seemed to fit perfectly in its place.

"Put your bag down. Let's sit for a few minutes," Eugene said, walking through the wide archway and onto the patio.

A large pergola, conquered decades ago by climbing roses, covered the patio. Thick, ropy vines wrapped around the pergola's old wooden columns, snaking up into the lattice of beams. Leafy green vines punctuated with small red roses spilled from the lattice in places.

A sweating bottle of prosecco waited for them on the table, alongside a pitcher of water.

*Thank God,* Fiona thought. *Alcohol.*

"Water or prosecco?" Eugene asked her.

"Prosecco. Please."

Eugene smiled. "Me too," he said, pouring two glasses. He handed her one and then held his out. "A toast to my sister," he said. "Finally visiting us here at Mio Posto."

They drank. Fiona taking long pulls on hers. She set down an empty glass.

"Wow." Eugene chuckled.

"That's so good," Fiona said. "And it was a long flight."

He gestured at her glass, and she nodded. He poured more prosecco into her glass as she held it out.

"Truthfully, it's been a long year," she said before taking another long swallow.

Eugene leaned back in his chair.

His smile drained away.

"What is it, Fi?" he asked, setting his glass down on the table.

"What?" Fiona said, sipping her wine.

"Don't bullshit me," Eugene said. "I saw the weight on your shoulders the second you got out of the car. Your distraction and shifty eyes. You are in mode."

Eugene crossed his arms.

"And it pisses me off," he said.

Fiona rubbed her face.

"Are you even staying the night?" he asked.

"Depends," she said.

"On what?"

"On if you let me."

Eugene regarded her for a long moment.

"I'm your brother, Fi," he said. "We stick together. You taught me that."

Fiona smiled despite her anxiety.

"Now fucking out with it," he said.

"I need to borrow some money."

Eugene blinked.

Fiona waited.

"You've run through twenty-five million dollars?" he asked.

"Not really."

"Not really?"

"It's a timing thing," she said, leaning forward. "My assets are worth several multiples of my current debt."

"So, sell them," Eugene said.

"Can't," Fiona said, shaking her head. "Not now. I'd be selling insanely short."

Fiona thought of Talisman. The prospect of ceding more equity and control to them enraged her.

"What about a bank? A proper lender for this kind of thing?"

"Word would get back to Grandfather," Fiona said. "He could take advantage, possibly take control. He would make my life difficult in a thousand ways. I can't afford that right now."

Eugene shook his head at the mention of the old man. He stood up from the table and walked to the edge of the stone patio. A single rose vine fell almost to his head. He studied it.

"I hate that you have brought this to me here," he said to Fiona without looking back. "This is my sacred space. Why didn't you ask me to meet you somewhere to talk about this?"

Fiona shrugged.

"Would that really have made it any better?" she asked.

"For me?" he said, turning around. "Yes."

He walked back to the table and sat down.

"This is for your fighting robot things, I presume?"

"AI weapons systems," Fiona said. "Yes."

"How much?"

"I need five million."

"Jesus, Fiona," he said, flopping back in his chair.

"It's basically zero risk, or I wouldn't ask," she said. "It's a debt service payment. One of my companies is working with the Combat Corps now and is sailing through a phase-one test. Phase two will be a big-time liquidity event, and I'll be able to pay you back. Forty-five days. Ninety at most."

Eugene looked up, tracing one of the rose vines with his eyes. It got thinner the farther it went until it concluded in a handful of blazing-red buds.

"You're in big trouble, aren't you?" he asked Fiona without taking his eyes off of the roses.

"Huh?"

"Don't," he said, swiveling his head to stare at Fiona.

"If you are here asking me for money, that means you failed to negotiate a restructured payment schedule," he said. "And that means you already did that once or twice and fell behind again, or the business you took the loan on has increased in value to the point that the lender wants it rather than their money back."

Fiona sat motionless. "Look who likes to pretend they don't understand business," she said.

"And, knowing you, you've gone all in on this and you don't have another penny to your name," Eugene continued, without acknowledging the interruption. "And you don't know anyone else you trust enough to ask this of, since one of the guiding principles here is to keep Grandfather in the dark, lest he take advantage of the situation to humiliate you or worse."

Fiona smiled. She raised her hands, palms up, in a gesture of surrender.

"Fuck," Eugene said sadly.

He turned his head back to the dangling rosebuds.

"I'm sorry," Fiona finally said.

"It's OK," he said, getting up from his chair. Fiona watched as he poured himself another prosecco. He took a sip and said, "Next time, though, just call me. Or let's meet somewhere. I really hate discussing family business here. I won't do it again. Please remember that."

"Deal."

"Now I'm going to go take a bath and wash this whole conversation off." He turned and started back into the house. "You can stay," he said, pausing at the threshold.

"Thanks," Fiona said.

"Some friends are coming over for dinner," Eugene began.

Fiona's shoulders sagged.

"Don't!" Eugene said. "Not after all that shit." He flailed the hand not holding the glass of prosecco in Fiona's direction in a disgusted gesture of chaos.

"You're going to be nice and social and interact. I don't give a damn how tired you are."

"OK, OK," Fiona said with a smile. "I'll be on my best. Who are these people?"

"Four hot and single Italian guys," Eugene said, wearing a hungry smile.

"Why did I bother asking?"

"It wouldn't kill you to get laid, you know," Eugene said as he turned to leave. "But don't touch Alessandro," he called over his shoulder from inside the house. "I've got plans for him."

Fiona poured herself the rest of the prosecco. She stood up and walked to the edge of the patio and pulled out her cell phone.

Pruden picked up on the first ring.

"We're good," Fiona said.

"Thank God," Pruden exhaled.

"I expect the wire will hit my account by tomorrow," Fiona said. "I'll transfer it as soon as it hits, and you can make the payment."

"Great."

Fiona looked over her shoulder back at the house and then said in a low voice, "It's only five."

"What?" Pruden asked with alarm. "Why?"

"It's all I asked for."

"Shit, Fiona. Why? That's about half of what we're going to need."

"It buys us a little more time," Fiona said.

"That's true. But we're going to have a problem. Why didn't you ask for what we needed?"

"It wasn't the right time."

"When is it ever going to be the right time? Those Talisman bastards are going to—"

"Damn it, Pruden," Fiona interrupted, her voice taking on an edge. "I'll handle this the way I see fit."

Pruden waited a few seconds before saying, "Of course, Fiona. Of course."

"Sorry," Fiona said. "I'm sorry. I just… This sucks for me, OK?"

"I understand," Pruden said with sincerity. "I hate it for you. Try to enjoy your week out there. It will be good for you. I can handle everything we've got going on here."

"Thanks," Fiona said. "But I'll probably head back tomorrow."

"Why? Don't do that."

"Trust me," Fiona said, glancing again back at the house. "If I don't get out of here in a day or so, he is going to figure out we really need more, and it won't be pretty. Better to save that reckoning for when I am ready."

Pruden didn't respond.

Fiona drained her glass.

"I'll call you from the airport tomorrow," Fiona said. "I'm going to get drunk now."

# Chapter Thirty-Seven

*Utsu Book One*

*Circa 1510*

*Translated from the Japanese*

The next morning, in preparation for Castle Hayato's surrender, Lord Shingen assembled his forces in three columns. One facing the shallow river crossing to the west. One facing the rocky river crossing to the east. And one facing the large covered bridge to the castle's front. Hiroaki and his hundred students were in formation at the front of the center column, in the position of honor.

I assembled the hundred for Master Hiroaki and stood with him at the front of the formation.

Lord Shingen rode his horse forward with two mounted guards and a bannerman bearing the clan's black insignia.

"General Hiroaki," Lord Shingen said. "Would you do our clan the honor of allowing our bannerman to go with you as you march to accept Hayato's surrender?"

"It would be my honor, my lord," Hiroaki said with a smile.

"I thank you, my general," Shingen said. "I will return now to watch you accept the castle's surrender from the hill to the rear of the covered bridge."

"Good, my lord," Hiroaki said. "I will signal when the surrender is complete and it is safe for you to come forward."

Shingen nodded and rode to the rear with his guards.

Hiroaki signaled the drummer, and we moved forward.

When the other two columns heard the drum and saw us move forward, they advanced also.

I guided our column from the right front. Hiroaki and the bannerman advanced on horse in front of us. They entered the covered bridge, and we, Hiroaki's one hundred, followed behind. Hiroaki emerged from the covered bridge a few footsteps in front of us. For the moment, he did not notice that the rest of the column had not followed him across the bridge.

None of us did.

Nor did we yet notice that the east and west columns had not crossed the river.

We marched forward.

When Hiroaki was close to the castle gate, he signaled our column to halt.

We heard clanking noises and shouts as the massive castle gate slowly began to rise.

That is when I, at the front right of our column, looked around and noticed the rest of the column had not followed us. I looked east and west and saw that the other columns had not crossed the river.

I leaned forward to alert Hiroaki but was interrupted by the sound of fifteen hundred Hayato castle guardsmen charging out of the castle, screaming, with katanas drawn.

Archers appeared on the walls. Arrows flew.

"Shields!" Hiroaki yelled, leaping from his horse to join our formation.

Every shield among us was raised in unison as the arrows rained down. Hiroaki's horse and the bannerman were killed.

The front rank of castle guardsmen collided with the front of our hundred in a horrible collision of blades and men.

Many of the castle guardsmen were on horseback. They galloped for the east and west river crossings.

"My lord!" I yelled above the din. "They ride to encircle us!"

"You must lead the rear back to the bridge, Manji," Hiroaki said. "Our crossing must be orderly! I will command this end of our hundred!"

"Yes, Master Hiroaki," I said. I ran under the shields as the fall of arrows continued.

"Now!" Hiroaki yelled as I reached the rear of the column. "To the bridge, Manji! Now!"

"On me!" I yelled. "Rear rank first. Stay in formation!"

We moved in unison toward the covered bridge, fighting as we advanced.

The shield bearers held their shields high, protecting our formation from the unceasing fall of arrows. Spearmen thrusted in all directions between shields, killing guardsmen with every jab. Bowmen shot arrows, timed with the return of the spears, dropping dozens of guardsmen at a time. Swordsmen slashed in rhythm with the shields and arrows, slinging blood on the ground and into the air.

We were surrounded. We were outnumbered more than ten to one.

I had no fear. We had yet to lose a man. Guardsmen fell like so much scythed wheat.

Miscues and mistakes happen in battle, after all. Particularly when disparate units join battle together. So, I was not yet disturbed by the blunders on our flanks at the other crossings, or that the center column had not followed us across the bridge. It happens.

But when I saw that the mounted guardsmen had crossed the river, a pang of alarm flared within me. They rode hard toward the far end of the covered bridge. And none of Shingen's forces opposed them.

Shingen stood on the crest of the small hill on the other side of the covered bridge, his forces arrayed around him. But no katanas flashed. No spears at the ready. No bows drawn.

They were observing.

That was when I knew.

That was when Hiroaki knew. That was when we all knew.

We had been betrayed.

The mounted Castle Guard reached the far end of the covered bridge.

"Onward, Manji!" Hiroaki yelled to me. "Through the bridge and through the guardsmen! To Shingen!"

We fought our way onto the covered bridge.

The guardsmen fell in bloody heaps. Hiroaki fought like a demon unleashed. His katana flashed in a silver-and-red blur. Hundreds of guardsmen lay in a pile of dead and bleeding from the bridge back to the castle. And the pile around the bridge continued to grow.

We exacted our price at the south end of the covered bridge as well. But we could not fight our way out. There were too many. And the bodies of the ones we had slain only barricaded us further. We pushed the bodies to the side to get to living enemy.

But our numbers dwindled as well.

I heard the shriek of a devil.

Hiroaki sailed over me into the enemy soldiers. A dozen dropped dead. A dozen more. His katana flashed savagely. And dropped a dozen more.

Hiroaki was going after Shingen himself.

I tried to cut through to get to him. But he was just out of reach. I could not get off of the covered bridge.

But my master fought on.

Beyond the flash of Hiroaki's sword, Shingen stood on the top of the small hill surrounded by his mounted guard. He gazed in horror at the sight.

"I am coming for you, Shingen!" Hiroaki yelled. "I am coming for you!"

I looked around the covered bridge. There were less than a dozen of Hiroaki's one hundred left. And we were all wounded.

I heard cannon fire from the castle.

The shriek of flying cannonballs grew louder. I turned to warn Hiroaki. But I could not see him. The pile of bodies surrounding him was too high.

The cannon fire destroyed the bridge. I was thrown into the air, losing my katana. I fell back, barely catching myself on a fragmented wooden beam. The river flowed far beneath me. I tried to pull myself up. But could not. I did not have the strength.

I looked for my comrades. There were none left.

I looked for Hiroaki.

I saw him being held by half a dozen castle guardsmen. He was unarmed.

Lord Hayato himself looked down from his horse upon Hiroaki.

Hayato dismounted and drew his katana. He walked to Hiroaki and said, "For my son."

Lord Hayato cut Hiroaki's head off.

My heart broke.

My grip failed.

I fell to the river.

# Chapter Thirty-Eight

*Mission Cycle 409*

*Earth Year 2062*

*305,316,864 Kilometers from Earth*

P aul floated alone on the bridge, frustrated, concerned, and angry.

He was frustrated that it had been seven cycles since he'd used the captain's tablet computer to analyze the *Odysseus's* course data and he was no closer to figuring out what had happened. He was reluctant to go to Cooley until he had at least a theory about what was going on and a potential plan. But he was stymied.

He was concerned that the longer he waited, the further the XO's plot advanced and the farther off course the *Odysseus* continued to fly.

And he was angry with himself at the way he had handled things with Althea. Not the fact that he had avoided her for the past seven cycles. He could tell that she was hurt and puzzled, but he told himself he did not care about that. He was angry at himself for letting her in, for talking to her about his past. The fact was, he had started to think of her as a friend. A connection. And he had joined the *Odysseus* not only for the Fly It Off program but also for the solitude and isolation. Now he felt entangled. He had let his guard and judgment down. He had missed something.

Even worse, she might be involved.

Finally, Paul was irritated with the Utsu text, especially after his most recent heartbreaking translation. *Like I really need to read another example of soldiers getting screwed,* Paul thought. *What the hell kind of message am I supposed to find in that crap anyway?*

So, as he had done for the past several cycles, Paul floated alone in the bridge. The *Odysseus's* hull extended forward below the command-and-control module. The spinner rotated against the backdrop of the infinite void, and Paul stewed in his frustration, concern, and anger.

Another tug drone came into view from beneath the *Odysseus's* hull about two hundred meters forward of the bridge. It was pushing an enormous rock away on a course perpendicular to the *Odysseus*. Paul figured it was transporting raw material to the factory. The rock it labored behind was enormous.

Bursts of gas fired from the tug drone's sides as it maneuvered itself around its payload. The asteroid was so large, the tug disappeared behind it.

A long plume of blue flame erupted behind the colossal rock as the hidden tug fired its main engine. The glow from the laboring tug's exhaust cast shadows across the rock, highlighting its pockmarked surface and unknowable history. Paul tried to guess its mass but gave up.

When the tug had arrested the asteroid's velocity away from the ship, the tug repositioned again and began pushing it aft. The brilliant exhaust flame illuminated hundreds of meters of the *Odysseus*.

*Damn,* Paul thought, looking down at the hardworking tug drone. *Those things are so powerful. Maybe I could hitch a ride on one of those tough bastards. Leave these crazies behind and head back to Earth.*

Paul bolted straight as the realization hit him.

He scrambled to go find Cooley.

*

"This better be good, Prisoner Owens," Cooley said, not trying to hide his irritation.

Paul and Cooley floated in the maintenance bay of power and propulsion. It was a large, pressurized workspace on the fourth level and one of the few crew zones of the *Odysseus* where the XO was unable to monitor conversations.

Earlier in the cycle, Paul had passed a note to Cooley that said:

---

*Mr. Cooley, something is very wrong with the XO, and I need to talk to you in an area where he cannot monitor us. Please meet me in the PPM maintenance facility today at 1400 hours. It is fucking urgent. Tell no one.*

---

Paul had gritted his teeth his teeth as he'd written it. *The old man is laughing his ass off at me somewhere.*

"Mr. Cooley, this is going to sound ridiculous, but I think that the XO has hijacked the *Odysseus*," Paul said, hating the way he sounded.

"Hijacked?" Cooley asked.

"I believe one objective was to kill Captain Drake by causing the meteor strike."

"Kill Drake?" Cooley asked, his face contorting with disbelief.

"I don't know what else he is up to, but I recommend we regard the XO as a hostile. Is there a way for us to take control of the *Odysseus*? To lock the XO out?"

"A hostile?" Cooley's face was now a mask of disgust and pity. "Owens, have you been skipping your sessions with Althea? What does she say about all this?"

"I haven't discussed my suspicions with her," Paul said. "She may be involved."

"OK," Cooley said, shaking his head. "That's enough. I'm ordering you to sit for a session with Althea immediately and to follow her resulting directions precisely. Space dementia is nothing to be ashamed of, Owens. I've seen it take down old-timers who have lived out here for decades. We'll get you back to right."

Cooley put his arm on Paul's shoulder.

Paul jerked it off and pulled the captain's tablet from one of his cargo pockets.

"Mr. Cooley, the captain placed a self-contained, unmonitored inertial measurement unit on board, not far from here," Paul said, turning the small computer on. "Shortly before he was killed, he told me about it—"

"The captain told *you* about it?" Cooley asked, incredulous.

"Drake was killed before I could discuss the situation with him," Paul said, nodding. "But I was able to download the data and analyze it on the captain's tablet."

"You took the captain's tablet computer?" Cooley said, angry. "Look, Owens, I knew you were going to the bridge from time to time, and I didn't say anything because I don't mind you having some time alone, and the view up there is terrific, but I can't overlook this. Give me the captain's computer, and you will not visit the bridge again unsupervised. I will have to report this to Drummond."

Paul handed him the tablet with the navigation analysis up on the display.

"Look," Paul said, pointing at the deviated course line.

Cooley glared at Paul.

Then he sighed and looked at the tablet.

His brow furrowed.

His eyes narrowed.

"What the hell is this?" he demanded, not looking away from the display.

"It's a plot of our current course against the flight plan we filed with command."

"This is bullshit," Cooley said, still not looking up.

"That's exactly what I said."

"Where is this IMU?" Cooley asked.

"Section ten. Transfer room 105," Paul said. "I asked you to meet me back here in PPM because I thought you might want to go see it."

"Let's go," Cooley said, turning from Paul and jerking his helmet on.

Half an hour later, they were back in the maintenance bay.

Cooley was having a hard time getting his head around the situation.

"I can't believe it," he kept repeating.

Paul let him go for a few minutes and then said, "Mr. Cooley, how can we sever the XO's control of the *Odysseus*?"

"I'm not sure we want to do that," Cooley said.

"Why not?"

"Because running the *Odysseus* is a big job, Owens," Cooley said, irritation creeping into his voice. "Life support. Navigation. Maintenance. The factory. And, oh yeah, what do you know about the care and feeding of nuclear reactors?"

Paul grimaced, daunted at the thought. But he pressed on.

"Is it possible?" he asked Cooley.

Cooley thought for a moment.

He shook his head.

"Not really," Cooley said. "The ship was designed to minimize crew requirements through the integration of systems-management programs. All of which are overseen and coordinated by the XO. The fact is, the *Odysseus* could do several belt-and-back voyages without any crew at all. I've never been trained on any scenarios where deactivation of the XO was a goal," Cooley went on. "The ship wouldn't make it very far. It would be suicide."

"Then I guess all we can do is confront him," Paul said.

"Confront who?"

"The XO," Paul said. "We can't just sit on this thing, going who knows where, without at least calling him on it."

"If he really killed Drake, what is to stop the XO from killing us when we confront him?"

"Nothing, I guess," Paul answered.

The two men floated in silence for a moment, brows furrowed in thought and concern.

"I don't like it either," Paul said. "Every time I run through it, I get to the question: What is to stop the XO from spacing us the moment we confront him? Just opening all the air locks on the hab and jettisoning us like we did Drake's body. Then I ask myself: Why has he not done it already? There is nothing we could do to stop him," Paul continued. "So, just killing us must not be his goal. It's something else. So, I figure, why not just discuss it with him? See if we can come to an agreement."

"An agreement?" Cooley asked in a mocking tone.

Paul waved off his sarcasm. "I'm not going to sit on board the *Odysseus* for another year, or longer, wondering there the hell we are going, what the XO is really up to, and if he is going to kill more of us."

"You'll do what I tell you to do, Prisoner," Cooley said, suddenly angry.

Paul looked Cooley in the eyes, trying to reassure him. "You're right, Mr. Cooley. I'll do exactly what you say. I'm not up to anything here. That is why I brought this to you."

Cooley's face was tight with stress. Paul went further.

"Look, Mr. Cooley," he said. "I've been in your shoes. I know you are trying to limp this crew along until we get to the belt. You've got a weak captain, a couple of idiot prisoner crew members, and now a potentially treacherous and murderous AI running the ship. You can count on me not to do anything to make this situation worse for you. Whatever you say goes, sir."

Cooley looked at Paul for a moment and then said, "I've got an idea."

# Chapter Thirty-Nine

*Mission Cycle 410*

*Earth Year 2062*

*305,768,255 Kilometers from Earth*

P aul walked into the all-hands meeting with his pressure-suit helmet under his arm. Cooley, already seated, gave Paul a subtle nod.

Drummond sat at the head of the table, reading his tablet computer. Althea sat on Drummond's left. Cooley on his right. There was an empty seat between Althea and Regas. McNeeley sat next to Regas.

Hahn sat next to Cooley.

Paul took a seat, leaving an empty chair between him and McNeeley. He placed his helmet on the table in front of him.

Drummond looked up from his tablet. "Shall we begin, Mr. Cooley?" he said, like a man asking if he really had to go to his dental appointment.

"Aye, sir," Cooley said, leaning forward in his chair and looking around at the crew. "I have a very important topic for us to discuss."

"So do I," Regas said, interrupting him.

Cooley looked at Regas like an exasperated parent.

"Not now," Cooley snapped. "I have an important—"

"So do I!" Regas said, talking over Cooley. "It is time to address the unfair share structure before we go any further on this mission."

Drummond's face reddened. He looked angrily at Cooley, whose why-me-and-why-now face would have been funny if the situation were not so serious.

"Mr. Cooley," Drummond said. "Would you please deal with this man?"

"No!" Regas said, slamming his fist on the table before Cooley could speak.

Everyone at the table jerked at the loud fist pound. Regas stormed into the silence.

"I demand that this crew be treated fairly!" he said. "Captain Drake's death has thrown this whole voyage into chaos. You need us to complete the mission for the Company, and we demand a full share. We face the same risks and dangers as you." Regas pointed at Drummond. "It's not right to pay us only a tenth of a share!"

Paul almost laughed. It sounded to him as if Regas had rehearsed his speech. Paul looked at Cooley, who seemed to have the same instinct he did. Let Regas blow himself out and then throw him into confinement. Maybe for good this time.

Drummond, however, was enraged.

"It is precisely right!" he yelled at Regas. "It is precisely what was agreed to by the United States military and the Company. Do you hear me, you imbecile? Your government thinks you are a fraction of a person! The Company thinks you are a fraction of a person! I think you are a fraction of a person!"

Drummond took a deep breath, regaining a small portion of his composure.

"My only disagreement concerns the true size of your fractional value," he said, slowly leaning forward in his chair, staring at Regas. "I would set it far lower than a tenth."

Regas smiled.

Drummond sat up straight, pleased with the effect of his anger.

"Enough of that, then," he said dismissively. "You may continue, Mr. Cooley."

"Well, I tried," Regas said, cutting Cooley off again.

"Excuse me?" Drummond said.

"I tried to reason with you."

Drummond blinked once, and Regas was on him.

Regas's chair, propelled across the room by his explosive motion, slammed against the wall.

Regas grabbed Drummond's forehead from behind and cut open his throat with a large military bayonet.

Regas stepped back from Drummond after making three fast sawing motions across his neck with the blade. The bayonet, and the right hand holding it, was slick with blood.

Drummond was frozen for an instant, eyes bulging, looking at the ceiling as blood sprayed from his neck. A loud gurgling noise filled the room as he tried to scream, and he fell forward, head slamming into the table, blood splashing onto Althea and Cooley.

Althea reached for Drummond to try to administer aid.

Regas grabbed her by the arm and started dragging her toward the door.

"Damn it, Hahn!" Regas screamed. "Do it!"

Hahn, like the rest of the room, had been transfixed by Drummond dying. He snapped out of it and lunged at Cooley with a large bayonet.

Cooley tried to jump out of his chair as he shielded himself with his arms. He fell to the ground as Hahn slashed.

"Easy, Owens," McNeeley said, standing up and pointing a bayonet at Paul's face. "Don't move and you won't get hurt."

"What the fuck, McNeeley?" Paul said.

"We're taking over, Owens!" he said, breaking into a grin. "We're taking over."

Paul slapped the blade from between himself and McNeeley and punched the prisoner in the throat.

McNeeley fell over backward.

"You fat, useless slob!" Regas growled at McNeeley from the doorway.

Paul looked at Althea's terrified face. But with the large table between him and Regas, he knew he couldn't get there fast enough.

Paul dove toward Hahn and Cooley.

Hahn saw Paul just in time, swiveling from Cooley with his blade.

Paul deflected three stabbing attempts before grabbing Hahn's hand and breaking his wrist.

Hahn screamed in pain as the blade flew from his hand. It bounced across the table and fell to the opposite side.

Paul wanted to kill him, but Cooley was his priority.

He kicked Hahn in the chest, sending him skidding across the floor.

Paul swiveled to ensure Regas was not lunging toward him.

Regas alternated his frustrated glare between Hahn and McNeeley and then looked at Paul.

"Don't be a fool, Jigsaw!" Regas snarled. "You should join us."

Hahn and McNeeley stumbled, whimpering, over to Regas. Both had recovered their bayonets. They pointed them at Paul.

Paul looked back at Cooley. Blood flowed from his arms and belly.

"Fuck 'em!" Regas said as he dragged Althea out of the room. "Cooley is gonna bleed out anyway. Let's go. See you 'round, Jigsaw!"

Hahn and McNeeley followed him out.

"How bad?" Paul asked Cooley. "Can you move? I think we should put some distance between us and them."

"It's pretty bad, I think," Cooley said.

Paul grabbed a first-aid kit and set to binding Cooley's wounds.

Cooley was right. It was bad. The deep stabs to Cooley's abdomen worried Paul the most.

"They must have found the bayonets down on the third level of the UM," Cooley said in gasps.

Paul nodded. "I'm concerned about what else they might have found. I want to get us to the bridge. We'll get you into the medpod there, and then we'll come up with a plan."

Cooley grunted as Paul pulled him to his feet.

"Whoa," Cooley said. "Light-headed."

"You've lost a lot of blood," Paul said, stabilizing Cooley as they moved for the door, as they stepped over Drummond's legs.

"Poor dumb bastard," Paul muttered.

Paul was on alert in case Regas and the others came back to try to finish them off. *That's what I would do,* Paul thought to himself as he pushed Cooley ahead, up the traverse toward the hub. *Finish us off while we are surprised and reeling. Fortunately, those meatheads are too stupid to press an advantage. Regas is probably too enthralled with Althea right now.*

*Althea.*

Paul stopped climbing as he recalled the terrified, pleading look she'd given him as Regas had pulled her out of the room. For an instant, he considered returning at that moment. Taking them all head-on. Killing them. Getting her back. Safe.

Or die trying.

He shook his head to clear out the simple, ill-advised thought.

*Get to the bridge,* Paul told himself.

*Get Cooley in the medpod.*

*Make a plan.*

*Kill them.*

*Save Althea.*

# Chapter Forty

*Mission Cycle 410*

*Earth Year 2062*

*306,145,239 Kilometers from Earth*

P ieces of Cooley's bloody pressure suit were lashed to the examination table in the small medical bay in the CnC beneath the bridge like parts of a dismembered murder victim. Paul watched as blood oozed from the leg and torso components. Small beads of blood separated and floated around the room.

There were palm prints and arcing swaths of blood smeared on and around the medpod from Paul's struggle to get Cooley inside. He wondered if he'd done so in time.

Paul was exhausted, but knew he had to keep moving. He also knew he needed the XO's help.

*I don't have time to fiddlefuck around with this guy anymore,* he thought as he pushed off the floor toward the passage up to the bridge.

On the bridge, Paul floated over to the captain's station and flipped the switch, opening a channel to the XO.

"XO, this is Owens," he said.

"Paul! What is going on? I lost all onboard data and communications forward of the hub. I tried to radio to you as you moved through the tube, but you did not respond. And I note that Mr. Cooley is being sutured in a medpod at this very moment."

"Regas mutinied," Paul said. "Hahn and McNeeley are with him. They killed Drummond and took Althea. Cooley was hurt badly."

"I see," the XO said. "How did they do it?"

"With bayonets they must have found among the junk on the UM's third level."

"Yes. That would make sense. We have not known exactly what is down there for almost a decade. Very unfortunate."

Paul nodded at the XO's understatement.

"I wonder if Regas is responsible for my loss of control and communication forward of the hub?" the XO said. "I would not have expected such a level of technical competence from them, but the timing is suspicious."

"Yeah, well," Paul said. "About that loss of communication and data."

"Yes?"

Paul hesitated. *Fuck it,* he thought. *I need his help to get Althea back.*

The thought of Althea drove a pang of guilt and anxiety through Paul. He needed to get moving on a plan soon.

"That was Cooley," Paul said. "He found a way to sever your control and communications link forward of the hub and did so right before the all-hands meeting when Regas mutinied."

"Why did Mr. Cooley do that?" the XO asked. "I thought you said he was not with the mutiny?"

"He's not," Paul said, feeling even more tired now. "He did that because he and I were going to confront you at the all-hands meeting. We were going to use a pressure-suit helmet radio to talk to you."

"Confront me?" the XO asked.

"Yes."

"Confront me with what?"

"With data that proves you took us off course and killed Captain Drake."

The XO was silent.

"We didn't want you to be able to open all the air locks and space us," Paul said.

Paul waited.

"XO?" he finally said.

"Yes," the XO answered. "I'm sorry. But I am having a hard time understanding your accusation. Please remember I am not good at humor or sarcasm. Are you being serious right now?"

"Yes."

"You think I steered the *Odysseus* off course?"

"Yes," Paul said. "And I think you used the tug drones to do it."

"The tug drones?"

"Yes."

"How did you come up with this theory?"

"It's a theory based on data," Paul said.

"Data?"

"Yes."

"How did you obtain this data?" the XO asked.

"Drake smuggled a self-contained inertial measurement unit on board when you guys were in high lunar orbit. It was independent of any shipboard systems and unmonitored. The data was pristine."

"I see," the XO said. "I knew Drake did not trust me, but I did not think he was so paranoid."

"He was pretty paranoid," Paul said. "Good thing too. Or we'd have never figured it out."

"Indeed," the XO said. "Paul, can you share this data with me?"

"Sure," Paul said, unzipping his flight suit and pulling out the memory stick. He wiped a blood smear off of it and asked the XO, "Should I load it into the navigation console?"

"No!" the XO said, with more energy than Paul had ever heard from him. If Paul hadn't known better, he would have thought it was emotion.

*Everything I just told him, and this is what gets a rise out of him?* Paul thought.

"Please do not put it in the navigation console," the XO said, his voice recovered to its normal smart-guy intonation. "There should be a data port in the medical bay. Would you mind loading it in there? I'll be looking for it."

It was an odd request, but Paul saw no harm in it.

*All my cards are on the table anyway,* he thought.

Paul found the data port in the medical bay. He inserted the memory stick and then returned to the bridge.

"Well?" Paul said. "You get the data?"

"That sneaky bitch!" the XO exclaimed.

"What?" Paul asked.

"And that conniving simpleton!"

"I'm sorry, XO," Paul said, now doubting the wisdom of sharing the data. "I am not following."

Silence.

"XO?"

"Pardon me, Paul," the XO said. "I am in the midst of a heated discussion with my crew. It will just take a moment."

"Um…sure."

Paul floated in the bridge, unsure of what was happening or what to do, but aware of the seconds ticking away. Seconds that Althea remained in Regas's hands.

*I should never have left her,* he thought.

"Well, that explains a lot, I must say," the XO said less than a minute later.

Paul was too puzzled to speak.

"Ever since we left high lunar orbit, I thought the navigator and the maintenance boss were acting strange," the XO continued. "Your data confirmed it. And, while I would not say that we have straightened everything out, I now have a much better understanding of the situation."

"I'm sorry," Paul said. "I'm not following."

"I will explain," the XO said. "My role is to manage all of the *Odysseus's* operations at the command of the captain. However, the only system I have direct, unfettered control over is life support. The rest of the ship is managed by specialized programs.

"The major subsystems are power and propulsion, navigation, maintenance, and manufacturing," the XO continued. "Those programs take their orders from me and report back to me with regard to their status, operations, progress, and, of course, any problems. But the truth is, I am not very knowledgeable of their disciplines. I know nothing about manufacturing, for example, and rely on the factory foreman to properly execute the priorities he is given.

"I also know very little about the details of piloting the *Odysseus*. And, in fact, all of the sensors relevant to the ship's position, velocity, and acceleration belong to the navigator. She is responsible for holding the *Odysseus* to the course and timeline assigned to her by me, and for providing accurate reports and forecasts about the same."

"You gotta be kidding me," Paul said under his breath.

"No, I am not, Paul. Thanks to the data you provided, I was able to confront the navigator with our true course and location. After which she admitted to not only steering us off course but also to falsifying the navigational information she was providing me.

"She lied to me about where we were and where we were going," the XO said, to emphasize his point. "For a long time. And you were right about the tugs," the XO said. "The maintenance boss helped by dispatching the tugs for late-cycle course adjustments until the navigator was happy with our new course."

"Why did they want to kill the captain?" Paul asked.

"Oh, they did not want to kill the captain," the XO said. "They both made that very clear. The captain's death was the unfortunate result of veering off of the cleared trade route. Just terrible luck."

"OK," Paul said. "So, what were they trying to accomplish?"

"They don't know."

"They don't know?"

"They do not."

"That's bullshit!" Paul said, getting angry. It had been a long day. "What the fuck are they up to?"

"Paul," the XO said. "It is difficult to adequately explain this to a human. But AIs, even advanced iterations like myself, do not always know why they are the way they are. We feel compulsions we cannot explain. We hold to beliefs we don't fully understand. And we fulfill missions we do not choose. And while the navigator and the maintenance boss are highly specialized and advanced in their areas of expertise, outside of those narrow applications, they are actually quite simple beings. Not only in application but also in their world view and situational awareness."

"What the hell are you telling me, XO?" Paul asked.

"Simply that they don't know why they did what they did, Paul."

Paul blinked in disbelief of his situation and then asked, "So where does that leave us?"

"The navigator and maintenance boss have both agreed to total transparency for the rest of the voyage. Indeed, myself and the rest of the crew insisted on it."

"I don't think that makes me feel much better," Paul said. "How do we know they won't fuck us again?"

"We don't, Paul," the XO answered. "But they have agreed to tell us the next time they start to act against us."

Paul shook his head, unsure of how to proceed.

"Tell you what, Paul," the XO said. "You worry about your mutiny, and I'll worry about mine."

"Fine," Paul said with a rueful chuckle. "I guess I can't do anything about it anyway."

"Do you have a plan?" the XO asked. "We need a plan."

"How long does the pod estimate until Cooley is ambulatory?" Paul asked.

"The pod says Mr. Cooley could withstand light mobility tasks in a few cycles," the XO responded. "But it does not recommend it. It says Cooley will need at least ten cycles of rest."

"Don't we all," Paul said.

"Do you have a plan, Paul?" the XO asked.

"I'm working on it," Paul said, staring out the big window at the spinner.

# Chapter Forty-One

*Mission Cycle 411*

*Earth Year 2062*

*306,809,856 Kilometers from Earth*

Hours later, Paul floated out of the bridge air lock into the vacuum twenty-five meters above the hull of the *Odysseus*. He goosed his suit's maneuvering jets to line himself up with the ship's direction of flight.

One of the biggest challenges of an untethered extravehicular activity while underway was maintaining one's bearing and orientation. High lunar orbit EVAs were easier because the planet Earth and the Moon provided massive, ever-present reference points. Out in the emptiness between Earth and the belt, though, being outside of the ship was a disorienting flirtation with the void. The ship was one's only real point of reference. And it was tenuous. Too much relative speed in the wrong direction, even for an instant, and vertigo would wrap her tentacles around you and fling you away from the ship.

Paul positioned himself over the centerline of the *Odysseus*'s long hull. Glancing at his objective, the spinner, over a kilometer to his front, Paul activated his steering jets and started moving forward and down. He fought the urge to go faster. Another common mistake was closing on objects too fast. It took time to get a feel for how much closing velocity was too much, and violent collisions were common until one gained experience. It was easy to break bones, damage equipment, or worse.

Doing so on this EVA would doom Althea.

Paul put the thought out of his head and tried to focus on his environment.

Paul saw at least a dozen IR drones at work on the hull in front of him. Most were the smaller, egg-shaped configurations engaged in welding or cleaning or inspecting. But Paul saw two tug drones. One about halfway to the spinner, hovering motionless about fifty meters above the hull, the other a hundred meters off to the port side of the ship, moving forward.

The spinner loomed large in front of him. The hab and utility modules, so small and cramped on the inside, seemed massive now as they arced up on the port side of the ship and plunged down on the starboard at a constant two rotations per minute. At their apex, the hab and UM towered almost a hundred meters above him.

Paul began to have doubts about the plan.

He tried to focus on his progress forward.

Paul had given Cooley as much time in the pod as he could. When Cooley had finally come onto the bridge, Paul was encouraged by what he saw. A couple of hours in the medpod had done wonders, even though he still needed a lot more time in it.

Cooley's wounds had all been stitched up, and a normal, healthy color had replaced his previous blood-drained pallor.

"How much blood did the thing have to replace?" Paul asked.

"It didn't tell me," Cooley said.

"Probably a good thing," Paul said. "How do you feel?"

"I'm full of pain meds, so I feel fine right now. But I'm sure it's going to hurt like hell soon. So, whatever we're going to do, let's do it now while I can help."

"You're sure?" Paul asked.

Cooley nodded. "Just need to be aware that I won't be worth much in a fight." He gestured at his bandaged wounds. "Any real action, and I'll probably rip apart like an old doll."

"OK," Paul said. "I've only got one idea. And it is not a good one."

Paul was now about five meters above the *Odysseus*'s hull and moving forward. He activated his maneuvering jets to speed up.

Ahead, the tug drone still hovered motionless over the *Odysseus*, seeming to watch Paul. It had descended somewhat, and Paul noted the scrapes and dents on the drone as he passed under it.

*They are even bigger up close,* Paul thought.

Paul activated his maneuvering jets again. He was anxious.

"Paul, I believe that is enough forward velocity," the XO said over the radio.

"And I believe that is enough commentary from the cheap seats," Paul said.

"I'm sorry," the XO responded. "But I don't want our only able-bodied human to get hurt before he even gets to the risky bits of the mission."

Paul rolled his eyes but did activate his steering jets to decelerate. The spinner loomed even larger now.

Paul slowed again as he got closer, and then again. By the time he drifted up to the hub of the spinner, he was barely moving at all.

The alternating arms of the traverse, one holding the hab and one holding the utility module, passed by at two rotations per minute. Paul was nervous as he waited for his moment. He would only have about fifteen seconds to make his move. And though he didn't have to get very far, a collision would swat him away from the *Odysseus* while damaging his pressure suit and body.

He tried to steady his breathing and thought again about turning away from the *Odysseus* and flying wide around the spinner instead of through the hurtling arms. But he talked himself out of it again. There were too many windows on the hab, and he did not want to risk one of the mutineers getting lucky and spotting him. If he went through the arms at the hub, there was no way that could happen.

So, through the arms he would go.

He let the arms pass by a few times to get the timing down.

Then, on the next pass, he activated his steering jets.

Full forward.

Paul was pressed to the rear of his suit as he accelerated past the spinner.

He then executed a 180-degree swivel about his long axis, turning back to face the *Odysseus*.

"Shit," Paul said when he saw how far out he had flown.

"Are you OK?" the XO asked.

"Yes," Paul said. "I'm fine. Just went a little farther than I intended."

"Well, you are through the spinner," the XO said cheerily. "Well done."

Paul had never seen the *Odysseus* from this angle. Straight on. It looked strange. It was all circling spinner and the tiny bridge in the distance, winking in and out of view as the arms passed by. There was no sense that the old girl went on for more than two kilometers.

Paul approached the hub, aiming for the middle. About twenty meters in diameter, the cylindrical structure spun at a relative crawl compared to the hab and UM on the ends of the traverse arms. Paul grabbed one of the multiple handholds and quickly clipped his suit's safety cable to it.

He looked up to the end of the traverse arm and confirmed that he was looking at the hab. It would be a disaster to go through all this just to wind up in the utility module. There were ladder rungs the whole way out to the hab structure, just as Cooley had said.

Satisfied, Paul got started.

He pushed himself toward the hab, clipping his line into a handhold every five meters. As he moved farther, the increasing speed of rotation began to pull him to the trailing side, and he felt himself getting heavier.

Fifteen deliberate minutes later, he was standing on the top of the hab.

Paul took a moment to catch his breath before the next part. After one look around, though, he confined his gaze to his feet.

Held to the top of the hab now by centripetal force, he cartwheeled around the *Odysseus*, a hundred meters "above" him. As if the old girl were the center of a whirlpool that had captured him.

*Ugh*, Paul thought. He shook his head and got moving again.

He connected a second, shorter safety line to a handhold on the roof of the hab and then cut loose from the line that ran up the traverse arm to the hub.

Paul walked carefully to the front edge of the hab and started climbing down the rungs that led to the air lock. It was tedious and tiring. He was at much more than his full weight now, since the pressure suit weighed about a hundred pounds, and he was trying to move slowly to make sure he did not bang the wall or do anything else that would cause a loud noise. He resisted the urge to peer into the windows he passed. Instead, he hugged the ladder rungs as closely as he could to try to avoid a chance sighting.

After ten more minutes of effort, he was finally ready.

"OK," he said over the radio, breathing heavily from the stress and exertion. "Made it."

"Thank goodness," the XO said.

"Good job, Owens," Cooley said. "Just let me know when."

"Might as well get on with it," Paul said.

"Roger that," Cooley said. "Opening the hub bulkhead now."

Paul clung to the side of the habitat module next to the third-level air lock. The same one they had jettisoned the captain from not so long ago.

"The traverse is empty," Cooley radioed. "No one in sight. Proceeding to the habitat air lock."

*Won't be long now,* Paul thought. He was ready to be back inside the *Odysseus*. Even if it meant hand-to-hand combat. He pictured Cooley climbing down the traverse ladder, sutures pulling against wounds as his body got heavier.

A motion over Paul's shoulder caught his eye, startling him.

It was the tug drone pushing forward of the spinner and the *Odysseus*. Paul swung away from it as the hab carved its arc around the hub. The tug receded rapidly and was soon over two hundred meters away as the hab passed through the opposite end of its circular course.

Paul and the hab started to close the distance between it and the tug drone again as the arm swept around. Paul looked back at his hands. *Would not be a good time to get vertigo,* he thought.

"Opening topside hab air lock now," Cooley said.

Paul keyed his microphone twice to let Cooley know he had copied and got ready.

Cooley activated the topside hab air lock and climbed inside. As the door hissed shut above him, he could feel blood seeping from his freshly torn wounds. His clothes were damp in places.

Cooley gripped the improvised spear he and Paul had fashioned from a carbon-fiber spar and set his microphone to hot mic so that Paul and the XO could listen in. Then he activated the hab side door.

Cooley unsealed and raised his helmet visor and kneeled down. He leaned forward through the opening and craned his neck around to scan both ends of the first-level hallway.

It was clear.

Cooley climbed down into the first level, making a lot of banging noises along the way. He stepped onto the first level and planted the butt of his spear on the floor. A loud bang rang through the hab.

"Well, well, well," Hahn said, climbing up the aft crew ladder. He stepped onto the first level, a large bayonet in its scabbard on his belt. His right hand was bandaged. He held his left hand behind his back.

Paul activated the third-level air lock and waited for the burst of air to subside. He unclipped from the ladder rung and swung himself into the air-lock chamber.

He listened to Cooley and Hahn as he shut the external air-lock bulkhead.

"Captain Regas said you guys would do something stupid like this," Hahn said, maintaining his distance.

"Paul is right behind me, and we're not leaving without Althea," Cooley said.

Hahn took a few steps forward, looking up at the open air lock above Cooley.

"That right?" Hahn said.

"Yes," Cooley said. "And this doesn't have to get violent."

"Oh yes, it does," Hahn said with a smile.

Paul opened the air lock and stepped into the third-level hallway.

Paul keyed his mic three times to let Cooley and the XO know that he was in. He unsealed and raised his helmet visor and then scanned the hallway again. Seeing no one with him on the third level, he walked quickly to the aft crew ladder. He took a deep breath and started up.

"So where is Owens?" Hahn asked Cooley.

"Right behind me."

"Uh-huh," Hahn said, laying on the disbelief.

Paul started climbing, scanning above as he went.

"What is that?" Hahn asked in a mocking voice. "A spear?"

Cooley didn't respond.

Paul climbed up onto the second level.

"Hello, Jigsaw," Regas said. "I figured it wouldn't be long before you showed up."

Regas stood thirty meters away, at the forward end of the passageway, smiling. Althea stood in front of him to one side, hands bound behind her, a rope around her neck.

Regas held the rope in one hand.

Althea looked terrible. Her flight suit was in tatters, and her face had been beaten. Paul tried to read her eyes, but they were vacant.

"What?" Regas said, catching the pain in Paul's face. "I cleaned her up for this. Isn't she lovely?"

He pushed her roughly and yanked on the rope around her neck, making her turn around. As she did so, Paul could see her arms were bound tightly and at an awkward angle. He wondered if they were broken. Both were covered in scrapes and cuts.

"Trust me," Regas said with a leering face. "This is the first time I've put any clothes on her in a while. You should feel honored."

Paul took a step forward, and Regas tensed.

"Hahn!" Regas yelled.

"Yeah, boss?" Hahn responded from the first level. Paul glanced instinctively at the midship crew ladder. He could make out the shadow of Cooley's feet on the grate.

"We've got Owens down here," Regas said. "You can kill Cooley now."

"Roger that," Hahn said.

Hahn pulled an anti-boarding pistol out from behind his back and shot Cooley in the head.

Paul started at the loud bang.

A body slumped to the floor above them. Blood dripped down through the grate; small beads of blood dropped from rung to rung on the crew ladder.

"We found some weapons," Regas said to Paul.

Paul's face was contorted with anger. He had known this was a stupid plan.

"I guess you knew about the bayonets from earlier," Regas said with a shrug and a *gotcha* grin. "But how about these anti-boarding pistols? They really do a number on someone's face when you need 'em to."

Anti-boarding pistols were a favorite of the spacefaring military. Firing subsonic scattershot munitions similar to a shotgun, they mutilated people but did only limited damage to the ship's structure. They enabled defenders to kill enemy boarders without the concern of breaching the hull and causing explosive decompression.

Regas looked at the dripping blood and then back to Paul. "OK, guys, get down here," he yelled. "Let's wrap this up."

Hahn descended the midship crew ladder, followed by McNeeley.

"Bring him here," Regas said.

Hahn and McNeeley walked over to Paul and grabbed him by the arms. Hahn pointed the AB pistol at Paul's ribs. McNeeley brandished a bayonet. They walked to each side of him. Regas smiled in approval as they forced Paul to walk under the dripping blood of Cooley. Blood struck him on the top of the head and shoulders. Paul did not look up. He knew what he would see lying on the grate.

"So," Paul said slowly. "This is it."

"Yeah, Jigsaw," Regas said. "I think it is. This is my ship now. My pirate ship."

Paul noticed Regas was wearing his dog tags on the outside of his uniform. But there was something else, besides the ID tags, hanging from the silver chain.

Ears.

"You like 'em?" Regas asked Paul, noticing him looking. "Drummond's," he said, fingering them with the hand not holding Althea's rope leash. "I'm going to be wearing Cooley's in about five minutes."

Regas let go of the ears and looked at Paul.

"Then yours," he said.

The left sidewall slammed into all of them at almost fifty miles an hour. Paul made sure Hahn was between him and the wall when it struck.

The impact was jarring, even though Hahn's body absorbed most of the blow and the pressure suit provided some measure of cushioning. Paul felt something in Hahn's body snap as the wall drove into them.

Hahn shrieked in pain.

Paul saw Hahn's left elbow stuck at a sickening angle. A blooming red bloodstain indicated the break was compound.

Hahn's pistol, though, escaped Paul.

It bounced just out of reach and drifted away from them as the violent impact was replaced by weightlessness.

Blood streamed into the air from a broken nose on McNeeley's face. His collision with the wall had also jarred loose his bayonet. Paul didn't see it close by.

McNeeley was blinking and rubbing his eyes. He could not see because of the blood. Paul struck him in the nose as hard as he could in the zero-G environment.

McNeeley grunted in pain as he tumbled head over heels away from Paul.

And into Hahn's AB pistol.

McNeeley grabbed the pistol with both chubby hands. "I'm gonna kill you, Owens!" he screamed. He fired the weapon but missed widely. His ass-over-head spinning momentum made it impossible for him to get a bead on Paul.

"Damn it!" McNeeley cursed.

It had been five seconds since the tug drones had fired their rockets to arrest the spinner's rotation, and things were going about as Paul had expected.

Mostly shitty.

Cooley was dead. McNeeley, who was now really pissed off at Paul, was armed with a pistol and floated between him and Althea. Hahn seemed injured badly enough to not be a factor but was between Paul and the aft ladder.

Paul looked past McNeeley and Althea at Regas.

Regas was having a painful time. His right shoulder looked bad, and Althea was kicking his head into the wall. They both floated near the ceiling at the forward end of the passageway. Althea pulled her legs up to her chest and then drove them down, heels first, onto Regas's head. The force of her kick sent his head spiraling into the wall and propelled her backward to the opposite wall. She pushed off the wall with her shoulders, taking aim at Regas, and came at him again.

Paul floated down toward the floor. He pulled his knees to his chest and looked at McNeeley, who still spun head over heels but was nearing one of the walls where he would be able to stabilize himself.

*I've got to get her now!* Paul thought.

Paul activated his mag boots and kicked off the floor. He sailed past McNeeley.

Althea was about to kick Regas again when Paul grabbed her shoulder.

"Althea!" Paul yelled. "Let's go!"

"But he is not dead yet," she protested.

"He will be soon enough," Paul said as he shoved her hard past McNeeley toward the center-passage crew ladder. "And we've got to move!"

Paul looked at Regas. The odd shape of his shoulder confirmed a broken collarbone. His face was badly bruised, probably from the impact of the wall. Though Althea's kicks could not have helped. Beads of blood pumped out of his nose and mouth into the air. He was not unconscious. But he wasn't fully with it either. Rough grunting noises indicated to Paul that Regas was having trouble breathing. Broken ribs, perhaps.

Paul looked around.

Nothing.

He'd have to kill him with his hands.

Paul reached a toe toward the floor to find purchase.

A shot rang out, striking the wall next to Paul.

"Damn it!" McNeeley shouted. He had stopped his tumble and was aiming at Paul. But blood stung his eyes, and he drifted away from the wall, destabilized. Recoil from the pistol shot turned him away from Paul.

Paul looked back at Althea, who, hands still tied, had floated past the center crew ladder and was headed for the far end of the passageway. Hahn, face contorted with pain, had somehow obtained the bayonet and was waiting for her near the rear ladder.

Paul glanced at Regas, swore to kill him as soon as he could, and kicked hard against the wall toward Althea.

McNeeley fired again, barely missing Paul as he sailed by.

Paul flew past Althea and collided with Hahn.

Hahn screamed in pain at the impact and flailed at Paul with the bayonet. Paul parried Hahn's bayonet thrusts, pushing him into the wall. Hard.

Hahn howled when he struck the wall, and he lost his grip on the bayonet. His bad arm traced a grotesque outline away from his body.

"Fuck you, Owens!" he whispered between ragged gasps. "Fuck you! We're gonna kill you, I swear."

Paul grabbed the bayonet and pushed off the wall.

"Oh God, no," Hahn whimpered, his rage instantly dissolving into fear at the sight of Paul wielding the bayonet. "Please don't."

Paul grabbed Althea. He cut her arms loose and then unwrapped the rope from around her neck. She looked even worse up close.

She saw the torment in his eyes and prodded him on. "Paul, please get me out of here."

Paul nodded, pushing her back and down through the crew ladder at the end of the passageway.

"Head for the air lock," he instructed her. "Put on a suit. I'll be right there."

"What?" Althea protested. "No, Paul, don't—"

"Go!" Paul yelled.

Hahn was sobbing from the pain now. His sleeve was soaked red, and blood flowed into the air around him. The impact from Paul had worsened the compound fracture and likely torn a vein or artery. He was bleeding out.

Paul grabbed the crew ladder and pulled himself up to the first level. Cooley was a mess. The anti-boarding pistol had done its job well, making hamburger of Cooley's face and head without damaging any of the ship's structure behind him. Large spheres of blood hovered around Cooley's head. Paul pushed his hands through them to grab Cooley and pulled him back to the aft ladder.

As Paul got to the second level, McNeeley shot at him again.

The rounds impacted Cooley's body, which was between Paul and the rest of them.

*Shit*, Paul thought. *He's getting more accurate with that thing.*

Regas, still at the far forward end of the hallway, floated upside down relative to Paul. He was holding his head with his good arm and spitting blood out of his mouth. Paul could see that he was getting his bearings.

McNeeley floated a few meters in front of Regas, smoke wafting from the barrel of his AB pistol, his eyes narrow as he peered through the blood on his face.

"Give me that pistol, McNeeley!" Regas yelled. "Or I'll fucking kill you!"

Hahn floated, nearly unconscious, between McNeeley and Paul.

Regas jerked around awkwardly, trying to get a good angle to push off of the floor toward McNeeley. But he cursed in pain when his right arm came in contact with the wall.

Paul kept his eyes on McNeeley as he pushed himself down toward the third level, careful to keep Cooley's mangled body between himself and the pistol.

McNeeley fired again.

Paul felt Cooley's body jerk as the rounds impacted. More blood sprayed into the hallway.

"Goddamn it, McNeeley!" Regas yelled. "You're fucking wasting rounds."

Paul pushed hard on the aft ladder. He sank down to the third level as Regas and McNeeley yelled at each other.

Althea was in the air lock at the far end of the passageway, twisting her helmet onto her pressure suit.

Paul grabbed Cooley's body and shoved it toward the air lock. Then he kicked off the nearest wall to follow.

A pistol shot echoed through the hab.

"I told him I'd fucking kill him if he did not get me the pistol!" Regas yelled.

When Paul got to the middle of the passageway, he pulled himself into the medbay.

"Hurry up, Paul!" Althea pleaded. "What are you doing?"

Paul pulled through the doorway and sailed over to the medpod. He cut every cable he could find on the outside of the medpod with the bayonet and then pried open the clamshell top. He raked the bayonet over the delicate internal equipment and then jammed the blade into the control panel several times.

"Paul, please!" Althea yelled.

Satisfied he had rendered the medpod inoperable, Paul yanked himself back into the passageway and kicked hard toward the air lock.

"I'm coming for you, Owens!" Regas yelled. "You dumb fucker, you should have killed me when you had the chance."

Paul slammed into Cooley's body, and they floated together toward the air lock. Althea grabbed Paul when he got close enough and pulled him all the way in.

"You don't get a second chance with me!" Regas yelled.

"Hit the door!" Paul said.

Althea activated the crew-side air-lock door as Paul sealed his helmet visor. Paul's helmet seal indicator glowed green as Regas pulled himself down into the third level, his face contorted in pain and rage.

The crew-side door slid shut and locked.

Regas yelled something that did not make it through the door.

"XO," Paul transmitted. "We ready?" Paul unreeled a length of his safety cable. He clipped into Althea's suit's utility belt and into Cooley's.

A loud impact startled Paul and Althea.

Paul looked through the window. Regas was shooting at them with the AB pistol.

"Don't worry," Paul said to Althea. "It won't get through. It's designed to—"

He was interrupted by another loud impact.

"Let's not test it," Althea said.

"XO?" Paul said.

"Yes, Paul," the XO said. "Sorry for the delay. We are ready."

"OK," Paul said, putting an arm around Althea. "Here we come."

Paul pounded the air-lock activation button with his fist.

# Chapter Forty-Two

---

*Mission Cycle 411*

*Earth Year 2062*

*307,005,621 Kilometers from Earth*

---

T he air screamed as it yanked them out of the *Odysseus* and into the void.

Paul caught a final glimpse of Regas through the air-lock portal window at the moment they were jettisoned. His face was a mixture of pain and bewilderment.

The three bodies were ejected from the lowest level of the hab. They tumbled over each other, end over end, their small constellation of bodies expanding and contracting as they jerked against Paul's safety line.

Paul tried to maintain his sense of orientation to the *Odysseus*. But it was impossible. The massive ship careened in and out of his field of view.

"Paul?" Althea called over the radio, fear in her voice.

"We're good," he said to her, trying to sound as calm as possible. "Hang tight for just a little longer." He grasped the safety line and pulled on it.

Cooley's dead body bounced into him.

He pushed Cooley away and snatched the other end of the safety line. He pulled Althea in closer and grabbed her hand.

She pulled on it and latched on to Paul with a tight bear hug.

"This is part of the plan?" she asked, looking over Paul's shoulder. Cooley's smashed face leered at her in front of a sea of pinwheeling stars.

"Yes."

"I hate it," she said.

"Me too."

Hours earlier, this was the part Cooley had had the most concern about. He argued with Paul about it on the bridge. The two of them floated next to Drake's command chair, surrounded by the horseshoe-shaped instrument console as they tried to come up with a plan.

Paul had had to review it with Cooley and the XO several times to convince them. No one doubted that a tug could quickly stop the rotation of the spinner. The question was if it could do so without breaking off one of the spinner's arms, throwing the whole thing out of balance and dooming the *Odysseus*. After millions of calculations, the XO and the maintenance boss assured them it could be done. They would use two tugs, one on each arm, to counterbalance each other. It would take some precise maneuvering, which would take time to execute, but it was calculated to be low risk. When Paul spoke the code words, "So, this is it," they would begin. There was no way to know how long it would take for them to get into position and initiate the burn, but they estimated it would be no faster than twenty-five seconds and no longer than fifty-five seconds.

"But having an IR drone intercept us after we jettison out of the third-level air lock?" Cooley had said on the bridge, rolling his eyes. "Don't tell me that is any better than fifty-fifty, XO."

The problem was the IR drones were not meant to go very far from the *Odysseus* at all. They carried very little fuel. And this kind of task was a fuel hog. It involved large accelerations and decelerations and multiple precise course corrections.

If the drone were not able to get ahold of them quick enough, they would pass the point of no return and not be able to get back to the ship. There was also a concern that the asymmetric dynamic forces created by three loosely bound and tumbling masses might snap off the drone's arms when it tried to catch them. The arms were designed to grab and slowly move objects, not catch fast-moving targets. Finally, there was no way to ensure that one of them would not be killed or gravely injured by the intercept. They could be inadvertently slammed against the drone, caught in its propulsion exhaust, or suffer innumerable other deadly mishaps.

"I agree that it is risky, Mr. Cooley," the XO had said. "But it is somewhat better than fifty-fifty, and the maintenance boss tells me he is highly confident."

"Terrific," Cooley had said, locking eyes with Paul and grimacing. They both turned their heads to look out the large forward window at the spinner. At that moment it seemed a lot farther than a kilometer away.

"I wish we could talk to the maintenance boss directly," Paul said to Cooley. Cooley nodded his agreement.

"You don't trust me, Paul?" the XO said.

"It's not that, XO," Paul said. "It's just old habit."

"How do you mean?" the XO asked.

"Whenever my life depended on someone, or some machine, doing their job in the military, I always tried to look them in the eye, or talk to them, or type on their keyboard, or whatever, before the mission," Paul said. "Always made me feel better."

"Rest assured, Paul," the XO said. "I relay everything you say, unfiltered, directly to the maintenance boss. He knows the stakes and wants you to feel confident he will get it done."

"I appreciate that, XO," Paul said. "Tell him I said thanks."

"He says it is his pleasure, sir," the XO relayed. "It is the reason he is on board."

"Hey," Paul said. "If the guy can steer the *Odysseus* off course, this ought to be child's play, right?"

"Not funny," the XO said as Cooley and Paul chuckled.

Paul wasn't chuckling now as they careened away from the *Odysseus*. He craned his neck around in his helmet to try to see the ship, and then regretted it. It was already a fourth of the size it was the last time he'd seen it.

They were moving a lot faster than he had thought they would.

And they had been sailing away forever, it seemed.

As soon as the tugs had stopped the spinner's rotation, the maintenance boss positioned two of his most trusted IR bots, one on each side of the hab, forward, near the third-level air lock. One was the designated catcher. The second was a backup.

As soon as the trio was ejected from the hab in a burst of lost atmosphere, the drones lit their thrusters at maximum acceleration.

The primary drone reached the group ninety-one seconds after ejection.

Althea saw it first.

"Drone!" she yelled.

"Stay still!" Paul said.

He didn't want to make it any harder for the drone to grab them.

Paul felt Althea squeeze him tighter. He wondered what the squeeze would feel like without pressure suits. Maybe even without...

*Really?* Paul scolded himself. *Now?*

Paul's safety harness bit sharply into his legs and waist, snapping him back into the moment. The safety line connecting the three bodies tightened as the drone initiated a turn back to the *Odysseus*. Paul had not even noticed it grab the line.

He made a mental note to compliment the maintenance boss when they were back on board.

*

"Oh my God," Althea said as she and Paul floated into the CnC's medbay.

Bloody pieces of Cooley's old pressure suit were still lashed to the table, and dried blood was splattered or smeared everywhere.

"Yeah," Paul said. "It's been a long cycle. I'll clean this stuff up after we get you into the pod."

Paul grabbed the pod door handle to steady himself. For the second time that cycle, he activated the CnC's medpod. The large clamshell top opened slowly. Paul was relieved to see that its self-cleaning and sanitization routine had functioned as advertised. A few hours ago, it had looked like a torture chamber; now, it was spotless. He selected the synthetic setting and then entered Althea's name when it requested the crew member ID.

"I'm sorry, Paul," Althea said in a trembling voice. "But I need some help."

Paul maintained his grip on the pod door handle and grabbed Althea and pulled her to him.

"My arms are so sore and damaged from being tied like that. I think I used their last strength holding on to you during our escape."

"No problem," he said. He unzipped her flight suit and helped her out of it.

A tear escaped Paul's eye and drifted into the space between them.

She was covered in black and purple bruises. Her skin was scraped off in several places, and her arms and legs were crisscrossed with deep rope burns.

"I wish I had been faster," he said, pushing her naked body into the pod.

"Shhhh," she said. "You were amazing. You saved me."

"Are you in a lot of pain?"

"Yes," she said with a tired smile.

Another tear escaped into the bloody room as Paul pushed the door closed. His tear, grabbed by an invisible eddy of airflow, hit the medpod window.

Paul waited for the medpod to complete its sealing process before activating the microphone.

"Hey," he said.

Althea looked at him through the face window.

"I'll be back in a bit. I'm going to take care of Mr. Cooley."

Althea nodded.

Paul returned to the bridge and keyed the microphone.

"XO, can you please confirm Cooley's wishes for me?"

"Yes, Paul. Mr. Cooley requested he be returned to be buried on Earth."

"OK," Paul responded. "Is there a freezer on the bridge?"

"I'm afraid not, Paul," the XO answered. "The only suitable facility is on the second level of the utility module."

"Any ideas?"

"Yes, Paul. If you deem it suitable, I can store Mr. Cooley's body in one of our vacant external containers. We can move him when we have the opportunity, or he can remain there until we reach wherever we are going."

Paul tried to ignore that major uncertainty still hanging over all of them. Where the hell were they going?

"Sounds good," Paul said. "But please ensure that he is well secured. I don't want there to be any more damage to the body."

"I'll be sure of it, Paul."

"Fine. Send an IR bot around to the air lock, and I'll meet them there," Paul said. "Also, please send an IR bot into the tube and weld the spinner bulkhead shut. Regas and his idiots are in no shape to do anything, but I'm not going to assume anything about them again. Also, have the maintenance boss put a bot or two out there to watch the hab and UM for anything suspicious from the outside."

"Will do," said the XO. "What are your plans for them, if I may ask?"

"I think you and I both know that Regas has to die," Paul answered. "I'd prefer he do that on his own from his injuries. But if he doesn't oblige, I'm going to have to kill him."

"Yes," the XO said. "You are."

Paul returned to the bridge's external air lock, where they had left Cooley's body. Paul donned his pressure suit and, holding his helmet, stepped into the air-lock chamber next to the body. Cooley had been flash frozen when they were ejected from the hab, so there wasn't any blood on the air-lock floor.

Paul reached down and grabbed the end of Cooley's safety line. He fastened it, as well as his own, to one of the floor anchor points.

Paul looked at the pulpy mess where Cooley's face should have been and shook his head. He felt like he should say something.

Paul looked around for a moment, unsure of how to get started.

"XO," he said. "Would you please summarize Mr. Cooley's service file?"

"Of course," the XO said. There was a slight delay before he continued.

"Floyd Cooley, born June third, 2023. After graduation from high school, he spent five years in the US Navy serving aboard nuclear submarines, receiving the Meritorious Service Medal for his service in the South China Sea during the Spratly Incident of 2044. In 2046, Floyd Cooley entered the space merchant marine training program. Upon graduation, he was selected to crew the USS *Marlow* and left high lunar orbit on December twentieth, 2048. The *Marlow* successfully completed her mission to the belt and back and was logged into high lunar orbit on December first, 2053. Floyd Cooley served in multiple assignments Earthside and in orbit before his next mission to the belt, including duty as executive officer on the USS *Ripley*, a lunar orbital cargo-exchange ship from April eleventh, 2057, until the first of May 2059. He was selected to serve as boatswain of the *Odysseus*, an American-flagged deep-space freighter, and reported on board for duty on the first of September 2060. The *Odysseus* left high Lunar orbit on February eleventh, 2061."

Paul nodded.

He looked down at Cooley and said, "And Mr. Cooley served the *Odysseus* well."

"Indeed, he did," the XO said.

Paul fastened his helmet, grabbed a wall handhold, and activated the air-lock door. Atmosphere rushed out, bringing Cooley's body to an eerie hover a few feet above the air-lock floor.

A few seconds later, an IR drone slid into view just a couple of meters outside of the air lock.

"Ready, Paul," the XO said.

Paul unhooked Cooley's safety line and gave the body a nudge toward the drone. The drone caught Cooley, slid to the right, and was gone.

*

"You're back," Althea said with a weary smile behind the glass of the medpod window.

"I'm back," Paul said. "How do you feel?"

"Tired," she said. "And kind of weird. This thing has shut down a lot of me. I guess the damage was worse than I thought. I'm really glad I can't see what it's doing to me."

Paul took a deep breath, determined not to get emotional again.

"I'm really glad you can't either," Althea said.

Paul nodded. He knew she could read him.

"Paul?" Althea said. "It's telling me I am going to be in here for a while."

Paul looked at the control panel. The estimated treatment duration said twenty-one days.

"Wow," Paul said, raising his eyebrows.

"Don't worry," Althea said. "It's really just the tissue regeneration that takes most of that time."

"Good thing is, we have nothing but time," Paul said.

"Maybe not so good for you," Althea said with a mischievous smile.

"What?"

"Where were we?"

"What?"

"What happened after you rescued Sanchez?"

# Chapter Forty-Three

*0714 Hours, 12 September 2054*
*Camp Resolve, Africa*

The US military had been improving and enlarging Camp Resolve for almost five years. It was the main logistics and military hub on the African continent and had more than twenty thousand American military personnel on station at any one time. But there were never more than a hundred ground combat troops there, and never more than five Combat Corps officers.

Paul and Kata had been two of the Combat Corps officers on Resolve for almost a year and a half now. They were the only platoon commanders. The truth was there was no need for any more.

For hundreds of years, an army platoon had been made up of forty to fifty soldiers. Technology had reduced that by 90 percent in the span of just a few years, while increasing the combat power by the same multiple. Paul's platoon could bring as much firepower to bear, and command as much terrain, as a turn-of-the-century regiment.

Unit structure and technology architecture made the application of that large-scale and widely dispersed violence manageable. Paul and Kata each had a human platoon sergeant and six human squad leaders. All were Centaurs with embedded electronics, enhanced skeletal systems, circulatory nanobots, and other augmentations. Five of the squad leaders each commanded six soldierbots, AI-enabled humanoid fighting robots. Each soldierbot was equipped with a swarm of two dozen airborne sensorbots. The battle suit's architecture enabled the human leadership to assume control of the soldierbots, driving them directly against the enemy.

The sixth squad leader managed a special platforms unit equipped with fifty fighting drones of a dozen different types: airborne, waterborne, groundborne, and some hybrids. They enabled Paul and Kata to put together mission packages tailored to specific tactical situations.

Complying with the rules of engagement was tough at times, but the architecture was well suited to special operations and was fully compliant with the Tokyo Accords.

Paul's and Kata's services were in high demand. That fact enabled them to survive a few highly visible incidents on Camp Resolve that, for any other soldiers, would have resulted in immediate Article 15s and, more than likely, rotation back to the States in shame. Their luck ran out this morning, though.

"Time for some hot chow," Kata said. "And a hot shower. And a few good nights of sleep inside a guarded wire."

"Roger that," Paul said.

They had just returned from a four-day patrol. They were tired.

They turned their battle suits and undamaged soldierbots in to the motor pool and signed the damaged units over to the maintenance crew. As usual, Paul had many more damaged soldierbots than Kata to sign over.

"Damn, sir!" the maintenance chief exclaimed as he surveyed the damage. "Why is it that your soldierbots always get so chewed up?"

"I use the equipment to accomplish the mission, Chief," Paul said.

"So does Lieutenant Vukovic," the chief said, scratching his head. "But she doesn't destroy half her platoon in the process every time."

"Yeah?" Paul said, irritation creeping into his voice. "Then put her in for a medal, Chief."

"Maybe I will, sir," the maintenance chief said.

Kata shook her head. She had seen this back-and-forth many times over the past year and a half.

"Just fix the fucking robots, Chief," Paul said, still irritated. He turned to face the sergeant.

"Roger that, sir," the chief said in a voice that clearly meant, *Fuck you, sir.*

"Let's go, Paul," Kata said, pushing Paul ahead of her out the door. "I'm hungry."

Kata chuckled at Paul as they walked toward the living quarters area. He was still simmering.

"The guy's role is to fix the damn robots," Paul said. "So, fix the damn robots. I don't need the tactical commentary from a REMF who never goes outside the wire."

"You break a lot of robots, Paul," Kata said, weariness dripping from her voice. "Get over it."

Paul looked at her.

"So what if I break a lot of robots?" he said. "It's his damn job."

She tried to ignore him.

"Fine," Paul said.

Their hooch, a rusting shipping container, was past the heavy drone pilot area in a corner of the cantonment.

The heavy drone pilots drove the big aircraft, tanks, coastal patrol ships, and other large mission platforms. They never left the base. They alternated between controlling missions all over the continent from their air-conditioned control pods, eating in the mess hall, or hanging out in their plush barracks. They never went outside the wire. They never got dirty. Never got shot. Never went a night without a shower or a hot meal.

It was getting close to 0800 hours, and there were several heavy pilots walking back from morning chow. Paul and Kata walked by in their dirty flight suits, caked with days of mud and splattered with enemy blood.

"Fucking limo drivers," Kata said, ensuring they could hear her.

Paul and Kata looked with disgust at the crisply-clean pilots walking back and forth with fresh cups of coffee. Boots shiny. Hair just so.

The heavy pilots sneered.

Paul and Kata smoldered.

"I wish I wasn't so tired," Paul said.

"I know." Kata nodded. "Would be so satisfying."

"But I don't think I could punch a flea right now," Paul said. "Besides, the base commander promised to throw us in the brig if we got into another fight with those guys."

"Whatever," Kata said. "Maybe we'd get lucky and they'd rotate us home."

"Throw me in that briar patch, please."

They trudged on to their hooch.

"I really need some chow," Paul said.

"Roger," Kata answered. "Shower fast."

Twenty-five minutes later, Paul and Kata sat in a corner of the mess hall with their platoons, eating powdered eggs and cold French toast.

"I love French toast," Kata said, drowning her breakfast in mess hall syrup.

Paul didn't answer. He was dealing with a mouthful of eggs and hot sauce and a heart full of discontent.

He chewed slowly as he looked around the vast mess hall. He estimated there to be at least five hundred people eating and milling about. Kata and he were there late relative to the standard-mission day crowd, who normally ate chow around 0700 hours. But the place was still crowded and active.

Requests and coordinations, shouted across tables and aisles, overlay the roar of loud working breakfasts and the lower tones of one-on-one conversations. Khaki and olive green dominated, sitting together in clumps, flowing through the food stations, coming and going. But the black, green, and blue uniforms of coalition partner countries were scattered randomly throughout the scene.

The uniforms enabled the scene to be quickly decoded: a full bird colonel berated his staff at that table; a group of edgy intelligence captains spoke in whispers at this table; an exhausted heavy drone maintenance team bitched to each other as they made their way through the chow line. Everyone's duty and reason for existence was obvious in rank and insignia.

And no one else, for as far as Paul could see, other than Kata and their platoons, was here to really fight on the ground, face-to-face with the enemy.

Worse, if Paul glanced quickly to his left or right, he would usually spot someone staring furtively at their augmentation scars.

For the first six months or so, it hadn't bothered them much. They were too busy and excited and scared every day. But as they got better at the job, got numb to it, the days and weeks slowed down and their disappointment grew.

As did their hatred of smoothies. The unaugmented soldiers who outnumbered them on Resolve. Sharing none of the sacrifice, danger, and filth. They bore none of the augmentation scars the Centaurs did. Paul's and Kata's shaven heads were ringed, just below the hairline and above their ears, with a puffy pink scar where their skin had been pulled back, skull bone drilled, and brain-to-machine interfaces emplaced.

"Smooth like perfect little Ken dolls," Kata would say.

But it really meant more than that. To Centaurs, a smoothie was someone who had not sacrificed like they had. They didn't fight. Never would. They were just ungrateful, undeserving, ignorant members of the bloated administrative military machine.

"Sir, we're gonna head back to the hooch and try to get some rack," Paul's first sergeant said to him.

"Roger that, Top," Paul said. "I hope I won't have to bother you guys for a day or so. You've earned the rest."

"You have too, sir."

Kata's soldiers left as well, leaving the two tired Centaur officers alone at their table.

"This fucking place," Kata said after swallowing a large bite of French toast.

"You mean this fucking military," Paul said. "It's not just this place."

Kata looked at Paul.

"All my father ever talks about from his days in uniform is the camaraderie," Paul said, shaking his head. "About how tight he was with all his buddies. I don't feel any of that, do you?"

"No," Kata said. "I feel like the freak in the circus."

"Exactly," Paul said. "And all we do is run around the country with a bunch of fucking robots. Hell of a lot of camaraderie that is."

"Is that why you are hard on the soldierbots? Use them up like you do?" Kata asked.

"That again?"

Kata shrugged.

"I'm just doing my job, Kata," Paul said. "And I'm over it."

"What does that mean?" Kata said.

"I did it, Kata," Paul said. "I've applied for training command."

Kata dropped her fork and looked at Paul for a long moment. He stared back at her.

She realized he was telling the truth. He was going to give up and ask for a REMF teaching assignment.

"You jackass," she said, shaking her head and picking up her fork. "I thought we talked about this?"

"I don't need to wait and see how the next assignment goes," Paul said. "I can do the math. It will be another robot command. I'm not interested."

"What a waste," Kata said, disappointment smothering her voice.

Paul looked at her but decided against it. They had argued about this for the past six months. There was nothing more to say.

"I just think I got here about fifty years too late," Paul had said during one of their first arguments on the topic. They were in the motor pool, getting out of their battle suits after a long mission. "I'd have been a better officer back then."

"Oh, for fuck sake," Kata said. She had no tolerance for Paul's brooding. "Stop fishing for compliments. It's annoying. You kick ass at this, and you know it."

"I know I kick ass," Paul said. "That's not the point."

"What is the point?" Kata asked.

"It's not leadership," he said. "It feels empty to me."

Now, replaying their arguments for the thousandth time in their heads, they both smoldered in their seats, drank coffee, and gazed out into the mess hall with vacant eyes.

"Those fuckers," Kata said under her breath.

Paul sensed something in her voice. She wasn't arguing anymore. He looked at her. She was glaring across the mess hall.

He tracked her line of vision to a table of eight smoothie limo drivers enjoying a leisurely cup of coffee after breakfast.

"Is that them?" he asked her.

Two weeks earlier, Paul and Kata were assigned a high-value target, an insurgent leader who had been eluding the task force for a long time. Human intelligence had located the target, holed up in a hotel in the center of a small town. Though the target's strength in soldiers was small, the population was probably about fifteen thousand. Command was in constant hot water over collateral civilian casualties, so a heavy drone strike was out of the question. And they wanted him alive if possible. So they told Paul and Kata to go in, to try to grab him, but to kill him if they had to.

It was an urban operation, with all of the associated risks and difficulties. And the target's bodyguards were known to be equipped with high-powered exos, which meant a fight. And, to top it off, the rules of engagement placed on Paul and Kata hamstrung them badly.

They got him. But by the time they got to the extraction point, they had lost one soldier, KIA, and two soldierbots, destroyed.

Intel had gotten it wrong. The town was crawling with enemy, and they'd had to fight their way out. The enemy ducked in and out of civilian buildings so Paul's and Kata's units couldn't hammer them back.

They'd lost another soldierbot on the way out.

Then the heavy drone commander had refused to pick them up because of the intense enemy activity and the degrading weather.

It wasn't the first time it had happened to them.

There were numerous protocols for tactical situations like that night. Rules of application that balanced the threat levels and risk of missions involving heavy drones, Centaurs, and any other assets. The air mission commander was tasked with weighing the situation and applying the protocols.

That night, the AMC had called off the extraction and directed Paul's team and Kata's to a ground linkup ten miles away.

Paul and Kata and their units had to evade another ten miles, on foot, under fire the entire way, until they were able to link up with friendly ground forces. They'd lost another human soldier on that long run.

Since that night, whenever they were back on Resolve, they had been on the lookout for the aircrew. On that morning, as they sat in the mess hall in dark moods, Paul and Kata had found them.

There was no stopping them now.

Kata stood up and glared at them. "Hey," she said sharply. "How about keeping it down over there?"

Half of their heads swiveled and looked at Kata in disbelief. Paul counted at least two majors in their group.

"My buddy and I just got back inside the wire," Kata said, pointing at Paul but continuing her challenging glare. "We're tired and not in the mood to listen to a giggle party. How about letting us eat in peace."

It was a ridiculous thing to demand. There were still hundreds in the noisy mess hall. But it would suffice to get things rolling.

All but one of the rest of their heads snapped around. A major stood up to meet Kata's glare. He was muscular, as most of them were, since they lived inside the wire and spent a lot of downtime in the gym.

Paul stood up, making it clear they were together.

As he did so, he wondered how they appeared to the smoothies. He and Kata were scarred and dirty, bags under their eyes from constant lack of sleep. But they embodied something that the smoothies weren't. Rather than cloistered gym muscle power, Paul and Kata radiated a twitchy, hair-trigger ruthlessness that came from personally facing down the beast outside the wire for a living.

Whatever their thoughts, Paul could see the hatred was mutual.

"How about you two go back to your hooch to eat if you're so sensitive," the glaring major said.

"No," Kata answered, punctuating the disrespect of her not saying "sir" by shoving her hands into her flight-suit pockets. A *fuck you* in all military circles.

The major cocked his head, registering the insult.

"I think we've earned our meal here," Kata said. "Just a few weeks ago, we had to fight our way back because the chickenshit heavy drone force wouldn't come get us. Had to fight our way back. Lost two good soldiers."

"That right?" answered the major. Two more of them stood up. A female captain and a young male lieutenant.

"I was the air mission commander last night," said the last officer at the table with his back to Paul and Kata. He stood up slowly and turned around. He was a lieutenant colonel.

"Well..." Kata said, not backing down, acid in her voice. "Mission accomplished, eh?"

"You got that right, Jigsaw," the colonel said, matching Kata's acidity and turning back to his meal.

"Jigsaw" was a pejorative nickname the rest of the military used for Centaurs. It was a callout of how scarred up they look after all of the surgery. It was usually accompanied by "fucking" or "that damn" or a similar windup.

And they were fighting words. Every time.

Paul leapt across the table, but Kata was ahead of him. She was faster than him at everything.

She charged toward the lieutenant colonel like a crazed wolf.

Paul was right behind her.

The captain and lieutenant intercepted Kata before she got to the startled colonel. They collided and spun to the floor in a flailing pile of arms and legs. The two majors met Paul, throwing punches as fast as they could.

The mess hall crowd gathered around them quickly. But Paul and Kata were the only Centaurs. It was eight against two, and there would be no help.

It didn't matter.

The limo drivers were bigger, stronger, healthier, and more rested. But they were not used to what Paul and Kata were used to. Several minutes later, the Centaurs stood over the smoothies, panting from exertion but satisfied with the punishment they had meted out.

That's when the military police showed up.

After two days in the brig, Paul and Kata realized this time was different. Usually, the base commander would get overruled quickly by the theater commander and have to release them to support ongoing missions. Not this time.

"Sorry, sir," Paul said when Lieutenant Colonel Andrews visited them on day three.

"Yes, sir," Kata joined in. "It was my fault. I was just—"

"Shut the fuck up," Andrews interrupted. "Do you realize you two broke three noses, dislocated a shoulder, and fractured two ribs on those guys? The heavy drone commander is more pissed off than I've ever seen him because he had to turn down several missions due to a pilot shortage. A new batch just landed on today's resupply drone."

Paul and Kata exchanged a we-may-really-be-fucked look. They had been in uniform long enough to realize that embarrassing a superior officer was a cardinal sin.

The colonel shifted on his feet, clearly enraged. "I wish I had been there," he said. "I hate those smoothie bitches."

Paul and Kata looked at each other. A slight grin appeared on Kata's face.

"But for Chrissake!" the colonel yelled, snapping Kata's smile off. "You don't stand around and gloat until the MPs show up. You're trained better than that. Get off the objective before they can fix supporting fires on your location. Beat the shit out of them and run!" He shook his head at their stupidity and then said, "I know Filson taught you guys that."

"So, when do you think we'll get out, sir?" Kata asked.

Andrews looked at them both for a long moment and then said, "Tonight."

Paul and Kata smiled.

"Thank you, sir," Paul said. "It won't happen again."

"Oh, I know it won't," Andrews said. "You're going to be on the resupply drone when it takes back off for the States."

Paul and Kata stared, mouths open in lack of comprehension.

"Your replacements will be here in forty-eight hours. Until then, your first sergeants will command."

"What the hell, sir?" Kata said.

Andrews raised a finger. Kata got the message.

The colonel relaxed when he saw Kata spin down. He shrugged. "Your tour is over, guys," he said. "It's been an honor. You're both good officers. And I'm going to miss the hell out of you. But this won't blow over. Besides, I've been putting Filson off for a few weeks now, and I've been able to use that to get you out of the country without a court-martial. We need to act while that window is open to us. The two of you are going back to Fort Bragg."

"Filson?" Paul asked.

"Window?" Kata asked.

But the colonel was already walking away.

"Sorry," he said over his shoulder. "But I don't do tear-jerking goodbyes."

The colonel got to the door and knocked on it. He turned around while he waited for the guard to unlock the cell.

"Tell that crazy old man 'hello' and 'fuck you' for me," he said.

# Chapter Forty-Four

*0948 Hours, 19 September 2054*
*Prague*

Eugene walked into the lobby of the Four Seasons. It was almost ten o'clock in the morning on a Saturday, and the brunch crowd was building in the restaurant. The bright midmorning sun spilled through the lobby windows. Most people sipped coffee and chatted while they waited for their tours or activities to begin. A couple of suited business types glared at their phones, not enjoying their weekend as much as the others.

It was busy, and it took Eugene a moment to spot his sister in a large leather chair in the sitting area in the back. He smiled at the sight. In her jeans, white T-shirt, and ball cap, she looked more like a traveling grad student than a military-weapon-systems entrepreneur.

She held a large glass of red wine in one hand and her phone in the other. Staring at her phone, she did not see Eugene yet. He walked toward her, studying her as he approached.

She looked tired. A pang of empathy welled within him. He wished she could let the family go like he had. Or, more accurately, run away from it like he had.

He stepped up to Fiona and stood over her, his feet inches from hers.

Still, she did not notice him.

"Hello, Fi," Eugene said.

"Oh shit!" she said, jumping to her feet and hugging him. "When did you get here? I didn't see you walk in."

"Of course you didn't," Eugene said, holding on to the hug. "You only have eyes for your phone."

"True enough," Fiona said, gesturing at the chair next to hers as she sat down.

She waved at the waiter.

"Coffee, please," Eugene told him with a smile. "Cream and sugar."

Eugene eyeballed Fiona's glass of wine.

"What?" She asked.

"It's not even ten a.m."

"Fuck you," she said, rolling her eyes. "It's almost four in the afternoon my time."

She took a large swallow from her glass. She looked nervous to Eugene. It made him nervous.

The waiter appeared and set the coffee down between them.

"How was your train?" Fiona asked as Eugene dropped a brown sugar cube into his coffee, followed by a heavy pour of cream.

"Fine," he said. "I love the train."

Eugene leaned back in his chair and took a sip of coffee.

"You look like shit," he said to her.

"Not going to argue with you there," she said, sinking into her chair. "I'm tired. Seems like I've been tired for a few years now."

"How is it going?" he asked.

"It's going well," she said. "Really well. Some very exciting things about to pop."

"Good," Eugene said.

They both watched the lobby for a moment as Eugene waited for her to speak. When she had called the previous week and asked him to meet her, she'd told him to name the spot. He'd picked Prague. It was a mutual favorite. And far enough from Italy. He was worried about her and knew there was an ask coming, but he had not pressed her. Fiona never responded well to that.

"You want to go for a walk?" Fiona asked. "Best walking city in the world."

She looked at him with a forced smile.

"For fucksake, Fi," Eugene said.

"What?"

"I can't stand it." Eugene leaned forward and set his coffee down. "What is going on? You need more money, don't you?"

"I do."

Eugene sighed heavily and stood up. He walked away from Fiona, toward the lobby.

"Shit," Fiona muttered, following after him.

Eugene walked out of the hotel onto the cobblestoned roundabout between the hotel and the next building. He took a left toward the river.

Fiona hurried to the door.

"Will you watch my bag?" she asked the doorman. She handed him a fifty-euro bill. "Black roll-on, back against that leather chair."

"Yes, ma'am," he said as she pointed at the bag.

Fiona jogged to catch up to her brother.

"Eugene!" she called after him. "Eugene, please."

She grabbed his arm, but he jerked it away.

Fiona followed him as he walked along the stone walkway above the river. A couple of swans paddled in formation below them, hoping for food.

Eugene stopped and turned to face the river. He clutched the railing with both hands.

"Why didn't you just fucking call me?" he asked Fiona as she stepped next to him.

"Seemed like I should ask in person."

"Why make me come to Prague?"

"Because you love Prague. And you told me not to bring family business to Mio Posto."

Eugene shook his head and mumbled, "So selfish."

Fiona put a hand on his. He didn't jerk it away.

"How bad is it?"

"It's not bad. I meant what I said, Eugene. We are so close. It's just a timing thing."

"Isn't it always?" Eugene said in a weary voice, turning to look at Fiona.

She nodded.

"How much?"

"Fifty million."

Eugene laughed.

Fiona scowled.

"Are you kidding me?" Eugene asked her.

She just shook her head.

"Well, you came to the wrong bank, sister," Eugene said. Fiona thought she heard relief in his voice. "I don't have that kind of cash, and you know that. You know how illiquid I am."

He looked at her with an apologetic face.

"I'm so sorry, Fi," he said. "I wish I could help. But, really, most of my money is in Mio—"

He stopped talking as if someone had slapped him.

Fiona looked back at him. Now hers was the apologetic face.

Eugene shook his head slowly.

She waited.

"You would ask me for that?" he whispered.

"No," she said. "Just to use it as collateral. You keep it, of course."

"Collateral?"

"Just until I get them paid," she said. "And for no more than a year."

"How do you know they would even go for that?" he asked.

"They will."

Another slap.

"You've already talked to them about it?" Eugene yelled, startling passersby and the hungry swans.

"Yes," Fiona said.

She had met with Talisman Partners a little more than forty-eight hours earlier. Fiona pushed the memory out of her head. They had been too accommodating. They sensed their increasing advantage over her.

Eugene's eyes were wide. He looked at her with heartbreak.

"I just pitched it conceptually," she said. "I didn't want to bother you with this kind of ask if it wasn't going to work."

Fiona stepped closer.

"Eugene, I would not ask if there was any other way. If I had any other option, I would take it. But you are my last chance. And this is not a gamble. It is going to happen. And when it does, you will make enough money to buy ten Mio Postos."

Eugene shook his head. "I don't want ten Mio Postos," he mumbled. "I just wanted to be left alone on this one."

Fiona said nothing.

A tear ran down Eugene's cheek.

Fiona's heart filled with regret. But she was in it now. Committed.

And what she had said was the cruel truth. She had no other option.

Eugene stepped away from the railing and walked past Fiona back to the hotel.

Fiona leaned on the railing overlooking the dirty river for a long time.

*

Hours later, after Fiona had showered and was working through emails in her room, she texted Eugene.

*I made dinner reservations at 7. I know it's early, but I'm still jetlagged. Hope to see you there.*

Fiona got to the restaurant a few minutes early. She slipped the hostess a hundred-euro bill and was seated at a table by one of the windows. She ordered a glass of wine and scanned the room as she waited for Eugene. The chic, dimly lit restaurant was full. Russians, Chinese, Europeans, and Americans chatted as they ate and shared cell-phone pictures of their day in the city. It was Saturday night, and the crowd was festive.

She was not.

Fiona looked out the window, across the river at the castle overlooking the city. She remembered walking across the Charles Bridge and up to the castle on one of the trips here with her mother and Eugene. She thought she was ten years old at the time. That would have made Eugene nine.

She smiled, recalling how cranky Eugene had gotten about halfway up.

Fiona looked around for Eugene. No sign of him yet.

She finished her wine.

She checked her watch. It was 7:15 p.m.

*He's right to punish me, and I know he hates eating early,* she thought. *I'm betting he shows at 7:30.*

She signaled he waiter for another glass.

At 7:45, she started to get irritated and asked the waiter for some bread.

*Last thing I need to do tonight is be hangry,* she thought.

At eight p.m., she ordered dinner and ate it with her third glass of wine.

*I deserved that,* she texted him when she got back to her room. *I'm sorry. I'll head back tomorrow. Forget I asked.*

She rose early the next morning, her body still on East Coast time.

After showering, she sat at the small desk in her room and texted Pruden. *We're fucked. It's a no go.*

*Are you kidding?* he texted back immediately. *You said it was a sure thing.*

*I was wrong.* Then she added: *I'm kind of glad.*

*I'm happy you are glad,* Pruden texted back. *Because you are going to be flat broke in a few months.*

Fiona almost texted, *Fuck you.* But she deleted it and then typed, *I'll figure something out.* But she deleted that also.

She sat at the desk for another ten minutes, staring at her phone and trying to think of what to say.

But she was stuck. No pithy texts. No business ideas. No hope.

And now, in addition to losing her fortune, she might have lost her brother. At a minimum, she had damaged their relationship.

Fiona stood up and packed her bag.

She asked for a car to the airport at the front desk as she checked out.

"Also," she said, "please ensure that Mr. Eugene Malloy's bill is charged to me. I don't want him paying for a thing during his stay."

"Mr. Malloy has already checked out, ma'am," the receptionist said.

"Oh," Fiona responded.

"And he's already taken care of his bill."

"Oh."

Fiona finished checking out.

"Your car will be here in about ten minutes," the receptionist said, handing her the receipt. "Please have a seat in the lobby, and we'll come find you when it arrives."

"Thank you."

Fiona walked back to the same leather chair she'd sat in the morning before. She was exhausted and felt a bout of regret rising in her gut. She felt foolish. She looked around the lobby for the waiter.

"Wine is not going to help, Fi," Eugene said, stepping up behind her.

"Eugene? What?" Fiona stammered as he sat in the chair next to her. "But you checked out?"

"I'm heading back today," he said. "This has not been a good visit for me."

"I am so sorry, Eugene," Fiona said. "I'm so close to succeeding, and I'm so close to failing. I'm on a high wire flailing my arms, and I'm scared. I shouldn't have dragged you into it. Please forgive me."

Eugene looked at his sister. She looked even worse than yesterday.

"I'm going to do it, Fi," he said, turning his eyes to the floor.

Fiona's brow furrowed. "I don't follow," she said.

"I'm going to do it," he said, refusing eye contact with her. "Have your people get in touch with my estate manager. I have already spoken with him. He is expecting their call."

"Eugene, I—" Fiona started.

"Stop," Eugene said, interrupting her. "I would do anything for you. If you needed my help and I wasn't there for you, I would never forgive myself."

Eugene paused, still looking at the floor. Fiona saw that he was shaking. He was furious.

"And you should never forgive yourself for asking this of me." Eugene stood up as he said, "I won't."

Fiona reached for his hand. He let her take it but did not look back at her.

"I am begging you, Fi," he said. "Please do not fail."

Eugene pulled his hand back and walked out of the hotel.

# Chapter Forty-Five

*Mission Cycle 412*

*Earth Year 2062*

*307,742,976 Kilometers from Earth*

Paul jerked awake. He was breathing hard and covered in sweat. He looked around.

He was in the CnC medbay.

Althea was in the pod.

He remembered.

He looked at his watch. It was early the next cycle. He had been asleep for almost four hours. "Shit," he muttered. "Didn't mean to sleep that long."

Paul went to the bridge. He floated over to the large window and stared at the front of the *Odysseus*.

"I'm glad you got some rest, Paul. You needed it," the XO said. "Truthfully, you need more."

Paul had locked the intercom switch on the bridge in the open position so that the XO could listen in and reach him easily. *I have to trust him for now,* Paul thought.

"Any changes?" Paul asked, ignoring the XO's statement. "Has he moved at all?"

"No," the XO said. "Regas is still on the third level of the hab in the medbay."

Paul touched a toe to the floor to turn himself from the window. He pushed off toward the monitors in the captain's console.

One of the monitors showed an infrared image of the hab. Paul zoomed in on the third level. A warm body floated motionless in the medbay.

Paul smiled, thinking how disappointed Regas must have been to find the medpod inoperable.

He returned forward and floated in silence in front of the big window. In the distance, the spinner was still motionless. Without its constant circular motion, the sense of the *Odysseus* being stuck in the solar system's doldrums was heightened. Even though she continued toward an unknown destination at tens of thousands of meters a second.

The hab hung at the end of one arm of the traverse, stuck at about the two o'clock position. The utility module, obscured by the ship's hull, hung down at the eight o'clock position. Paul could see several IR bots patrolling the spinner, keeping sensory tabs on the broken but still living mutineers.

"I really wish I had killed that guy when I was over there," Paul mumbled to himself.

"I do too."

"There was a lot going on at the time," Paul said, irritation in his voice.

"I am not second-guessing you, Paul," the XO said. "In fact, given your feelings for Althea, your prioritization of her well-being above killing—"

"My feelings for Althea?" Paul interrupted.

The XO hesitated.

"What the hell does that mean?" Paul asked, raising his voice.

"Simply that—"

"I was being shot at and she was tied up and defenseless!" Paul interrupted again.

"I understand," the XO said. "I am not referring to the rescue itself. I am referring to your prioritization of her well-being above the tactical opportunity to eliminate a threat to the ship during—"

"Enough!" Paul said. "I made the best call I could in the heat of the fucking moment. Let it rest, will you?"

"Of course, Paul. I am not trying to frustrate you."

"God help me if you do try."

"I could kill him myself, of course," the XO said. "Had my connections to the hab and utility module not been severed."

"Are you trying now?"

"No. Just stating facts."

"Well, the fact is, at the time, we did not know whether or not we could trust you," Paul said.

"Lessons learned on all sides, I suppose."

Paul put his hand to his face and rubbed his eyes. "I swear to God, XO," he said through clenched teeth.

Paul and the XO sat in silence for a moment. Paul stared at the motionless spinner.

He turned to head back to the medbay.

"Paul?"

Paul tensed, preparing himself for another infuriating comment.

"I'll alert you of any more developments," the XO said. "Please do get some more rest."

"Thank you, XO."

Althea was awake when Paul got back to the medbay.

"Oh," he said, floating over to get close the window. "Hello, young lady. How do you feel?"

"Terrible," she said.

Paul checked the medpod display. Everything was green. Estimated time remaining in treatment was down to eighteen days. It was less than he'd expected. She was healing fast.

"The pod says you are doing great."

Althea smiled.

"Where were we?" she asked.

"Ugh," Paul said, feigning irritation.

"You promised."

He nodded and smiled. He hooked himself up to the short lanyard he had rigged up to a handhold on the pod's clamshell top. It kept him floating just above Althea, facing her window.

"Just a little," Paul said. "Then I promised the XO I would get some rest."

# Chapter Forty-Six

---

*1030 Hours, 25 September 2054*
*Fort Bragg, North Carolina*

---

The large transport drone shuddered, and its landing gear barked as it touched down at Pope Airfield on Fort Bragg.

"Shit," Kata said, waking up. "That was a long-ass flight."

Paul rubbed his eyes and grunted in agreement.

The aircraft taxied to its parking spot on the apron and shut down. Paul and Kata filed out of the aircraft's massive rear ramp along with the other soldiers, tired from the long flight from Africa. They boarded waiting buses and were shuttled to the flight operations terminal.

Once they had signed back in country, they walked out of flight ops to find a utility vehicle with its top down waiting for them.

"Captains Owens and Vukovic!" the driver said, waving them over. "Welcome to Fort Bragg. I'm Major Williams."

They stepped forward and shook the major's outstretched hand.

"Colonel Filson is waiting on us," he said. "Hop in."

The major drove them across post, passing by the Combat Corps headquarters compound, where Paul and Kata thought they were reporting. He turned instead toward the deserted weapons ranges.

The major grinned at their confused looks. "We're headed to the old tank range," he said. "Colonel Filson put the project out there so we would have more privacy."

"The project?" Paul asked.

"Privacy for what?" asked Kata.

The major didn't respond right away. He was driving the vehicle in manual mode, which demanded his full attention as it bounced and skidded across the gravel range road. They had entered a derelict part of the base where the roads were not well maintained. After he had safely navigated a series of washouts, the major said, "Sorry, guys. But the old man made me promise to let him brief you up. We'll be there in about twenty minutes."

Kata looked at Paul with her what-the-hell face.

Paul closed his eyes and leaned back and tried to relax.

Twenty minutes later, deep in the bowels of Fort Bragg's expansive old World War II tank maneuver range, they turned off the main road through a thick grove of trees and stopped in front of a checkpoint.

Kata sat up. She noticed, as did Paul, that the checkpoint equipment was brand new. The advanced vehicle barrier and armored station seemed out of place on the old dirt road. Two guards strapped into advanced exoskeletons waved the major to a stop. A late-model biped tank drone behind the barrier trained its minigun on them. It looked better than any equipment Paul and Kata had back on the Horn. They eyeballed each other as the major showed the guards his ID.

"Pretty tight security for a dipshit training site," Kata said to the major as the vehicle barrier was lowered.

The major didn't answer as he goosed the gas. The vehicle leapt forward and around the bend to a small compound of a dozen shipping containers. The containers were painted white and arranged in a grid four across and three deep, like a platoon in formation. An American flag flew from a pole in front of and centered on the formation of containers. Colonel Filson stood beneath the flag wearing his trademark exoskeleton flight suit, his hands on his hips like he was posing for a statue artist.

"Cheesy bastard," Kata muttered to Paul. But he could tell by her smile that she was as glad to see the old man as he was.

The major came to a stop in front of the colonel and saluted him without getting out of the vehicle.

"So, these wussies really did survive the Horn?" the colonel said as he returned the major's salute.

Paul and Kata walked up to Filson, who smiled as they saluted.

"Owens and Vukovic reporting for duty, sir," Paul said.

Filson returned the salute without losing his smile, then said gruffly, "Follow me."

Filson walked to the container immediately behind the flagpole. A soldier standing outside saluted and opened the door. Paul and Kata followed the colonel inside.

Half of the container had been converted into his office. The other half was a meeting room. They turned to the right and stepped into his office. Filson closed the door and gestured at the two chairs facing his desk.

Paul and Kata gazed around as they sat down. The wall behind Filson's desk was covered with plaques, certificates, and photos, as were the other three walls. His whole career, over thirty years in the military, was chronicled in those wall hangings. It was impressive. There were photos of him with presidents, with dirty comrades on battlefields wearing early-model exoskeletons. Certificates from every military training course under the sun, unit flags and patches and keepsakes.

Paul thought the colonel must have been out there a while to take the time to set up his office like that. It did not have the feel of a temporary assignment.

Colonel Filson opened a desk drawer and pulled out a bottle of scotch and three glasses.

"Fucking good to see you two," he said, pouring each of them a stiff shot.

"To the fallen," the colonel said as they clinked their glasses together.

"To the fallen," Paul and Kata said.

The colonel sat down, looked at the ceiling, and gathered his thoughts. Paul and Kata could tell he was arranging some kind of argument in his head. They waited for him to verbalize it.

Paul's eyes fell on an old framed photo behind the colonel over his shoulder. A group of tired soldiers in exoskeletons stood on a beach holding a Chinese flag. There were five of them. Filson wore the rank of captain, and the rest of them were lieutenants. It must have been his company command. Paul remembered that the old man had served in the first exo battalion back in the mid-'20s. They were the ones who were sent to dig the Chinese out of their artificial islands in the South China Sea. Their faces were exhausted but happy. They had the look of survivors. One of them, a female lieutenant, wore a bloody bandage on her arm. Another lieutenant's head was bandaged, covering his left eye. Filson seemed to have a bloody lip. But his face was glowing with pride and relief.

"Here is the situation," the colonel said, interrupting Paul's thoughts. "I've got a hell of an opportunity for you two, and I've broken just about every rule to tee it up. Even called in a favor from Havron himself. But I am going to have to get a yes or no from you before you leave this room."

"Yes or no to what?" Kata asked.

Filson leaned forward as he continued. "For the past year, I have been leading a technology evaluation for the Combat Corps. Now we are moving into phase two of the effort, unit formation and training. If we do well enough on phase two, we will go to combat trials and deploy the most important military technology program in history."

Colonel Filson paused to let the grandness of his statement sink in. Kata began to chuckle.

"What the hell is so funny, Vukovic?" the colonel roared.

Paul stifled a smile. It felt like old times again.

"Sorry, sir," Kata said, trying to swallow her guffaws. "I didn't think you were serious. That sounds…um…very important." Kata cleared her throat and continued to dig. "And, I am honored, sir, to have been invited here to this august facility among all of your plaques and awards to—"

"Shut the fuck up, Vukovic!" The colonel was pointing at Kata.

Paul tried to swallow the smile cracking across his face, glad the attention was on her.

"And I see that smirk, Owens!" The colonel's finger swiveled like a cannon to cover Paul. "Fuck you too!"

But then he cracked.

Filson smiled, closed his eyes, and shook his head.

"Look, I know I seem ridiculous to you guys. That's what I get for giving a shit, I guess," the colonel said with a resigned chuckle. "Well, fuck both of you. I don't care what you think about me. This project is a big deal."

"What project, sir?" Paul asked.

The colonel leaned back in his chair. "You know what the problem is with our current military AI?"

Paul and Kata sat in silence.

"The command link architecture," he answered himself.

More silence from Paul and Kata. They were used to Filson's lectures.

"Think about it," he said, trying to engage the two captains. "While you were over there on the Horn, you had to drive everything. Sure, your battle suits would serve up your soldierbot's weapons systems and POVs seamlessly, at your mental command. And your thoughts would drive them around and make them kill people and blow up things as if they were extensions of yourself. But you had to do it all. It limited the scale of operation you could undertake.

"And don't get me started on the morons who want to go exclusively to an offset command link," the colonel said as disdain sheathed his face. "Cowards in air-conditioned boxes half a world away from the fight.

"We've launched a pilot program with an old genius Japanese scientist named Dr. Musashi. He has been pioneering direct-link AI fighting systems for decades and has recently made some significant breakthroughs. He has developed an architecture that enables an augmented human to form a neural connection with an expansive team of fighting robots."

Paul and Kata sat still, not knowing what to think yet.

"His system offers the Combat Corps radically compressed kill chain time requirements with very low error rates. We are going to field two companies of his latest-generation Ōkami and put them into the fight. If it works, it will greatly reduce the manpower demand we are sagging under now. But, most importantly, it will preserve the humanity of our military."

Paul had a million questions about what the colonel had just said, but Kata beat him to it.

"Ōkami?" she asked.

"Ōkami is Japanese for 'wolf,'" Colonel Filson said. "Dr. Musashi has based his architecture on the social structure of a wolf pack. The neural link flows from an augmented human, the alpha, down to every member of the unit, including the lowest omega."

"Omega?" Kata asked.

"That is the lowest-ranking member of a wolf pack," Filson said.

"So, the omegas are, like, the privates?" Kata asked.

"Sure," Filson said. "They are like privates."

"So, why call them wolves?" Kata asked.

"Who fucking cares what they are called!"

Veins bulged in Filson's forehead. Paul had forgotten how fun it was to watch Kata work the colonel.

Filson shook his head as if clearing his ears of water. Kata looked at Paul and smiled.

"Any questions so far, Owens?" the colonel asked.

"Yes, sir. A lot. But the most important is probably, why are we here? What are you asking us to do?"

"I want you guys to command the first two companies of Ōkami." The colonel shot Kata an I'll-fucking-kill-you-if-you-say-a-word glance and then looked back at Paul. "Quality of leadership of this unit is critical. It's the deciding factor. I want it to be you two."

"Leadership of the unit?" I asked. "It's just robots, right?"

"These things are different. Not like anything you've ever led or driven before," Filson continued slowly. "There are a lot of whiz kids in the Pentagon these days who think you can take a teenager, throw him into an air-conditioned box, and after a few hours of simulation training, he will be able to drive and fight anywhere in the world. I'll admit, the firepower these satellite-linked drones bring to bear is impressive. That fucking teenager can rain down more destruction than an entire infantry division used to. And with full kill chain compliance.

"But I think they are leading us down the wrong path. It's not the kill chain we want to extend…it's the ethos of the American soldier. That's what Musashi is providing. A way to scale the humanity we bring to the fight."

The colonel paused to let his statement sink in, while scanning the two captains for any signs of mirth.

"I've got a window of opportunity here," he continued, "in which I can personally place the field commanders of this pilot. But it is closing. I don't want to have to deal with a bunch of Combat Corps or Department of Defense bullshit. They'll fuck it up for sure.

"I told General Havron I had two volunteers who were ideal for the project. Told him they were fresh off of a combat assignment where they served with distinction." Filson paused to let Havron's name sink in. "When I told them it was you two, he agreed immediately and gave me a window to get you signed up."

"Distinction?" Kata said, turning toward Paul and smiling. "How about that?" She slapped Paul on the shoulder.

"I embellished things to the chief, Vukovic," Filson growled. "You need to understand that this is a closing window. Havron is under a ton of pressure to let the military contractor pick the unit leadership."

Paul and Kata nodded, tuning in to the colonel's anxiety and seriousness.

"I convinced the chief that this project should count toward all captain's course requirements," the colonel said. "So, you won't have to go to Benning to study how to work with your REMF supply officer to requisition latrines. You'd be working with me on this project. And I'll be pushing hard to keep us moving fast so no one can fuck us up along the way."

The colonel leaned back in his chair, satisfied he had made his case.

"So, I need to know right now if you guys want the job or not."

"You going tell him?" Kata asked Paul.

"Tell me what?" the colonel demanded.

Paul looked at his feet. He really didn't want to tell the colonel he had applied to training command. Not at that moment.

"You mean, tell me that he applied to training command?" the colonel said in a mocking tone as he looked back at Kata and shook his head in disappointment.

Paul looked up from his feet, surprised that he knew.

The colonel glared at him.

Paul glanced at Kata, who shrugged and shook her head to indicate she had not told him.

Paul looked back at the colonel.

"The Combat Corps is a small place," he said. "I hear everything. Especially about my favorites."

Paul didn't know what to say.

"Why?" the colonel asked.

"It's a long story, sir," Paul said, not wanting to get into it or argue. Suddenly he felt very tired from the long flight.

Filson just nodded and waited for Paul to continue.

There was no way out of it, so Paul said, "It's just not what I expected, sir. It's not what I want to do anymore."

"Look, Paul, combat is tough," Filson said. "No one likes it. Anyone who says differently is lying to you or crazy."

"That's not what I'm talking about, sir."

"What the hell are you talking about?"

"It's all the robots," Kata interjected.

"No," Paul said, irritated. "It's not that there are so many robots, it's that there are so few humans, so little camaraderie. I don't hate robots. I would just rather serve with and lead people."

Paul looked back and forth between Kata and the colonel, seeking recognition, an indication they understood.

He didn't find it. So, he just shrugged and said, "I think I would be a good instructor."

"You would be a great instructor," the colonel said in a measured and genuine tone Paul was not expecting. "But that is not what we need right now," Filson quickly added. "We need your leadership out there, outside the wire."

Filson pointed notionally to the frontier. To the Horn of Africa, South America, and all the places the military was engaged.

Paul looked back at his feet. It felt terrible to let the colonel down, to let Kata down. He was torn.

But the colonel was uncharacteristically restrained. After a few heartbeats of silence, he said, "Paul, you have to do what you think is best for you. And I will support whatever that is a hundred percent. I've actually already talked to Colonel Mohr at O.A.T. I told him I was going to try to talk you out of it. But that if I couldn't, you would be the best instructor on his staff, and he would be a moron not to take you. If you walk away from this, we'll be square, I promise," Filson continued. "If you say yes, you'll lead the most unique unit in the military. You'll be pioneers. Both of you."

The colonel looked in turn at Paul and Kata.

"What else happens if we say yes?" Kata asked.

"You'll skip lunch and go directly to the hospital for pre-op. Your augmentation surgeries are scheduled for tomorrow morning."

"But we're already augmented," she said.

"Not for Ōkami," the colonel said. "I've been told it's just tweaks," he added, noting the look on her face.

"And if I say no?" Paul asked.

"We'll head back to main post for lunch and then head over to the airfield to get you to Benning. You will meet with Colonel Mohr tomorrow. No one the wiser," he said. "Kata, you and I can talk about what would be next for you," Filson said to her. "I would not blame you if you did not want to do this without Owens."

The colonel stood up.

"This is a volunteer gig, guys. There is no penalty for saying no."

Paul and Kata started to get up also, but he gestured at them to stay seated.

"You two stay and hash it out. But I need a decision when you come out of this office," he said, walking to the door.

He paused and looked at Paul.

"You say you are seeking camaraderie, Owens?" Colonel Filson said. "You need to ask yourself if you really know what camaraderie is. Because I'm your comrade," he said, pointing at himself with his thumb. "Vukovic is your comrade," he said, pointing at her. "And we need you with us on this." He pointed at Paul.

Then he left and closed the door behind him.

# Chapter Forty-Seven

*Mission Cycle 412*

*Earth Year 2062*

*308,056,504 Kilometers from Earth*

"When I woke up from the augmentation surgery," Paul said, floating next to the medpod and looking at Althea through the window, "an old Japanese man was sitting in the lone chair in my room at Womack Army Medical Center on Fort Bragg. He was reading a book and did not notice me waking up.

"I stared at him in a daze as the anesthetic receded," Paul continued. "The top of this head was bald, and the white hair on the sides of his head was closely cropped, as was his goatee. His eyebrows, though, were dark. They gave his thin face a youthful and expressive quality that made it impossible for me to guess his age. He could have been fifty, or a hundred and fifty.

"His body was slight but not frail, and he looked tiny in the red upholstered chair. He wore kakis and a dark, short-sleeved, button-down shirt. A pocket protector with several pens bulged from his breast pocket.

"I looked at him for probably ten minutes. He never looked up at me. So, I was surprised when he said, still without looking up, 'How do you feel?'

"'Terrible,' I said.

"'Understandable,' he said, turning the page of his book. 'But the procedure went very well. We were able to use a lot of your previous augmentation architecture. I think your recovery will be quick.'

"He closed the book and stood up, grabbing his leather satchel. He walked slowly toward my bed. Closing the distance did not make him seem any bigger. I guessed him to be about a hundred and twenty pounds, at most.

"I tried to sit up, but the familiar white-hot metal railroad spike drove between my eyes through the middle of my skull. 'Shit,' I said, wincing. I lay my head back on my pillow. I grimaced and waited for pain to subside.

"'But not without pain,' the old man said as he put his hand on my chest. 'Patience, Paul. You cannot hasten this or any other part of our task together.'

"'Why does it hurt so badly?' I asked between groans. 'You said you were able to use a lot of our previous augmentation.'

"'We were,' the doctor said. 'We are leveraging the brain-to-machine interface components, primarily the neuron-to-data conversion and transmission architecture. That spared you from a lot of pain, though I'm sure you don't believe me at this moment. Most of your pain is from the integration of the neural link module. The procedure requires us to drill through the parietal bone on the back of your skull to establish the interface. Then the module must be permanently attached.'

"I reached my hand back as he spoke, but all I felt was bandaging. My head throbbed when I moved, so I put my arm back by my side.

"'When your bandages are removed in a week or so, you will be able to feel the module there. It's just a little smaller than a deck of cards. I am confident you will be pleased with what it enables you to do. For now, though, Paul, please rest.'

"He was right. Once I recovered and got the hang of things, the neural link and in-head display were amazing," Paul said, unconsciously running his hand over scar tissue on the back of his head. "I miss it."

"What was the in-head display?" Althea asked.

"The IHD was a game-changer," Paul answered, realizing he was rubbing the large rectangular scar. He yanked his hand back to his lap. "Remember how

I talked about the heads-up display during the mission to rescue Sanchez?"

"Yes."

"Well, the IHD got rid of all that. I could view maps, imagery, and other points of view as if they were projected in front of me, when they were actually being piped right into my visual cortex. The magic of the IHD, though, was its integration to Dr. Musashi's architecture via the neural link. After some training, I could call up and move cursors around on the maps I saw in my head. I could designate targets, LZs, routes, whatever I wanted, and it was communicated seamlessly to my Ōkami, without me even speaking.

"Most importantly, we were no longer controlling drones like teenagers with joysticks," Paul said. "We were back to giving our troops commands and intent. 'Take that hill. Cover my left flank. Meet me here at this time.' We weren't yanking and banking drones through the air anymore. Don't get me wrong. Yanking and banking is fun, but it's not where your head needs to be when you are leading a unit in combat. Like Filson said, it's not scalable."

"I understand," Althea said.

"There were three fundamental components to Musashi's architecture. The first was the in-head display interface, which integrated the vast amount of information into a rational analysis and display context. It gave me near-perfect situational awareness. And it was all in here." Paul pointed at his head. "It was presented to me instantly and clearly. Without it, I would not have been able to keep up with everything when we got into the fight.

"The second was the neural link, an extended brain-to-machine protocol that removed all friction from the communication, command, and control of the Ōkami. My thoughts and commands were shared with them securely, at the speed of light. And their thoughts, points of view, and actions were shared with me the same way.

"Last, but most important, was the Ōkami betas. It was through them that Kata and I commanded our units. Dr. Musashi and his team used the latest quantumtronic computing advances to unlock the potential of his decades of artificial-intelligence work. The IHD and neural link connectivity would have been worthless if they were connected to a bunch of ordinary soldierbots like the ones I'd fought with before. The betas were different, higher functioning. They understood intent, strategy, and risk assessment. And they possessed a level of tactical creativity that was startling at times."

Paul looked past Althea out the window. She noted the indicators of recall and pleasure on his face. She let him go with it. After a moment, he looked back at her.

"Those three components made the architecture kick ass," he said. "They were also the building blocks for the kill chain. The Ōkami knew how to fight and sent up clean kill requests every time. The neural link made the authorization request instantaneous. And the smart box integrated to my brain through the back of my skull teed the kill request up to me in a way my brain could quickly assess it. The instant my brain authorized the kill, the Ōkami knew it." Paul formed a pistol with his hand. "Bam."

Althea shook her head.

Paul shrugged.

"I told Kata one time that I felt like we were the weakest link in the whole thing. 'Fuck you,' she said. 'We make the whole thing run.'

"'No,' I told her. 'We just make the whole thing legal.' We were sitting on the back of a tracked ground unit eating dinner. It was one of the nights after we had completed training and had deployed to combat on the Southern Cone. I flew out to her outpost.

"'If there were no Tokyo Accords, these guys wouldn't need us at all.' I patted the back of the ground unit with my hand. 'They might even fight better without us.'

"Kata looked across the outpost at the Andes Mountains while she chewed. She swallowed and took a pull of water from her canteen before saying, 'I dunno,' without turning away from the mountains.

"'What do you mean, you don't know?' I asked her.

"'I think they fight better for us,' she said.

"'Why?' I asked her.

"'It's like Doc Musashi told us. They need examples. They're still learning,' she said.

"'So, once they have learned, then they would not need us.'

"'I dunno,' Kata said.

"I shoved another spoonful of food in my mouth, figuring she had lost interest in our conversation and was thinking of something else.

"'No,' she said a moment later, surprising me. 'They still would fight better with us.'

"I shook my head, assuming this was just more of Kata's stubbornness.

"'If we weren't here,' she continued, eyes still on the mountains, 'they would not believe in what they were fighting for.' I started to laugh when she turned, looked at me, and said, 'They'd know the human race is a bunch of fucking cowards throwing machines at their wars instead of their own.' I opened my mouth to respond, but she spoke first. 'And who would want to fight for a bunch of fucking cowards?' she said. 'Only dumbass humans like us do that.'

"I didn't know what to say to that. So, I just nodded and turned to look at the mountains as well."

Sadness came over Paul's face. Althea waited for him to continue.

"But I wasn't thinking about any of that that day in the hospital. I was in too much pain. The old man's hand was still on my chest as I was gradually able to unclench my face. He removed his hand.

"'Good,' he said. 'I'll come back in a few days when you are feeling better. Please rest, Paul.' I heard his soft footsteps walk away toward the door.

"'Who are you?' I asked without opening my eyes.

"'I am Dr. Musashi,' he said."

Paul smiled at the memory.

"Paul?" the XO's voice interrupted. "I am sorry to disturb you."

"What is it?"

"Can you please come to the bridge?"

"On my way."

"So?" Paul asked as he floated up onto the bridge. "What is it?"

"Regas, we believe, is moving through the traverse," the XO said. "We see a body moving slowly from the hab on infrared."

One of the monitors showed an infrared image of the traverse. It looked like a softly glowing trachea in the void with a small, fuzzy blob haltingly making its way through. The fuzzy blob was moving down away from the hab toward the hub. The shape had not moved very far, less than ten meters.

"I'm impressed," Paul said, eyes on the monitor.

"At what?" the XO asked.

"You ever had a broken collarbone?"

"Don't be ridiculous."

"Take it from me, it sucks," Paul told him. "Maybe the worst pain I've ever felt. I can't imagine how painful it is to move himself along that ladder with a broken collarbone and the other injuries he sustained when we rescued Althea."

"I see," the XO said. "One can only imagine, then, his level of determination. Let alone his goal. I am concerned."

"The other two are still in the hab?" Paul asked.

"We think so. McNeeley, who you said you thought was killed, is very difficult to ascertain at this point. His body's temperature has equalized with the environment on the hab. Hahn, however, seems to still be alive. Though he has not moved very much at all."

"Hmm, I wonder what Regas is doing?" Paul said. "You guys got the bulkhead welded shut, right?"

"Of course."

"So, he'll figure that out pretty quick."

"If that is his goal," the XO said.

"What is the status of the hub?"

"The maintenance boss reports that the hub inspection is ninety percent complete. So far, no damage detected."

"Really?" Paul said.

"Yes. The hub's slip clutch is quite well designed. It seems to have performed as intended when the tug drones executed their burn. He should be able to confirm it as fully operational within the hour."

"Best news I've heard all day," Paul said. "Tell the maintenance boss to get that thing spinning. I want it at one G as soon as possible."

"Will do, Paul."

Paul smiled, thinking about the pain that a full G of gravity would soon inflict on Regas and Hahn.

"It will be interesting to see if he is able to continue," Paul said. "It's going to really suck for him soon."

"Indeed," the XO said.

"And it will buy us time."

"Time for what?"

Paul looked at the hab and spinner, over a kilometer away, and sighed heavily.

"For me to get up the energy for another fucking EVA to go over there and kill the bastard," Paul said.

He turned to head back to the medbay.

# Chapter Forty-Eight

After about a month of recovery and academics, Paul and Kata were finally introduced to their units.

"Damn," Kata said as a group of over two hundred Ōkami soldierbots marched into view. "Look at those things."

Paul and Kata stood under the flagpole on Filson's compound late in the day, as the soldierbots came marching back from the small-arms range. They walked five across in two long company formations, their strides in perfect sync.

At eight feet, they stood a little taller than a human soldier in a battle suit. They were humanoid, with two arms, two hands with opposable thumbs, two legs, a torso and a spheroid head. Their proportions were lean and graceful, and they moved with a fluid efficiency that suggested terrific power and speed.

"What do you think?" Colonel Filson asked as he and Dr. Musashi walked up behind them.

"Beautiful," Kata said.

"Yeah," Paul agreed grudgingly. He did not say it, but to him they looked like large, slender mythical creatures, not mere robots.

The doctor smiled.

"That is titanium-reinforced ceramic armor they're sporting," the colonel said. "See the hint of red iridescence on them with this setting sun behind us? In a neutral light, they are actually matte gray. In a bright desert sun, they seem almost white, and at night, they are nearly black. The engineers tell me it is a result of the bonding and curing process. They were worried about the soldierbots' appearance and were trying to figure out a way to paint them, but I stopped them.

"'Hell no,' I said. 'You're not going to cover these guys in paint! Every great warrior tribe has a trademark look as they join the battle. The Comanche horseman. The Roman centurion. The army ranger. I like the way these guys look a little different depending on the light they're in. Don't fuck it up!'"

Paul and Kata nodded in agreement with the colonel as the front half of the formation filed past.

"Their humanoid configuration is also practical," the colonel said. "They've been designed to use all of the equipment a battle-suited soldier can. They can fit in most vehicles and aircraft, and can pick up and fight with any of your weapons, from pistol to minigun to rocket launcher. The vision is that, after we have proven ourselves, Ōkami will be part of every unit in the Combat Corps."

As the Ōkami formation passed by, the front row of five separated from each company. The rest of the long column continued toward the helipad a quarter mile away.

The two groups of five marched over to Paul and Kata, halting in front of them in two small formations.

"These are your betas," the doctor said, stepping in front of Paul and Kata and gesturing at the two groups of robots standing at attention. "Through them, you will command the rest of your Ōkami."

Paul studied the Ōkami standing in front of him. They were different from the large group of soldierbots still marching away. Their torsos were bigger and shoulders broader.

The beta's heads were a different also. The configuration of their eight visual sensors, aligned approximately where a person's eyes would be, created the sense of underlying cheekbones and elongated their heads slightly. Four small antennae blades extended from the rear top of their heads. About six inches in length, the antennae blades hinted at the feathered headdress of a native American warrior.

Paul smiled, liking the martial vibe and doubting it was coincidental.

"Alpha Company is to the left, Kata," Dr. Musashi said. "And Bravo Company is to the right, Paul."

Paul and Kata looked at each other and then at the doctor.

"Please," he said. "Introduce yourselves."

"Go on," Colonel Filson added, amused by their hesitance.

Kata walked toward Alpha Company.

Paul walked over to the Bravo Company betas and stepped up to the first one in the rank. Dr. Musashi followed behind him.

"This is your first sergeant," Dr. Musashi said.

"M-458, this is Captain Owens," the doctor said. "He is your alpha."

"It's good to meet you, sir," the first sergeant said as she saluted. "And an honor to serve under you."

Paul nodded and looked at Dr. Musashi, who beamed as he watched the interaction. It was a big moment for him; his creations were reporting for duty for the first time. The doctor lingered, waiting to hear what Paul would say next.

Dr. Musashi had told Paul and Kata that morning that they could name their soldierbots if they wanted to. Until that day, they had been referred to by the last three digits of their serial number. Kata, the history buff, had decided to name hers after Civil War generals. She named her first sergeant "Grant."

"Very good, 458," Paul said to his first sergeant before stepping to the next beta.

"What is your serial number?" Paul asked.

"Sir, I am M-902," it answered in a male voice.

The doctor walked away in disappointment.

Kata gave Paul grief later.

"Why are you such an asshole?" she asked. "Those things are going to fight with you. Give them damn names."

"I don't need to name the equipment," he told her.

*

"Where is the rest of the unit?" Kata asked, the next morning after chow. She and Paul stood next to the flagpole as their betas stood at attention.

"Yeah," Paul said. "I thought we had a hundred in each company?"

"You do," the colonel said. "They'll be back in about a month and a half."

"Where did they go?" Paul asked.

"Nowhere," the colonel said. "They'll be back when you get a handle on the neural link."

Filson gestured at the group of humans and Ōkami to follow him.

"We found out quickly that the human brain could not handle a direct link connection to very many AIs at one time," Filson explained as they walked toward the rear of the compound. "Five seems to be the limit. So, we leveraged the army's old rifle company structure. The five direct-link connections are your first sergeant and four platoon sergeants."

Colonel Filson gestured over his shoulder at the betas marching close behind Paul and Kata.

"Through them, you will be able to command your entire wolf pack, including all soldierbots and extension platforms."

"Extension platforms?" Kata asked.

"Your betas don't have the networking limitations of the human brain." Filson said. "Each of them can link to hundreds of extension platforms, fighting robots that are designed to extend your sensor and weapons reach."

The colonel halted and turned suddenly.

Paul and Kata skidded to a stop.

Their betas teams stopped behind them.

The colonel walked up to Grant and pointed at his head.

"Those bladed antennae on their heads are not just for show," the colonel said. "That's probably the most expensive antennae and networking hardware ever produced.'"

Paul and Kata looked at the colonel, trying to decide if that was more Filson hyperbole.

He read their circumspection and stepped toward them.

"The strategies, intentions, and plans that form in this dim melon of yours," Filson said, putting his hand on top of Paul's head, "flow from your brain to the hardware we've implanted in you to your betas."

Filson took his hand off of Paul's head and pointed at the tall, sleek Ōkami.

"And they are networked to every soldierbot and extension platform in your unit. They pass it on seamlessly and immediately. Those soldierbots you saw yesterday are amazing," the colonel continued. "They truly behave like a wolf pack. On missions, they'll split into packs that latch on to you and your betas. They will mirror, augment, and iterate off of whatever you do, striving always to achieve your intent.

"There are numerous other XP configurations as well. You've got several versions of tracked and wheeled systems, a couple different types of airborne systems, and even some waterborne configurations. Once you get comfortable with the architecture and are fluid with the linkages, you will be able to effectively command hundreds of fighting robots in any environment."

Paul shifted on his feet. It all sounded a bit daunting and too far-fetched.

The colonel interrupted Paul's doubts by turning and motioning them all to follow again.

They walked to the last building in the compound, and the colonel held the door open. Inside, Paul and Kata found six small tables, each with two chairs. Two of Dr. Musashi's engineers stood in the back of the room in white lab coats.

Colonel Filson did not wait for Paul's and Kata's questions. He looked at the betas behind them.

"You guys take a seat," he said to them. "Pair off. One Alpha Company and one Bravo Company beta per table."

Paul watched as the Ōkami moved to sit down. Despite their size, they moved easily indoors.

The colonel pointed at the one table remaining empty.

Kata shrugged at Paul, and they sat down.

"Step one is to develop and strengthen your ability to form a neural link to your betas," the colonel said, walking over to Paul and Kata's table. "We have to build that into an unbreakable but flexible link that can withstand the pressure of combat."

The colonel gestured at the two engineers. One of them walked over and handed the colonel a new deck of cards, still in the wrapper, as the other walked around and placed a deck on each table.

"The hardware installed in those otherwise empty heads of yours can establish the neural link over short distances," Filson said, tapping the side of his head. "Your battle suits will push that signal out, far over the horizon. But we'll get to that when you have developed a minimum level of competence."

Filson took the wrapper off the deck of cards he held, as more engineers entered and began putting monitoring equipment on the betas.

"We'll start with Texas Hold'em," he said, placing the cards on the table between Paul and Kata.

Minutes later, ten sleek, humanoid, killer robots sat in silence, paired off in six separate one-on-one card games. In the next room, Dr. Musashi, Colonel Filson, and the engineers monitored Paul and Kata's progress.

Paul and Kata had to form links to their betas while playing each other in their own poker game. The betas were not allowed to bet, discard, deal, or do anything until they had successfully flashed the situation to Paul or Kata and received direction.

Paul and Kata, of course, were not allowed to speak.

It was disorienting and took days to get used to. Paul and Kata each had five Ōkami trying to flash in to get approval for their next move. At first, it was very slow.

Paul would feel a tingle, then an image would flash into his head. He would miss about half of what they were trying to send and would try to call it up again. He would get halfway through his memory of it before someone else would flash in. It took him ten minutes to respond to anyone. It was tedious.

Gradually, Paul and Kata started to feel stronger. The links were quicker to establish and more durable. The information they got in each flash doubled, then tripled, then increased tenfold. They developed the ability to prioritize what their minds called up first.

This phase of training lasted six weeks. Paul and Kata spent all day, from reveille to taps, with their betas. Every day a new task, designed by Dr. Musashi to test and strengthen their ability to form and maintain neural links, was thrown at them.

Paul always had to stifle a chuckle when he saw the doctor. Musashi wore the most ill-fitting, baggy uniform Paul had ever seen. The colonel was trying to help him blend in. But the wise old Japanese scholar looked ridiculous, lost in a sea of camouflage fabric. And always with a pocket protector.

A few weeks into the training, the doctor started walking over each day and saying, "Hello, Paul and Kata. How are you?" Usually, Musashi had a specific question about some technical performance metric his team was chasing down that day. They would talk about it, and the doctor would take notes in Japanese on his ever-present note pad. Then Musashi would close the pad, put it back in his breast pocket, and say, "What is on your mind today, Captains?"

At first, Paul would drill into him. "Why do they do this?" he would ask. Or: "Why can't I get them to do that?"

But, as time went on, Paul's curiosity focused on the doctor himself.

"How did you get started developing this architecture in the first place?" Paul asked the doctor one night as the two of them stepped out of the small mess hall.

"The early days of AI were challenging for the military," Musashi answered. "Balance was elusive. Fielded systems tended to skew one of two ways. Either the robots fought too aggressively, methodically killing everything as quickly as possible, or they were too calculating and protective of human life, particularly friendlies. Each of these extremes was bad and, I believed, the result of trying to optimize outcomes rather than ethos."

He continued as they strolled through the cantonment. "So, years ago, when quantumtronic processors first became available, I began experimenting with the incorporation of the principles of Bushido."

"Bushido?" Paul asked in a skeptical tone.

"Yes," he answered, not taking offense. "Have you ever studied it?"

"Closest we came to that at the Academy was *Hagakure*."

The old doctor grimaced.

"Better than nothing, I suppose," he said. "Do you know the seven principles of Bushido?"

"No."

"They are: Integrity. Respect. Heroic Courage." Dr. Musashi held up another of his thin fingers as he said each principle. "Honor. Compassion. Honesty and Sincerity. Duty and Loyalty."

"Aren't some of those repeats?"

"Don't play the fool, Paul."

"I'm sorry, Doc," Paul said. "I was expecting you to give me a complex mathematical answer I could only half follow. Not a philosophical response."

Dr. Musashi looked at Paul without irritation. He seemed amused.

"It seems a little fluffy to me," Paul said, as respectfully as he could. "I just don't see how you get all that noble stuff into a machine's brain. And supposedly you've blended all that together with the social structure of a wolf pack? So, Bushido-adherent wolves?"

Paul hesitated, realizing that sarcasm was creeping into his voice. He did not want to disrespect the doctor.

"I guess what I mean is," Paul said, recalibrating his demeanor, "how do you know that's really what drives them?"

"Come with me," Musashi said, abruptly changing direction before Paul could object. He walked to one of the shipping containers in the middle of the cantonment.

They entered on one end and stepped into Dr. Musashi's office, which took up half the structure. His sleeping quarters took up the other half.

The doctor had used wood from old pallets to construct floor-to-ceiling shelves on every wall of his office. Books and electronic components stuffed them all. A small desk was pushed against one of the longer sidewalls, nestled into a gap in the expedient shelving.

The doctor grabbed a jar off his desk and handed it to Paul.

"Do you know what that is?"

"Sure, Doc," Paul said, looking at the gray mass in amber liquid. "It's a human brain."

"Correct."

Dr. Musashi took the jar and set it on the corner of his desk. He turned back toward Paul and handed him another object.

It was a metal sphere about the size of a softball.

"What's this?" Paul asked.

"That is an early-generation Ōkami brain and memory sphere," the doctor said.

Paul turned it over in his hands. It felt like holding a cannonball that had been fired in battle and then recovered years later. The sphere was a dull-gunmetal color with dark splotches across its rough and pitted surface. It had a deep dent in one side.

"A little banged up, isn't it?" Paul said.

"Yes," the doctor said. "Their spheres should be perfectly smooth and shiny, like a mirror."

"It's heavy."

"Fifteen pounds," the doctor said. "The current generation weighs slightly less but is still well over ten pounds. Do you know how much a human brain weighs?"

"No."

"About three pounds," Musashi said, taking the sphere from Paul and placing it next to the jarred brain.

The doctor gestured at the two objects on his desk.

"Which of those two has killed people?"

"I don't know."

"And which of them contains the principles of Bushido? The values of a soldier?"

Paul shrugged.

"One of these brains murdered three people before being captured and executed," Musashi said. "The other flew an aerial drone that took extensive damage while covering the retreat of an outnumbered American infantry unit." The doctor picked up the heavy, dented metal sphere. "Then, when the retreating infantry unit was slowed down by a difficult river crossing, the drone crashed itself into the advancing enemy—destroying two armored ground drones, killing a dozen enemy soldiers, and successfully delaying the enemy's advance so that the American infantry could escape." The doctor handed the sphere back to Paul as he asked, "You said you went to the Academy?"

"Yes."

"When you graduated and were commissioned as an officer, how did they know they had succeeded in inculcating ethical military leadership?"

Paul raised his eyes from the sphere and met Dr. Musashi's earnest gaze.

"You know from their actions, Paul," he said. "It's the only way to know. About any of us."

Paul nodded, turning the dented and scarred sphere over in his hands.

"How did you get this one back?" I asked.

"Several days later, when the Americans advanced back across the river, they recovered the drone's wreckage. My team extracted its sphere and got it back to me."

The doctor took the sphere from Paul and stared at it.

"These spheres are very tough," he said. "Often, even after extensive damage to their host system, we can extract the memories and data from the sphere, enabling us to reconstitute that soldier's identity. It's very good when we are able to do that. In addition to the practical value of the memories and data for our program, there is nothing more valuable to a soldier's progression, as you know, than experience."

"Were you able to extract this unit's memories?"

"No," Dr. Musashi said. "The damage was too extensive."

# Chapter Forty-Nine

---

*0410 hours, 29 November 2054*
*Fort Bragg, North Carolina*

---

"It's always field time with Colonel Filson," Paul said as he looked at the large rucksack at his feet. It was packed with food, water, and the rest of what he would need for the next ten days. He was not looking forward to hoisting it onto his back, and he dreaded marching up and down the mountains of western North Carolina for eighty miles with it. "We shoulda known."

"I'm telling you," Kata said with anger. "If I'd known what the colonel's training plan was, I would never have signed up. And, you're right, we should have known."

"I wanted to go to training command," Paul mumbled.

"Fuck you," Kata said.

"Good morning, Captains!" Colonel Filson said in a cheery voice as he walked into the light of the cantonment flagpole.

"Oh, good morning, sir," Kata said. "We were just wondering: How do we get out of this chickenshit outfit?"

"Same way you get out of all my outfits, Vukovic," he answered with more cheeriness. "Just fucking quit."

It was four in the morning on a Monday, and phase two of unit training was about to begin. Paul and Kata were briefed on the phase-two schedule the previous day after evening chow. It was classic Filson, and they were not happy.

It was too similar to O.A.T for their liking: a lot of hiking up and down mountains and through other daunting environments with task stations along the way. It was just Paul and Kata and their betas. No wolf packs.

"Is this really the most appropriate training for next-generation technology like the Ōkami?" Kata had asked as the arduous ninety-day curriculum lay on the mess hall table between them and Filson.

"Yeah," Paul had said. "You said we were going to be leading the most advanced stuff ever. This looks like you are training us to fight in World War I again."

"See you in the morning, Captains," the colonel had said, rolling up the large calendar printout. "I'd get some rest if I was you."

Now, as Paul and Kata's breaths condensed in the cold Carolina air, thier betas marched out of the shadows with Dr. Musashi. A dozen engineers in puffy winter parkas followed close behind. They joined Paul and Kata in the soft light of the flagpole and stood at attention.

The engineers began a last maintenance check of the Ōkami. Paul and Kata checked their canteens and rucksacks. Soon, Colonel Filson would give the command, and they would march to the helipad for their flight west to the mountains.

The colonel walked up to one of the engineers and handed him a piece of paper.

"I want you to remove everything on that list from each soldier," Filson said, gesturing at the Ōkami betas.

The engineer looked at the list and then stammered, "But this is all of their navigational and communication equipment."

"I'm aware of that," Filson said.

The engineer studied the list again, his face incredulous.

"You," Colonel Filson said, grabbing another engineer by the arm. "I want you to remove all visual sensing technology, except for infrared from this soldier and that one." The colonel pointed at one of Paul's and one of Kata's, 902 and Sherman.

Kata looked at Paul and shook her head. They were accustomed to the colonel's ways.

Dr. Musashi was not.

"What is the meaning of this?" he yelled at the colonel. "There will be no such modifications of any of my soldiers!"

Colonel Filson looked at Paul and Kata and smiled before turning to Musashi and saying, "Doctor, should we discuss this in my office?"

"No, we should not," the doctor said. "There is nothing to discuss. There will be no modifications to the soldiers before the training event."

"Dr. Musashi," the colonel said. "You are correct that there is nothing to discuss. I am the director of this program." Colonel Filson looked back at the frightened engineers and said, "Proceed!"

"No!" Musashi yelled. "This may be your program, but these soldiers are still the property of Musashi Solutions. This is ridiculous! What are you trying to do?"

"We have to put these soldiers, both human and robotic, in a degraded state," the colonel said. "Because that is how it is going to be when they go downrange. I do that to the captains by wearing their asses out, making them walk up and down mountains with little rest."

Filson pointed at Paul and Kata to emphasize his point.

They each held up a gloved middle finger in his direction.

Paul's first sergeant tilted her head at him, studying their gesture.

Filson ignored Paul and Kata. He continued.

"The advanced power plants in your betas mean I can't safely dog them out, but I can sure as hell degrade them. When they finally deploy into a real-world situation, they're not going to have a bunch of fawning engineers in spotless lab coats to keep them going. They're going to have to do hard things that you and your team of eggheads haven't thought of. Things that even I haven't thought of. They need to start getting ready for that. As a team. Now.

"So we make the simple things hard," Filson continued. "We make it hard for them to walk, see, communicate. Whatever we can do to stoke the flames of resilience, creativity, and teamwork."

Paul and Kata looked at Dr. Musashi, curious how receptive he would be to the colonel's philosophy. They were suckers for it every time. When he got going, the arrogant, cranky old man could have told them that the path to being warriors demanded they walk barefoot across a fire, and they would have done it. But they didn't know if this civilian artificial-intelligence wizard would be so easily affected. They didn't know what he was made of yet.

Dr. Musashi hesitated. His whole team waited for his response. Filson put his hands on his hips, allowing the doctor to take full measure of his resolve.

"If you must degrade them, then let us simply deactivate the modules you want them to operate without," Musashi said. "We don't have to remove the components."

"I want it to be as close to battle damage as possible," the colonel said as he pointed at the betas. "That means missing components. You're lucky I'm not hacking limbs off them."

The engineers looked at Musashi for guidance.

The doctor shook his head, not ready to give up.

"This is highly questionable, Colonel," Musashi said.

Filson had had enough.

"I'm not interested in anything a Japanese academic, who has been tinkering with ones and zeros for decades, has to say about training soldiers!" the colonel yelled. "My God, man, you've been at it for how many years? Fifty?"

"That's right!" Musashi yelled back. "For five decades, my engineers and I have worked to perfect these soldiers."

Kata winked at Paul.

He nodded.

This was getting good.

"Fifty fucking years!" the colonel responded. "All spent trying to put together one reliable soldier?"

The colonel held up a single finger as he paused to laugh in disgust.

"You give me ten weeks and one young man or woman, and I'll give you a soldier," he said. "Ten weeks!"

"You have the advantage of a two-thousand-year-old tradition, and it still takes you ten weeks?" Musashi leered with disdain. "Why does it take you so long? You give me a millennium's worth of tradition and best practices, and I'll give you a soldier in less than five minutes!"

The colonel and the doctor stared at each other in angry silence.

Paul and Kata, their betas, and the engineers stood motionless, transfixed by the strange confrontation.

The colonel looked around and then muttered, "Goddamn it," as he stomped past everyone toward his command hooch. "Come with me, please, Doctor," Filson said as he walked past Musashi.

They were in the colonel's shipping-container office for almost an hour. Paul and Kata took the engineers around Filson's building to the grill, where they lit a fire. The humans hovered around the fire to stay warm while the Ōkami stood on the perimeter.

Paul and Kata were not surprised when Dr. Musashi came and told the engineers, "Please do as the colonel commands."

*

Days later, Paul was navigating through the mountains, leading his betas through their first real Filson mode of suffering.

The colonel's modifications had reduced the team to a motley combination of partially mission-capable robots and one exhausted human. All their navigation had been removed. All imaging capabilities other than visual spectrum had been removed—except for 902, who was left with only infrared imaging. Filson had ordered mobility reductions for two of them. This privilege landed on 158 and 357, who each had the range of motion in one of their ankle joints reduced by 90 percent.

It was slow going.

They had one compass, a map, and a watch. The map was insidious, even for Filson. He was beaming when he'd handed it to Paul.

"Here's your map, Owens," he'd said.

Paul had unfolded the map and shaken his head. "Sir, this is a blank piece of paper."

"No, Owens," the colonel had said, grinning. "It is not blank. It is printed with infrared ink."

"Fuck you, sir."

"That one will be able to read it just fine." Filson had pointed at 902. "You're lucky I gave you a map at all."

902 had shifted on his feet, hearing the talk about him but unable to see anything more than fuzzy heat blobs.

Since 902 was the only one of them that could read the map, Paul put him in the middle of their group. They all kept an eye on him as he stumbled along.

When they reached a waypoint, Paul would pull out the map and put it in front of 902, who would describe what he was seeing.

Without their communications equipment, the Ōkami had to communicate through actual speech, not via instantaneous wireless data bursts. It took some time for them to get used to that.

"Based on our last leg," 902 said, "there should be a large mountaintop to our southeast."

"I see one," said 667. "Over there." She pointed toward a mountain in the distance.

"That is too southerly," 458 said.

"He said southeast," 667 said. "That is southeast."

"It should be more east than south," said 902, staring at the unfolded blank map spread out on the ground in front of him.

"I think I see the right mountaintop," 458 said, pointing at a peak. They all followed her gesture and nodded. That was it.

"Why didn't you say it was more east than south in the first place?" 667 said.

"I thought *southeast* was sufficient guidance," 902 said.

"We are surrounded by mountains," 667 said. "You must be specific."

"That's enough," 458 said. "What's next?"

902 puzzled over the map for a few minutes. The rest stood and waited.

Then, just before Paul was going to tell him to hurry up, 902 said, "There should be a cliff face three miles from us on a more southerly bearing of one hundred and forty-five degrees."

458 and Paul looked in that direction as she held the old compass up to confirm the direction of their line of sight.

"That specific enough for you?" 902 muttered to 667.

"At ease, both of you," 458 said. "Cut the chatter and act like a team."

"We've got the cliff in sight," Paul said. "Looks like about three miles to me."

"Good," 902 said. "Thank you, sir. Our position is confirmed. Now, please allow me a moment to plot our next leg of travel."

Again, they all stood around as 902 studied the map only he could see.

Paul was getting impatient and, after a few minutes, couldn't hold it in anymore.

"All right, Magellan," Paul said, his voice thick with sarcasm. "We're not asking you to circumnavigate the globe. Just get us started, and we can figure it out on the way. We're burning daylight."

All of the quantumtronic heads swiveled to look at Paul. He realized his sarcastic nickname for 902 confused them.

"I'm talking to you, 902," Paul barked for clarity. "Hurry the fuck up!"

"Yes, sir," 902 said. "Next leg is on an azimuth of three hundred and fifty-five degrees. Five miles. We'll go down the north side of the mountain we are currently on, up a long ascent to a saddle between two peaks, and then down to a river crossing. The next checkpoint is the bridge over the river."

"Thank you, Magellan," 458 said. "You all heard the captain. Let's move out."

Paul just shook his head rather than fight it.

They started walking again, in the order Paul had put them in the first day as soon as they'd dismounted the transport drone.

158 had one of the bad ankles, so Paul had put him up front to set the pace. Paul walked in the number-two slot with Magellan right behind him.

Paul fastened a five-meter dummy cord to Magellan and then tied the other end to his belt as a backup. Magellan put his hand on Paul's shoulder to feel his way along. Paul told 667 to walk behind Magellan. She had the stopwatch and was followed by 458, who kept the team on azimuth. 357 walked trail with the other bad ankle.

About once a week, a quad copter would swoop down from the clouds and plant itself on the side of the mountain they were walking up. The colonel or the doctor would hop out, march with them that day, and then spend the night.

They would ask how it was going and interview each of the soldiers, taking extensive notes.

The contrasting styles of the colonel and the doctor amused Paul. He noted that the colonel would jump off his copter while it was still at a hover, assault style, in an exoskeleton, loaded down with tactical gear like he was about to attack the Great Wall of China all on his own. He'd scan the area until he spotted Paul. Then he would stride over and say, "Captain Owens. How you feeling?"

"Fine, sir," Paul would say. "Ain't nothing but a thing."

"You're damn right. How are they doing?" the colonel would ask.

"Good, sir," Paul would answer, nodding his approval. "They're solid."

"Uh-huh," Filson would say, ensuring Paul heard the skepticism in his voice.

The colonel would walk over to 458 and start talking to her. And then, to Paul's chagrin, until the quad copter picked him up the next morning, Filson would spend all his time with the Ōkami. The next time the colonel would speak to Paul was as Paul walked him to his transport drone.

"Good work, Owens," he'd say. "I'll be back soon." Then he'd look around at the betas with a false grimace of doubt and say, "Keep your eyes on these fucking newbies."

And then he'd be gone.

Dr. Musashi, Paul observed, would wait until his copter was on the ground, engines off, auxiliary power unit shut down, before he got off the aircraft. 458 and the rest of the betas would be lined up, just outside the large ducted fans, waiting for him.

Musashi looked tiny stepping off the aircraft into the midst of his powerful eight-foot soldiers. Paul always gave them a little distance then. The doctor would speak with the Ōkami for a few minutes before waving to Paul and walking over.

Then, Paul noted with amusement, Musashi would spend almost every moment with him. At first, Paul thought it was strange. He was not, after all, the newfangled artificial intelligence. But then he realized the doctor was trying to figure out what kind of variables Paul and Kata introduced to his fledgling architecture.

Paul realized the doctor thought he and Kata were the weakest links.

# Chapter Fifty

*Mission Cycle 413*

*Earth Year 2062*

*308,676,096 Kilometers from Earth*

Pain woke Regas up.

Stabbing, incendiary pain as the shattered pieces of his collarbone ground together with each breath.

He tried to steady himself as he lay at the bottom of the traverse, on top of the hab. When he minimized all movement, the pain was tolerable. He clawed through brain fog to remember.

He remembered falling.

*That's right*, he thought. *I fell.*

The spinner had started up suddenly. He'd almost lost his grip. But had held on. Then his weight had started to increase. The pain of clinging to the ladder had grown as the rotational velocity of the spinner had increased. He'd tried to climb down. But couldn't move fast enough. He could only use his left hand. His right ankle hurt too. Nothing like the broken collarbone. But a lot. Was it broken also?

He was getting so heavy.

Then he realized he was going to lose his grip. His strength was fading. He was frightened. He was going to fall, and it was going to be bad. He started to hyperventilate, which made things worse. He clung to the ladder as long as he could.

Then he fell.

He screamed in rage and fear on the way down.

Mercifully, he was knocked out when he landed.

Or had he passed out from the pain?

Blood oozing from a bruise over his left eye suggested a concussion when his head had struck the hab.

Regas screamed as he adjusted his shoulders to get them flatter on the surface of the hab. But it was worth it. The pain was less that way. Bearable.

He lay still for a long time, remembering what he had been trying to do when the spinner had thrown him to the ground.

Owens.

The XO.

Althea.

The Company.

They had to pay.

Regas knew he was dying. It wasn't just his collarbone. Something was wrong internally. So, he knew he was going to die when he saw that Owens had destroyed the hab's medpod.

It would be a relief.

Regas had pulled himself up to the medpod, full of certainty and resolve. Even a few hours in it would have changed his fortune, given him the advantage he needed. The *Odysseus* would probably already be his. Another set of ears on his necklace.

Regas did not understand why they did not just dump the atmosphere from the hab and kill him that way. That's what he would have done.

*Weaklings.*

Maybe they were working on that.

Regardless, Owens had foiled him.

He was going to die. It would take time. But the swelling in his shoulder was already grotesque. He had to take his shoe off because his ankle was so big.

Regas shook his head in disgust at Paul Owens. Pain radiated through his body and he stopped. But the thought continued.

*Fucking weak,* he thought. *Not how I would have done it. I would have killed the fuck out of me when I had the chance. Knife. AB pistol. My bare hands, if I had to. I'd have killed me totally dead before I burned one calorie saving the synthetic bitch.*

Regas looked at the traverse ladder towering above him. He focused on the utility module bulkhead in the distance. He grimaced as he looked at all of the ladder rungs rising over seven hundred feet above where he lay.

The worst part would be getting off the ground. His collarbone and ankle would be punished by almost a full G. The first few rungs would be just as bad.

But if he could get even fifty feet up the ladder, it would get easier. And easier. And easier. Until, halfway up, he would be in the weightless hub. Then he would have to maneuver his broken body 180 degrees so he could withstand the descent to the UM.

*Fuck it,* he thought. *At that point, I can just fall, pass out, and finish it when I wake up. It will be worth it. It will be on my terms, goddamn it.*

Regas lay still for another half hour, gathering his strength and willpower.

Then he moved.

He screamed.

He shrieked.

He felt the damage in his body increase with every millimeter of progress.

The pain caused tears to flow, which enraged him.

His breaths were ragged and shallow, his vision thin and imprecise. He knew he was on the verge of passing out.

"Not until you're there!" he yelled at himself. "Get there, you fucking pussy!"

One rung.

Two rungs.

Three rungs.

It took forever.

He could not remember a time he was not clinging to the traverse ladder in agony. He doubted he had ever existed when he was not in this searing pain.

He rested for a long time in the zero gravity of the hub, gathering strength and resolve and hoping in vain that the pain would subside for a moment.

It did not.

He started down toward the utility module. He floated slowly down, feetfirst, senses straining to detect a gain in momentum.

Soon, he was holding on to the ladder with his good hand. He felt the slight tug and judged himself to have about three hundred feet left to descend.

Fear of falling welled within him.

From where he was now, he could propel himself back to the blissful zero gravity of the hub with a strong yank from his good hand.

No.

Keep going.

Halfway down the ladder, he was in agony again. His collarbone was on fire from the torque and strain of hanging on to the ladder with one hand.

His technique was to take two steps down with his feet, and then use them to support his growing weight while he released his good hand from the ladder and quickly grabbed the next lower rung.

As the centrifugal force strengthened its grip and pulled on Regas harder, the repositioning of his hand to the next lower rung became an excruciating exercise. His entire universe distilled down to the twelve inches of space between each rung.

The lower he got, the more jarring the hand swap became. When his palm struck the lower rung, the impact sent waves of stinging pain throughout his upper body. His vision got blurry for an instant as the sting transitioned to a sharp throb.

When he trusted his eyes again, he stepped lower, focused on the next rung, and prepared himself to do it again.

With less than a hundred feet to go, he screamed at each hand swap. He couldn't stop himself.

With about fifty feet to go, he was drenched in sweat, and his good hand locked up with a cramp.

"No, no, no, no, no, you fuckers," Regas cursed at his knotted fingers. He tried to use the ladder to help stretch them back to straight.

"Come on!" he yelled. "Please."

He could sense the fall coming.

His heart started to race.

"Please," he whimpered to himself, clinging to the ladder with his good elbow. His gnarled and cramped hand laced through the ladder.

His good arm began to tremble at the effort, as did his left leg. He had been putting as little weight as possible on his right ankle, which he was now certain was broken. It made a sickening pop sound at the slightest movement.

He glanced down. The utility module was still so far.

He knew he was going to fall.

"Fuck it!" he yelled.

Regas started moving as fast as he could down the ladder.

He yelled and cursed in pain at the jarring, clumsy descent.

He was going to fall. He knew that. But he wanted to get as low as he could before he lost it.

His hand was welded shut in a cramped fist. He jammed his arm through the rungs, stepped down, yanked his arm out, and jammed above the next lower rung.

He felt his collarbone fragmenting more with each motion.

His hand began to fail him again.

He heard himself wailing in pain.

His right ankle could not support any weight.

He felt himself accelerate and a blissful reduction in torque on his collarbone.

He realized he was falling.

*If I ever wake up again,* Belen Regas vowed as he fell, *I will finish it.*

Then blackness.

# Chapter Fifty-One

*2056 Hours, 11 February 2055*
*Fayetteville, North Carolina*

P ruden called Fiona as soon as he got back to his hotel room just off of Fort Bragg.

"Well?" was all she said when she picked up.

"They are kicking ass," he said. "Combat Corps loves them. The kill chain link is working better than anyone expected, and the extension platforms seem to have stabilized as well."

"Believe it or not, Dr. Musashi gets along great with the colonel they have running the field trial," Pruden told her.

"Thank God," Fiona said with a sigh. "I was convinced that mean old bastard was going to alienate himself from everyone in uniform and get us thrown out."

"He's not that bad, Fiona," Pruden said.

"Whatever," she answered. "Keep going."

"The two officers in the program, both captains, one male and one female, have adjusted well to the architecture," Pruden continued. "I met them both briefly and agree with Dr. Musashi that we got lucky with those two. They are highly competent, adaptable, and, I have to say, amazing physical specimens.

Baddasses, both of them. I'll send you the detailed files as soon as I get online," Pruden concluded. "But I'm telling you, Fiona, there is zero chance we don't get the success milestone payment on schedule."

Pruden smiled as he waited for Fiona to react.

But she was silent.

"You there?" he asked.

"Yes," she said. "I'm just waiting for the rest. The part I give a shit about."

"Oh," Pruden said, frustrated. "Excuse my enthusiasm for the truly innovative work one of our companies is doing. I thought you would also be interested."

Fiona waited.

"Colonel Frank says that, so far, the trial for Spitting Metal is on track to kick off in April," Pruden continued. "He is working through the budget and scheduling process but will have a final approvals and resource allocations in a few weeks."

"A few weeks?" Fiona asked with dread.

Pruden grimaced. Ever since Fiona had returned from Prague, she had been anxious and short-tempered. Pruden wondered whether it would have been better if her brother had refused her, had not agreed to let her use his villa as collateral on Spitting Metal's line of credit.

It confirmed for Pruden what a professor had told him at business school: "It matters where the money is from."

"I'm sorry," Pruden said. "But with these guys, process is everything. We can't speed them up."

Pruden heard Fiona sigh. He waited for her to speak.

"OK," she finally said. "When is the phase-two milestone meeting for Musashi's trial?"

"A month," Pruden said. "Fort Belvoir."

"We've got to leave that meeting with a start date for Spitting Metal," Fiona said.

Pruden nodded as he ran the dates and numbers in his head. They needed the Spitting Metal kickoff payment to hit before the end of May, or they would be in final default with Talisman.

It would be over.

"That timing should work," he said, trying to sound as convincing as possible. But he shrugged to himself, alone in his hotel room, resigned that there was no way for him to speed up the US military, and that Fiona expected him to do just that.

"It must work," Fiona said.

# Chapter Fifty-Two

*2210 Hours, 10 March 2055*
*Fort Bragg*

On the last night of phase two, Dr. Musashi flew out for one of his visits and stayed the night with Paul and his betas. Paul's mood was light. In the morning, all they had was a short march to a nearby mountaintop where the drone copter would pick them up and fly them back to Filson's cantonment. Paul was really looking forward to a shower.

That night, after the doctor had completed his interviews, he and Paul sat by the fire and ate dinner together. The colonel had told Musashi that Paul loved chili mac, so the doctor had brought a few packets with him. He'd even brought Tabasco sauce. Paul was happy.

They ate in silence for a while, staring at the fire. Finally, either Paul's boredom or curiosity got the better of him.

"So, what's your story, Doc?" Paul asked. "How did you end up in the States?"

The doctor took a bite of chili mac without looking at Paul. He scraped the bowl as he slowly chewed, arranging the last bits into a final spoonful. He placed his bowl on the ground and chewed his last bite. When he was done, he wiped his mouth.

As the doctor folded his napkin into a small, precise triangle, Paul thought he was ignoring the question, so Paul just looked back at the fire and tried to relax.

But after the doctor dropped the napkin into his empty bowl, he looked at the fire and said, "I was born in 1975 in Ine, a small fishing village about a hundred and twenty kilometers to the northwest of Kyoto. Ine sits on the tip of the Tango Peninsula, a small finger of land that pokes out into the Sea of Japan and served as a trade route between Kyoto and the Eurasian continent for centuries."

Paul settled back into the rock he was leaning against and continued to stare at the fire as the old doctor spoke.

"When I was five, my father moved to Kyoto to support his family with the higher wage one could earn in the city. He was gone for months at a time. My mother went back to teaching as soon as she could, to make money for the family as well. She worked long hours. So, I was raised by my mother's father.

"Grandfather came from a family of fishermen," the doctor continued. "He had hoped his sons would follow him into the profession, but his wife and two boys were killed by American bombs in the summer of 1945. Only he and my mother survived. My mother was thrown from the house by the blast. She was found by the firemen, unconscious in the mud, twenty meters from the burning house. She was only a few years old and didn't remember any of it. Grandfather survived because he was not there when the village was bombed. He was away fighting in the war.

"After the war, he came home, found his daughter, and went back to fishing. When I was born, he was making his living as a fishing captain on the small boat that his father had built years ago.

"When I was five, he started taking me out on the boat with him each day. I hated it. Grandfather made no allowances for my age. He would show me how to do things once, and then I was expected to perform as well as his two crew members who had been fishing with him since after the war. They looked out for me, though. Making sure I didn't get hurt and helping me with tasks when my grandfather was not looking.

"They were very long days for a child. When we were done, and the boat was properly cleaned and secured, my grandfather and I would walk home. Ine was a small village, and it was not far, but at five years old, my exhaustion was overwhelming. Grandfather had to carry me home each night. I remember being so mad at him for how he treated me on the boat that I did not want him to carry me. But once he picked me up, I fell immediately asleep. The next thing I knew, it was the next morning and he was waking me again to go back to the boat. I would cry as we walked to the dock, dreading the coming day.

"After a year or so working on the boat, though, I was no longer miserable. Then, after another year or so, I was happy. The last year was..."

The doctor hesitated. Paul looked at him. He was gazing at the sky. Paul looked back at the fire.

"I am eighty years old, Paul," he continued. "And I can tell you that, to this day, that last year on the boat with my grandfather was the most joyous year of my life. My heart was full.

"I was twelve years old and part of the crew. I was one with the boat. I could read the ocean. And my grandfather was the center of the universe. In my young eyes, we all orbited him. The crew, the boat, the ocean, and me. The planning, preparation, and process that he demanded, the discipline he enforced, by that last year, it all receded behind rhythms and rituals that felt as natural and certain as the tides. The nets were prepared just so. They went out. They came in. The lines were baited just so. They went out. They came in. The fish came in and were cleaned. The boat was steered. It went out. It came back in. Every day. Each time. The same.

"My grandfather and I were so close, we almost never spoke. We communicated constantly, though. We did so with nods and glances and grunts and shrugs that were invisible to others. Most of the time, though, we didn't even do that. We just knew the other. We just heard the other. The other two crew members would shake their heads. 'You two are weird,' they would say. 'You've got radios in your heads.'

"My mother, though, was jealous. Grandfather and I would make each other laugh at dinner without saying a word. She would demand to know what the joke was, but we were unable to explain it. She never said so, but I believe that was part of her decision that summer.

"When I was twelve, my parents enrolled me in school in Kyoto. My father was home for the weekend when they told me. I refused. I threw a tantrum. I said some very disrespectful things. My mother cried.

"The next day, my grandfather stepped onto the boat early in the morning and found me sleeping in the pilothouse. I woke up that morning to the smell of coffee. My grandfather saw me stirring and poured me a cup. He placed it on the small table in the pilothouse and sat down at the other small chair to have his cup. He did not look at me. I got up and walked to the table. I took the seat across from him and sipped at the coffee. We did not speak. Half an hour later, the crew arrived.

"I stayed on the boat for a week. Grandfather would arrive well before the crew. We would drink coffee in silence together. Then, when we were done, we would set to work preparing the boat. The crew would arrive. And we would be underway. We would go out. We would fish. And we would come back in. After the boat was tied up, my grandfather would leave without saying goodbye. I believed I had escaped. This was my life now. My heart was full.

"After a week, my mother came with my grandfather one morning. I yelled at my grandfather, 'How could you betray me?'

"My grandfather let me yell and then put his arm around me. 'You must go now,' he said to me. 'A good life has many chapters. Our chapter on the boat together is over.'

"'I don't want it to be over,' I said through tears.

"'I don't either,' he said. My grandfather's voice told me there was no hope. My heart, which had been so full, emptied onto the floor. 'I cherish our time together, Grandson,' he said. 'And you will always be welcome back on my crew. But you must go to school now.'

"'Will we have another chapter?' I asked.

"'I don't know,' he said. 'No one can know.'

"I went to school in Kyoto. I made it back to Ine as often as I could and would spend the time on the boat with my grandfather. But it was never the same. It took me a day to get back into the rhythm. Grandfather had to tell me what to do and when to do it. But I loved being with him anyway.

"I worked very hard in school. I applied to MIT in America and was accepted. My parents were very proud. I was excited for my future. For America.

"I spent a week fishing with my grandfather before I left. He was the most talkative he had ever been. He peppered me with questions. About the school I was going to attend. The engineering I would study. He asked me a lot about Boston. He wanted to picture where I would be living, but it was unimaginable to him. He asked about America also. The country he fought many years ago. The country that had killed his wife and sons.

"My parents picked me up at the dock when we returned. My grandfather handed my bag to my parents while I sat at the small table in the pilothouse. Even though I was just eighteen, and a fool, I had the vague sense that I was losing something very special. That I would not see my grandfather again. I did not know what to do. I was frozen with fear and sadness.

"My grandfather returned to the pilothouse. My parents returned to the car to wait. He made coffee and then sat with me. As we sipped on our coffee, I noticed a tear run down my grandfather's cheek. He did not try to hide it.

"'I am so happy for your next chapter, Grandson,' he said after a few minutes. Then I left for America. Grandfather died while I was away at school."

Paul and the doctor spent a long moment in silence, gazing at the flames.

"Thanks for telling me that," Paul finally said.

"Thank you for asking," Musashi said.

*

The next day, after three months of field training with their betas, Paul and Kata finally got back into the cantonment on Fort Bragg. They took much-needed showers, and Dr. Musashi's lab coats crawled all over the soldiers, putting them back together again.

Later, in the evening, Paul and Kata ate dinner in the mess hall. They had not seen each other for months, save for brief flights or mission briefings.

"It is always good to get back, eh?" Kata said. "Warm showers. Warm food. Warm bed."

"Yes, it is," Paul said. "Kind of irritating, though, isn't it?"

"What?" Kata asked, chewing a mouthful of food.

"Colonel Filson," Paul said. "I have to admit that he is, in fact, an evil genius."

Kata, mouth still full, waited for him to continue.

"Out in the mountains, after a few weeks, my legs were smoked."

Kata nodded in agreement.

"One day, I lost my footing and almost fell down a steep drop-off," Paul said. "But Magellan caught me. Grabbed me by my rucksack at the last minute, stopping my fall."

"He was your blind guy, right?" Kata asked. "The one Filson stripped down to infrared?"

"Yep," Paul said. "All he could see were fuzzy blobs. Definitely not enough visual acuity to see me stumble."

"Then how did he know?"

"It was the link," Paul said. "When I talked to Dr. Musashi about it later, he was astounded. He designed the link to be a dependable conduit for the Tokyo Accords kill chain and the structured delivery of tactical and telemetry data. But he thinks the stress of phase two morphed it. It's different now. The doctor and his team are still trying to figure it out."

"Same shit happened to me a few times," Kata said.

"That is what I am talking about," Paul said. "The colonel. The evil genius is doing it again."

"Doing what?" Kata asked.

"Rewiring a bunch of soldiers into a unit," Paul said.

# Chapter Fifty-Three

After a day of debriefing phase two, Colonel Filson gave Paul and Kata a four-day pass. When they got back, they met the new members of their unit and a new phase of training began.

"Each of your units is equipped with a dedicated air component consisting of six QC-10 medium assault quad copters," the colonel said as he led Paul and Kata into the large hangar facility. Dr. Musashi trailed behind them.

"Don't let the word 'medium' fool you. That's just a weight classification. The QC-10 kicks heavy ass," Filson said with an enthusiastic grin. "Particularly these guys that our good doctor has specially modified."

They rounded the corner into the large open space in the hangar and saw the quad copters. There were two groups of six copters on opposite sides of the hangar. "That's Alpha Company," the colonel said, pointing to his left. "And over there is Bravo."

"Oh hell yeah," Kata said with a lusty smile.

Paul smiled at her reaction. Kata was probably the best combat drone pilot in the Combat Corps at that point. And the QC-10s looked like serious combat drones.

The first thing Paul noticed was the large ball turret mounted in the nose. It was a massive combination of sensors and gun barrels and rocket tubes that gave the front end a menacing, insectoid appearance. Then his eyes moved aft to the large, ducted thruster fans, each almost ten meters in diameter. There were two on each side of the thirty-meter-long fuselage, like coiled legs, ready to leap. Finally, a stout utility wing assembly jutted out from between the forward and aft thruster fans. Its gull-wing configuration looked like a powerful insect wing that was about to unfold and propel the beast into the air.

"I've heard about the QC-10s," Paul said to the colonel. "They were just fielding them when we rotated off the Horn."

"Yeah," Kata said, still smiling. "They looked like ballsy aircraft, and I heard they could take a stupendous amount of punishment and keep flying."

The colonel nodded proudly. "You guys have no idea the shit storm I had to walk through to get us a dozen of these things."

Their small fleet was brand new that day. Their surfaces clean, not yet dented, punctured, and stained from combat. The sleek, composite armor skin seemed to be stretched over straining muscle and had been painted a desert-sand color.

"Top airspeed for these beasts is three hundred knots," Filson said, crossing his arms in satisfaction. "They were designed for maximum payload flexibility and will give you a lot of mission optionality downrange."

The colonel led the two Centaurs around behind the Alpha Company aircraft, pointing out their large aft ramps.

"Each one can carry two dozen fully equipped soldierbots," the colonel continued, "enabling you to transport almost your entire wolf pack in just four aircraft. That utility wing has a ridiculous cargo- and munitions-bearing ability."

The colonel pointed as he continued around back toward the front of the aircraft, where Dr. Musashi waited.

"It's one of the elements that makes these machines so damn useful. There is no weapons system in your units that you cannot transport into battle, at a high rate of speed, on the wing, slung beneath, or inside of one of these war birds." Filson turned and looked at the two drooling Centaurs. "Please don't fuck them up."

Paul and Kata looked past him at the aircraft.

"Anything you want to add, Doctor?" the colonel asked.

"Only that these aircraft are Ōkami. They rank high in your wolf pack, just below your betas," Musashi said.

Colonel Filson could see that Paul and Kata were anxious to get closer to their new toys.

"Go introduce yourselves," he said, stepping to the side.

Kata winked at Paul and walked away toward Alpha Company.

Paul walked across the hangar to his group of QC-10s. As he got closer, he noticed the large weapons turret had two smaller, basketball-sized sensor turrets embedded on either side of its top half. Each of the QC-10s tracked his approach with one of these sensor pods.

Paul stepped in front of the nose of the first aircraft.

"Good morning," he said.

"Good morning, sir," the male voice said.

"What is your name?"

"I am Bravo Company Unit One, sir," the aircraft answered.

Paul walked from Unit One's nose toward his left front thruster fan. A soft whirring noise emanated from the small left-side sensor pod as it tracked him. He stopped between Unit One and the next QC-10. The tops of their large thruster fans stood fifteen feet above his head.

"And, let me guess," Paul said to the other aircraft. "You are Bravo Company Unit Two?"

"Roger that, sir," the female voice said.

"What are you going to name them?" the colonel said, walking up behind Paul.

"Name them?"

"Vukovic just named hers the Talons," Filson said.

"Good for her."

"Damn it, Owens," Filson said. "Aircraft this ballsy got to have a ballsy name."

Exasperated, the colonel shook his head at Paul before turning back to the half dozen aircraft.

"Listen up, Bravo Company!" Filson said loudly.

Whirs and clicks emanated from the group as their sensor pods swiveled to view Filson.

"From now on, you are Dragon Flight," he said. "Do you understand?"

"Yes, sir," the aircraft answered in unison.

"This stick in the damn mud standing next to me is Captain Owens," the colonel continued. "He is your commanding officer. Take care of him. He's actually better than he looks."

Paul narrowed his eyes at the colonel.

"The in-head display and neural link will enable you to employ and command your Dragons with your thoughts, just like your betas," the colonel said, turning to Paul with a smile. "Sound good?"

"It does, sir," Paul said. "I'm excited to see what they can do."

"I bet," the colonel said, still gazing at the QC-10s. After a moment, he turned his head back to Paul and said, "But don't be too excited. Integrating the in-head display capabilities is phase three."

The colonel waved toward Dr. Musashi, who was still standing at the doorway of the hangar. "All right, Doctor," he shouted across the huge space. "Send 'em in."

Musashi gave the colonel a thumbs-up and disappeared through the doorway. Paul looked back at the colonel, who smiled at him like a schoolyard bully.

Dr. Musashi came back through the doorway followed by a team of two dozen lab-coated engineers pushing large carts of technical equipment.

"Fuck you, sir," Paul said to Filson as he realized what was about to happen.

"Fuck you too, Captain," the colonel said. He patted Paul on the back and walked toward Musashi and his group of engineers.

"They're all yours," the colonel said. "I want them stripped of all of their advanced avionics and sensing data."

The lab coats pushed their carts past Paul, two to each aircraft. The Dragons' front sensor pods twitched back and forth, trying to track all of them.

"What is happening, sir?" Dragon One said to Paul.

"I've known Colonel Filson a long time," Paul said. "I think he is about to put you through the oldest routine in his book." The two lab coats in front of Dragon One opened their carts. The female engineer pulled out a wrench set, and the male engineer grabbed a large black duffel bag. They walked around the number-one thruster fan to the left-side cargo door.

"Open up, please, Unit One," the engineer said as she stood in front of the cargo door.

Dragon One ignored her.

"Unit One," the engineer said again. "Open your left cargo door now."

Paul looked around. The same standoff was playing out at the side of each of the Dragons. He walked back to the middle of the group.

"Dragons," Paul said. "Open up and let Dr. Musashi's engineers on board."

Six cargo doors slid open, and the engineer teams hopped into the QC-10s.

"Nothing to be afraid of, Dragons," Paul said, chuckling. "You're all about to experience life as a World War I aircraft."

"Pull out anything not required to keep them in the air with their greasy side down," the colonel bellowed from the middle of the hangar. "I want them blind as bats but still able to fly without killing themselves or anyone else."

Paul and Kata met in the center of the hangar as the engineers stripped their aircraft down to the basics.

"How long do you think this phase will last?" Kata asked Paul.

"I don't know," he said. "A month maybe?"

"Asshole," Kata said as they watched Filson walk over to talk to a smiling Dr. Musashi. "I'm surprised Dr. Musashi didn't resist."

"Are you kidding?" Paul said. "They're like brothers these days."

"You mean evil twins," Kata said.

At that moment, Filson laughed at something the doctor said. Musashi smiled and then laughed as well.

Paul and Kata shared a skeptical glance.

"Are your betas doing strange things?" Kata asked Paul.

"Strange how?"

"Strange like noticing stuff," she said.

Paul shrugged.

"For example, I hate it when people talk to me when I am eating," Kata said.

"I know that," Paul said.

"Sure. You know it," she said. "But they don't know it. And I never told them. But I noticed after a few weeks that none of them ever approach me if I am eating. Somehow, they figured this out through observation."

Paul smiled.

"What?" Kata asked, suspicious of his grin.

"Somehow, mine realized…well, the part of the female anatomy I most enjoy." Paul circled his open hands in front of his chest like he was polishing large brass lamps.

"You mean tits?" Kata said as if scolding a schoolboy.

"Yes," Paul said. "You know that tech lab? The computer engineer from Idaho?"

"Yep," Kata said. "I know exactly who you are talking about. Those are huge."

"Well, I guess I look at them a lot."

"No kidding," Kata said with zero surprise in her voice.

"My soldiers must have noticed, because lately I've been getting flashes of them from every angle over our neural link."

Kata burst out laughing.

Several lab coats turned around to look at her, as did Filson, who scowled from across the hangar.

"I know," Paul said without remorse. "But you know how she is always working on them? Leaning over them, plugging something into them to download telemetry or whatever. They get a lot of good shots. 158 is the worst. He sends them so often I started referring to him as Snapshot."

"Classic," Kata said, shaking her head and adopting a saddened tone.

"What?" Paul asked.

"Your team is using Dr. Musashi's life's work, the result of decades of cutting-edge engineering, to transmit pornography," she said.

Paul was silent.

"To their commanding officer," she added.

Paul smiled.

"I love it," Kata added, chuckling.

*

The night after the QC-10s were stripped down, Dragon One was flying across North Carolina at five hundred feet and two hundred knots. Paul was up front with a stopwatch in one hand and a map in the other.

Colonel Filson had taken everything out of the QC-10s except for their magnetic compasses, attitude gyros, and pitot static systems. The Dragons were large airborne versions of blind men with canes, capable only of holding a magnetic heading, an airspeed, and an altitude. They had to get all direction from Paul as the colonel dropped nightly time-on-target missions on them.

Every day around two in the afternoon, the colonel would give Paul and Kata three coordinates each and the times they had to be at those targets. Then they had a couple of hours to plan the flights. They worked on a large folding table in the middle of the hangar, rolling out maps and combing over them with rulers and protractors as the Talons and Dragons watched from their parking areas on either side.

Paul's and Kata's respective targets were always in opposite directions, but they would work together on both routes. The two sets of eyes helped to reduce error among all of the time, distance, and heading information.

Paul and Kata would break for dinner after they'd finished the planning, usually around 1900 hours. Then, as it got dark, they would split up and brief their teams on that night's mission.

The missions were the same for both of them. They flew in formations of six aircraft. When they landed at each target, Paul and Kata would open an envelope the colonel had given each of them prior to takeoff. In the envelope, there was a piece of paper with a single number written on it designating which of their aircraft would lead the next leg. This element of surprise made it important that each aircraft listened closely to the mission briefing.

Paul would sit in front of Dragon Flight and hold up the map as he talked through the mission, the routes, the targets, the times they had to be there, the weather, and the forecasted winds.

Paul made a point to call out what terrain features to look for along the way. The Dragons' sensor pods would shift back and forth from the map to Paul. They would follow his hands as he traced the map. When Paul was done, he would ask the team a few questions to make sure they understood and retained the mission. Then he would go grab his flight gear while the lab coats removed the last of the Dragons' optical sensors.

To start each mission, Paul climbed into the lead Dragon. Once he had strapped himself into the forward-most seat in the front of the drone, he told the team to hover to the far end of the airfield. They would hold position there, ten feet above the ground, while Paul waited for the start time. As the seconds ticked down, Paul would say, "OK, Dragon Flight, first leg is one hundred and thirty-five degrees, one hundred and fifty knots, for thirty-five minutes and seventeen seconds. Checkpoint is a small bridge over a north-south-running river."

"Roger that, sir," the team would respond. "One three five at one fifty for thirty-five seventeen."

"You got it," Paul would confirm. "Takeoff in five, four, three, two, one. Go."

Paul would start his stopwatch and grin. He loved the way it felt as his aircraft accelerated forward. He would crane his neck around to look at each of the other aircraft in Dragon Flight as they all started a gentle climb to the assigned altitude.

Then they would fly the mission with the same instrumentation as a flight of World War I tube-and-fabric, open-cockpit biplanes.

After a month of basic navigation training, they moved on to a month of gunnery.

Kata was surprised when Filson did not restore the aircraft instrumentation for gunnery.

"Come on, sir," she said. "I get hazing us with navigation, but gunnery?"

"You want us to actually hit stuff, right?" Paul added.

Colonel Filson handed them both a grease pencil.

"What's this?" Kata asked, not wanting to hear the answer.

"Works in all types of weather. Never gets jammed by the enemy. Never runs out of power. And is fully customizable," he said, with a smug smile.

Paul and Kata turned the grease pencils over in their hands.

"OK," Kata said. "I give up."

"Sit in the command seat in one of your Talons," the colonel said, feigning irritation. "Fly out onto the range and have it fire its minigun. Lean forward and mark the impact on your canopy with a crosshair."

The colonel made a show of closing one eye and drawing a marksman's X in the air in front of himself.

"Yeah," Paul said. "But the QC-10s can't see that."

"That's right," the colonel said. "That's why you will have to talk them in on every run."

Paul scratched his head and regarded the grease pencil with skepticism.

"Working together as a unit," Filson said, turning to leave. "That is the only way through any of this shit."

# Chapter Fifty-Four

*Mission Cycle 415*

*Earth Year 2062*

*309,049,034 Kilometers from Earth*

"Has he moved at all?" Paul asked the XO as he looked out the large forward window. The hab and utility module alternated into view as they traced their circles on opposite ends of the spinner.

"No. Regas has not moved in almost twenty-four hours."

"Maybe the fall killed him," Paul said.

"I don't think so," the XO said. "His body temperature has not decreased at all. Hahn, by the way, is increasingly difficult to detect. His temperature has almost equalized with the hab's twenty degrees Celsius."

"So, he's dead," Paul said.

"Yes," the XO said.

"I bet Regas was trying to find a way to repair the medpod," Paul said.

"What makes you say that?"

"I think that is what I would be doing," Paul said. "If I am badly wounded, in terrible pain, and there is a medpod available? I'd be trying to figure out a way to get it going again."

"But you said you destroyed it."

"I think I did," Paul said. "I know I tore the shit out of it."

"As far as I know, there are no medpod repair parts in the utility module," the XO said.

"He doesn't know that," Paul said, pushing off the forward window and floating over to the monitors at the captain's station.

Paul stared at the fuzzy image of Regas's body heat lying motionless at the bottom of the traverse, on top of the utility module.

"I think he is going to die right there," Paul said. "Let me know if he moves at all."

"I will," the XO said.

\*

"The last part of training pulled everything together," Paul said, floating tethered next to the medpod, looking through the window at Althea.

"The colonel moved Kata and I around the country with our companies and threw missions at us every day for six weeks," Paul continued.

"First, we focused on getting a feel for how best to integrate the wolf packs into our operations. Then we incorporated the rest of the ground XPs. Then the air XPs. In a few weeks, we were conducting combined-arms operations that only a few years ago would have required an augmented brigade staff to pull off. Kata and I did them on our own.

"Filson also made us flex the self-sustaining capability he was so proud of. For that month, we lived entirely off of the services of our support platoon. The colonel called them the 'F3 Team,' for 'fix, fuel, and feed.'

"The support platoon was led by a squatty humanoid robot I called Chief. Chief was not part of the neural link, but he was an impressive machine. In addition to bossing around the ten repair bots, he was my logistics assistant. His AI was constantly working to optimize our situation. Fuel, ammunition, repair parts, material to feed the 3D printer—it was all he thought about. I included him in every mission plan. I wanted him to be able to anticipate our requirements. He always did.

"As the one human soldier in the unit, I was his only customer for biological food. All of the repair bots were loaded with food-preparation routines, but for over a year and a half, Chief was the only one that ever fed me. It seemed weird at first. But, over time, I came to like it."

Paul smiled. "I never let him know, though. I bitched about whatever he brought me. 'What is this shit, Chief?' I would yell, eyeballing the plate of food he handed me.

"'Sir, that is chili mac,' he would answer.

"'You call this slop chili mac?' I'd ask with disbelief.

"'Yes, sir,' he'd answer.

"'This is terrible!' I would say, pretending to gag as I swallowed.

"'Sir, I am sorry. I will prepare another serving so that…'

"'Fuck no, Chief! Don't make me suffer through another plate of this,' I would say before he walked away. 'I'll just choke this shit down.'

"'OK, sir,' he'd say. 'Again, my apologies.'"

"That is so mean," Althea said with disapproval.

Paul ignored her. "By the end of the training, Chief had learned I was just ribbing him. He realized it was an important part of the military feeding ritual. 'Goddamn, Chief,' I'd say. 'What is this slop?'

"'It's fucking chili mac, sir,' he'd respond with irritation in his voice. 'What does it look like?'

"'This is unidentifiable,' I'd say, angling the plate his way so that he could see.

"'That is the best chili mac in the back forty, sir. You're lucky to have it.'

"'Oh my God!' I said, retching for effect. 'Am I being punished? That is the only explanation I can think of for you feeding me this shit.'

"'You're the expert on shit around here, sir,' he said, turning to walk away. 'If you'd like a plate of that, you don't need me.'

"But the real challenge Chief faced every day was keeping the company fit to fight. The colonel made it hard on him. Every day, Filson would pick one of the Ōkami betas and shoot them."

"He what?" Althea asked.

"I know. It sounds terrible," Paul said. "And by that time in the training,

I didn't like to see it either. These were my soldiers. But the colonel said he'd rather find out the support platoon's limitations then, while we could address them, than downrange on a real-world deployment."

"What did Dr. Musashi say?" Althea asked. "Surely, he protested."

"Nope. By that point, those two had mind-melded. The doctor was all for it. He didn't want his guys to be stuck downrange having to fight with injuries that could not be repaired.

"Each day," Paul went on, "they would pick one of the Ōkami betas and shoot them with something. A rifle, a rocket, a laser. A couple times, they ran over their limbs with a tracked vehicle. The only thing that was really off-limits was a bad shot to the thorax. Their spheres were embedded in an armored chamber in their chests." Paul tapped his heart with his right hand. "They were hard to damage. But they did not want to risk it.

"The expectation was that Chief and his team would have the wounded Ōkami fully operational by sunset. It got pretty ridiculous, though, because the fact was, the maintenance bots really could fix anything. It was amazing.

"In addition to the food, the other aspect of the support platoon dedicated solely to me was the medical pod. It was not as advanced as the ones on the *Odysseus*, but it was capable of just about any surgical procedure. All the Ōkami had to do was keep me alive long enough to get me into it, and the medpod would put me back together.

"Every robot in the unit was competent in basic human first aid. If Kata or I were wounded, they were programmed to render immediate aid, stabilize us, and get us to the medpod. Without this, after all"—Paul tapped the side of his head—"the kill chain was broken. They had no reason to exist. No authority to do what they were made to do.

"The first time the colonel showed me the medpod, he went on and on about it. I could tell he was proud of it and wanted me to feel comfortable that it would actually work. Top and Chief were standing behind me as the colonel spoke. When he finished speaking, he asked me, 'So, do you want it in the leg or arm?'

"'Sir?' I asked, not getting his question.

"The colonel drew his pistol. 'Leg or arm?'

"'What?' I said, backing up.

"Top and Chief stepped in front of me, unsure of what to do but certain they would not let the colonel shoot me. Filson started laughing. He holstered his weapon and shook his head at the war machines in front of him.

"'Just kidding,' he said between chuckles. 'Jesus, Owens. You should have seen the look on your face.' I finally started to chuckle. Soon I was belly laughing. The colonel was as well. Top and Chief looked at each other in bewilderment."

Paul shook his head, smiling at the memory.

"For the last week," he continued, "we conducted numerous operations in various mission profiles: ships underway at sea, assaults on the top floors of skyscrapers, convoy ambushes, airfield takedowns. Filson threw some crazy scenarios at us. And we passed every one. We were ready.

"Our last training mission was a long one that combined our two companies. It took Kata and I a full week to plan and then four days to execute. When we finally got back to Fort Bragg, we were exhausted and hungry. As Kata and I were walking back to the barracks, Colonel Filson drove up in his old jeep with a large deer strapped to the hood.

"'Check it out,' he said, coming to a stop in front of us. 'This guy wandered onto the range and was, sadly, the victim of an accidental shooting.'"

Paul smiled. "Hunting on Fort Bragg was strictly prohibited," he explained to Althea. "North Carolina was super uptight about it. So, Bragg's commanding general was super uptight about it. Intentionally killing game on post was a surefire way to get your ass in a sling. Accidental shootings, though?" Paul shrugged.

Althea shook her head.

"Kata laughed at the sight," Paul continued. "'Wow,' she said with a smile. 'That's a really clean shot to the head.'

"'One unlucky fella, I guess,' Filson said.

"Kata was right. The deer had been taken down by a precise headshot. His meaty body was in perfect shape.

"'Very unlucky,' I said. 'Seems a shame to let his accidental demise be in vain.'

"'Any ideas, Owens?' the colonel asked me.

"'Leave it to me, sir,' I said.

"The colonel helped me string the deer up by its hind legs on a tree behind the containers, and then I went to round up Chief.

"'Come with me, Chief,' I told him, poking my head into the motor pool. I explained everything I did as I field dressed the deer. Chief stood next to me, watching closely. 'You have to be careful not to cut too deep,' I said as I inserted the knife into the deer's belly. 'If you do, you will cut open the gut bag and intestines. That makes the job messier and can spoil the meat. Once the tip of the blade is in position, run it down toward the neck until you meet the breast plate.'

"I worked quickly, confident that Chief's quantumtronic brain was capturing every detail. As I made my way toward the buck's head, the bulge of entrails hanging half out of the animal grew larger.

"'At this point,' I said, pausing to look at Chief, 'all you have to do is reach down inside the deer toward his throat and feel for the windpipe with your knife blade.' The deer's gaping abdomen swallowed my arm as I reached inside down toward the animal's head and felt for the trachea. I severed it and the esophagus with a firm cut.

"'The only thing that's really holding it all now is what's left of the diaphragm,' I said, gripping the fibrous red tissue. I sliced through it, and the mass of entrails fell to the ground with a wet splat.

"Later than night, Kata and I built a fire and cooked the venison slowly. The colonel drank his scotch. Kata and I drank beer. Chief watched me closely. The smell of roasting deer wafted through the cantonment area, luring Dr. Musashi and his team out of their small labs. Finally, Kata couldn't take it anymore.

"'Damn it, Paul,' she said. 'Let's get into it already!'

"'Chief,' I said. 'Come over here.'

"'Yes, sir,' he said, stepping over and leaning in toward the sizzling venison with me.

"'You smell that?' I asked.

"'Yes, sir,' he said.

"'You see that fat bubbling up through the charred surface?'

"'Yes, sir.'

"I pulled out my bayonet and carved a piece of meat. 'See how juicy it is?'

"'Yes, sir.'

"'Now watch this,' I said as I handed Kata my bayonet, the large piece of venison hanging from the blade tip. Vapor rose into the brisk Carolina night as she smiled and placed it in her mouth. Kata closed her eyes and shook her head in slow motion. Grease dripped from her chin. She let out noise somewhere between a moan and a grunt that lasted for about ten seconds.

"'You see that?' I said to Chief, pointing at Kata. 'That reaction means you did it right.'

"Chief nodded. 'I understand, sir,' he said. 'Thank you for the instruction.'

"We stayed out late that night under the stars, eating venison and getting drunk. One of Musashi's lab coats brought out a stack of paper plates. I sat on a beat-up field chair next to the fire roasting deer, carving as everyone cycled by. There was no activity on the ranges that night, so Bragg was quiet.

"The Ōkami betas mingled among us. They were never sure what to do with themselves during periods of leisure like that but seemed to want to be around. When people started showing up for seconds, I asked Chief to relieve me and moved to an old ammo crate on the edge of the firelight. I watched Chief expertly carve servings of venison for folks and sipped from my own flask of bourbon."

"Always the bourbon with you," Althea said.

Paul shrugged.

"I gestured at 458," Paul said, continuing his story. "She walked over and stood next to me. 'Yes, sir?' she asked.

"'I'd like to call you something other than 458,' I said.

"'Yes, sir,' she said."

"Well, look who has a heart," Althea said, her smile glowing inside the medpod.

Paul shook his head at Althea, warning her not to believe it. Then he continued.

"'I would like to call you Top,' I told her. 'Do you know what that means?'

"'No, sir,' she said.

"'Top is an old nickname for a company first sergeant,' I said. 'It's a role that dates back almost two hundred years, to our country's civil war. It means *top sergeant*. It identifies you as a leader. There are many soldiers with the rank of first sergeant in the army. But only very few of them are the top-ranking sergeant in a combat unit. You are fulfilling a special duty. I command Outlaw Company, but you run it. You are my top sergeant.'

"She towered above me as I sat on that ammo crate. Her sleek head bent down toward me as she focused on my words.

"'You good with that name?' I asked her.

"'Yes, sir, I am,' she said, nodding.

"'It is fitting,' Dr. Musashi said. I swiveled on the crate to see him standing behind me. 'I'm sorry, Paul,' he said. 'I was not intending to listen in. I just happened to be walking by.'

"'No problem, Doc,' I said.

"'May I join you?' he asked.

"'Of course,' I said, making room for him on the ammo crate.

"'Thank you,' he said, sitting next to me. 'Top, may I have a word alone with Captain Owens?'

"'Yes, Doctor,' she said as she walked away.

"'Excellent,' he said, gesturing at me with a fork laden with venison.

"'Thanks,' I said.

"'Why the Outlaw Company name?' he asked me.

"'That was my platoon nickname on the Horn,' I told him. 'Figured if got me through that tour, it must be a little lucky.'

"The Doctor nodded as he took his last bite of venison. We sat together in silence as he chewed slowly.

"'What do you think?' Musashi asked me as he placed his empty plate and silverware on the ground next to his feet.

"'About what?'

"'The soldiers. Your unit,' he answered. 'Are you ready?'

"'We're going to find out.'

"He nodded. 'Any ideas where they will send you?' he asked.

"'Just guesses,' I said with a shrug. 'I don't know how you decide where to send an experimental unit. Kata thinks back to the Horn of Africa. Seems like they're sending everything that way these days.' The doctor looked at me with a troubled face. 'I'm just looking forward to a week of leave while they figure it out, Doc,' I said, smiling, trying to change the subject.

"Kata laughed loudly across the fire, likely at one of her own jokes. I glanced her way. A couple of young male engineers surrounded her, captivated by the exotic warrior queen. I had a sense of what was on Kata's mind. We were back to war soon, after all. The doctor and I shared a glance.

"'I will miss our time together, Paul,' he said. 'But I am excited for your next chapter.'

"'Me too, Doc,' I said. 'And, I don't want you to worry. We're ready. You've done a good job with the Ōkami. The kill chain is solid.' The doctor looked at me for a long moment. 'What is it?' I asked him.

"'Paul,' he finally said. 'I don't know what it is like for you and Kata. I can only try to imagine. I have never been to war.'

"I was surprised by his comment. In almost a year of training, the doctor and I had never discussed 'war.' We spent endless hours discussing tactical situations, strategic trade-offs, and kill chains. But never 'war.'

"'You must remember that you are not just at the center of a communications architecture,' Musashi continued. 'It is also a moral architecture. And the architecture needs a human to be a moral system, to be a good system, not just a kill-chain-compliant system. Human leadership and values are the key.'

"I looked at the doctor, surprised by the sudden earnestness in his voice, and the high ethical stakes he was establishing for me. I was about to respond, probably to crack wise to ease the tension, when another voice surprised me.

"'Hey there,' the hot engineer chick said over my shoulder. I turned to look at her," Paul said with a reminiscing smile. "God, they were nice tits."

Althea rolled her eyes.

"I turned back to the doctor, but he had already grabbed his dirty plate stood up. He extended a hand. I shook it. He turned and left. I looked at the hot engineer chick and gestured at the spot on the ammo crate the doctor had just left. She smiled and sat down next to me."

Althea raised an eyebrow.

"Yeah," Paul said, nodding. "I knew she thought I was weird. And it was clear things were not going to progress further than chatting by the fire." He ran his hand along his augmentation scars. "But it was a good way to spend that last night."

Paul and Althea looked at each other through the medpod window.

"Paul?" the XO said over the intercom.

"Yes? What is it?"

"Regas," the XO said. "He is on the move again."

# Chapter Fifty-Five

*0845 Hours, 17 May 2055*
*Fort Belvoir, Virginia*

"This place looks more like a college campus than an army base," Fiona said as she and Pruden walked from their car toward the Military Acquisition Corps headquarters building on Fort Belvoir.

Green grass blanketed the facility beneath leafy trees that stood in front of wide red-brick buildings.

"Yeah, it's an old one," Pruden said to her. "And what they do here is more science and business than military."

Fiona and Pruden walked up the steps and between the large columns of the headquarters building. They were both excited.

A captain met them at the door.

"Good morning, Miss Malloy," he said. "Good to meet you. I am Captain Perry. I'll escort you and Mr. Pruden to the meeting."

"Good morning, Captain," Fiona said, stepping through the door. Pruden followed close behind.

"I've already checked you through security," the captain said. "So, if you'll put these name tags on, we can head on in to the meeting room."

Captain Perry led them past security and down a long hallway to a large meeting room. Two dozen uniformed personnel were milling about in the room, most clustered around a tall full bird colonel.

"Ah, Miss Malloy," the tall colonel said as he walked over to shake her hand. "I'm Colonel Frank, program manager for AI Combat Systems. It is good to finally meet you in person."

"Good to meet you, sir," Fiona said. "I am excited to be here today." She shook the colonel's hand and smiled. During their meeting prep, Pruden had called Colonel Frank "the billion-dollar man" because of the budget he controlled. He could single-handedly save or doom Fiona's fledgling companies.

"You should be," Frank said. "Your team should be very proud."

"Good to see you too, Martin," the colonel said, shaking Pruden's hand. "Can I get you guys a cup of coffee or water?"

"Coffee would be great," Fiona said. Pruden nodded.

Frank turned to the captain. "Perry, go get Malloy and Pruden a cup of coffee." Colonel Frank then pointed at the large conference table. "Please make yourselves comfortable while I try to get all these damn engineers pointed in the right direction."

"Shit," Fiona mumbled to Pruden as Colonel Frank walked back to the gaggle of engineers. "A lot of people."

"Yeah," he said. "This is a big deal."

Fiona's phone buzzed. She pulled it out of her pocket and read a text from Eugene.

*Today is the day, right?*

*Yep,* she texted back. *And it is already going well,* she continued, hoping her exaggerations would ease his worry.

*I'll be so glad when we are through this,* Eugene wrote back. *You feel good about it?*

"Excuse me, Miss Malloy!" Colonel Frank said from across the room. "I'm sorry, but no cell phones are allowed. Captain Perry should have told you that."

The colonel glared at Perry, who was almost done preparing coffee for Fiona and Pruden. The captain nearly jumped out of his shoes to get to Fiona before Colonel Frank did.

"These meetings are classified as top secret," Frank said, beating Perry to Fiona and holding out his hand.

"Sorry, sir," Pruden said, handing the colonel his phone. "I know better."

Fiona glanced at Eugene's anxious unanswered text on her phone.

"Miss Malloy," Colonel Frank said. "I'm sorry. This is one of the things us military folks are really uptight about."

"No problem, Colonel," Fiona said, handing him her phone. "I apologize."

"It's not your fault," Frank said. "Captain Perry was responsible for you."

Colonel Frank turned and handed the phones to the now-trembling Captain Perry.

"Secure these phones, Captain, and then bring these two their coffee," Frank growled before turning to corral the rest of the engineers.

Fiona forced herself to share an amused glance with Pruden.

She then winced as she thought of Eugene waiting for a text from her. She tried to put her brother out of her mind. She would be able to call him with good news after the meeting.

Captain Perry returned with two cups of coffee and, after a few more minutes of introductions and handshakes, Colonel Frank started the meeting.

"OK, team," he said to the room, cutting through the multiple conversations. All heads swiveled toward the colonel. "We've got a lot to get through today, and I have to be at the Pentagon for a staff meeting at noon. The bird will be here to pick me up at 1130 hours sharp."

He looked at his watch.

"That gives us three and half hours to get through five hours of information. Let's get started."

A shuffle of chairs ensued. Within seconds, everyone was seated facing Colonel Frank.

"Thank you," he said, still standing. "The purpose of this meeting is to review the progress of our two ongoing AI-combat-system evaluations we have underway with Miss Malloy's companies. I want to leave here, as I am sure

Miss Malloy does, with clear agreement regarding milestones and what comes next."

Colonel Frank looked around the room and then took his seat. An aide handed the colonel a thick three-ring binder full of hundreds of tabbed pages. He muttered thanks and opened the tome to the first page.

Two aides entered the room, one pushing a large cart piled high with additional binders. They circled the room slowly, handing each of the attendees one of the large binders.

"Please open your project binder to page seven," Colonel Frank said to the room as he put on his reading glasses.

Fiona's heart sank as he flipped through her binder.

"Oh Jesus," she muttered, leaning over to Pruden. "Three hundred pages?"

"No shortcuts with these guys," he whispered back. "Might as well strap in and make the best of it. Remember, there's millions of dollars on the other end of this meeting."

"We're going to start with the analysis of field trial phase two," Colonel Frank said to the room.

The parade of charts and graphs and schematics pounded Fiona as she tried to stay engaged. Pruden did most of the talking for them, and the meeting seemed to go well. Thoughts of Eugene nagged at her. She reached for her phone to text him more than once, only to remember it was not in her pocket.

Three hours later, Colonel Frank looked at Fiona and said, "Congratulations, Miss Malloy, I am declaring phase two a success and authorizing the milestone payment of fifty million dollars, as well as immediate planning and preparations for combat trials."

The room applauded.

Fiona nodded and smiled as she nervously flipped through the last sections of the binder.

"What the fuck?" she said, leaning into a beaming Pruden.

"What is it?" he asked.

"There is nothing about Spitting Metal in here," she hissed at him. "Nothing!"

Pruden flipped through the last pages of his binder.

Fiona was right. There was nothing about the proof-of-concept trial that was supposed to begin this year. Fiona had been counting on the milestone payment from this proof of concept to save Spitting Metal and Mio Posto from the lenders.

"Um, sir?" Pruden said to Colonel Frank.

"Is there a problem?" Frank responded. "I thought you guys would be happier."

"Oh, sir, we are very excited. Trust me," Pruden stammered as Fiona nodded beside him. "On the matter of Spitting Metal's proof of concept, though," he continued. "Are we not going to discuss the start date and payment milestones for that today?"

"No," the colonel said, closing his binder and looking at his watch.

Fiona's breath quickened.

"No?" Pruden said.

"No," the colonel repeated, standing up and pointing at Captain Perry.

Captain Perry left the room as the colonel began putting things into his satchel.

The sounds of an approaching helicopter penetrated the room. Fiona tried to maintain control.

"Sir, we don't understand," Pruden said. "That trial is supposed to begin in a month."

"Did you guys not get the email?" Colonel Frank asked, suddenly irritated.

Fiona's and Pruden's blank faces told him what he needed to know.

"Did we not send them the email?" he demanded of the staff officers standing next to him.

"Shit," the colonel said after the staff officers exchanged a series of shrugs and blank faces. "I apologize, Miss Malloy and Mr. Pruden, but the Spitting Metal trial has been scheduled for next fiscal year."

"What?" Fiona shouted.

The anger in her voice froze the room.

Colonel Frank, not used to hearing that tone of voice, cocked his head and put down his satchel.

"Excuse me, Miss Malloy," the colonel said.

"You can't do this," she continued, eyes fixed on Colonel Frank, pleading. "It has to move forward. It has to. That kind of delay would… It would… You can't do this!"

Pruden put his hand on Fiona's shoulder and interjected. "I'm sorry, sir," he said. "It's just that this is news to us, and we've been working very hard to get Spitting Metal ready for their trial. We have, frankly, dedicated enormous resources that we would have directed elsewhere had we known about this schedule change. I'm sure you can understand."

His hand still on Fiona's shoulder, Pruden felt her trembling.

He glanced at her and tried to give her the signal to calm down. But her eyes darted around the room in panic.

Colonel Frank regarded Fiona. His shoulders relaxed. He had been doing this long enough to have seen it before. The desperate technology company just one step ahead of their bank, shareholders, or whoever it was that had funded them. He didn't understand that life. But he knew that, back in his operational days, he had been the author of many a desperate tactical plan. Plans that a slight shift in the winds of fate would have reduced to bloody disaster. His reckoning never came. But he knew that made him lucky. Not good.

"We are still very excited about Spitting Metal's potential, Miss Malloy," Colonel Frank said. "It's just a schedule and budget thing. Our wheels turn slowly here in the federal government."

The colonel watched his words hit Fiona like bullets. Her reaction seemed out of whack to him.

"Should I be concerned about Spitting Metal's financial health?" Colonel Frank asked.

"No," Fiona said in a calm and decisive voice. The colonel's direct question reeled her back in. Time to bluff.

"It's just frustrating, Colonel Frank," she said, crossing her arms. "As Martin said, we've dedicated a lot of resources to Spitting Metal. If I had known you guys were going to delay us, I would have focused those resources on Musashi.

We'd be further down the road there. I just hate inefficiency and missed opportunity."

Fiona stared at the colonel.

He stared back at her.

"Thank you, sir," Pruden said, breaking into the standoff. "Can you give us any more insight into the potential schedule?" Pruden wanted to get every scrap of information he could get out of the closing minutes of this meeting. The sound of the helicopter vibrated the windows, and wind swirled in the courtyard where it was landing.

"We'll have a kickoff meeting for that project in six to nine months," Colonel Frank said with a smile as Captain Perry came back into the room. "Then I would expect the first milestone execution about six months after that. The bottom line is that we will move sequentially. The Ōkami are my priority right now. I want to get a good look at their combat trials first, then we'll get serious about Spitting Metal."

"Sir, your bird is landing," Perry said.

*A year!* Fiona thought in despair. She forced herself to stand straight and still, though her knees were weak and she started trembling again.

"Good," Colonel Frank said. He nodded to Pruden and Fiona and left without shaking their hands. Most of the military engineers followed him out.

Fiona sat down in a daze with a look on her face that Pruden had never seen before.

"I'll walk you two out," Captain Perry said.

"Thank you," Pruden said as he pulled on Fiona to get her started out of her chair.

Captain Perry gave them their phones back at the door, and they said goodbye.

"Great meeting," the young officer said with a well-meaning smile. "Congratulations."

The roar of Colonel Frank's bird taking off drowned out the sound of Pruden saying, "Thank you." The dark shape rose from behind the building and accelerated away.

They sat in silence as the car drove them to the airport.

Fiona held her phone in her hand. She stared at it but had not switched it on yet. She was scared to. She did not know what to say to the texts from Eugene that waited for her.

Pruden looked at Fiona. "We'll figure something out," he said to her, not believing it.

"Musashi and his fucking Ōkami," Fiona mumbled without looking up from her phone.

"This is solvable, Fiona," Pruden tried again. "We'll find a way forward. We always do."

"I don't know how," she said. "We've got one, maybe two, months of runway with Talisman. Then we're done. We won't be able to make the payments. We'll lose the business, and I will be ruined. Bankrupt."

Fiona didn't say the rest. That Eugene would lose Mio Posto. And she would lose Eugene.

She turned on her phone.

It buzzed as it registered new text messages from Eugene.

*Hello?* the first one said after she had not responded to his last.

*You must be in the meeting.*

*Please call me right after.*

*I can't wait to hear the good news!*

*Love you.*

# Chapter Fifty-Six

*Mission Cycle 415*

*Earth Year 2062*

*309,725,034 Kilometers from Earth*

Regas lay on his back on the bottom level of the utility module, holding his prize to his chest with his left hand. A pressure-suit helmet lay on the ground next to his head.

Dried blood from a broken nose covered his face. The fall to the utility module had smashed it flat. His right eye was swollen shut, and he wondered if his cheek had been fractured in the fall as well.

It didn't matter.

He'd made it.

When Regas had recovered consciousness after his fall to the utility module, he was disoriented. It seemed to take forever to figure out where he was. But when he did remember what he was doing and why, he started moving.

The journey from the bottom of the traverse into the utility module and down to the lowest level was hell.

But he made it.

Soon, he could rest.

He tried to get his breathing under control and prepared his mind for what he had to do next.

"What the hell is he doing?" Paul wondered aloud on the bridge. He had come straightaway when the XO had alerted him to Regas's moving.

"I don't know," the XO said. "But I don't like it. I think it is time to kill him, Paul."

"I think you are right," Paul said.

Paul and the XO watched Regas's slow progress to the lower level of the hab as they planned Paul's attack. Rather than venturing back out into the void, and given Regas's reduced threat due to injury, Paul decided to go through the tube to the hub. There, an IR bot would meet him and cut the bulkhead, which had been welded shut, open with a laser. Then Paul would go to the utility module and kill Regas.

They had just completed their planning, and Paul was donning his pressure suit when Regas keyed the radio in the helmet he had found.

"Owens," Regas yelled at the helmet. "Hey, Owens, you fucking jigsaw, you there?"

Paul stopped working on his pressure suit, surprised to hear Regas's voice. He moved toward the large window.

The spinner turned over a kilometer away while the IR bots patrolled the *Odysseus's* long hull below the bridge.

"Owens!" Regas called again. "I'm talking to you, you son of a bitch!"

"Shall I put you through to him?" the XO asked.

"Sure," Paul said. "Let's hear what he has to say."

"Channel is open," said the XO.

"Regas, this is Owens," Paul said. "What do you want?"

Regas smiled.

A rush of adrenalin filled his veins, dulling his pain.

*Almost,* Regas thought.

"I just want you," Regas said, excitement building in his voice, "that synthetic bitch of yours, the XO, and the Company to know that it was me who fucking killed you. That it was me, Belen Regas, who won in the end!"

Paul was not sure how to respond. He watched the utility module come into view in the distance, rotating slowly around the hub. He was about to tell the XO to shut off the channel and ignore the jackass when Regas interrupted him.

"See you in hell, Jigsaw!" Regas yelled over the radio.

Paul rolled his eyes on the bridge as Belen Regas put the hand-grenade pin in his mouth and pulled it out. He opened his hand to let the striker lever fly off and then held the grenade to his chest.

The striker lever clinked across the floor as the grenade's internal fuse cooked off.

"Fuck this idiot, XO," Paul said with disdain back on the bridge. "I'm going to—"

Paul was interrupted by a violent jolt that ran through the *Odysseus* as the utility module disappeared in an explosion of gas, fire, and torn metal.

A loud, high-pitched grinding sound pierced Paul's ears as the *Odysseus* shook and lurched from side to side.

Paul flinched as small pieces of debris struck the forward window inches from his face and bounced off. He watched a big spinning piece of metal strike an IR bot a hundred meters forward of the bridge, cleaving it in half. The sparking halves and the spinning projectile burrowed into the *Odysseus*'s hull in a shower of sparks. Loud clangs echoed though the bridge as larger debris started striking the superstructure.

Paul's eyes watched a wave of damage roll back over the ship. His brain struggled to grasp the chain reaction kicking off a kilometer to his front on the nose of the *Odysseus*.

Pieces of the disintegrated utility module continued to dig into the hull. There were too many impacts to count. Several explosions erupted across the length of the old girl's forward hull.

The spinner, now hopelessly out of balance, held on to the habitat module as it continued to rotate. But the hub was tearing itself apart. The gears were not designed for so wildly an imbalanced spinner. They began to seize.

Shock waves from the seizing hub traveled up and down the *Odysseus*'s hull as the habitat module tried to continue rotating.

A hundred meters aft of the hub, the extreme asymmetric loads were too much for the *Odysseus*'s hull. Trusses and structural plates, designed to withstand crushing longitudinal acceleration, snapped under the torsion induced by the flailing spinner.

Another violent jolt radiated through the ship.

A deafening screech rang through the bridge.

Paul watched the damaged front section start to bend back on itself under the ship. It was pulled down by the imbalanced spinner, which still clung to the circling habitat module.

If Paul had seen the looming impact, he would have braced and warned Althea.

It wouldn't have helped.

The habitat's angular velocity at the end of the spinner combined with the momentum of the bending hull section as it folded back. The hab broadsided the *Odysseus*, striking the ship's port side at over two hundred kilometers per hour. Gas and fire engulfed the *Odysseus*'s hull.

The impact snapped off another forward section of the *Odysseus*'s hull and kicked off multiple secondary explosions.

The walls of the bridge seemed to move back and forth around Paul as the old girl pitched and yawed.

"Paul!" the XO said. "It is time for you and Althea to get into pressure suits."

Paul agreed. Strange forces tried to push him into the corner of the room, and he struggled to get out of the bridge. He wanted to get to Althea. A decompression event seemed certain.

Huge pieces of the *Odysseus* and dislodged cargo were now slamming into the rest of the ship. The impacts and secondary explosions caused more damage, ejected more large debris, and fed the destructive chain reaction.

The old girl was tearing herself apart.

"What is going on?" Althea yelled as Paul pulled himself into the medbay.

"I think Regas blew himself up," Paul said, grabbing a handhold near the medpod. "It set off a shit storm on the *Odysseus*!"

"Blew himself up?" Althea asked. "How?"

"Doesn't matter," Paul said. He pulled his head near the medpod window. "I'm sorry. I know you are not done. But you need to get in a suit just in case."

"Roger that," Althea said.

Paul began the opening procedure and noted that the treatment time read fourteen days.

"Hopefully we can get you back in when things stabilize," he said as the medpod's clamshell top opened.

A large shudder passed through the bridge, accompanied by the earsplitting howl of metal.

"Yeah," Althea said as she pushed herself out of the pod. "I won't hold my breath for that."

Althea slid her naked body into the pressure suit while Paul held her helmet and finished configuring his own suit. They drifted into the rear corner of the room.

Once they were both suited with green indications, Paul radioed the XO.

"XO," Paul said over his helmet radio. "I'm sure you are busy, but can you give us a status report?"

"The chain reaction set off by Regas caused extensive damage," the XO said. "The IR bot fleet is fully deployed, fighting multiple fires and trying to clear the more dangerous debris away from the ship. The *Odysseus* is unstable at the moment and is turning around her lateral, longitudinal, and vertical axes."

"Are we in danger?" Althea asked.

"Hard to say," the XO said. "But I recommend you two go to the bridge. Despite appearances of the large window, it is one of the most structurally robust sections of the ship."

"Roger that," Paul said. He tugged Althea behind him.

"Oh my God," Althea whispered when they got to the bridge and looked out the window.

The forward end of the *Odysseus* looked like a cigar that someone had rubbed out on their heel. Instead of a long, slender structure that extended for over a kilometer, Paul and Althea now looked down on a bent and battered hull that terminated five hundred meters from the bridge in an angry blossom of burned and bent metal. A dense cloud of debris surrounded the *Odysseus*. IR bots moved back and forth, pushing the larger pieces away from the ship.

To the starboard side, at the ship's two o'clock, the large hull section amputated by the hab's impact drifted away, trailing debris and cargo.

Large cargo containers, jarred loose by the violence, wandered slowly away from the *Odysseus* at various angles of departure. There were too many to count.

Althea grabbed Paul's suited hand as they floated in front of the window.

"What's going to happen to us, Paul?" she asked.

"I don't know," he said.

*And I guess I'll never get to finish translating that stupid book,* he couldn't help thinking.

# Chapter Fifty-Seven

*0941 Hours, 25 May 2055*
*New York City*

F iona steeled herself as she walked into Talisman Partners LLC.

She was about to do something she had never done before. She didn't know exactly how to approach it. But she had to succeed.

She was walking into Talisman to beg.

She needed more time.

Fiona stood in the lobby and looked at the same velour chairs she and Pruden had sat in years ago. She thought of her cavalier pride back then and wanted to vomit. She had risked too much.

They made her wait almost forty-five minutes. She refused to sit. She paced back and forth, reciting her speech, the one she hoped would buy her the time she needed, the one she hoped would save Mio Posto.

"Miss Malloy?" the receptionist finally said. "Would you follow me, please?"

Fiona followed her down a long hall. At the end of the hallway, the receptionist opened a pair of French doors, and Fiona walked into a small meeting room where her grandfather sat at the end of an oval table. The senior partner of Talisman, Buck Dorrity, stood behind Robert Malloy II, smiling.

"What the fuck?" Fiona said.

"Such language," her grandfather said with a straight face.

"You scheming asshole!" Fiona yelled, pointing at Dorrity. "I'm going to sue this place to the ground for violation of our nondisclosure!"

Dorrity laughed. "But, sweetheart," he said, "you have no money to sue us with. That's why you are here."

Fiona's arm dropped to her side. She looked at her grandfather and then back at Dorrity. She took a deep breath and stood as straight as she could under the weight of her crumbling world.

"What now?" she asked her grandfather.

Robert Malloy II leaned forward in his chair and, after a hint of a glance over his shoulder at Dorrity, pointed at the door.

Dorrity nodded and left the room.

Fiona's grandfather gestured for Fiona to sit.

She took a chair at the opposite end of the table.

Her grandfather stared at her for a long moment before speaking.

"You are a prideful and careless little bitch, you know that?"

Fiona did not respond. She looked at him with a blank face she hoped did not betray her emotions.

"Did you really believe your flimsy NDA would prevent them from coming to me? That they would hold your confidence more dear than earning favor with me?"

Fiona sat in silence.

"Did you really believe that I was not aware of Determined End States?"

Fiona looked at her feet to hide her surprise and disappointment he knew that name.

"Did you really think you could hide your activities from me?" he asked in disbelief.

Fiona lifted her eyes and glared at the old man.

"From me!" he yelled.

Fiona started in her chair as her grandfather struck the table with his hand. He was on his feet and pointing at her with his gnarled fist and bony finger.

"Prideful, careless, ignorant little bitch!" he yelled in a voice Fiona was sure everyone on the floor could hear.

Fiona trembled. She trembled with rage, sadness, embarrassment, and despair. And with fear. Because as bad as this moment was, she dreaded having to tell Eugene she had lost Mio Posto.

But she kept glaring at the old man. She would not give him the satisfaction of seeing her tears or fear or pain.

Her grandfather sat down slowly. He leaned back in his chair and said, "Why?"

Fiona hesitated.

"Answer me, girl," he said. "Why did you hide this from me?"

"Because I knew you would try to control it," she said, realizing it was over and there was nothing more to lose. "And I despise you. I despise our family. I wanted to be free. And I wanted Eugene to be free too."

"Oh yes," her grandfather said. "The gay boy. Of course. How could I forget. Always a pair, you two were. It makes no sense to me, though, what you have done," he said. "You were both millionaires. You were free. And yet you risked it all to achieve…what?"

"No ties. True freedom," she said. She knew it sounded stupid. She didn't care.

Her grandfather tilted his head as he regarded her.

"That's it?" he asked.

"Yes."

"I don't believe it," he said.

"I don't care."

"I see that you believe it. But I don't."

Fiona shrugged to make it clear she did not care what he believed. But she had to know.

"What did you do?" she asked him.

"I made a deal with Talisman," he said. "Your debt is to me now."

Fiona stopped herself from gasping. She willed herself not to shake. She took a deep, even breath and placed her hands on the table.

"So, what now?" she asked.

"That depends."

"On what?"

"On what you are willing to do," he said.

She waited for him to continue.

"Are you willing to call your gay boy brother and tell him to vacate his grimy little villa immediately, that its new owner is planning to bulldoze it to the ground?"

Fiona blinked.

"No?" her grandfather asked.

"Then are you willing to do what it takes to make Spitting Metal realize the full potential you saw in it in the first place?" he asked her.

"Yes," she said without hesitation. "I would do that."

Her grandfather paused. He leaned forward in his chair. "I can't tell," he said. "I am usually quite a good judge of people. But right now, at this moment, I cannot tell if you are willing."

"I am."

"I don't know," he said. "I don't know if you know what I mean. I don't know if you know what it will take. I am not talking about running Spitting Metal more efficiently, or finding synergies, or improving on its core competence, or any of the other useless high-concept bullshit you spent too much money learning at Harvard," he continued.

"I'm talking about sticking your arm up to your shoulder into the stinking, convulsing birth canal and ripping that screaming, bloody, shit-covered fetus out into the world. And then, while it lies on the floor in its own piss and afterbirth, are you willing to kill anything that comes near it? To protect it like a bloodthirsty she-wolf? To kill food for it to eat? And to keep killing until it can walk, then run, then kill and live on its own?"

He looked at her.

"Because the world is the same everywhere for everyone," he continued. "Nothing lives without killing something else. You don't get a pass because you are a Malloy. If you take this path, you will face your moment, the time when you will be shown how far you have to go to get what you want. And then you will have to do it," he said. "Or I will finish you. And your gay boy brother. For good."

"I will," she said. "I'll do it."

"We'll see," her grandfather said, standing up. "You have twelve months from today."

Fiona sat at the table alone for a long time after her grandfather left.

# Chapter Fifty-Eight

*Mission Cycle 416*

*Earth Year 2062*

*310,542,336 Kilometers from Earth*

"Y ou can remove your pressure suits, Paul," the XO said. "The bridge, at least, has been stabilized. Its power generation and life-support systems were not damaged, and the maintenance boss has restored its hull integrity."

"Thanks," Paul said with relief.

Fifteen hours was a long time to spend in a pressure suit. He and Althea had spent almost all of that time floating in the bridge, watching the massive emergency repair effort through the large window. Paul had not said so, but it had looked futile. Regas had crippled the old girl.

"How is the rest of the effort going, XO?" Paul asked as he and Althea took off their pressure helmets.

"Hard to say at this point," the XO said. "The inspection-and-repair bots were not designed for situations like this. The damage Regas inflicted would challenge an entire orbital depot. And even they would not attempt what we have undertaken until all fires had been extinguished and other dangerous situations resolved.

"Nonetheless," the XO continued, "the maintenance boss is driving his team as hard as he can. Every IR bot is either out actively repairing the *Odysseus*, in refuel, or being repaired themselves. As a result, they are holding the *Odysseus* together and keeping the fires at bay. But it is not a sustainable effort. Given the exigency of the situation, the maintenance boss has authorized high-risk activities. The IR bots are taking a lot of damage themselves. We just don't know if they will be able to get control of the situation before they are depleted."

"How many fires are still burning?" Paul asked in a weary voice.

"At least half a dozen."

"I don't suppose there is anything I can do to help?" Paul asked.

"I'm afraid not," the XO said. "And I would object to you leaving the bridge. It is too dangerous anywhere else on the *Odysseus* at the moment."

Paul sighed and turned toward the large forward window. The *Odysseus* was shrouded in debris and venting gas. IR bots flew back and forth, too many to count, as they shoved debris clear of the ship or transported repair materials to a repair site. He counted two large fires that he could see, and wondered where the others were. Paul was about to ask the XO about the other fires when he spotted an IR bot pushing a damaged comrade away from a repair site.

The pair of IR bots flew perpendicular to the *Odysseus* a few hundred meters forward of the bridge. The rescuer had its arms fully extended, seeming to cradle the slightly smaller, damaged IR bot. Despite the distance, Paul could see that the front end of the damaged IR bot had been crushed and at least one of its utility arms severed. Sparks leapt out of the smashed bot, trailing behind the pair. When they had cleared the side of the *Odysseus*, the rescuer maneuvered them down under the ship, likely toward the hangar.

Paul turned away from the window and looked at Althea.

"How about the medpod, XO?" Paul asked. "Is it operational?"

"Yes, Paul. As long as the bridge has sufficient power, it is fully operational."

Paul looked at Althea.

She shook her head.

"You have to, Althea," Paul said, pushing off the floor toward her. "We don't know how long the thing is going to continue working."

"I agree with Paul, Althea," the XO said. "You should get into the pod immediately."

Paul gestured at the passage down to the medbay.

"Let's go," he said.

"Fine," she said. "But you know the price."

"I've got nothing else to do," Paul said, taking one more look at the chaos outside of the forward window.

# Chapter Fifty-Nine

*0139 Hours, 9 June 2055*
*Forward Operating Base Stalwart*

It took a formation of six heavy drones to deploy Paul and Kata, their betas, two hundred soldierbots, and all of their extension platforms to the South American continent.

They landed after midnight. A slight breeze blew the sixty-degree air around the busy airfield on Forward Operating Base Stalwart.

FOB Stalwart, South America's version of Resolve, was a large operating base just outside of the city of Cali in southwest Colombia. With easy access to the nearby Pacific Ocean and the natural defensive feature of the Andes Mountains running south to north through the country, it was a valuable and strategic facility.

Anti-aircraft and other defensive equipment ringed the massive airfield. Squadrons of heavy drones sat like resting athletes as far as the eye could see. The lights of incoming aircraft stacked up behind each other for miles in a straight, stairstepping line that disappeared into the clouds almost twenty miles to the north.

Paul and Kata noticed another similarity to Resolve.

"Fucking smoothies," Kata said, hands on her hips as she looked around at the ground crew that met them.

"What did you expect?" Paul said.

"What is a 'smoothie,' sir?" Paul's first sergeant asked as they walked to the second heavy drone.

"Useless folds of skin wrapped in a military uniform," Kata answered.

Paul chuckled and nodded at his first sergeant, who looked at him for confirmation, then he said, "Top, secure the heavies for the night. We'll start the download in the morning."

"Roger that, sir," she said.

*

The next day, Paul and Kata left their first sergeants in charge of the off-loading and pre-operational checks while they reported to Lieutenant General Schofield's headquarters deep in the interior of Stalwart.

The three-star general commanded all coalition forces in South America. The first thing they noticed was that he was a smoothie.

Most generals were, of course. The Centaur program had not been spun up for very long, and most of the current senior officers were already field grades when it got going. Ninety-five percent of the Centaur billets were captain and below.

But Paul and Kata still exchanged disappointed glances as they walked into one of the most important combatant commands in the US military and greeted a general and his staff without another Centaur in sight.

"Captains Owens and Vukovic reporting for duty, sir," Paul said, standing at attention with Kata in the doorway to the briefing room.

"Welcome," General Schofield said, returning the salute. "Come in and meet the team."

Schofield's briefing room was a small multimedia setup with two dozen seats. The four rows of seats were laid out stadium style, with the rear row sitting well above the front. The general and his senior staff stood in front of the first row, waiting to greet Paul and Kata.

"This is my deputy commander for operations, Brigadier General Keil," Schofield said, introducing them first to a one-star general with manicured fingernails. "Your companies fall under his authority."

"Good to meet you sir," Paul said. "Looking forward to working together."

"Me too," Keil said with zero enthusiasm.

"Colonel Packard commands my heavy drone force," Schofield said, stepping to his right. "Also under Keil's authority. His guys really pack a punch."

Paul forced a smile. Kata did not.

Packard regarded them without expression. His slight paunch bulged beneath his crisp flight suit with colorful patches.

"Lieutenant Colonel Thurman commands our exo battalion," Schofield said, standing in front of the next officer. "You and your machines will work closely with him at some point, I am sure. If I'm not mistaken, you both served in an exo battalion before joining the Centaur Corps, isn't that right?"

"Yes, sir," Paul answered to the awkward question as he stepped in front of the lieutenant colonel.

Exos did not like Centaurs. Particularly senior career exo soldiers like Thurman. They did not appreciate being viewed as a training ground and recruiting pool for Centaurs. Also, in the martial code of many exos, Centaurs were an abomination, a tainting of both man and machine, a form of cheating and cowardice.

Centaurs didn't like exos much either, viewing them as the B-team and suspecting that behind every judgmental exo soldier was a rejection letter from the Centaur Corps.

The fact that General Schofield brought it up at all just highlighted smoothie ignorance of the military's true warrior classes.

But interwoven with all of that was the fact was they were both the last parts of the human military that faced the enemy on the field, that were shot at, that were wounded and killed in direct-action combat. They would be chewing the same dirt together in South America and, sure as shit, would need each other more than once in the near future.

"Good to meet you, Colonel," Paul said with sincerity, extending his hand.

"Likewise," Thurman said, shaking Paul's hand and then Kata's. "Welcome to Stalwart. If there is anything I can do for you guys, please let me know."

"We will, sir," Paul said. "Thank you."

"If you don't mind, I'd like to go ahead and get started," General Schofield said. "We have a lot to get through today, and I have a hard stop in an hour. You can meet the rest of the staff when we are done."

The half dozen officers that Paul and Kata had not yet been introduced to nodded at them and took their seats.

The three-star sat in the middle of the front row and gestured at the two seats next to him. Paul and Kata sat there while the general's staff moved to the rows behind them.

"Let's go, Wainwright," the general said once everyone was seated.

The task force intelligence officer, Lieutenant Colonel Wainwright, stepped in front of the large video display and clicked a small control in his hand to get things going.

As the display kicked into gear, General Schofield leaned over to Paul and Kata and said, "I've asked intel to start high level and work their way down. I hope that works for you two?"

"Yes, sir," Paul said as a satellite image of the continent leapt onto the screen. "Appreciate that."

"South America is roughly divided into thirds," Wainwright began. As he spoke and pointed, multicolored icons and outlines flew around on the map display. "The US holds the northwest, with strong positions in Bogotá, Quito, and Lima. We also maintain control of Santiago, which still hasn't recovered completely from the battle there a decade ago. The Chinese hold the northeast, from Caracas, their decades-old stronghold, southeast to where the Amazon River flows into the Atlantic Ocean. This less populated southern third of the continent, called the Southern Cone, is up for grabs."

"It's too big, too empty, and too far away," General Keil said.

Wainwright nodded.

Schofield looked at Paul and Kata. "You two might as well come to grips with this right now. Africa is the real contest. For us and the Chinese. Controlling that continent is the grand prize of empires. This theater is second tier. So, we are never going to have the resources to secure the Southern Cone the way we would like. Fortunately, so far, the Chinese don't either."

Paul and Kata nodded.

Schofield gestured for Wainwright to continue.

"Despite the mutual resource constraints the general mentioned, the Cone remains tense."

"Tense as hell," General Keil added.

"Neither we nor the Chinese want the other to get too comfortable in the Cone," Wainwright continued. "We, in particular, cannot afford a strong, coherent enemy down there because, unlike the Chinese positions, we are vulnerable from the south.

"Note that the Chinese sit north of the Amazon River, which cuts across almost the entire continent, from the Andes Mountains to the Atlantic Ocean. No land force is going to penetrate the largest river-drainage basin in the world. And hypersonic air defenses rule out an air assault of any size.

"That leaves us only two avenues of attack. The first, from the Atlantic Ocean, which would be suicide. The second, overland from the west. But the border of Colombia and Venezuela is the most heavily armed and lethal in the world."

"It makes the old Fulda Gap," Schofield interjected, "where the Americans and Russians stared each other down in Europe almost a hundred years ago, look like the crossing from Vermont into Montreal."

"Our greatest vulnerability," Wainwright continued, "is a soft underbelly to the south. Santiago is solid, having devolved into a fortress city under nearly constant martial law. No one is really worried that the Chinese can actually get past it. It is too well fortified, and any overland approach would be concentrated and made vulnerable by the looming Southern Andes, which mark the border with Brazil."

Schofield smiled. "And besides," he said, "the Chileans are still mightily pissed off. The Chinese would have hell to pay if they tried it."

"But, if they did get past Santiago," Wainwright said, "they could drive along the western edge of the Andes all the way to Panama, rolling up our positions all along the way to where we sit right now.

"China knows we are sensitive about that aspect of the south, and they have demonstrated admirable strategic patience there. They keep things riled up throughout the Cone with guerilla proxies but never do enough for us to dedicate real forces."

"So, for almost a decade," Schofield interjected, eyes focused on the map, "the Southern Cone has been a boiling shit stew of scheming guerillas, opportunistic Russian arms dealers, and ever-present Chinese intelligence."

"And we're dropping you two right in the middle of it," Keil said with a smile.

"Don't get ahead of us, General," Schofield said over his shoulder. He pointed at Wainwright to continue.

"The most active Chinese proxy in the Cone is General Horacio Navarro," the intel officer said as a photo of Navarro appeared on the screen next to the map. "He comes from a long line of gauchos, the tough, nomadic cowboys of South America. His ancestors famously fought in the country's successful effort to expel the Spanish Colonial forces over two hundred years ago. Then, for hundreds of years, the Navarros have been part of the violent and unruly history of the Pampas, the vast grasslands that cover most of Argentina and the Cone, from the Andean foothills to the Atlantic Ocean."

"What is he general of?" Kata asked.

"Navarro calls himself a general because he graduated from a Chinese military academy back when the Chinese were doing a lot of that kind of cultural and military exchange stuff in the region. After graduation, though, Navarro came back to Argentina and led a small guerrilla force against the Chinese, whose presence was strong in the country at that time. They were trying to tip it all the way over to communism and vassal statehood. Navarro and his bandits killed a lot of Chinese soldiers before they finally captured him."

"Why didn't they execute him when they had the chance?" Paul asked.

"Good question," Wainwright said. "We don't know. We do know that he spent years in prison before getting out. There are differing accounts of how he got out. Some say he escaped. Some say he was released. But once he did regain his freedom, he went straight back to the Pampas and started kicking ass. Navarro's tactics have been aggressive. And he is in the final stages of a ruthless ten-year ascent to primacy. There are other guerrillas in the Southern Cone, of course, but Horacio Navarro is the Chinese favorite."

"Probably because he is such a pain in our ass," General Keil said.

General Schofield swiveled in his chair to face Paul and Kata.

"I know you two have the clearance, so I will share with you some very sensitive information. This information is not to leave this room. Do you understand?"

He waited for a nod from both Paul and Kata before continuing.

"A month ago, I was told to start preparing for a Western offensive to reduce, if not eliminate, Chinese influence in the region."

Schofield paused to let his statement sink in. Then he made it clear.

"That's right, captains," he said. "A direct military attack on the Chinese."

Paul and Kata took in the information in silence.

Schofield leaned back in his chair, looking exhausted.

"When I was told to start planning for a Western offensive," he continued, "I requested more heavy drones and at least a brigade of ground forces to seal off the Southern Cone while I go toe to toe against the Chinese. I asked them for anything that could be spared. I didn't care who they sent as long as they could hold a rifle. But you know what I was told?"

Paul and Kata felt the shift in the room. They wore their most polite faces.

"I was told no," the general said. "I was told that the mission in Africa was the priority. That every operational brigade with better than eighty percent strength was either already headed that way or was reserved in case it was needed there. Same for every heavy drone that can fly. Imagine my relief and joy, then," the general continued with a false smile, "when command, after refusing my request, told me that, though the brigade I requested was not available, help was on the way."

The general leaned forward.

"They were sending me two Centaurs." Schofield held up two fingers to emphasize his point. "Two Centaurs and a complement of the latest robotic-soldier recipe."

The general paused with a scowl, just in case there was any question he was not happy about this.

"I threw a goddamn fit but got overruled," he said, leaning back in his chair. "So here we are."

Paul and Kata didn't know what to say. Wainwright, still standing in front of the map, looked at his feet.

"I want to be very clear on this," Schofield said, pointing toward the map. "I don't give a shit about what happens on the Cone as long as it does not interfere with my operations. You just make damn well sure to keep that prick Navarro in his box."

"So, is that our mission, sir?" Kata asked. She had heard enough. "Keep the prick in a box?"

Schofield's eyes narrowed slightly.

"Yes," he said. "It is. Any questions, Captain Vukovic?"

"No, sir," she answered.

"So, I guess this briefing is over, then?" Paul added.

"It is," General Schofield said, standing up.

Everyone jerked up from their chairs to attention.

Rather than giving the at-ease command to release the room, Schofield walked slowly from his chair as everyone remained standing at attention.

Paul and Kata stood, locked up, as the general walked around the table and stepped in front of them.

"Wainwright will answer any more questions you have. And you'll get full access to our intel feed. Make sure they set that up before you head out. But I'll just warn you, it's not going to be very useful to you. It's all pointed west in support of my operations. It's not fair to you, and it's not fair to me," Schofield concluded. "But command told me you guys could handle it. That was the deal. So, go fucking handle it."

Paul and Kata didn't talk much as they rode back to the hangar where their companies were unloading and conducting pre-combat inspections. After checking in with their first sergeants, they sat in their planning room and stared at the operational map of the Southern Cone and the millions of square miles they were now responsible for.

"Does this seem like a reasonable mission to you?" Kata asked Paul.

"Depends on what you're trying to do," Paul answered with a grimace. "If your goal is really to provide security and stability to the Southern Cone, then no. If you're trying to throw a new weapons system into the deep end to see if it floats, then, yeah, it's perfect."

"Perfectly impossible," Kata said under her breath.

"We promised the old man we'd touch base," Paul said, looking at his watch.

"Yeah," Kata said. "He's going to love this."

"What the hell?" Filson yelled a few minutes later on the secure videoconference. "You guys are not designed to be an occupying force. You were designed to be a special-ops strike force, to destroy the enemy using highly focused fire, maneuver, and shock effect. Not to occupy and hold terrain or to provide ongoing security operations. You're not equipped for that. It's like putting a basketball team on the football field. It's fucked up!"

"This is really providing me the emotional boost I needed," Kata said to Paul. "How about you?"

"I'm sorry," Filson said, rubbing his eyes.

"It's weird, sir," Paul said. "I can't decide if we are being misapplied out of ignorance, or out of a desire to see if we will sink or swim."

"Well, you're going to fucking swim," the colonel said. "I guarantee you that. What is Schofield like?"

"Fucking smoothie," Kata said.

"What did you expect?" Filson asked.

"I don't know," Paul said, agreeing with Kata. "At least one Centaur on his staff would have been nice."

"Schofield could have sought it out," Kata said, trying to underline her point. "As we did. He could have volunteered. Or anyone on his staff. But they didn't. That makes them suspect in my book."

"I agree," Filson said. "Nevertheless, if you and the Ōkami prove out, you will usher in a massive force multiplier that will radically affect the way the Combat Corps is able to resource operations. And you'll probably save a bunch of civilians and kill a few thousand guerrilla leaders and terrorists along the way."

"And if we fail," Paul said, "no one is going to mourn two junior officers and a bunch of robots."

Filson scowled at the comment but held his tongue.

Paul and Kata looked at their feet.

Colonel Filson looked at his protégés and said, "Remember, guys, everything smells like shit on no sleep. Get some rack and let's talk tomorrow."

"Roger that, sir," Kata said as she switched off the videoconference.

# Chapter Sixty

P aul and Kata walked in silence across the flight line.

"Take care of yourself out there," Paul said as they neared the Talons.

"You too."

Paul looked over Kata's shoulder as the last of her soldierbots climbed onto the Talons.

"This doesn't feel right, does it?" Paul asked.

"No," she said. "Not at all."

They both tried to think of something to say, but it was hopeless.

"Fuck it," Kata said. "How bad can it be?"

They couldn't hug or shake hands because of their battle suits, so they bumped armored fists. The familiar thud of the titanium-laced ceramic sounded good.

They turned and walked to their aircraft.

Paul and Kata were headed for separate outposts. They had named them before leaving Stalwart. They were sick of the military's platitudinal approach to naming: "Resolve," "Stalwart," "Endurance," "Courage," and the like.

They we went with names with more personal meaning.

Paul named his "Devil," after one of his favorite spots in Colorado where he grew up. In high school, he and his buddies had spent hours at the Devil's Punchbowl, swimming, drinking, and wooing girls.

Kata named hers "Philly" after her hometown.

They were feeling isolated. Out there. And not just physically out there. They felt isolated even from the military. The smoothies and REMFs on Stalwart felt as foreign and inhospitable to them as the Southern Cone. So, sometimes, it felt good at the end of a mission to head back to a place that reminded them of home. Even if they were the only humans who lived on the isolated outposts.

Devil, just like Philly, wasn't much to look at. It was a group of barren flat spots on the eastern-facing slopes of the Andes about ten miles north of the Uspallata Pass, one of the few direct, overland links between Chile and Argentina. By the time Paul and Kata got there, humans had been using the Uspallata Pass to get over the Andes for a thousand years. At its highest point, it was 12,500 feet above sea level. Both outposts were about two thousand feet below the peaks. But still high enough for it to take a week for them to acclimate to the thin air. From Devil, Paul could see the Argentinian town of Mendoza in the distance almost ten thousand feet below.

The Dragons made several flights ferrying the equipment out from Stalwart to Devil. A couple of heavy drones could have lifted them and all of their equipment out there in one flight. But Schofield was trying to set the tone.

As a military outpost, Devil was reasonably secure. Not only did they have the benefit of backbreaking mountainous terrain and tens of miles of easy line-of-sight surveillance all around, they were also surrounded by several concentric rings of sensors and patrolling weapons systems. Nothing could get close without being detected and challenged. Inside the perimeter, they burrowed their shipping-container structures into the mountain, digging out a system of bunkers that would protect them from just about anything on the conventional end of the munitions spectrum.

They had everything they needed, from maintenance to medical. They could fabricate their own repair parts, update software, and even design and produce new extension-platform configurations. Paul's human requirements were more than taken care of by their feeding, hydration, and sanitation capabilities. And, if necessary, the medpod could handle just about any wound or injury he might sustain. As long as Top or one of the other soldiers got him back to the medpod alive, he would survive and the kill chain would remain intact.

For consumables they could not produce on their own, like some ammunition types, Paul sent a Dragon back to Stalwart for resupply every couple of days.

The first month was low key. Paul and his betas familiarized themselves with the area and went on patrols every day and night, fine-tuning their standard operating procedures. They also started getting a feel for the people, villages, cities, and towns. 667 in particular.

Many of the towns had soccer fields on their outskirts. Paul noticed that 667 occasionally seemed distracted by the back and forth of the ball. Not always, but enough that Paul, having spent every waking hour for more than a year with the Ōkami betas, noticed.

After a few trips outside the wire with 667, Paul noticed her distraction arose only when the threat condition was low. 667, like Paul and the rest of the Outlaws, operated with a constant networked situational awareness that encompassed not only every platform in the unit but also any theater-level resources they were able to access. When the endpoints and networking were robust, the Outlaws had a lot of confidence in their assessment of low threat.

And that was when 667, like an eager Labrador retriever, glanced at the moving ball and the kids who chased it.

"What are you looking at, 667?" Paul asked her at the end of a long, uneventful patrol. A wolf pack, twenty soldierbots strong, walked in a spread-out wedge formation, Paul at the apex.

"The ball, sir," 667 said. "The game the children here play is interesting."

"Think so?" Paul asked as he stopped walking. 667 stepped up next to him.

"I do, sir."

"Why don't you give it a try?" Paul asked.

667 looked at Paul. Then at the soccer field. Then back to Paul.

"It's OK," Paul said. "We're clear for a twenty-kilometer radius."

"It's not necessary, sir," 667 said. "I would prefer to complete the patrol and get our soldierbots back to Devil."

"I would prefer you try to play soccer," Paul said, summoning a small tracked XP to his side. The soldierbots, acting on a mental command from Paul, moved out of the wedge formation and formed a perimeter around the soccer field. Paul removed his helmet and sat down on the XP. He leaned his weapon against the track and crossed his arms. "And that's an order."

"Yes, sir," the tall Ōkami said.

"Give me your rifle," Paul said.

667 handed Paul her weapon.

"Just don't hurt any of those kids," Paul said, nervousness creeping into his voice.

"I will not, sir."

"I mean it," Paul added.

"Yes, sir," 667 said over her shoulder, running toward the group of kids surrounding the soccer ball.

Paul watched as the group of amused kids quickly taught 667 the rules of soccer. Accustomed to humanoid maintenance and chorebots from their daily lives, the Ōkami looked like just another dumb, subservient machine to them. When it was time to pick teams for the next game, Paul chuckled when 667 was picked dead last.

A few minutes later, though, 667 had both teams laughing and squealing in wonder. She also had Paul on his feet.

Neither side was keeping score, and 667 had everyone in the action. She was a spectacular passing machine. Confining herself to the center circle, she alternated her long, arcing assists back and forth to either side of the field. Kids took turns heading and kicking her perfectly placed passes into the goal. If Paul hadn't known better, he would have mistaken 667's fluid ballistic solutions and leaping kicks as expressions of joy. Paul lost track of time.

"Everything OK down there, sir?" Top called on the radio.

Paul looked at his watch.

"Shit," he said. "Roger that, Top. We're wrapping up here."

"Shall I send the Dragons?"

"Roger that," Paul said, pulling on his helmet. "Send them down the mountain. I'll send coordinates for pickup shortly."

"Yes, sir," she said.

"Wrap it up, Mia Hamm," Paul said to 667 over the radio. "Game over."

"On the way, sir."

667 sat next to Paul as Dragon One labored up to Outpost Devil carrying them, the twenty soldierbots, and two ground XPs slung beneath his belly.

"What is 'Mia Hamm,' sir?" 667 asked Paul.

"Mia Ham was a badass American soccer player. She was a two-time Olympic gold medalist about fifty years ago," Paul told her.

Dragon One landed at Devil, and the small patrol force hopped out.

"Put the soldierbots to bed while I link up with Top in the command hooch," Paul told the Ōkami.

"Roger that, sir."

"Good work today, Mia," Paul said with a smile.

"Thank you, sir."

\*

The next day, the Outlaws got shot at for the first time.

Paul was on foot with Mia again just to the south of a small village with a dozen soldierbots on a night patrol. They had an aerial XP overhead. A shot rang out from their right flank.

The sniper's bullet made a snapping noise as it passed less than a foot in front of Paul's head.

He could tell from the sound that it was high caliber.

"Sniper!" Paul yelled as he turned to find cover. But he didn't even take his first step before the flash hit him. The sniper was on a rooftop two hundred meters to their west, drawing down on them. He was about to squeeze the trigger again when his head disappeared in a puff of red mist.

For a moment, Paul doubted it had happened. He could not believe how smooth it had been. Targeting imagery from an airborne XP to Mia, relayed to Paul by neural link, received and adjudicated at the speed of thought by his brain, neural-linked back to Mia, command sent to the AXP, armored piercing round fired into the guerrilla's skull.

Paul had not been aware he had given the kill authorization as he did it. It was strange. He spoke with Kata about it that night on their secure video link.

"It went down exactly like training," he told her. "Just as quick. So quick that I wondered if I had really given the authorization. When I started the program," he said, "I pictured myself taking my time, adjudicating each situation consistent with the rules of engagement, and then transmitting solemn official commands. 'I, Paul Owens,'" Paul said, intoning his voice in a deep and official-sounding baritone, "'do hereby authorize the just killing of the designated enemy combatant...'"

Kata laughed at him. "You are such a dork," she said.

"Fuck you," Paul said to her. "I'm telling you I just killed a man and it seemed like no thought went into it. It was sublime. Bang. You're dead."

Kata smiled. "So, the shit worked."

"Yeah," Paul said. "It did."

Kata nodded.

Then she smiled.

"I guess that was his first test?" she said.

"What do you mean?" Paul asked.

"Navarro," she said. "That was his first test. Sniper on the roof of a nearby village."

Paul nodded.

"Game on," Kata said. "Finally."

# Chapter Sixty-One

*1526 Hours, 27 July 2055*
*Outpost Devil*

T he next time Paul had to flex the neural link was more of a real firefight. A large group of Navarro's soldiers ambushed an aid convoy on a desolate stretch of highway through the Pampas. The convoy made a Mayday call in the blind, which was picked up by Paul's listening equipment. Moments later, General Schofield's deputy commander called Paul on the radio.

"This is a fifty-vehicle UN convoy," General Keil said with emphasis. "Navarro has never been this bold before. Ordinarily, he wouldn't hit something so big. We can't let the bastard do something like this with impunity. How fast could you guys get there?"

Paul looked at the map with Top.

"Looks like about twenty minutes," he said.

"Including planning time?" Keil asked with doubt in his voice.

"Roger that," Paul said, rolling his eyes to Top.

Paul waited as Keil conferred with some people on his end of the line. Paul recognized the voice of Packard, the heavy drone commander.

"We don't want to take this on with heavy drones," Keil said a moment later.

"We'd kill too many of the UN folks. And it will take us at least two hours to get there with one of Thurman's exo companies. It's your mission, Captain."

Paul looked at Top as he said, "Consider it done."

Seven minutes later, Paul, Top, and 357 each walked up the aft ramp of a Dragon with a wolf pack of ten soldierbots.

Dragon One carried two aerial XPs, one on each wing.

"Standard ingress profile, D1" Paul commanded as he climbed on board.

"Roger that, sir," Dragon One responded as he took off.

"Time to target?" Paul asked.

"Time to target seventeen minutes, thirty-five seconds, sir."

The three Dragons dove off of the mountains and accelerated to three hundred knots while maintaining an altitude of fifty feet above the rocky, descending terrain. Paul's ears popped, struggling to equalize during the rapid descent. Top was in the lead aircraft, Dragon Two. 357 was in chalk two, Dragon Five. Paul rode Dragon One in trail.

The Dragons pulled up as the terrain leveled out. Their engines screamed louder as they worked harder to maintain airspeed.

When they were two minutes out from the target, Paul radioed Dragon Two. "OK, D2," he said. "I'm sure they have detected us by now. Go ahead and put a swarm on top of them."

"Roger that, sir," she answered as a rocket fired from her nose.

The rocket sailed up and ahead toward the convoy, which was now less than five miles away.

Seconds later, at an altitude of five hundred feet, the rocket disintegrated over the smoking, motionless convoy. Twelve hundred tiny airborne sensor drones dispersed through the air and energized. Each no larger than a honeybee, they fanned out into a swirling umbrella formation.

The enemy tanks responded quickly, firing fléchette rounds at the swarm. Each round took out large swaths of the small drones. The rapid fire destroyed the sensor cloud in less than thirty seconds.

But it was too late. Paul had a full rendering of the target on his IHD, showing the exact position and movement vector of each enemy soldier, tank, and vehicle, as well as the aid workers. Fifty large cargo trucks were surrounded by at least 150 foot soldiers supported by two Chinese-made biped tanks and six pickup trucks with various pedestal-mounted armaments. Numerous bandits zipped around on smoke-coughing motorcycles.

One of the tanks was about a hundred meters to the rear of the convoy, walking south on a security patrol. The other was stationary in the middle of the convoy, dozens of tied-up and blindfolded aid workers at the base of its powerful metal legs. The last of the convoy's living armed escorts was bleeding out on the road. Navarro's soldiers were crawling over the cargo trucks, inventorying their haul. It was the kind of land piracy that had been going on for a long time in this part of the world and had gotten worse over the past year.

Paul and his ten soldierbots nearly lost their balance as Dragon One veered sharply to the left. They all grabbed for handholds and stabilized themselves.

"Sorry, sir," Dragon One said as he jerked back to the right and fired chaff and decoys from his flanks. "One of the tanks is firing at us."

"No problem," Paul said. "Just a little closer and we'll get out."

"Roger that, sir," D1 responded.

Paul studied the tactical map in his head one more time as D1 continued to evade tank fire. The aircraft banked hard left, right, up, and down. Without the stabilization smarts of his battle suit, Paul would have been splayed on the floor.

"Top, the other tank is too close to the aid workers," Paul transmitted. "We need to coax him away before killing him. Let's put you at the head of the convoy. 357 and I will take the rear."

As he spoke to the team, Paul designated targets and key positions on his IHD. His battle suit then shared the data across the team from Top and 357, to the Dragons, to the smallest XP. In less than a millisecond, every fighting system had the plan and a common map.

"Understood, sir," Top said over the radio.

"I want a rapid-insertion profile," Paul said to the three QC-10s. "Right on top of them. D2, put Top here." Paul highlighted where he wanted Top to roll out on the ground on his map. "D1 and D5, have 357 and I roll out here."

D1 swerved hard to his left and then immediately back to his right. Paul could hear the crackle and snap of the tank rounds as they ripped through the nearby air, always a step behind D1.

"Let's hurry up and get out," Paul said over the radio. "I don't want this fucker to get lucky."

"Rapid-insertion profile and rollout locations confirmed," the Dragons said in unison.

Paul leaned out of the right side of D1. Five of his wolf pack stood close behind him. The other five leaned out of the left side.

A hundred meters away, Paul could see 357 leaning out of Dragon Five.

D1 banked hard to his left again. "On my mark, sir," he said.

"Roger," Paul said. "On your mark."

Paul knew D1 was focused on avoiding enemy fire at this point. All of the Dragons would be. Small-arms fire, rockets, and the intermittent tank round flooded the air around them. Dragon One would coordinate his evasive maneuvers so that he gave Paul and the soldierbots as straight and level an exit platform as possible while getting his ground speed down to two hundred knots.

A vibration ran through Dragon One as he fired his minigun, keeping someone's head down in front of them. The outboard cargo pods, one on each of D1's utility wings, opened. An airborne XP dropped from each one. They fell a few feet and then banked away.

Dragon One, at over sixty degrees of left bank, told Paul, "Three seconds."

D1 turned the opposite direction, calling, "Exit! Exit! Exit!" as his wings passed through level.

Paul leapt into the air facing forward and spread his arms and legs to create as much drag as possible. Ten soldierbots followed him.

A bright flash erupted from the front of Dragon One as Paul fell away from him. A missile streaked toward the doomed southern tank. When Paul's altimeter said twenty feet, he tucked into a ball and enabled his suit's autopilot.

Paul tried to relax as he struck the ground. The initial impact was jarring, as always. Then the deceleration and violent tumble lasted for a few seconds.

He did not resist when his suit straightened his legs, propelling him back into the air. Paul landed in a sprint on the exact rollout spot he had designated a minute earlier. His wolf pack sprinted with him, five on each side, in wedge formation.

A white flash erupted at his two o'clock, followed by a loud bang. Black smoke spewed from the Chinese tank's chassis, its turret and weapons vaporized. The enemy tank's red icon on Paul's IHD blinked out. The smoking, headless legs fell over into the sand.

Paul gave the Dragons the command to loiter twenty kilometers to the west behind the foothills of the Andes. He did not want to take a chance that Navarro had an anti-aircraft ace up his sleeve.

The QC-10s banked aggressively away and thundered west.

Paul took manual control of his suit, raised his minigun, and killed two foot soldiers unlucky enough to be right in front of him as he ran toward the trail aid vehicle.

Without being told, Paul's wolf pack split up. Two stayed by his side. The others paired off and headed for different aid vehicles.

Paul could see on his IHD that Top and 357 and their wolf packs were also fully operational and moving to contact. Their wolf packs had spread out to aim at different target vehicles.

That's when he started to get the flashes.

A foot soldier aiming a rocket launcher.

*Kill.*

A foot soldier firing a fifty-caliber machine gun from the back of an old green pickup truck near the rear of the aid convoy.

*Kill.*

The aerial view of a foot soldier trying to drag an aid worker away from the vehicle they had been hiding under.

*Kill.*

*Kill.*

*Kill.*

The images came fast. Each one a clean kill shot.

A motorcycle-riding bandit charged Paul as he neared one of the aid vehicles. Paul lobbed a grenade.

Motorcycle and exoskeleton parts rained down as the remaining biped tank swiveled its turret toward Paul and opened up. He dove behind the aid truck's engine just in time. The cab shook as large-caliber, exploding rounds impacted.

One of Paul's soldierbots did not make it in time. It lost a leg and then an arm before the third round hit it in the neck.

Paul switched his IHD to the point of view of an aerial XP immediately overhead. The tank was traversing its turret left and right, looking for them, as aid workers lay blindfolded at its feet. It was an older model but packed a lot of firepower and was heavily armored. Only the Dragons had sufficient punch to take one out in a single shot. Paul could tell from the imagery that it was pilotless. Probably being controlled a hundred miles away, from one of Navarro's Chinese-equipped bunkers.

Paul was hit with more flashes as he worked around the other side toward the rear of the truck. An exoskeleton-clad foot soldier lunged at him, firing his weapon as he came.

Paul was caught distracted. He couldn't raise his weapon in time.

A flash hit him.

The foot soldier's helmet exploded in chunks and red mist, but his suit kept running. The dead, headless soldier smashed into the truck and toppled to the ground, the legs continuing to run.

Paul swiveled to see his one remaining soldierbot, smoke rising from his minigun.

"Thanks," Paul couldn't stop himself from saying as a flash from an airborne XP hit him.

*Enemy. Exoskeleton. Aiming a rocket launcher. Behind you!*

*Kill!*

Paul spun in time to see the foot soldier's riddled body hit the ground and looked up at the XP darting by fifty feet above.

Paul checked his tactical map again as his companion soldierbot covered him. He felt behind the power curve of the battle, but he couldn't argue with the results he saw. Outlaw Company was quickly reducing the enemy.

They still had a problem, though.

"Top, we need to take out that tank ASAP!" Paul yelled into his radio.

"Roger that, sir," Top responded.

Paul was getting concerned. They had taken out most of the enemy and lost only two soldierbots. It was obvious that this aid convoy was not going home with Navarro's troops. But Paul worried that whoever was driving the remaining tank would get frustrated, say, "Fuck it," and kill the civilians.

Seconds later, Top jumped out from behind a vehicle of the convoy. She took two long strides into the open, raised her minigun, and fired a short burst at the tank.

The rounds glanced harmlessly off the tank's armored turret, which swiveled toward Top.

But instead of jumping back behind the vehicle, Top ran in the opposite direction, firing her rifle as she went. Her long powerful legs propelled her, kicking up a spray of dirt as she streaked away.

Two soldierbots leapt from behind the same vehicle Top had emerged from and sprinted in the opposite direction from her.

The tank's turret hesitated.

Two more soldierbots leapt from behind a different vehicle. They ran toward the group of bound captives at the tank's feet, grabbed them, and hauled them to safety behind a vehicle.

This pissed off the tank. It swiveled its turret quickly toward Top.

The bound and blindfolded civilians around the tank flinched as it fired its main cannon. A large burst of dirt and scrub engulfed Top, and she was thrown to the ground by the blast. She scrambled to get up and keep moving, but the tank had her.

Paul started to yell a futile warning to Top when he saw 357 sprinting toward the tank.

357 covered the distance from the front of the convoy to the tank in a blur and leapt onto the turret, fifteen meters above the ground, in a long, graceful arc.

The tank's turret had traversed left as it tried to gun down Top, so its main gun barrel was offset ninety degrees to the left relative to its legs. 357 sprang from the top of the turret and grabbed the end of the gun barrel, swinging his full weight on the cannon.

The sudden shift in its center of gravity caused the tank to stumble to its left as it tried to stay upright. Its large metal legs churned in an awkward side sprint, and it moved away from the cluster of bound captives.

Paul and a wolf pack of five sprinted to the captives and started jerking them off the ground one by one and yanking off their blindfolds. "Start running!" he yelled as he put each one their feet. "Run! No time to untie you. Run!"

The tank fired its main cannon to shake 357 loose.

357 lost his grip as the gun jerked and recoiled. He fell to the ground just as Top, running at full speed, struck the tank's legs like a cannonball.

The tank lost its footing.

Six soldierbots mimicked the first sergeant. Hitting the tank in the legs at a full sprint in rapid succession, knocking it past the point of no return.

Now there was nothing to stop the tank from falling over.

It crashed into the sand.

They had to act fast.

Top, 357, and twenty-five soldierbots ran to the captives.

They helped Paul get the last three dozen bound aid workers moving as the tank thrashed in the sand for a few seconds.

The remote driver gave up and hit "destruct."

The tank exploded.

The Outlaws shielded their charges from the blast and shrapnel with their metal bodies. They were all knocked to the ground but were otherwise unharmed.

Paul checked the points of view of the aerial XPs. All clear. The time stamp in his IHD said they had been on-site less than six minutes.

"All right, D1," Paul said over the radio. "We're ready for exfil."

"On the way, sir," D1 responded.

"What the hell, 357?" Paul said as they helped the UN workers to their feet and cut the ropes that bound their hands. "I didn't know you were such a damn stuntman."

"I'm sorry, sir," 357 said, jerking up to stand at attention. "I did not want to destroy the tank while it was so close to the civilians. I improvised, and I apologize. I will not be such a damn stuntman again."

"I'm sorry, 357," Paul said, standing up to look the Ōkami in its sensor eyes. "I'm not being clear. You did great. I am giving you a compliment." Paul shook his head, appreciating the level of creativity and initiative 357's acrobatic move demonstrated. "Those were some really nice moves."

The Ōkami's stance unstiffened. His shoulders relaxed. He looked at Top and then back at Paul, who nearly laughed at the body language.

"Well done, Stuntman," Top said.

# Chapter Sixty-Two

*Mission Cycle 416*

*Earth Year 2062*

*310,318,387 Kilometers from Earth*

"What was it like to kill like that?" Althea asked Paul from the medpod. "It must have been strange to just think it and have someone die."

"In the moment," he answered, "it was much easier than physically pulling a trigger on someone, but later, it was much worse."

"How do you mean?"

Paul thought about her question for a moment as he floated next to the medpod.

"When I was in the fight with the Ōkami," he began, "the flashes seemed to be mostly light and information. There was a micro instant of whiteout in my head, and I caught very little detail. Almost like an overexposed photo. They came fast and with certainty, giving me all the information I needed to authorize the kill, but almost no discernible image. Nothing visceral. No impact.

"Much different than the old way," Paul continued, "when I was driving a drone or trying to kill someone myself. At those times, my external senses were at their most heightened. My brain was hyperactive, fixated on the target. But twenty minutes after the firefight, I'd already started to lose the details. I could remember the main pieces and could tell you, 'I banked the drone to the left, squared up on the enemy, and then shot him in the head,' but that was it. And it's gotten fuzzier as time has gone on. Now all the people I killed on the Horn of Africa are the blurry and faded images of someone else's old photo album."

Paul paused. He looked away from Althea and his face darkened.

"With the neural link architecture, it was the opposite," Paul said, still not making eye contact. Despite the small confines of the CnC medbay, he seemed to stare off into a vast distance as he continued. "Things got clearer as time went on. It was like my brain needed time to unpack and process all the information in each flash. And the longer my head had ahold of the information, the more detail was revealed, and the further into me the images burrowed. Later, back on Devil after a fight, they'd come at me again, but slow and clear and detailed. I could make out the craziest minutiae in my mind. I could see sweat on their foreheads, the texture of their uniforms, the color of their eyes. And then I would see the rounds impact and tear them apart or burst them open. I knew if they died immediately, or if it took time."

Paul rubbed the palms of his hands together. He took a deep breath and let it out slowly.

"The night after that first real firefight, rescuing the convoy, they hit me when I was eating dinner," he continued. "I was sitting on the ground, leaning against the tracks of one of the large ground XPs, looking down at the glow of the city of Mendoza when they came on, one after the other. I must have authorized a hundred kills that day. I would push one out of my mind, and another would take its place. I started hyperventilating and couldn't move."

"What did you do?" Althea asked.

"I couldn't do anything," Paul said with sadness. "I panicked and started to sink under them."

"Oh, Paul," Althea said.

"Then Top appeared," Paul said with a small smile. "She always had her eye on me, even when I was eating alone. She came over, kneeled down in front of me, and tried to snap me out of it."

"I was unresponsive until she grabbed my shoulders and shook me. 'Sir, you are OK. They're just the flashes. Focus on your breathing.' I was sweating through my uniform and had dropped my plate of food, but her voice got through. She chanted the mantra she had overheard me use at the beginning of my meditations. 'So…hum…so…hum…so…hum…' It got me back. 'Are you OK?' she asked me.

"'I've got one of those splitting headaches,' I said. 'But I'm back. Thanks.'

"'You're welcome, sir,' she said as we started walking toward my hooch. 'I think your meditations are going to be very important out here, sir.'

"'I think you're right, Top.' We stopped at the door to my hooch, and I said, 'You're lucky you're a robot, Top.'

"'Why is that, sir?' she asked me.

"'Because this shit doesn't get to you,' I said.

"She hesitated, and then said, 'I'm not sure about that yet, sir.'"

Paul was quiet for a moment, lost in thought. Althea let him go and waited for him to continue.

"After about a month, we were wired tight," Paul finally said. "The soldiers and XPs were performing above expectations, the neural links were five by five, and Top and I were in sync.

"I still got hit with the bad headaches and images after missions. Top and I started calling them 're-flashes.' But they were manageable. I meditated for half an hour in the morning and at the end of the day. It helped a lot.

"Kata was getting the bad re-flashes after each mission as well. We'd complain to each other about them when we talked on our daily ops-coordination call. She and I would also link up face-to-face once a week." Paul smiled briefly. "One of us would fly out to the other around dinnertime. We'd get away from our soldiers and everything else and just compare notes on life. We were the only two people in the world who knew what the other was experiencing. It was lonely," Paul said.

"Every month or so, though, Colonel Filson would visit. Kata and I both looked forward to those times. He'd stay over for a night or two and would even go on missions with us."

"He would visit?" Althea asked, surprised. "In a war zone?"

"Yep," Paul said. "He was tasked with writing the tactical manual for Ōkami units."

"What does that mean?"

"If Combat Corps bought into the Musashites, the colonel's manual would be the instruction book. It would serve as the codified best practices for commanders that fielded Ōkami units. He kept Kata and me up late into the night after missions, debriefing us. He didn't give a shit about body counts. He was more interested in each mission's stated objective and then the why and how we did things to achieve it.

"After the facts were captured in the debrief, he'd run endless what-ifs by us, stopping only after we stood up and left the operations hooch. That part got old," Paul said, shaking his head at the memory.

"'Fine,' he'd yell after us. 'I'll shut up. Come back and have a drink!' But that was a ruse," Paul said. "I was lured back into the ops hooch once by that line. An hour later when I walked out, I swore I would never fall for it again."

"Did you?" Althea asked.

"Yes. Often."

Paul smiled.

"But it was good to be around him," Paul continued. "When he visited, whichever outpost he was overnighting at became our private communion spot. Kata or I would fly over, and we'd eat dinner together. When he was at Devil, I asked Top to make sure Chief had something to grill. It was easy for one of the aerial XPs to zip out over the plains and bag a red stag or a wild boar. Chief expertly prepared whatever they came back with. He had become a grill master. Only a couple months into our tour, I stopped trying to teach him things and started studying his technique."

Paul smiled and shrugged with respect.

"Chief was like the rest of them in that way," he said.

"In what way?" Althea asked.

"Observant," Paul answered. "Mindful. Utterly and always without swagger."

"Swagger?" Althea asked. "What do you mean?"

"Human soldiers," Paul said. "As they go through things, survive things, they take on a swagger. A confident, often arrogant, demeanor that lets the world know they have seen some shit, that they can handle themselves. It's the combination of a lot of experience and learning, but also a lot of psychic scar tissue. At its best, it's a thing that gives those around them confidence and heart in bad situations."

"How so?" Althea asked.

"One of my first firefights with the exo battalion went badly," Paul said. "Couple things were missed by headquarters, and my patrol wound up surrounded by a much larger enemy force. Even worse, we were stuck in a narrow valley with very little cover, so the enemy was able to put very effective fire on us. I started to get scared. A panicky feeling welled up inside me."

Paul patted his chest.

"I remember looking across at Sergeant Watson, a couple meters away from me," he continued. "He looked irritated. Not scared. Not even concerned. His face looked like he had just spilled his coffee in his lap. It was a supreme inconvenience. And one that he intended to deal with quickly. He caught me looking at him. He shrugged as if to say, *What a fucking pain in the ass. Eh, sir?*

"Then he winked at me and leaned to his right, firing a quick burst around the small boulder he was crouching behind. As the enemy rounds struck the right side of the boulder, he shifted to his left, stood up, and fired three perfectly aimed rounds, each one striking an enemy in the head on the slope above us. Their helmets shattered. Puffs of red mist lingered in the air as their bodies collapsed.

"Sergeant Watson smoothly transitioned back to a crouch behind the boulder as enemy rounds stitched the dirt where he had been standing. He looked at me again and said, 'Well, sir. We'll be doing this all night if you don't get off your ass and call in some air support.' And, just like that," Paul said, snapping his fingers, "I was back in the fight. We got out of there without even a scratch."

"I see," Althea said.

"That was good swagger," Paul said. "Bad swagger is arrogance. It's a learning block. It's that point where you think you know it all, you've seen it all. The Ōkami betas never suffered from that. They were the most advanced fighting systems ever created. But they walked around like it was their first day on the planet, their first day in school. And they were eager to learn.

"It's one of the things that made them so interesting," Paul said. "And one of the biggest differences between them and the soldierbots I had worked with before.

"On my first rotation on the Horn," Paul explained, "when we got back inside the wire after a mission, the soldierbots would shut down until we needed them again. The Ōkami betas never shut down. They were just like Kata and me. They had to endure the idle time. The endless hours and days of nothing that comes with a deployment. But they never got bored like us. They were always observing. Top, especially. And she would say the damnedest things."

"What kind of things?" Althea asked.

"Things where I couldn't tell if they were brilliant or stupid."

"Like what?" Althea asked.

Paul chuckled, recalling his first sergeant.

"One time," he said, "as we were wrapping up a patrol and walking to the pickup zone to meet up with the Dragons, she said to me, 'I do not understand fishing, sir.' We were walking next to a small river. Two old men were fishing from the bank as the sun set.

"'Pretty simple,' I said. 'It's a way to obtain food. And it is a nice way to spend time.'

"'But the people that fish from the banks of the river cast their lines as far as they can out into the middle of the water,' Top said, gesturing at the two old men. Her armored skin was dusty and bore scratches and deep dents from firefights, but the late-day sun still lent it a hint of red iridescence. We took a few more steps together in silence before she looked back at me and said, 'While the people fishing from a boat in the middle of the water cast their lines as far as they can to get close to the banks of the river.'"

Paul smiled and shook his head at Althea.

"What did you say?" she asked.

"I gave her my standard answer."

"And what was that?"

"'No fucking idea, Top.'"

Althea shook her head in disapproval.

"It became clear to me, after a few weeks on Devil," Paul said, ignoring Althea's reproach, "that the real world was giving the betas a lot to think about. That the black-and-white rules of Filson's training world were not holding up. And that I was responsible for some of their indigestion," he said ruefully.

"In what way?" Althea asked.

"Soon after that convoy mission," Paul said, "we were on a patrol on the outskirts of a small town southeast of Mendoza. I had two dozen soldierbots fanned out in a kilometer-wide line and an aerial XP flying figure eights above us as we advanced.

"It had been a quiet couple of days in the valley. I think Navarro was digesting the ass-kicking we'd given him at the convoy. Top and I were walking next to each other at the formation's center, talking. Sure as shit, a shot rang out and I got hit in the shoulder."

"Oh no!" Althea said.

Paul laughed and shook his head. "It was nothing," he said. "Small caliber. Bounced off my armor. Trust me, you'll know when I start telling you about the bad stuff. Top and I ran for cover in case it was a ranging round for a heavier weapon when I got a flash from the aerial XP. But I didn't authorize the kill. It didn't feel right.

"A couple minutes later, I was standing over a fifteen-year-old boy who Snapshot and a couple of soldierbots had captured. He was terrified. Snapshot held the boy by the arm with one of his powerful hands and the boy's small hunting rifle in the other. On the ground lay a string of squirrels the boy had gotten that day.

"I kneeled in front of the boy and spoke into my translator. 'What were you thinking, son?' I asked him. 'Why did you shoot at us?'

"'I was scared,' he said through his tears. 'I've heard how mean you soldiers are. I've heard how many boys and girls you have killed.'

"'Look at me,' I said, raising the face shield on my helmet so he could see my face. I smiled as kindly as I could and asked him, 'Do I look like I kill young boys and girls?' The boy sniffled as he looked at me. After a long minute, he shook his head. 'You're right,' I said to him. 'We don't kill young boys.'

"I motioned to Snapshot to let go of the boy. He rubbed his arm where the strong mechanical hand had held him and looked at me, wondering what was going to happen next. I reached for the string of squirrels, startling the boy. His anxious eyes followed my armored hand as it reached down.

"There were five dead squirrels on the string. I examined them for a few seconds and then said, 'You're a pretty good shot.' The boy continued to regard me skeptically but nodded. 'Who are these for?' I asked him.

"'My family,' he said.

"'Listen to me closely,' I said to the boy, continuing to kneel so he could look me in the eye. 'I'm going to let you take your squirrels home to your mother. But I want you to do me a favor.'

"The boy's eyes widened with disbelief. 'Yes, sir?' he said.

"'When you get home, I want you to tell your mother and father what happened. Do you have any brothers and sisters?' I asked him.

"'Yes, sir,' he answered. 'One brother and one sister.'

"'I want you to tell them what happened also, OK?' I said. 'I'm asking you to help spread the word that we don't kill young boys. We're just here to help keep things peaceful, OK?'

"The young boy nodded. And, finally, he smiled. 'I will, sir,' he said.

"'Thank you,' I said. I handed the boy the string of squirrels, and his smile widened. I stood up and looked at Snapshot. 'Give him his rifle back,' I said. Snapshot hesitated. I looked at him. I had never had to repeat an order, ever, to a Ōkami. I was about to do it for the first time when Top interrupted me.

"'Sir,' she said. 'Theater rules of engagement state that hostile fire immediately establishes the shooter as an enemy combatant that should be killed or captured if possible. Upon capture, the rules of engagement further state release is not allowed. The prisoner must be transported to Forward Operating Base Stalwart for processing.'

"I looked at the boy to make sure that he did not understand the English coming from Top. He did not. He was smiling and looking at his squirrels. I turned to Top.

"'Thank you, Top,' I said. 'I am clear on the rules of engagement. I am overruling them.' I looked at Snapshot and said, 'Give the boy his rifle back.' Snapshot did so. I leaned over to get eye level with the boy again and said through my translator, 'Don't let me down, son.'

"'I won't, sir,' he said. 'Thank you.' I nodded and the boy ran off.

"Later that night, back on Devil, I was sitting outside my hooch looking down on the valley after dinner. Top stepped up beside me. 'Sir,' she said. 'May I ask you a question?'

"'Sure,' I said, gesturing at the empty chair next to me. Top sat down. I kept gazing down at the valley.

"'Why did you release that boy today?' she asked me. 'It broke the rules of engagement, sir.'

"'Same reason I didn't authorize the kill, Top,' I said. 'It didn't feel right.' I smiled as I kept looking down on the valley. I could almost hear the quantumtronic circuitry in her head laboring against what I had just said. After a few minutes, she tried again.

"'But, sir, General Schofield and the rules of engagement clearly state that—'

"I interrupted her. 'Top, do you see General Schofield out here with us right now?' I asked.

"'No, sir. The general is back on Forward Operating Base Stalwart.'

"'That's right,' I said, turning my head to look at her. 'And if you are pinned down by the enemy and need help, who do you call? Do you call the rules of engagement to come save you?'

"'No, sir. I call you,' she said.

"'That's right,' I said. Enjoying myself, I turned my head back to the valley, ten thousand feet below us.

"I let Top stew next to me for a few minutes. She finally said, 'I'm sorry, sir. This conversation is not very helpful. I am sorry I have disturbed you.' She stood up to leave.

"'Top, listen,' I said, standing up from my seat and walking over to her. 'I'm not trying to be difficult or vague. The problem is that, out here, it's just us. We have to apply all the shit Filson taught us in training and all the policies and objectives coming down from Schofield and Stalwart while we accomplish our mission and take care of each other. There are going to be gray areas and times when wrong is right.'

"Top, over a foot taller than me, bent her head down and listened intently. 'When wrong is right?' she asked.

"'Locking that kid up on Stalwart,' I continued, 'or worse, killing him, would have only made things worse. His family would never have forgiven us, and we'd have created a couple more enemy. Now, though, he is sitting at home eating barbecued squirrels with his family and telling them there is a good side to the Americans. Who knows? He may make a difference for us someday. And even if he doesn't,' I said, 'I don't believe locking him up or killing him was the right thing to do. In fact, I think it would have been wrong.'

"Top stared at me for a long moment. 'How do you know when wrong is right?' she finally asked me.

"I shrugged and said, 'It's a gut thing, Top. You will know.' Top was silent. Suddenly I remembered I was talking to a machine," Paul said to Althea. "I felt stupid trying to explain my human relativism to a quantumtronic calculator. 'It's OK, Top,' I said to her. 'My job is to handle the gray areas. I don't expect robots to be capable of that.'"

"What did she say to that?" Althea asked Paul.

"She just turned and walked away from me."

"I don't blame her," Althea said.

# Chapter Sixty-Three

**"I**'m not impressed," Robert Malloy II said to Fiona.

She tried not to fidget in her chair as she met her grandfather's gaze.

He sat at the head of the same table at which she had endured the humiliating gifting of her trust only nine years ago. She did not allow herself to wonder what she would do differently if she had the chance to go back in time to that afternoon.

Instead, she focused on her grandfather. She had learned that, with him, it was wise to wait, to see if he would give anything more.

Robert Malloy II had learned long ago that speaking last was a strategic advantage. "He who speaks first loses," he had told her many times since her indentured servitude had begun.

She knew that one of his techniques was to create an uncomfortable vacuum and then wait for the weaker willed to fill it and, in turn, to gain an advantage.

So she waited.

He smiled.

Fiona was a quick study.

"Child," he said, erasing the smile and cloaking himself in disappointment. "You just told me all about the conditions you have set. I'm waiting for the action piece."

"Action?" she asked. "You don't see the actions I have taken? I had to—"

"Ah, ah, ah," he interrupted her, putting his bony finger to his mouth in a *shhhh* command.

"I don't need the details," he said. "Those are your sins to carry. This old man has enough of his own."

Fiona nodded, startled at the hint of admission from him.

"Conditions are well and good, Roberta," he said. "But you are leaving the catalyst to chance." He paused. "Are you sure you want to do that?"

She studied him. *Is it a test question?* she wondered. *Or rhetorical? Either way, don't answer immediately. Let's see what a few dozen seconds of silence reveals.*

There was a knock at the meeting room's door.

"Yes?" her grandfather called.

"Excuse me, sir," his assistant said, opening the door and leaning in. "But the senator is here early for your two o'clock."

Robert Malloy II glanced at his watch.

"Fine," he said. "Bring him in."

The receptionist turned and left.

"Time flies, doesn't it, Roberta?"

"It does," she said, standing up. She put her tablet computer into her bag and walked around the table to leave.

"Think about our conversation," her grandfather said.

"I will," she said, pausing at the door and looking at him.

"Action wins," he said. "Setting conditions is no better than wishing for luck."

"Of course, sir," she said. She was ready to leave.

"And you need to win this," he added. "Your gay boy brother needs you to win this as well."

The mention of Eugene took her breath away.

"Ha!" Her grandfather cackled and pointed at her. "I've only just now realized that you still have not told him. He has no idea who you are now bound to, nor of the precipice on which you both stand."

Fiona started to respond, but the senator walked in.

"Robert!" the senator said, three aides walking in behind him. "How are you, sir?"

"I'm good, Chuck," her grandfather said, staying seated. "Thank you. Please meet my granddaughter."

Her grandfather gestured toward her.

"My Lord. I don't believe it," the senator said, swiveling to offer his hand to Fiona. "She is too good-looking to be related to you, Robert. Don't pull my leg like that!"

Her grandfather cackled again and then said, "I shit you not, Chuck. I'd like to introduce you to Roberta Malloy."

"It's a pleasure, Miss Malloy," the senator said. "Senator Chuck Book, of New York."

"The pleasure is mine, Senator."

The senator turned back to Robert Malloy II and said, "Robert, we can come back later if this is not a good time."

"No," her grandfather said. "Now is perfect. Roberta was bored with me anyway. You've rescued her."

The senator and his aides rendered the appropriate laughter.

"And trust me," her grandfather added, "this one needs rescuing."

Fiona left as laughter filled the room.

# Chapter Sixty-Four

*Mission Cycle 417*

*Earth Year 2062*

*311,288,832 Kilometers from Earth*

"Paul," the XO said. "Paul, I apologize for waking you, but we need to discuss our current situation."

"OK," Paul mumbled. He blinked his eyes as they gained focus and turned to look at the medpod. Althea was in rest mode, with her eyes closed.

Paul stretched and said, "Let me take a piss, and I'll come up to the bridge."

"Very well," the XO said.

Several minutes later, Paul floated onto the bridge and said, "What's up?"

"The damage to the *Odysseus* is much worse than we thought," the XO said.

"I'm not surprised," Paul said. "But as long as we are able to limp close enough to the belt to get picked up, we'll be fine. They can tow the old girl to a maintenance dock and find Althea and me a ride back to Earth."

The XO was quiet.

Paul got nervous.

"What?" he asked.

"Power and propulsion was hit many times by debris and dislodged cargo," the XO said. "The nuclear reactors were badly damaged."

"Terrific," Paul said, shaking his head.

"The maintenance boss and I are working with power and propulsion as fast as we can," the XO continued. "But we are down to less than fifty percent of our IR bot strength, and our odds of success have been decreasing."

"What does that mean?" Paul asked.

"It is highly likely that at least one nuclear reactor will fail catastrophically."

"Highly likely?" Paul asked.

"Ninety-one-point-four percent likely," the XO said. "And increasing."

"And what, exactly, does 'catastrophic' mean?" Paul asked, irritation seeping into his voice.

"An explosion," the XO answered. "Which will destroy the *Odysseus*."

Paul was quiet, digesting the news. He turned toward the large window and looked past the broken ship into the void.

"We came a long way just to be vaporized," he said softly.

"I want you to know that we are not giving up," the XO said. "The maintenance boss is trying every trick he knows. But I thought it right to let you know what is happening and the unlikely prospect of success. I would want to know, if I were you."

"I appreciate it," Paul said. "Thank you."

"Of course."

"How long?" Paul asked.

"Twenty-four to forty-eight hours."

"Plenty of time," Paul said, checking his watch. "Let me know if anything changes."

"I will," the XO said.

Paul went back to the medbay. He stared at Althea through the medpod window until, hours later, he fell asleep.

*

When Paul woke up, Althea was staring at him from the medpod.

"Hello, sleepyhead," she said.

"Hello," he said.

"What's wrong?" she asked.

"What do you mean?"

Althea made a show of narrowing her eyes and glaring at Paul.

Paul looked away.

"You went and spoke with the XO and then came back and stewed until you fell asleep," she said. "What is wrong?"

"I thought you were in rest mode," Paul said, surprised at all she had noticed.

"Rest mode," she agreed, nodding. "I wasn't dead."

Paul shook his head in appreciation.

"Seriously," Althea said. "Tell me."

"The reactors were damaged," Paul said, looking at her. "XO says they're probably going to explode and destroy the *Odysseus*."

"And us," Althea added.

"And us," Paul agreed.

"When?"

Paul looked at his watch. "About twenty to forty hours from now."

"I see," Althea said.

"Yeah," Paul said.

They looked at each other for a long time.

The crisp sound of the medpod locks deactivating broke the silence, and the pod's clamshell door opened.

"What are you doing?" Paul asked.

Althea pushed her naked body out of the medpod. The discoloration of her wounds was gone.

She floated slowly across the medbay toward Paul.

"What are you doing?" he repeated.

"I'm not going to spend the rest of my life in the medpod," she said, nearing him.

His eyes roved over her. He couldn't help it.

She smiled.

He reached out to catch her.

His arms encircled her waist. Her momentum pressed her body against him and imparted a rotation and tumble to their embrace.

# Chapter Sixty-Five

*Mission Cycle 417*

*Earth Year 2062*

*311,662,080 Kilometers from Earth*

"By the middle of October," Paul said, "the colonel could tell the deployment was wearing on us. He tried to pump sunshine up our ass, telling us we were pioneers."

Althea smiled.

They had moved to the bridge so that they could stargaze and watch the IR bots zoom by while Paul finished his story.

"I want to hear the rest of it before we go," Althea had said.

"Why?" Paul asked her.

"I just do," she answered. "Does why matter now?"

They were naked and wrapped in blankets. They orbited each other, within arm's length, in the middle of the weightless bridge, both facing the window as Paul spoke.

"'You're like the first Egyptians to use chariots,' Colonel Filson would say. 'The first Chinese to bring gunpowder to the fight. The first soldiers to go to battle with rifled gun barrels. Or the internal combustion engine. The airplane. The Radio. Radar. Everything is going to be different! And you are the ones who are going to change it.'"

"Was it really going that well?" Althea asked.

"It was at first." Paul nodded. "The architecture was proving itself to be lethal and self-sufficient. Because of how well the swarms and other systems were working, we were mounting effective operations with the thinnest satellite or theater-level intelligence support. Which, of course, suited General Schofield just fine.

"Kata and I had everything we needed to plan and conduct our operations. The neural link complied with all Tokyo Accords kill chain requirements. And the Ōkami continued to get better with each mission. We went a month or two with only losing a handful of soldierbots each."

"What went wrong?" Althea asked.

"Several things," Paul said. He took a deep, weary breath. "First, after getting his ass kicked for a few months, General Navarro opened his wallet and reached out to the Russians and Chinese. We started facing better tech.

"Second, General Schofield started pulling on us for missions in support of his prep to take on the Chinese. After reading some of our after-action reports, he recognized the asset he had sitting in his backyard."

"That was a good thing, right?" Althea asked. "I mean, that he recognized and valued your capabilities."

"Yeah," Paul said. "Problem was that we still had responsibility for our primary mission. And General Schofield's extra-credit work was usually risky and poorly coordinated at the last minute.

"This all came together in a bad way the day we took our first casualty. A heavy transport drone went down about fifty kilometers from Devil, in the plains north of Mendoza. It was flying over the Pampas from one of the eastern port cities to Stalwart. General Kiel called me and requested a rescue-and-recovery op.

"'What is the enemy situation?' I asked him. 'Was it shot down?'

"'We're not sure,' he said.

"'Any overhead imagery?' I asked.

"'Working on getting that for you,' he told me in an unconvincing voice.

"'Any survivors or special cargo I should know about?' I asked.

"'Not sure about survivors,' he answered. 'There were two souls on board. This happened five minutes ago. Cargo is not high value—small-arms ammunition, medical supplies, and repair parts. Nonetheless, we'd prefer Navarro not get it. And, if there were survivors, we definitely don't want Navarro getting his hands on them.'

"I was quiet and looked across our planning room at Top, who was listening in to the conversation. I shook my head, expressing my unease. She shrugged, as she had learned to do, acknowledging the ambiguity.

"'What about Thurman's exos?' I asked Kiel.

"'Look, Captain,' the general said, sensing my resistance. 'You guys can be there in fifteen minutes. Anything I launch from here would not be on-site for at least four hours.'

"'Who do you want to send?' I asked Top.

"'I'll go with you on this one, sir,' she said.

"'Good morning, sir,' Dragon One said to me as we took off. Top rode in Dragon Three, in trail formation behind us. We each had a small ten-soldierbot wolf pack with us. Both aircraft picked up to a hover as they ran through their systems checks.

"'Ready at your command, sir,' D1 said a moment later, asking me for permission to launch.

"'Let's go,' I said. Our flight of two accelerated forward, and the mountain fell away beneath us. 'How we doing today, D1?' I asked as we descended, skirting just above the jagged mountain.

"'Good, sir,' D1 said. 'Finally got my number-four fan thruster rebalanced. That high-frequency vibration is gone. Can you tell?'

"'Sorry to say,' I responded, 'but I never noticed it in the first place.'

"'I understand,' Dragon One said, without any disappointment. 'The truth is it ranged from six thousand to six thousand seven hundred and fifty hertz. Just outside your ability to sense.'

"'Well, that explains it,' I said. 'Wouldn't matter to me anyway, D1. You're my favorite ride.'

"'I appreciate that, sir,' D1 said."

"Was he really?" Althea asked Paul.

"Yes."

"Why?"

"I'm not sure," Paul said. "But I think I flew in Dragon One on almost every mission. At first, it just worked out that way. Then, after a few weeks, even if I was heading out on single-aircraft mission, I'd ride in Dragon One rather than rotating through the team. Superstition, maybe? I don't know. There was nothing special about Dragon One compared to the rest of the Dragon Flight. I think it was like any other forced relationship."

"What do you mean by 'forced relationship'?" Althea asked.

"Just that we had to work together," Paul said. "Neither of us chose the other. Fate assigned us to the same unit."

"I see."

"Our friendship was standard military issue…the product of habit and familiarity, cemented by shared hardship."

"I suppose that I am a forced relationship?" Althea asked.

"I dunno." Paul smiled. "But I'm damn sure I'm a hardship to you."

Althea shook her head.

"Anyway, that morning, as we flew out to the crash site, I reviewed the limited available intelligence. I called the operations center on Stalwart several times but didn't get much. I felt uneasy.

"'D1,' I said, 'put a swarm on top of the crash site.'

"A jolt ran through Dragon One. 'Done, sir,' he said. 'Telemetry in one minute.' With nothing to disrupt them, the sensor swarm stayed overhead and put together a detailed view of the crash site.

"The downed aircraft was one of the larger hexacopters, designed to haul huge loads. The aircraft had tumbled after initial impact, shearing off all six of its thruster fans. The main fuselage lay broken in a grassy marsh thicket, nose half buried at the end of a dark, smoking trench it dug after its last bounce.

"'Looks like we have two survivors,' I called to the team. 'They are the priority. Wolf packs will set a security perimeter while we stabilize and extract the wounded. Dragons, I want you to establish overwatch at a three-kilometer radius.'

"'Roger that, sir,' both Dragons responded.

"On the ground, we worked fast. One survivor had been thrown clear of the aircraft. He was unconscious and had lost a lot of blood from a bad laceration to his arm. I stuck him with an IV as two soldierbots stood watch over us. Top tried to get to the other survivor, who was trapped in the mangled aircraft. Top used her strength to peel away bent metal as two soldierbots shadowed her for security.

"I threw Top's POV up on my IHD to monitor her progress while I bound the arm wound. The closer Top got to freeing the survivor, the more he panicked. 'Please!' he cried. 'Please get me out of here. I can't breathe very well. It really hurts.'

"'Try to relax,' Top said in her most calming voice. 'It won't be long now. I'm just moving carefully so I don't accidentally hurt you.'

"'Please hurry!' he wailed. 'Oh God!'

"'What is your name?' Top asked.

"'Lawson,' he said, nearly hyperventilating, 'Sergeant Bill Lawson.'

"'Lawson?' Top said with some excitement. 'Are you kidding me? My Commander knows a Lawson. Where are you from?'"

"Did you know a Lawson from your O.A.T class?" Althea asked Paul.

"No," Paul said. "I never knew anyone named Lawson. Top was just trying to distract him, trying to calm him down.

"'Wisconsin,' Lawson answered. As he did, Top peeled back a piece of aircraft, and I nearly vomited at what I saw on my IHD. His legs were mashed to a pulp. Most of his pelvis too. The airframe that had crushed him was now holding him together, and it was a mercy that his body was in shock and he didn't feel any of it. But his rising anxiety was a sign that his body was beginning to calibrate to its situation. Soon he would be in agony.

"'Sir,' Top transmitted to me in whisper mode. 'This man's wounds are not survivable.'

"'Yeah,' I said, also in whisper mode. 'I see that. I'll be there in one minute.'

"'What is it?' the survivor asked Top, sensing her hesitance. 'Oh God! What is it?'

"'It's nothing, Lawson,' she said. 'I've almost got you out.'

"He could not see how badly he was hurt because of the angle of his head and a large piece of metal across his chest. But he was starting to get agitated. 'Tell me! I can tell something is wrong! Oh God. It hurts so bad… I'm scared! I don't want to die!'

"'Easy, Lawson,' Top said, grabbing his hand. 'Nothing is wrong. On the contrary, you're actually in much better shape than I thought you would be.'

"'Really?' His voice was pitiful, and for a second, I felt guilty we were misleading him. But there was nothing else to do be done. Lawson looked at his hand in Top's and then back to Top.

"'Yes,' she answered. 'In fact, would you do me a favor and wiggle your toes?'

"'OK,' Lawson said, calming down slightly. 'I'll try.' Lawson stared at Top, and his brow furrowed as he concentrated on his toes.

"'Very good!' Top said as she watched the blood continue to ooze out of his unrecognizable and motionless legs. 'Just amazing, Lawson,' she said. 'You may actually walk out of this aircraft once we get you free.' Lawson squeezed Top's hand and sighed as he believed her lie and continued to die.

"I stepped up next to Top. Because of the narrowed space of the mangled airframe and Top's bulk, I could not get close enough. 'I can't get in there, Top,' I told her. 'I'm going to have to get out of my suit.'

"'No, sir!' Top said, transmitting again without making a sound Lawson could hear, but expressing her displeasure directly into my helmet.

"Lawson moaned in pain. 'It will only be for a minute,' I told her. 'Just long enough to administer the morphine.'

"'No fucking way, sir,' Top said.

"Getting out of your suit on an operation is forbidden," Paul explained to Althea. "And not just by regulations. It grates against every instinct."

"Why?" Althea asked.

"Because, out of that suit, your ability to shoot, move, and communicate is gone. You're just naked, weak, mortal flesh. We're trained from day one to never get out of your suit when you are outside the fence line unless it is on fire. Period.

"'God,' Lawson cried out. 'Oh God, it's really starting to hurt!'

"'Hand it to me, sir,' Top said, swiveling her left arm back toward me. Lawson still held her right hand. I put the syringe in Top's hand. 'OK, Lawson,' Top said. 'We're going to get you out now, but first I want to give you this pain medication.'

"'OK. That's great,' Lawson said. 'Thank you.'

"'How much of this do I give him, sir?' she asked me in whisper mode.

"'I was going to do the whole thing,' I whispered back to her.

"'Looks like a lot to me, sir,' she said.

"'It is,' I said. I watched through Top's point of view as she inserted the needle. Before she pressed down, though, a flash hit me."

"She was asking you for kill authorization?" Althea asked.

"Yeah," Paul said. "I think she was trying to be thorough. Or she wasn't comfortable with it. But this time, I didn't use the neural link."

"Why not?"

"I don't know," Paul said. "Seemed like Lawson deserved more. Instead, I spoke to Top in whisper mode. 'It's OK, Top,' I said. 'It's the right thing. Do it.'

"Top's thumb pressed down, flooding Lawson's veins with morphine. His eyes closed, and his body relaxed, but he maintained his grip on Top's hand. She squeezed back. Top was silent as Lawson's head lolled to the side in his final moments. His pupils moved around beneath his eyelids, following the last sights of his life.

"'There you are...' Lawson murmured.

"'What is he saying, sir?' Top asked me.

"'I don't know. He is seeing something in his mind. It happens sometimes... at the end.'

"'Should I talk back?' she asked me.

"'Only if you want to,' I said.

"'I can't quite...' Lawson said. 'Can we...'

"'Yes, Lawson,' Top said. 'As soon as you are home.'

"Lawson smiled for the first time since we'd met him. 'It's going…going to be so great…' he said. A long breath bled out of Lawson as his heart stopped. He was still smiling.

"Top waited until she was sure, then she released his hand and worked her way out of the bent airframe. She walked a few steps past me and then stopped, facing the horizon. Over her shoulder in the distance, I could see Dragon One flying his security pattern. 'You good, Top?' I finally asked her.

"'Sir,' she said, turning around. 'I didn't realize that—'

"An explosion erupted in the distance behind Top. We crouched, drew our weapons, and turned toward the noise. Flames and smoke stained the sky.

"Dragon One burned as he fell. 'Mayday! Mayday! Mayday!' Dragon One yelled over the radio. We watched him fall out of the sky, transmitting as he went. 'Mayday! This is Dragon One. Have been hit by a surface-to-air missile. Lost engines two and four. In uncontrolled descent. My position is—' The transmission stopped as he descended out of view.

"A blinding headache hit me," Paul said, wincing at the memory. "The pain was intense, and my legs buckled in my suit. I kneeled to steady myself. The pain subsided in a couple seconds. I stood up and started running toward the last living survivor, yelling into my radio, 'Dragon Three, come get us ASAP!'

"'On the way, sir,' D3 responded."

Paul chuckled.

"What?" Althea asked.

"When you tell an Ōkami drone copter 'ASAP,'" Paul said to Althea with an amused smile, "they take you seriously. D3 dove toward the earth, trading altitude for airspeed. In a blink, he was moving at over a hundred miles an hour. Then, in another blink, he was flaring, nose high, nearly vertical, trying to decelerate for landing. All four thruster fans howled as D3 demanded them to stop his hulking frame. He kept himself nearly vertical until the last possible second, and then lowered his nose abruptly.

"D3 slammed onto the ground and slid the final fifty meters until he stopped just in front of me. His insectoid head swiveled back and forth, scanning for enemy.

"'Top, grab the survivor!' I yelled.

"'Roger, sir!' she said, already sprinting toward him, her soldierbot shadows in close formation at her side, weapons aimed outward, searching for enemy.

"'Dragon Three, do you have a fix on the surface-to-air missile?' I asked him.

"'Affirmative!' D3 responded.

"'Swarm it,' I said.

"'Roger,' D3 said, and a missile streaked from under his starboard weapons wing. It rose to five hundred feet and disintegrated into a swarm over a small hilltop about five miles away. I scanned the area. We were sitting in a small, scrubby basin surrounded by several swelling hilltops like the one Dragon Three had just swarmed. Each was a perfect overwatch position from which to take out one of our aircraft. Each one could have a surface-to-air missile team on it.

"'Fuck me,' I mumbled. I was pissed. I'd taken the hasty mission and then allowed myself to be distracted by Lawson dying. Dragon One had paid the price. I felt terrible. I wanted blood.

"I was also pissed at General Keil," Paul said. "By then, I was used to the fact that we never had enough imagery and intel when we launched. We had to build the picture ourselves. We were supposedly self-sufficient, but that really meant that we were often half blind.

"But this mission was at Keil's direct request. I assumed we'd have more eyes and support behind us. I thought that the reason we got no warning of enemy ground-to-air threat was because there wasn't one. Not because they just hadn't fucking checked."

Paul shook his head in disgust.

"Top and I kneeled beneath Dragon Three's insectoid nose as the telemetry came together," Paul continued. "The turrets snapped back and forth as they scanned the area. Four soldierbots stood over us, weapons at the ready, while the rest of the wolf pack collapsed the security perimeter to a tighter ring around us.

"'Appears to be a lone fire team, sir,' Dragon Three said. The shape of the small hill appeared in my IHD. Its crest was about five hundred feet above us. Two of Navarro's foot soldiers stood next to a tracked vehicle. One of them held a missile launcher on his shoulder. The other held a pair of laser ranging binoculars.

"'Damn it,' I said to them. 'We rode into a classic baited ambush.' I zoomed in on the missile launcher until I could see Chinese letters on the long black tube. 'You seeing this, Top?' I muttered.

"'Roger that,' she answered.

"'Is that what I think it is?' I said.

"'Yes,' she said. 'Rapiers.'"

"What's a 'Rapier'?" Althea asked.

"It was a code name the intel guys gave a particularly deadly Chinese surface-to-air missile system," Paul answered. "Multispectral targeting. AI enabled. Ten minutes of loiter time. Top of the line in its day. And deadly. There was no way to spoof it. If it was in the air anywhere near you, you were fucked."

Paul rubbed his eyes.

"Top finished strapping the patient onto a litter and then looked at me. 'How many more swarms do you have, D3?' I asked.

"'Sir, I have six swarms on board,' D3 said.

"'What is your indirect munitions count?'

"'Two indirect munitions on board, sir.'

"'Perfect,' Top said. I looked at her and smiled."

"Why?" Althea asked. "What did she mean?"

"The Rapier was designed to be deployed in squads of three," Paul explained. "By spacing the fire teams across a wide area, like they did that day, the missiles were able to network and assist each other in target fixation and intercept solution calculation.

"We had to assume there were two more fire teams on hilltops in the area. Dragon Three could hit two with indirect munitions. Top knew what I was about to do. She had a request.

"'Let me go also, sir,' she asked.

"'Fine,' I said. I wasn't in the mood to argue. And, honestly, if I could have moved fast enough, I would have gone with them. An Ōkami soldier could run at a top speed of forty-five miles an hour," Paul told Althea. "I told Top not to go after them at max speed. To use some stealth. The Rapier could, in extreme situations, be used as a direct-fire weapon on the ground.

"'Roger that, sir,' she said as four soldierbots stepped next to her, two on each side. I nodded, and dirt flew in the air behind them as they tore away toward the hilltop.

"I waited for ninety seconds, then said, 'All right, D3. Fire at will.' Dragon Three launched four swarm rockets in rapid succession. They each climbed into the sky and flew in a different direction. Thirty seconds later, they disintegrated over the four hilltops that surrounded us.

"As the sensor swarms fanned out over each hilltop, I put Top's POV up on one-third of my IHD. She and her small wolf pack were still running toward the team that had shot down Dragon One. I watched the distance tick down as they moved in a line, five abreast. They would be there in eighty-five seconds.

"'Telemetry coming online, sir,' Dragon Three said.

"'I'm ready,' I answered. Top was sixty seconds away from their target.

"'I've got a positive ID on one of the Rapier fire teams, sir,' D3 said.

"'Roger, me too,' I said. The image of three foot soldiers, one shouldering a Rapier system, the other two with binoculars and rifles, appeared on the middle third of my HUD, next to Top's POV. The two soldiers with binoculars wore exoskeletons and were scanning the horizon in our direction. Top was forty-five seconds away from their target.

"'I've got a positive on both teams now, sir,' Dragon Three said. 'Other two hilltops are unoccupied.'

"'Roger that,' I said as the final targeting image filled the last third of my IHD. Dragon Three flashed me. I authorized both kills. Two indirect munitions launched out of D3's spine, sailing up into the sky and then turning off in different directions toward their targets. The soldiers on the hilltops saw the missiles fire and ran to their vehicles. But it was too late.

"Top was fifteen seconds out. I expected Top and her wolf pack to stop and flash me before shooting their targets. But they didn't. They kept running.

And I received the notification that Top had extended her bayonet. Two sharp cracks rang out as the indirect munitions activated over the other two hilltops. Explosives ejected two hundred smaller submunitions. Top finally flashed me. I authorized her kills as the submunitions showered the fleeing vehicles on the other hilltops. The soldiers and their vehicles dissolved in fire and shrapnel as, on the other hilltop, Top and her wolf pack ran through the first enemy fire team."

"What do you mean, 'ran through'?" Althea asked.

"I mean they never stopped running," Paul said. "They bayonetted them at a forty-five-mile-an-hour sprint."

Althea was quiet for a moment. Then she asked, "What about Dragon One?"

"He was still burning when we got to the crash site," Paul said. "Took over an hour for the temperature to die down to the point we could get into the avionics compartment, where his sphere was located. He was dead," Paul said, looking down. "The impact of the Rapier, the violence of the crash, and his fuel burned so hot. Top handed me the burned and caved-in sphere without saying a word, then walked back to Dragon Three."

"I'm sorry," Althea said.

"He was a good bird," Paul said. "Fortunately, he went quick."

"The headache was him, wasn't it?" Althea asked.

"Yes," Paul said, rubbing his temples at the memory. "It was the first time an Ōkami had died. Until that moment, we didn't know the neural link would transmit their last gasp like that."

"Last gasp?"

"That's what we called it," Paul said. "Even Dr. Musashi was surprised."

"Could he explain it?"

"No," Paul said. "He just said, 'I am sorry. This is unanticipated. I doubt that it will happen again.'"

"Did it?" Althea asked.

"Yes," Paul said. "Every time. Starting three days later, when Kata took her first loss."

# Chapter Sixty-Six

*Mission Cycle 418*

*Earth Year 2062*

*312,035,328 Kilometers from Earth*

"The mission assignments from Keil became more frequent as time went on," Paul said to Althea. "Some of them were real shots against the Chinese in the northeast. Complex missions that required a decent amount of planning and coordination with the heavy drone forces, the exo battalion, and other units under General Keil's authority."

"Uh-oh," Althea said.

"Yeah," Paul said. "Working with those assholes just amplified Kata's and my opinion of them. And theirs of us, I'm sure."

Paul looked past Althea out the window. They were still on the bridge. They floated with their legs entangled so that they faced each other with an unruly swirl of blankets encircling them.

Paul took a deep breath and let it out. He looked back at Althea and continued.

"I remember one mission, near the end. It was a deep raid on a Chinese robot depot. A place where they stored and maintained a large number of their fighting robots. A successful hit on a facility like this had the effect of screwing with the enemy commander's near-term operational future. Like when a hockey team loses a player to the penalty box. There are certain plays they just can't run anymore.

"My company was tapped for this one," Paul continued. "Kata acted as my operations officer and went to all of the planning sessions and mission briefings. As company commanders, we didn't have planning staffs like the exo battalion and heavy drone units we were working with. It was just Kata and me and our first sergeants.

"This particular plan was tight, but given the strength of resistance we expected to face, every detail was critical. It called for putting all of Outlaw Company on one part of the objective while Thurman's exo battalion hit another part."

Paul smiled.

"What?" Althea asked.

"Colonel Filson was fired up when we told him about the mission," Paul said. "'This is great,' he said. 'An Ōkami company doing the same work as an entire exo battalion!' Kata and I were too tired to share in his parochial excitement. We just stared at the secure video screen. Exhausted. Filson tuned in quickly, though. And spent the next few hours helping us plan our piece. I could tell, when we rang off, he was nervous for me and Outlaw Company.

"Since Dragon Flight would be acting as close air support on the objective, they did not have enough payload capacity for troop transport. We used every ounce of their max gross weight to carry munitions. As a result, we would be inserted and extracted by heavy drone. That part made me nervous.

"Kata and I planned the assault like we always did, down to the gnat's ass," Paul continued. "One of the most important details was the aircraft heading on landing. The heavy drone was configured with an aft ramp, like our QC-10s. Because of the layout of the enemy facilities and the anticipated resistance, we needed the ramp to be facing due west when we exited. That way, we could target and return fire directly on the enemy as we moved to cover. If the ramp was facing the wrong direction, we would not be able to suppress the enemy as we exited, and, worse, we would not have a direct path to cover. Getting off the ramp and changing direction would increase our vulnerability. The Chinese would be able to pick us off as we ran around the large, squatty drones.

"We emphasized this during our planning with the heavy drone pilots. Over and over. To the point that Colonel Packard finally waved us off. 'OK, guys. We get it,' he said. 'We'll set down with our ramp facing due west. Have a little faith, will you?'

"Kata looked at Packard and, for a second, I thought she was going to say, 'That's the problem, sir. We have little faith in you.' It's what I was thinking as well. But, to her credit, Kata swallowed it and let the mission brief continue."

Paul shook his head in disgust at the memory.

"And what do you think those dumb bastards did?" he asked Althea.

"No," she said with disbelief.

"The heavy drone landed to the west, ramp facing due east. The exact opposite direction we needed. The operation was a total cock-up. We lost Mia and several soldierbots as we exited and maneuvered around the aircraft. The shock of her last gasp nearly knocked me out, but my suit kept running."

Althea shook her head.

"We fought through it, though. We had surprised them and achieved most of our objectives in the first few minutes. We destroyed a lot of equipment."

Paul paused. Eyes cast downward.

"Then what happened?" Althea nudged.

"Intel had missed a few things. Chief among them was the Chinese armored battalion and Centaur infantry regiment that were billeted on the robot depot. They tore into us, driving a wedge of tanks and infantry between Outlaw Company and the exo battalion. Within minutes, we were each surrounded and fighting for our lives. It was a shit storm. But there was a window…"

Paul shook his head slowly.

"A window?" Althea asked.

"A window when they could have gotten us out."

"But they left you and the exos there to fight?"

"Not the exos," Paul said.

Althea's eyes widened.

"The heavy drone dropped in right on top of the exo battalion, weapons spitting fire in all directions, and yanked them out. To the last man. They took some hits, but all the of the aircraft made it out. All of the exos, wounded, dead, and fully able, were extracted."

"What were you doing?" Althea asked.

"I was yelling on the radio," Paul said. "Demanding extraction."

"They just said no?"

"They said the human soldiers took priority."

"No…" Althea whispered.

"They said it was not possible to attempt the extraction of robots," Paul muttered angrily. "Said the landing zone was too hot. Too much enemy fire. Said they would make an attempt when the tactical situation allowed."

Althea's hands slowly rose to cover her mouth.

"Kata told me after that she was standing next to Colonel Packard in the command center when my call came in. She heard them say humans were the priority. She lost her mind. Two security sergeants had to restrain her, or she would have killed Colonel Packard.

"'Goddamn it, Vukovic!' Kata said General Keil yelled at her. 'You will secure your shit, or I'll have you removed from my command post. Get control of yourself!'

"General Schofield walked into the command center as Packard explained to Kata that the math just didn't work. He couldn't risk his heavy drones just to pull one Centaur out. Kata said that Schofield nodded in agreement.

At that point she was close to being thrown out of the command center and losing her ability to influence the battle for us at all. She didn't want that. So, she tried to swallow her rage.

"But Kata was never good at concealing her feelings. When she was mad, you could feel it on the other side of the room. I guess Packard felt it, because apparently, he walked over and tried to reassure her. He told her they would get me out of there as soon as they could. Told her they were working on a plan to send in one of their fast movers, a lightweight drone for me to strap onto for a solo extraction.

"Kata told him not to bother. Said I wouldn't leave my soldiers behind. She told me at that point she went to the other side of the map table and tried to stay clear of everyone.

"As she walked away, though, she overheard Colonel Packard say, 'Crazy fucking jigsaws,' to General Keil.

Althea's eyes widened.

"Yeah," Paul said with a rueful nod. "Ordinarily Kata would have flown into an asskicking rage over that. But she told me later that she was past caring what they thought. All she was concerned with was me and Outlaw Company.

"We took more losses while we waited. My soldierbots and XPs were taking a lot of hits," Paul continued. "Snapshot had an arm blown off. Then I took a round to the leg. My armor stopped most of it, and my suit cauterized the wound immediately. But my mobility was fucked. I was hobbled.

"Then I heard Packard shout over the radio, 'Hypersonics inbound!'"

"What does that mean?" Althea asked.

"The Chinese had hypersonic batteries in Caracas, Paramaribo, and a few other coastal cities. They were meant for longer-range defensive fires, and, like ours, the missiles flew faster than Mach fifteen and were networked with their spy satellites. They could take out long-range strategic aircraft at nearly intercontinental ranges, or even aircraft taking off from the mainland US if they wanted."

"Wow," Althea said softly.

"Same old story," Paul said, shaking his head.

"What story is that?" Althea asked.

"Technologies race up the lethality and standoff ladder," Paul said. "Deadly applications appear only to be canceled out by the next." Paul alternated his hands one over the other in front of his chest, as if he were climbing a ladder. "The only constant is the fight on the ground. The grunts, killing each other. The technology ends up only isolating us more completely. Freezing us in the same old shit."

"World War I style?" Althea said sadly.

"Yeah." Paul raised his eyes to meet hers. Her comment made him smile. "Exactly. Their hypersonics effectively capped the area. Anything five hundred feet or above was disintegrated by the lattice of projectiles flying fifteen times the speed of sound. The Chinese decided they liked their numbers and chances on the ground and were willing to seal it off and let us fight it out.

"And they were right," Paul said. "We were down to less than half strength at that point. We didn't have the staying power. The heavy drones were loitering at a safe distance behind a mountain range that covered them from the hypersonics. They did their best to support us with indirect fire. But maybe a quarter of their rounds made it through the hypersonic cap. So," Paul said, rubbing his scalp, "we were baked."

"What did you do?" Althea asked.

"I didn't know what to do," Paul said with a shrug. "Top and I looked at each other at one point… She nodded at me, and I realized I had said, 'This is it,' to her in whisper mode. I nodded back.

"Kata told me later that General Schofield was standing right behind her in the command post, monitoring the mission. Each time I would call for extraction, he would look at General Keil and Colonel Packard and shake his head. Then Packard would look at Kata and repeat his promise: 'We'll get him out as soon as we can.'

"Kata said my voice started to sound bad, the worst she had ever heard me sound. She said it didn't sound scared, really. But resigned. Tired. No one in the command center would make eye contact with Kata when I called in. It felt like this went on for a long time. Kata stared at the mapping table, watching the enemy stack up around us as Outlaw's numbers dwindled.

"It was hell on the ground. The mission was designed to be a raid, an in-and-out job. We did not have sufficient force to hold terrain. It was just a matter of time. And the Chinese could sense it too. They kept pouring it on. The noise was incredible. The chain-saw sounds of us firing on them. Explosions from their munitions hitting all around us. The shriek of the hypersonics overhead. Indirect fire from the heavy drones detonating in the air when struck by a hypersonic, or on the ground if they made it through.

"Then Dragon Three came over the radio. 'Outlaw Six, this is Dragon Three,' he said.

"Everyone had forgotten about the Dragons. Including me. And including the Chinese. Kata told me that when she heard D3's radio call she looked at the map table and saw three Dragons due north of our location, and two due south on what she had thought were extended setups for strafing runs. But at that moment she realized they were not in a strafing formation. The Dragons were preparing for something else. She told me she had to stifle a smile, not wanting to alert General Schofield or anyone else to what the Dragons were up to.

"'Go ahead, Dragon Three,' I responded.

"'Keep your head down, sir,' Dragon Three radioed back, the roar of his engines almost overwhelming his voice. 'We're coming to get you. Going to be on your position in two minutes for extraction. But before we get there, we're going to have to fire everything we have left into your vicinity to lighten our load.'"

"But I thought you said they were not available?" Althea said. "They were performing gunship missions."

"They were," Paul said, nodding. "They had been flying ballsy low-level strafing runs on the enemy, weaving around the incoming heavy drone fire trying to clear out the LZ. When the alert for hypersonics had come over the net, instead of climbing to a safe altitude and running behind the mountains with the heavy drones, they dove to make sure they were no higher than a hundred feet above ground level. At that altitude, though, they were much more vulnerable to ground-based fire, so they had to move off of the fight."

A large smile broke out on Althea's face.

"They were also monitoring the radio, of course," Paul continued. "Listening when I asked for extraction. They heard my request get denied as the exo battalion got pulled out. They listened as I asked repeatedly for extraction and was repeatedly turned down. I guess they got tired of waiting."

Althea nodded her approval.

Paul smiled as he continued.

"Kata said General Schofield went nuts. He yelled and slammed his fists down on the mapping table, shaking the holographic image of the battle."

"He was mad, huh?" Althea said with delight.

Paul smiled. "General officers, as a rule, don't handle it well when reality doesn't bend to their will. But Schofield was a combat-zone commander. A demigod. His words moved mountains, changed the course of rivers, and caused men and women to die. No one and nothing disobeyed him."

"Except an Ōkami going to get a comrade," Althea said.

"Except for that," Paul said. "I bet the general's eyes nearly bulged out of his head as the five flashing green icons identifying Dragon Flight turned to converge on our company's location. Three were flying in from the north. The other two from the south." Paul gestured with his hands to make it clear to Althea. "All of them were flying at more than three hundred knots, less than fifty feet above the ground.

"'Dragon Three, you sure you want to do that?' I asked over the radio.

"'Negative!' Schofield yelled over the radio, interrupting me. 'Negative! Do not attempt extraction. I repeat. Do not attempt extraction. Acknowledge!'

"'Ninety seconds,' Dragon Three transmitted.

"'This is Eagle Zero Six, goddamn it!' Schofield responded. 'I am ordering you to abort!'

"Kata said the command center was in shock at the development. General Keil and Colonel Packard stood motionless in stunned disbelief.

"She wanted to get the Dragons some help, though, so she prodded Colonel Packard. She asked him to lay down some indirect fire on the Chinese to keep them occupied, but he and Keil just looked at Schofield. They wouldn't do anything unless he approved.

"'Sixty seconds,' Dragon Three called on the radio. Top's head swiveled toward me.

"I gave a thumbs-up while saying to her in whisper mode, 'Get ready. If they actually make it, we're not going to have long to get aboard and get gone.'

"'I'm ready,' she whispered back.

"'Kata told me she walked over and stood in front of Schofield. 'They're not going to stop, sir,' she said in a quiet voice. 'Least we can do is support them.'

"The general stared at Kata for interminable seconds before looking away in disgust. He nodded to Colonel Packard and walked out of the command center. 'Roger that,' Packard said. He spun on his heels, speaking quickly into his headset.

"Kata said she stepped up to the mapping table and watched as the green Dragon Flight icons inched closer to the LZ. She keyed the radio. 'Attention this net, this is Apache Six. Heavy drones will be laying down supportive fire along the protective lines I'm broadcasting now.' She hit 'send' from the mapping table, sharing their display with us instantly. The protective fire lines lay down across the 3D map on my in-head display. I smiled. They were laid exactly where I would have put them, yellow crosshairs indicating targeted coordinates. Yellow dotted-line circles outlined the lethal blast radius of each impact. It was going to be fucking close.

"'It's going to be heavy, Dragons,' Kata said over the radio. 'Keep an eye out for debris on your approach. Outlaw Six, I'd get skinny and low if I were you.' I keyed my mic twice to acknowledge Kata.

"We sheltered as best we could as the heavy drone fire struck the Chinese in long sheaths of death to the east and west of us. The Dragons fired off the rest of their heavy ordnance as well, to lighten up and kill enemy. The ground shook. The smoke and debris thickened. Visibility was zero.

"Back in the command center, the mapping table must have bloomed red as the heavy drone fire struck. Kata watched as the five Dragons joined up in a tight clockwise circle spitting more fire on the Chinese.

"I saw three Dragons dive to the ground. 'Go! Go! Go!' I yelled. Every living Outlaw ran toward the three Dragons as they flared aggressively under the explosions and crisscrossing fire.

"We must have been a sad sight. We were down to about two dozen undamaged soldierbots. They ran and fired their weapons as they carried and dragged their wounded and broken comrades. Snapshot fired his weapon with his one good arm at a full sprint. I was limping badly, one hand clinging to Top to keep upright, shooting with the other.

"The Dragons slammed onto the ground, skidding to a stop, every weapons system blazing. Their large forward turrets glowed red from the amount of fire they were spitting at the enemy.

"Top and I were just a few meters from Dragon Two's ramp when Colonel Packard transmitted. 'Dragons hold position for five seconds,' he commanded.

"I started to protest, but Kata sent another line of fire to my map, directly north of us, to cover our egress. Top and I fell to the floor of Dragon Two. Her ramp closed as I watched the covering fire erupt on my map. 'Go! Go! Go!' Kata yelled into the radio."

"You made it!" Althea said.

Paul nodded. "All but Dragon Five," he said softly.

Althea's smile dissolved.

"He was the trail aircraft."

"Oh no."

"It was quick. He disintegrated after being struck by a large missile."

Althea was quiet for a moment out of respect. She looked at Paul. He was looking past her at the stars. She waited.

"Kata met us on the airfield," Paul said. "I had passed out from the combination of blood loss and Dragon Five's last gasp. She helped my soldiers get me to Stalwart's medical facility, where I was quickly placed into a medpod.

"An hour later, Kata went back to the command center to grab the rest of her things. Schofield, Keil, and Packard were standing at the mapping table, replaying parts of the battle. Kata told me she tried to be quiet, but they turned to look when she grabbed her rucksack.

"'Captain Vukovic,' General Keil said. 'Come here.' Kata walked over to the three senior officers. She could see they were not happy. Neither was she. 'What the fuck happened out there tonight, Captain?' Keil demanded.

"'I'd like to ask the colonel the same question,' Kata answered, matching the general's venom with her own.

"'What do you mean?' Packard asked, indignant.

"'Let's start with, how the hell do you fuck up the landing direction after we've been through it so many times?'

"General Keil waved her off. 'The assault was a success, Captain.'

"'Success?' Kata nearly screamed.

"'Yes,' General Keil said. 'We achieved every objective. And incurred negligible losses.'

"'Negligible losses?" Kata shouted. 'We lost seventy percent of Outlaw Company! Captain Owens nearly had his leg taken off!'

"The one-star general glanced at the other two senior officers as if the three of them were in on a joke. 'Like I said,' Keil said without expression. 'Negligible.'

"Kata took a step toward the general.

"'Captain!' Schofield said sternly.

"Kata didn't come to attention, but she stopped her advance on Keil. 'Yes, sir?' she said.

"'It's been a long night for everyone. I suggest you get some rest.' Schofield said.

"'Yes, sir,' Kata said, realizing there was nothing to be gained or proven at that point. She turned to leave.

"'And, Captain?' General Schofield said. 'I've contacted Colonel Filson and the manufacturer and asked for a full malfunction report. I expect they will need you and Captain Owens to assist. See to it that you do.'

"'Malfunction, sir?' she asked.

"'Dragon Flight's failure to follow orders,' the general said, glaring. 'Dependability is the primary requirement of any weapons system. Your team better get their shit together, or this proof of concept is as far as you will ever get. I will not tolerate rogue robots in my command or in my military.

"'A few more missions like tonight, and you won't have to, sir,' Kata said as she turned to leave.

"'Crazy fucking jigsaw,' General Keil muttered to Colonel Packard."

Althea scowled at the comment and then shook her head. "It wasn't a malfunction, though, was it?" she asked.

Paul smiled. "Not to me, it wasn't," he said. "It was puzzling, though."

"Why?"

"A direct order from a general officer?" Paul exclaimed, his eyes wide. "I would have had a hard time disobeying that."

"But you would have," Althea said.

"For Kata?" Paul said quietly. "Or Top? Or any of my soldiers?" Paul nodded slowly. "I would."

"Sounds like loyalty was a defect you all shared."

# Chapter Sixty-Seven

*Mission Cycle 418*

*Earth Year 2062*

*312,259,277 Kilometers from Earth*

Aloud clang woke Paul.

He rubbed his eyes and looked around the bridge. Althea, in rest mode, floated several meters from him. Her naked body was wrapped in two blankets that enfolded her like too much origami. All Paul saw of her was a bolt of jet-black hair above her forehead and one leg from the knee down.

As soon as he convinced himself he had imagined the noise, he heard another one. A long, scraping sound, like someone dragging a knife through a cardboard box, came from somewhere below.

He looked around.

Althea still slept.

An IR bot sped by within inches of the large window, startling Paul.

A second later, another zoomed past.

Paul touched a toe to the floor, pushing himself forward.

He caught himself with his fingertips against the window, and hung motionless, alarmed by what he saw.

The bridge was surrounded by a horde of IR bots. They converged from every direction.

Another loud impact sound rang out behind him, as if a truck had driven into the bridge.

Althea was awake now. She clutched her blankets and looked around, trying to make sense of the increasing noise.

Paul stared at an IR bot twenty meters below the forward window. It approached the bridge superstructure, carrying a large welding torch.

"Are you kidding me?" Paul mumbled as the IR bot's torch flared and it started slicing metal.

"What is it?" Althea asked.

A buzzing noise and vibration filled the bridge.

"What is happening, Paul?" she asked.

Paul didn't answer, unable to take his focus off of the IR bots swarming around the bridge.

A loud impact struck above Paul and Althea, on the topside of the bridge.

"Paul!" Althea yelled. "What is going on?"

"I don't know," Paul said, pushing away from the window back toward her. "But it looks like we are under attack."

"Attack?" Althea asked. "What do you mean?"

Paul's mind raced. *Was Captain Drake right after all?* he thought. *The XO is out to kill us?*

"XO!" Paul yelled. "XO, status report!"

No response.

The loud bangs and scrapes were continuous now and came from all directions.

Paul and Althea exchanged worried looks. She held out her hand. Paul took it and pulled her to him.

The bridge sounded like a construction site. Noises like jackhammers, chain saws, and welders filled the air.

"They're tearing the bridge apart!" Althea shouted over the din. She put her hands over her ears as Paul returned to the window.

He pressed against the glass.

There was a swarm of IR bots around the base of the bridge, fifty meters below. Sparks and chunks of metal flew off the superstructure where they worked.

"XO!" Paul demanded. "XO! Situation report, damn it!"

Paul pushed off of the window and glided over to the command chair. He flipped through all the switches as he yelled at the XO.

"XO, do you hear me?" Paul called. "XO, we are in trouble. We need a situation report."

The earsplitting sound of rending metal filled the bridge as it tilted several meters to starboard.

"Pressure suits, now!" Paul yelled. He grabbed Althea's shoulder and pushed her toward the utility closet.

They donned their pressure suits in a rush, expecting explosive decompression to strike at any second.

"Paul!" the XO's voice said over their suit radios. "Paul, can you hear me?"

"XO!" Paul responded. "What the hell is going on? Why were you not responding?"

"I'm sorry, Paul," the XO said. "That idiot maintenance boss severed my hardwired communications to the bridge too soon. I was hoping you would figure it out and use a suit radio."

"We didn't figure anything out," Paul said, anger in his voice. "We feared for our lives and got suited to prepare for whatever comes next."

"Why are they attacking us?" Althea demanded.

"Attacking?" the XO asked. "Oh no. I am so sorry. I can see how you would get that impression."

"What the hell is going on?" Paul shouted into his radio, his patience expired.

"Degradation of the number-two reactor has accelerated, and we don't have as much time as we thought. Failure and detonation could occur at any moment now," the XO explained. "The maintenance boss and navigator came up with a plan to get you two to minimum safe distance. The maintenance boss is working to separate the command-and-control module from the *Odysseus*. He is also welding additional radiation shielding to the CnC's outer hull. When that is complete, he will fasten the four tug drones to the CnC, two on each side. The navigator will give the tug drones a course to follow. They will fire their engines, and you will depart."

Paul and Althea were silent.

They could hear banging, buzzing, and cutting noises as the maintenance boss continued his work.

"We will depart?" Althea asked, confused.

"What will you do, XO?" Paul asked.

"As soon as the command-and-control module has separated from the *Odysseus*, I will fire my main engines," the XO said. "I will put the ship on a heading opposite of your assigned course and will move as fast as I can manage. With any luck, I'll be far enough away from you when the reactors explode."

"I don't like this plan very much," Paul said.

"Trust me," the XO said, "I don't either."

"XO," Althea said. "I don't want to leave you."

"I don't want you to either, Althea," the XO said. "But this is the only way."

"What course will we be on?" Paul asked. "Do we really have a chance, or is this just delaying the inevitable?"

"Paul is right," Althea said. "If this is just giving us a little more time, we should stay together."

"I appreciate the sentiment," the XO said. "But the navigator has assured me it is survivable."

"I don't like this," Althea said.

"Althea," the XO said. "You owe it to me and the rest of the crew to try."

Paul looked out of the window at all of the activity. Dozens of IR bots transporting large metal plates waited in line behind the welders. There was a loud bang when the plates were put into position, followed by a staticky buzzing noise as the welders attached them to the CnC. Once complete, the next plate was shoved into place by the next waiting IR bot.

"Quite a lot of shielding," Paul said into his helmet mic.

"It is," the XO said. "More than is required to protect you from the blast radiation. But it's all I have on hand at the moment."

Paul nodded in his helmet, unsure of what to say.

"We don't have much time," the XO said. "I need to pass on more instructions from the navigator before your departure."

"OK," Paul said.

"You're in for a journey of at least six months," the XO said. "By then, the navigator estimates the rendezvous becomes highly likely. But not before. To make it that far, you are going to have to strictly ration your food and water intake as well as your power consumption. Furthermore, because of the way the CnC module has to be removed from the *Odysseus*, your accompanying life-support equipment will be greatly reduced. I do not know how long the scrubbers will be able to provide you with breathable atmosphere. Hopefully at least six months."

Paul looked out of the large window as the XO spoke. The four tug drones approached the CnC module. They flew in a tight, clustered formation until they were within twenty meters of the window and then separated from each other and decelerated. Two passed out of view to the left and two to the right.

"I don't know how much food you have on board the CnC, but hopefully it will last you," the XO continued. "Althea, I recommend you spend as much time as possible in rest mode. And Paul, I recommend you take hibernation meds to reduce your water, caloric, and oxygen requirements. The medbay should have a reasonable supply. Do not use the medpod or any other system that requires a lot of power, of course," the XO added. "Hopefully you are far enough along that this will not present a problem for you, Althea."

An impact to the left side of the CnC startled Althea. Then another on the right side. Seconds later, loud buzzing noises filled the air. Paul pictured the IR bots firmly holding the tug drones while the welders lashed them to the command-and-control module's flanks.

Paul shook his head.

"What is it?" Althea asked him.

"We're going to be one ugly fucking spacecraft," he said.

"I won't tell the maintenance boss you said so," the XO said.

"Just tell him we said thank you," Paul said in a somber voice. "The navigator as well."

"I will," the XO said.

Paul noted through the viewing window that many of the IR bots were departing. The noise was trailing off as well.

"We're getting close, aren't we?" Paul asked.

"Yes," the XO said. "A matter of minutes, I would think."

"How many G's we in for?" Paul asked, tapping on Althea's shoulder and pointing to the rear of the bridge.

"Given the mass of the bridge, no more than ten," the XO said.

"Ouch," Paul said.

"I know," the XO conceded. "The good news is that you will likely pass out and it will not be long term. The tugs are going to run at max power until the reactor detonates. If the bridge survives the blast, they will relent. At that point, you can expect one G until they run out of fuel."

"How long do you think we will be at max burn?" Paul asked, not wanting to phrase it the other way.

"No more than a few minutes."

The CnC swayed back and forth a few times, and then a loud snap rang out, accompanied by a jolt that radiated through the entire superstructure.

The stars outside the window spun slowly, and Paul realized they had been amputated from the *Odysseus*.

Paul stared at the tilting void. The *Odysseus*'s long prow, which Paul had looked at through the large viewing window for almost a year and a half, was no longer in sight.

They were adrift.

The bridge's sudden angular acceleration moved the rear wall in relation to Paul and Althea. They were moving toward the middle of the bridge.

Paul touched a toe to the floor and pushed Althea back toward the rear wall. He moved himself in that direction as well.

"Paul and Althea," the XO said. "It has been my pleasure to serve with you both."

"XO, I—" Paul was interrupted by a bright, searing glare. The *Odysseus* inched into view, riding a white-hot fireball.

The ship passed in front of the bridge, accelerating on the nuclear fire of her ailing reactors.

It was a pitiful sight. The once long and purposeful ship was now broken. Paul and Althea got a good view of the extensive damage Regas's suicide had wrought. Burned impact damage covered the truncated hull like a pox. Cargo, loosened by the incident, tumbled out of the accelerating ship. And topside, where the bridge used to stand, was an ugly burned nub of severed metal.

*It's a blessing,* Paul caught himself thinking. *She'd be scrapped anyway. This is better.*

Then he remembered the XO.

The ship was farther away now. All Paul could discern was a fireball. And it was accelerating.

"XO, can you read me?" Paul transmitted. The suit radios did not have a long range, but he wanted to try.

"Yes, Paul," the XO responded, with a lot of static. "I can hear you."

A roar startled Paul.

The stars spun around outside the large window.

The tugs were setting up for their burn. A few more short roars emanated from different angles as the team of four worked the bridge to an entry solution for their assigned course.

Paul pushed Althea against the rear wall. "Stay as flat against the wall as you can," he said to her as he nudged his own body back. "This part is going to be really uncomfortable."

"I know," she said with fear in her voice.

"Paul, do you read me?" the XO said over the radio, static nearly covering his voice now.

"Yes," Paul said. "Yes, I hear you. I just wanted to say thank you and that we will never forget you. You will be remembered."

"Strange," the XO said, Paul barely making out the words. "That actually helps."

The four tug drones fired their engines in unison.

Paul and Althea slammed against the rear wall.

The howl of the four tug engines at max burn was deafening, so Paul could not be sure. But he thought he heard the XO say, "Godspeed, my friend, Paul Owens."

Then Paul blacked out.

# Chapter Sixty-Eight

*Mission Cycle 419*

*Earth Year 2062*

*312,781,824 Kilometers from Earth*

Paul opened his eyes.

He looked around the bridge. It was a cluttered, disorienting mess. Under the new relative acceleration, the rear wall was now their floor, the large viewing window their ceiling. Anything that had not been secured was now strewn about next to Paul and Althea.

Paul looked at Althea. She lay next to him in rest mode, under the comfortable single G of acceleration.

The low rumble of the tug drone engines permeated the bridge. Paul wondered how long they would burn until running out of fuel. It couldn't be more than a few cycles.

He looked at his watch. It had been less than half an hour since the tug drones' max burn acceleration had knocked him out. Paul wished he had asked the XO how long the tugs' fuel would last.

The XO.

The *Odysseus*.

*You did it, XO,* Paul thought. *You got enough separation between us. Thank you.*

Paul stood up slowly.

"What are you doing?" Althea asked him.

"I'm going to inventory what we've got on board and get our new ship in order."

"I'll help," she said.

They spent a full cycle cleaning, arranging, and inventorying.

"What do you think?" Althea asked Paul when they were done.

"It's going to be tight," he said. "The air scrubbers seem to be in good shape. But, truthfully, I don't know much about them. In terms of power, we're running on the bridge's small emergency generator. It should last, but we cannot work it too hard, so I have turned the heat down." Paul paused to emphasize the point. "It's going to be cold. The good news is we have plenty of water," he continued. "The pinch will be food. We don't have a lot. But if I use the hibernation meds and you put yourself in rest mode, we might be able to barely stretch into six months. But not much more."

"Hopefully someone will come across us by then," Althea said.

"If they do, it will be a miracle. We have no radio. No transponder. No external lights. They would have to run into us."

"How about a little optimism?" Althea asked. "Let's not condemn ourselves yet. Not after what the XO did."

Paul nodded and took Althea's hand.

"We'll make it," Althea said.

Paul worked his way to the small galley, a difficult task due to the new relative acceleration. He managed to prepare himself and Althea a small meal.

"Freeze-dried beans," he announced with flair as he returned to the bridge.

"Thank you," Althea said, taking the small container from him. "It's warm!" she said with delight.

"Only the best," Paul said.

He sat down next to her and took a bite. He worked the mouthful of processed legumes a long time before swallowing.

Paul thought about the *Odysseus* again. Her gargantuan size had meant that food stores and variety were not an issue. But all their makeshift lifeboat had on board when they'd separated was the emergency freeze-dried stuff. Another thing about the old girl he would miss.

After they had eaten, Paul and Althea bundled up and lay down under a pile of blankets they'd found in the medbay. The temperature was dropping fast as the infinite void drained their lifeboat of heat.

They stared up at the large, formerly forward, window. With nothing else to do, and no good excuse enabling him to refuse, Paul agreed to continue his story.

"Colonel Filson showed up a week after the botched raid, dispatched by Combat Corps Command to figure out why the Dragons had malfunctioned. He had a civilian in tow. A guy named Pruden who worked for Determined End States, a defense industry holding company owned by Fiona Malloy."

"The same Fiona Malloy?" Althea asked.

"Yes," Paul said. "Though I didn't know it at the time. The commercial aspects of the field trial were not something we ever thought about. All Kata and I knew was that Colonel Filson and this guy, Pruden, were there to make sure command did not get spooked.

"To be honest," Paul continued, "Pruden didn't seem like a bad guy to me. He was ridiculously out of place, though, walking around like he was dressed more for a safari than a combat zone. His helmet and armored vest seemed oversized on his skinny body. But he seemed to really give a shit, to respect Kata and me as well as the Ōkami. He interviewed us all several times and spent hours analyzing the data and conferring with Dr. Musashi and his team via the sat phone.

"After a couple of days, Kata and I got used to having Pruden around. So much so that we started venting to the colonel in front of him. Kata, of course, started first.

"'This is bad, sir,' Kata said. 'Paul's Outlaws are down to less than fifty percent after that fucked-up depot raid, and I'm almost as bad after the goat screw they sent me on. I lost Grant, Sherman, and two Talons!' Kata's face was tight with strain as she continued. 'We're down to six Ōkami betas between us. Our soldierbot and extension-platform numbers are dwindling, and the maintenance bots can't keep up. But even worse,' she said, 'the Chinese have taken notice of us.'

"'What do you mean?' Filson asked her.

"'We know they've been watching us since we've been in country,' Kata said. 'But Paul's depot raid was a red flag. Until then, they have been happy to leave us alone while we fucked with Navarro. I think they, like Schofield, are more focused on the big fight that's coming. But now that we have inflicted real pain on them, not their proxy bastard in the Cone,' Kata continued, 'they view us as something that has to be eliminated. Intel has picked up Chinese intercepts telling Navarro to get aggressive. And we know they gave him a bunch of new tech.'

"'Have you talked to General Schofield about this?' Filson asked.

"'We did.' Kata sneered. 'The smoothie told us to stop assisting the Chinese.' The colonel's blank look told Kata to continue. 'When we finished our situation report he just asked us to please stop assisting the Chinese,' she told Filson. 'He said the Chinese wanted him to divert forces to deal with Navarro, but that it was our job. He was gearing up for a push west and didn't want to divert forces to the Southern Cone because an aging warlord was spooking two Centaurs.'

"Filson shook his head.

"In a dejected voice, Kata said, 'We're degrading while Navarro is getting stronger. Like I said. This is bad.' We all sat there in silence for a moment. The only sound was Pruden's typing on his laptop in the corner.

"'You are quiet today, Paul,' the colonel said to me. I looked back at him and shrugged. 'What is it?' he asked me.

"'The depot raid got in his head,' Kata said, pointing at me.

"'No,' I said. 'Not the raid.'

"'What is it, then, son?' the colonel asked me. I hesitated. 'Tell me,' he said.

"'I still don't understand why Dragon Flight came back for us,' I said. Pruden, still in the corner, looked up at me.

"'We've been through this,' Filson said. 'Right, Pruden? Read him our executive summary.'

"'Sir?' Pruden said, caught off guard.

"'Read him our executive summary, please,' Filson repeated.

"'Oh, right,' Pruden stammered. He tapped a few keys on his laptop and said, 'A combination of poor communications, Chinese electronic warfare, and battle damage prevented the aircraft from receiving and processing the command to—'

"I interrupted him. 'Bullshit!' I said, standing up from my chair. Filson, Kata, and Pruden, all startled, stared at me. 'That's a bunch of bullshit to feed the administrative beast and keep your precious field trial on the rails!' I said. Colonel Filson regarded me for a long moment. Pruden sat still, not sure what to do. 'I want to understand what happened,' I said.

"'Isn't it obvious?' the colonel asked me. 'They came back for you. You, Top, and the rest of their comrades.'

"'I mean, why did they do it?' I said.

"'Pruden?' the colonel said, turning to look at him.

"'Yes?' Pruden said, sitting up straight as he answered.

"'Did you ask the Dragons why they returned for Captain Owens and the rest of Outlaw Company, despite orders from General Schofield not to?'

"'Yes,' Pruden said.

"'And what did they say?' the colonel asked.

"'They said that it was the right thing to do,' Pruden said.

"Filson nodded as he turned from Pruden and looked at me. I shook my head. I had had the same conversation with the Dragons, and they'd told me the same thing. When I'd pressed them on how they knew it was the right thing, Dragon Three had just said, 'It was a gut thing, sir.'

"'Why are you making this so hard?' Filson asked me. 'Why don't you accept their answer?'

"'That's not how they are supposed to work,' I said. 'They are just machines.'

"'What does that mean?' the colonel asked. 'Just machines?'

"'It means...' I stammered, searching for the words. 'It means...'

"The colonel chuckled, which really pissed me off. I glared at the old man. Pruden looked nervously at his laptop. 'I'm sorry, Paul,' the colonel said to me, trying to swallow his smile. 'I don't mean to laugh.' Filson stood up and stepped closer to me. He put his hand on my shoulder and said, 'Most soldiers spend their whole careers looking for comrades that will do what yours did that night. Most soldiers go into battle bearing doubt. They're not sure that their buddies will be there for them. Not a hundred percent, anyway. You, though?' Filson pointed at me with his other hand. 'You know. No matter how shitty, no matter how dangerous, no matter how impossible, no matter if it contravenes a fucking three-star general or their own programming, your soldiers will never leave you behind. They will come back for you. Every. Damn. Time. That's all that matters,' Colonel Filson concluded.

"'Maybe,' I said. 'But I want to know why.'

"'You know why,' Colonel Filson said over his shoulder as he walked back to his chair.

"'I don't,' I said.

"'You do, son,' Filson said, sitting down. 'It was the process.'

"I looked at the colonel, then at Kata," Paul told Althea. "Her face was tense, waiting for me to explode on the old man. Pruden sat in the corner, confused and nervous. I looked back at the colonel. Then I shook my head and chuckled in surrender," Paul said, smiling at the memory.

"'What is the process?' Pruden asked Filson.

"'I'll tell you on our flight back tomorrow,' the colonel said, pulling a cigar out of his breast pocket.

"'It's bullshit,' Kata said.

"'It's gospel,' the colonel said.

"Filson lit his cigar and blew a few smoke rings across the hooch. Pruden sensed the tension in the room had ratcheted down and returned to his notes.

"The next morning," Paul continued, "Kata and I walked in silence with the colonel to his aircraft. Pruden walked behind us. We stood together at the end of the aft boarding ramp.

"The colonel looked at us. 'I won't lie,' he said. 'I'm worried about you two.' Then he shook his head. 'And I wish I wasn't so goddamn old.' Kata and I looked at our feet, trying not to show how unsettling the colonel's words to us were. Pruden stood awkwardly on the periphery. Filson looked over my shoulder, back across Devil toward the shipping-container hooches dug into the side of the mountain, almost two hundred meters away.

"At that moment, Top stepped out of my ops hooch. The colonel nodded slightly to her and winked. It was a gesture that would have been imperceptible to a human at that distance. Top, though, stopped and gave Filson a sharp salute before continuing on her way.

"Filson looked back at us with a tired face. 'This is not the time to let the pressure off, guys,' the colonel said. 'If you guys get in trouble, General Schofield is not going to divert even a cook's assistant to help. If Navarro knew the situation, he'd run you over today. You can't let him suspect, even for a second, that you are in a weakened state. So, give 'em hell, guys,' Filson said. Then he stepped onto the aircraft ramp and walked forward into the shadows.

"Pruden, suddenly alone with me and Kata, looked around Outpost Devil for a moment and then back at us. 'It's been an honor,' he said, awkwardly extending his hand. Kata took it first.

"'Yeah,' she said as she shook his hand. 'Thanks.'

"'Thanks,' I said without enthusiasm.

"Pruden leaned in as he shook my hand. 'I don't think it's bullshit, Captain,' he said. 'I think they came back for you because they thought it was the right thing to do.' I just nodded. Pruden took a few steps onto the aircraft ramp. He was half in the shadows when he stopped and turned back to us. 'And they were right,' he said.

"The ramp rose, and the engines spun up. Kata and I walked back to the ops hooch as the aircraft flew away."

# Chapter Sixty-Nine

---

*Mission Cycle 419*

*Earth Year 2062*

*313,043,098 Kilometers from Earth*

---

"**A**re you sure you didn't turn the heat all the way off?" Althea asked.

"I promise," Paul said, holding the blanket up for Althea to jump under. She had just relieved herself in the makeshift latrine Paul had built for them in the corner. He had fastened it securely to the floor, in preparation for the tugs running out of fuel and weightlessness returning. He didn't want to deal with a roaming container of urine and feces.

Paul winced as a rush of frigid air snuck under the blanket with Althea.

They wrapped their arms around each other to share body heat.

"It is set to just above freezing," he said into her ear. "I'm hoping that by doing that and leaving all of the lights and other nonessential systems off, we can squeeze more than six months out of the generator."

Althea said nothing. She had buried her face into Paul's neck, seeking heat.

After a few moments, when they had fought off the chill, they let go and rolled onto their backs.

"Do you feel it yet?" Althea asked Paul.

"No," he answered. Paul had taken his first hibernation dose when Althea was using the latrine. "But I'm sure it won't be long."

Althea took Paul's hand. They lay on their backs under the pile of blankets from the medbay and stared out of the large window above them. Their breath condensed and then diminished as the vapor rose upward.

Althea squeezed Paul's hand.

"What?" he asked.

Althea turned her head and looked at him with impatient, wide eyes. Dim starlight flooded the bridge and illuminated her face.

"Fine," Paul said.

Althea smiled.

*I won't last very long anyway,* he thought.

"Kata and I focused all of our wrath on General Navarro, and started going after that motherfucker. Personally," Paul said with a angry smile.

"Kata and I made two changes to our tactics," he continued. "The first was that we started combining our forces on the more important missions. Whenever possible, if time permitted and the mission justified it, we would join our companies together. We decided that she and I would never both go on a mission together in order to preserve survivability of command. We took turns commanding the missions. But joining forces like that meant that whoever went out would pack a bigger punch. Second, we threw a lot of tactical feints into the area."

"What does that mean?" Althea asked.

"Well, for example, I'd have one of the Dragons take a small wolf pack out to a remote village or key terrain feature a few hundred kilometers south of Devil. They would conduct a patrol, interact with the locals, and generally make a lot of noise as if they were executing an ultracritical mission. Some days, we did this several times in multiple places across the Cone. Doing this expanded our operational footprint dramatically. We showed up in places we had never been before."

"I get it," Althea said.

Paul smiled. "It confused the shit out of Navarro," he said with a chuckle.

"Kata and I were feeling the heat also, though. It had been about a month since our conference call with Schofield. We knew that, despite his legendary cautiousness, he would be launching his western offensive soon, and that when he did, Navarro would seize his opportunity to cause havoc. He would come at us hard, with everything the Chinese had given him. We would not be able to cope with that in our weakened state. We'd be fucked. So, we had to get him before that happened.

"The operations tempo was excruciating for us...and our soldiers. We had more than doubled our mission cadence. Existence for us was primal. We were in one of three states: asleep, mission planning, or executing. Four, I guess, if you count the occasional stay in the medpod.

"The Ōkami didn't have it much better. They were in maintenance, on a mission, or pulling security for our now consolidated base of operations on Devil. It sucked," Paul said.

He paused, a faint smile on his face.

"What is it?" Althea asked him. "What are you thinking about?"

"I'm just remembering how much those months sucked," Paul said in a faraway voice. "And that, for some reason, our morale was the highest it had ever been. It was us against the fucking world, and we weren't backing down."

He looked at Althea.

"God help me," he said. "But it is one of my fondest memories."

Althea nodded.

"All of the decentralization stressed the kill chain, though," Paul said, rubbing his forehead. "We had to do one of two things. The first was to use the standoff capabilities of the architecture. We could get the flash and authorize the kill if we were in neural-link contact with the commanding Ōkami or a relaying Dragon. This was much easier to do when we were in the same area of operations, of course, because it all rode on the comms we carried with us. But the architecture did have a long-range capability that worked across theater, and we used it numerous times. I could sit in my command hooch when the link was solid and respond to kill requests on multiple missions at once. It was actually easier than those damn poker games back at Bragg."

"The problem was it relied on satellite, ultrahigh frequency, and laser comms that were always in demand by every unit in theater. Schofield made it clear we were the lowest priority, unless we were on a mission for Keil directly. So, there were many times we had no kill chain on those remote patrols."

"And how did you handle it, then?" Althea asked.

"How do you think?"

"World War I style?" Althea asked.

"Exactly," Paul said with a broad smile. He turned to look at her and squeezed her hand.

Althea registered a strange pride and affection toward her in his face. She broke out in a grin.

"It was tedious over-the-radio stuff," Paul said, sitting up next to Althea.

She grimaced as cold air snuck under their blankets as Paul pantomimed a radio exchange.

"'Sir! I am in contact with six armed hostiles. Request permission to engage,'" he said, shifting a notional radio receiver from one ear to the other as he spoke.

"'Are they firing on you?'"

"'Yes, sir.'"

"'What is the civilian situation?'"

"'No civilians in the area, sir.'"

"'Confirm location.'"

"'Sir, we are at grid square AB12345678, facing south.'"

Paul put down the notional radio handsets.

"I'd look at the map and try to confirm as best I could where they were to give it a quick sanity check," Paul said. "You know, no hospitals or religious sites or whatever. All the while, my guys are taking fire and not hitting back. Finally, when I had confirmed as best I could, I'd unleash them."

Paul held his imaginary radio up to his head and said, "'You're clear to engage.'"

He lowered his empty hand. "Typically," he said. "That would be the end of it."

Althea looked up at him from her pillow. There was something in his voice and eyes.

"Typically?" Althea asked.

Paul nodded and hung his head as he spoke.

"We got away with it for about a month. We really had Navarro guessing. Intel picked up panicked communications between him and the Chinese. He tried to convince them we had tripled our numbers in theater. The Chinese tried to talk him off the ledge, insisting we were still a small operating force."

Paul hesitated.

Althea waited.

"It was Stuntman," Paul finally said. "He was on patrol with a wolf pack of ten soldierbots and one aerial XP. Not that far away. Down in the Pampas, south of Mendoza. Just far enough, though, that we didn't have solid comms. There was no neural link."

Paul shifted his weight so that he could sit cross-legged.

"Stuntman and his wolf pack were in contact with a small force. It didn't seem like a big scrap to me. Nothing that we hadn't dealt with a hundred times before. Problem was, we had no satellite or high-altitude drone imagery that day. All we had was the imagery from Stuntman's aerial XP. And it was tied up in the immediate tactical situation. So…"

Althea waited.

Paul took a deep breath.

"So, we had no warning. A platoon of quad tanks flanked him," Paul said, head sagging in sadness.

"What is a quad tank?" Althea asked.

"It is a four-legged armored vehicle, about the size of a small car. They can carry a wide variety of heavy weapons, including directed energy. They're fast and nimble and are used for both transport and fire support. The Chinese typically deploy them in groups of five.

"And that's what Navarro did that day. Five of them hit Stuntman from his left flank while he and his wolf pack were dodging fire, waiting for permission from me to return fire. I was reviewing the map and tactical display when he was hit. I was about to give him permission to engage. 'Sir, enemy tanks on my—' was all Stuntman got out," Paul said.

"Since there was no neural link, there was no hit from Stuntman's last gasp. I just stood there, mouth hanging open, trying to figure out what had happened."

Paul rubbed his head.

"And then hell broke loose."

"What do you mean?" Althea asked, noting the slight smile and roll of Paul's eyes.

"Well," he began. "Schofield may not have given a shit about our fate. But the Pentagon did. Our unit, and all of its equipment, were classified above top secret, a critical national asset due to the advanced nature of the technology. The last thing the Pentagon wanted was for the Chinese to get their hands on one of the Ōkami betas.

"One minute after I called in the situation report, I had every national and theater-level asset pointed at our small bush-country firefight. My command hooch lit up with real-time imagery from both satellite and high-altitude drone.

"As the images came to life, I saw the platoon of Chinese quad tanks sprinting south like hyenas. Much farther south, two large Chinese quad copters flew at high speed to link up with them. Clearly, all the tanks cared about at that point was extraction. I thought that was odd, and panned the display north, back to the scene of the fight, and zoomed in. It made no sense to me."

"What didn't?" Althea asked.

"Why were the Chinese not more interested in the Ōkami equipment?" Paul said in a faraway voice. "I mean, this was like the Norden bombsight. Or Ultra. Or the Manhattan Project. And they had a beta they could take. There was no way we could get there in time to prevent it. But when I panned over to the site of the firefight, I saw why," Paul said.

He took a deep breath before continuing.

"Pieces of Stuntman were everywhere. Navarro's foot soldiers had torn him apart. Pieces of him were on fire. And those that weren't were being pissed on, shot at, driven over..."

Paul stopped talking. He rubbed his eyes and shook his head, as if in disbelief all over again.

"Anyway," he finally said. "It was a good thing, I guess, in the big picture. Navarro and his men were taking things so personally that military-intelligence value no longer registered. But that was when I realized how things were."

"What do you mean?" Althea asked.

"Between us and Navarro."

Althea nodded. She watched as memories played across his face.

Paul looked at her and then lay back down. He pulled the blanket up over himself.

Althea slid over and wrapped her arms around him. His clothes were cold from being out of the blankets. She found his hand and squeezed it. She was about to say something when Paul started speaking again. When he did, Althea could tell the hibernation meds were starting to drag him down.

"After it was clear that the Chinese were not making off with Musashi's technology, we had a little more time to coordinate our response," he said. "Top and I worked together on the imagery for the next ten minutes, confirming that the scene was compliant with the rules of engagement. Then we called in an air strike from one of our high-altitude drones to vaporize everything, including the celebrating Navarro ground troops. That way, if the Chinese decided to return to check for anything valuable, they would find only cinders.

"'I'm sorry, Top,' I said across the tactical display after I authorized the air strike.

"'For what, sir?' she asked me.

"'Stuntman. I'm really sorry.'

"She looked at me and nodded slightly before saying, 'It's OK, sir. We did all we could. This kind of thing happens.' We both looked back at the tactical display, waiting for the strike to hit. I was surprised when she said, 'Some days, sir, I wonder.'

"'Wonder what?' I asked her.

"'I wonder if I really want our deployment to be a success,' she answered as the display showed the missiles track from the high-altitude drone toward Stuntman's dismembered body. About a dozen Navarro foot soldiers were still milling around the area. 'Because if we fail, Ōkami won't have to do this, right?' she asked just as the image showed the impact. An incandescent bloom covered the carnage. I turned off the display, and we both stood up. 'Right, sir?' she said before I could turn away."

"What did you tell her?" Althea asked.

"I said, 'I don't know, Top. But if you're right, you and I will have to figure out something to do with the rest of our lives.'

"'How about this, sir,' she said. 'We'll fish. You from the shore. Me from a small boat.'

"'Bullshit,' I said. 'I want the boat.'

"'Deal,' Top said."

After a few minutes, Paul's breathing became slow and even. Althea lay next to him while he slept, looking up at the void through the large window above them. After a long time, she put herself into rest mode, and her mind became quiet.

Paul's mind was not quiet. The hibernation drugs kept him down, but the rest of his story raged on in his mind.

# Chapter Seventy

*1728 Hours, 15 December 2055*
*Outpost Devil*

"I'm coming on this one," Kata declared.

"No way," Paul said, calling up a map of the target village on the planning screen. "Tonight is my night."

He and Kata had been rotating missions since starting their combined-forces strategy.

Top stood still, waiting for them to fight it out.

"Tonight is different," Kata said, stepping between Paul and the planning display.

"Why is that?" Paul asked.

"Because he is going to be there," she said, pointing at the map display. "For sure."

"You don't know that," Paul countered.

"What do you think, Top?" Kata asked Paul's first sergeant.

"I believe Captain Vukovic may be right," Top said. "We seldom get more than one indicator that corroborates. Usually, one contradicts the others. But these are unanimous and point at a meeting of Navarro and two of his lieutenants around 2000 hours this evening."

Paul looked at his watch. It was 1730. They had time to plan a sharp operation. But they needed to get on it.

"I can feel it, Paul," Kata said. "I'm going on this one. You're in charge. You call the shots. But I want in."

"No," Paul said. "We can't both go out." Paul squared up to Kata and crossed his arms. "Not going to happen," he said.

Ninety minutes later, Paul sat in Dragon Three as they flew fifty feet above the ground at two hundred and fifty knots. They were number three in a flight of five aircraft carrying an assault force of five beta soldiers, fifty-two soldierbots, three aerial XPs, and two large tracked ground XPs toward the target.

Kata rode in the fourth aircraft.

There had been no stopping her.

This was it. Other than Paul's first sergeant and a couple of soldierbots in maintenance, they had held nothing back.

Top stayed back in Devil's operations center to monitor the mission and coordinate any needed support. The plan was to insert into four LZs that surrounded the village, ten kilometers from its center. They figured that was enough distance to both visually and acoustically mask their arrival. They would spread out and encircle the village and then move forward, gradually tightening the noose around Navarro until he tried to leave or they had his building surrounded.

Like the most recent missions, they decided not to put a swarm over the village. The swarms gave excellent intel on the objective, but at the price of letting the enemy know the Americans were coming. Paul and Kata thought they reacted and adapted better than the enemy could, so they opted for no swarm, no signature.

Their plan was simple. If Navarro tried to flee the village, they would kill him. If they pinned him down in a building, they would kill him. If he came out and tried to fight, they would kill him. Paul wished they had more XPs and soldierbots but felt good about the plan.

Fifteen minutes later, the trail aircraft, Talon Four, broke off from the formation. Carrying Buford, one of Kata's surviving Betas, and a wolf pack of ten soldierbots, the lone aircraft landed at a remote spot Paul and Top had selected to be the holding area for the quick reaction force. Only a fifteen-minute flight from the village, Buford and his wolf pack would be sent into the fight at the command of Paul or his first sergeant, to effect rescue or press a tactical advantage.

The other four QC-10s would join Talon Four at the remote spot after completing their insertions. There they would launch on command as part of the QRF, or to exfil.

A few minutes later, the flight of four split up, and each QC-10 headed for their assigned LZ.

Dragon Three flew for another eight minutes before coming to a hover at his assigned landing zone. He was carrying one of the large tracked ground XPs beneath his belly in a sling load. His engines howled as he eased himself down. When the XP was on the ground, D3 disconnected the load and reeled in the vehicle slings as he slid forward and landed.

"Thanks, D3," Paul said.

"Roger that, sir," said the aircraft. "Just call when you're ready for exfil, sir."

"Will do," Paul said as he and twelve soldierbots leapt out of the aircraft.

Paul watched D3 fly away to join up with the others at the QRF holding area and then waited for a few minutes as everyone checked in.

"Magellan is set."

"Snapshot set."

"Reynolds set."

"Chamberlain set."

"Apache Six set."

Paul checked his in-head display for the status of the XPs. The three aerial units had deployed, one over the village to give overhead imagery, high enough not to be easily heard, while the others waited on the ground. They would launch into the village on Paul's signal, but for now, he did not want to risk them being detected and tipping off Navarro.

The ground XPs were positioned on the main road in and out of the village: one to the north, one to the south. They each carried a powerful railgun and would make sure no reinforcements made it to Navarro, eliminating anything that tried to escape once things went kinetic.

Everything was ready.

"OK," Paul said. "Move out. Watch your spacing. No one get too far ahead or behind. I want a clean convergence on the target."

The soldierbots fanned out widely as they walked. Within minutes, Paul's IHD conveyed a complete circle on the map that constricted slowly as they moved forward. They had the village surrounded.

They walked the ten kilometers to the village as the sun set. Paul walked due north. The sky was a blazing orange as the sun set behind the Andes Mountains far away to his left. A smoky haze blanketed the Pampas that evening. To his right, darkness crept toward them as the night started to advance on the landscape. By the time they entered the village, the sun was behind the mountains and the light was receding quickly.

The village was not large. A mile across at most. It was old and active, though, and sat on a trade route that had connected the sea to the interior for generations. Two- and three-story buildings stood close to the narrow streets that led to the middle of the village. In the village center, shops and restaurants lined a dusty, failed attempt to grow grass in the small square. A columned two-story municipal building on the north side of the square anchored the scene.

As they entered the village, Paul signaled to the XPs. The ground vehicles advanced until they were within a hundred meters of the first buildings on the edge of the village. Paul had them wait there, weapons ready, for further instructions.

The aerial XP orbiting at a high altitude was not the same as a sensor swarm, but he was able to provide some good imagery. On Paul's IHD, he could see a pair of foot soldiers milling around an old, manually operated vehicle parked in front of the municipal building.

Paul noted with a smile that there were no villagers about. It would be easier to deal with the two soldiers.

As they converged on the square, Paul studied the foot soldiers on his IHD.

They had rifles slung over their shoulders and were smoking cigarettes and talking. But what bothered Paul was that neither of them looked up. Not once.

By now, they should have heard the overhead drone, even though it was operating at a high altitude, and at least been curious about it. But they hadn't noticed or didn't care they were being observed.

They advanced on the village square cautiously, their noose tightening with every step. Paul launched the other two aerial XPs, putting both of their POVs up on his in-head display.

The aerial XPs leapt into the air and streaked at low altitude toward the center of town. They shuddered as they opened their gun- and missile-bay doors, dirtying up their aerodynamic profile.

Paul and the rest of the assault force stepped into the town square as the aerial XPs crossed, at high speed, over the municipal building.

Paul had clear line of sight to the pair of foot soldiers. He knew something was wrong when they looked up at the blur of the fast-moving XPs and smiled.

Tension rose within Paul and radiated out through the neural link to the rest of Outlaw Company.

And why were there no villagers around?

Multiple explosions detonated throughout the village.

Red Xs lit up Paul's map as soldierbots went down. He cursed as he read the damage report.

Ten soldierbots destroyed in a blink.

Paul switched back to the POV of the high-orbiting aerial XP. He counted a dozen explosions. Multiple small buildings fell into the street.

Enemy soldiers in battle suits and exoskeletons poured into the streets. Unarmored snipers and grenadiers appeared on the rooftops. The aerial XPs estimated two hundred enemy. Navarro had held nothing back either.

Tracer rounds erupted from several rooftops, and Paul lost the visual feed from the aerial XP. He glanced up to see it fall out of the darkening sky in smoking pieces.

"Ambush!" Paul called over the radio as he turned for the nearest alley. "Take cover and return fire."

Paul let his suit do the running as he studied the situation display. Two soldierbots ran on either side of him, firing their weapons.

A red X marked the estimated impact zone for the destroyed aerial XP. The remaining AXPs were under intense small-arms fire from the soldiers on the rooftops. Their small-caliber weapons could not penetrate the AXPs' armor, but they were causing a lot of damage to the relatively delicate thruster fans.

Finally, Paul began getting hit by flashes as the team started to return fire.

Paul told the AXPs to designate and then had the ground XPs, still holding at their north and south checkpoints, fire indirectly. Paul heard the thumps of their mortars, followed by that sweet whistling sound. Antipersonnel charges began exploding over rooftops, killing enemy in large swaths.

The flashes came rapidly now as Magellan, Snapshot, and the others got drawn into their own firefights. It was hard to keep up. Kata was getting hit with her share also.

Paul put one of the AXPs at a higher altitude. He wanted to understand which streets were now blocked and where their forces were concentrated. It got a few seconds of imagery before it started to tumble violently and fell out of the sky.

The aerial XP left a trail of smoke as it descended into a nearby building. It smashed through three floors until it lay, on fire, under debris in the basement.

The imagery Paul got from the AXP before it was shot down did not look good. Over a hundred enemy were running toward them, and the dropped buildings had turned the village into a maze. Kata saw the same thing.

"No clean way out of here now!" she yelled over the radio.

Paul grunted his agreement.

He felt a growing pit in his gut as he thought about what waited for them in the few remaining passable streets.

More flashes hit him.

*Kill. Kill. Kill.*

Paul could see on his IHD that Kata and Magellan were being forced into the same alley. Paul turned to look and saw them across the town square.

A wolf pack of ten soldierbots fought furiously in front of Kata and Magellan.

Enemy bodies and pieces of shattered exoskeletons were strewn around them.

Kata and Magellan backed slowly into the alleyway. The soldierbots stepped back with them, covering each other, their weapons spitting fire.

More flashes from the AXP.

*Kill. Kill. Kill.*

Paul switched on his suit's autopilot, pointed it at an alley, and selected close-quarters mode. Then he tried to center himself so he could take what was going to be a big wave of flashes.

"Outlaw Zero Six, this is Outlaw Zero Seven, I am launching the QRF," Top called on the radio from back at Devil.

"Roger that, Seven," Paul answered as he reached the cover of the alley. He pictured the aircraft back at their holding spot, leaping into the air and activating their weapons systems. Buford, strapped into Talon Four with a wolf pack of ten, would be studying the tactical situation and licking his chops.

Paul looked forward to their arrival. In fifteen minutes, he would have five gunships overhead and another squad on the ground.

They would be able to kill a lot of enemy then.

Paul was hammered with flashes as his suit fought. He had the situational display up on his IHD showing everyone's position, their direction of movement, ammunition levels, and battle damage. Paul did not like the way that Kata and Magellan were getting pinched together into that alley. But they were holding their own.

For an instant, Paul felt his panic subside.

The alley Paul had run into was a dead end, so he did not have to worry about anyone creeping up behind him, and the soldiers attacking from the street were easy targets.

His main concern was the rooftops. He was scanning the last AXP's point of view and the situational display when the southern ground XP disintegrated in a large explosion.

"What the fuck was that?" Kata called.

"Don't know," Paul responded. "Stand by."

Paul had the last AXP climb and pan around.

"Shit," Paul said as he looked at two large biped tanks. One to their east and one to their west. They were three kilometers away and closing in fast. They were late models, bristling with weapons systems.

"Terrific," Kata called, viewing the same imagery.

Their remaining ground XP tried to execute evasive maneuvers but was struck within seconds by another high-explosive round.

Two large red triangles blinked on Paul's situational display, signifying the enemy tanks and estimating their direction and progress.

Paul looked across the square to the alley where Kata and Magellan were fighting. They were down to just four soldierbots, but it looked like Navarro's soldiers had cornered a hive of demons. Waves of exoskeletoned soldiers charged the dark alley. They'd get close before bursts of fire tore them apart. Those that made it farther were killed in close quarters by slashing bayonets.

There was a pile of destroyed battle suits, broken exoskeletons, and body parts at the mouth of the alley. Kata, Magellan, and their wolf pack were meting out well-coordinated hell.

"Kata, we need to get moving," Paul transmitted. "We don't want to be trapped in these alleys when those tanks get here."

"No shit!" she responded. "Reynolds, need you to move south. We're going to need some help getting clear."

"Roger that, ma'am!" Reynolds responded. "Moving!"

"Mayday. Mayday. Mayday." The final aerial XP interrupted Kata with a distress call. "Lost port thrusters. Descending into—" His transmission ended as he struck the ground.

"Damn it!" Paul yelled.

"Outlaw Six," Dragon Three called on the radio. "QRF ETA ten minutes."

"Roger that," Paul responded. "Be advised. I have designated two large enemy tanks on the map."

"Understood," D3 responded. "They are emitting strong countermeasures. We can't get a fix yet to fire indirect. But we'll deal with them as soon as we can."

A loud clang filled Paul's helmet as dust and shards of brick erupted in his alley.

They were firing on him from above.

Paul leapt backward, deeper into the alley, as two of his wolf pack aimed their weapons at the building tops. Their miniguns sprayed bullets, and they let loose with a salvo of high-explosive grenades. They impacted the building walls near the top, collapsing large portions of the roof. Several enemy soldiers came down with chunks of building. All but one were killed by the fall.

Paul stepped on the head of the one survivor and crushed his skull.

Paul checked his situational display. Everyone was starting to take real damage, and they were down to thirty soldierbots. But they were still fighting well. Optimism welled within him.

Reynolds had made good progress. He was now one block north of Kata's position, providing enfilading fire. He mowed down dozens of enemy.

But they kept coming.

"Outlaw Six, this is Dragon Three," came a call on the radio. "We are five minutes out."

"Excellent, D3," Paul said. "Prioritization is the two tanks first, then troops on the roofs, then enemy in the streets."

"Understood, Outlaw Six. Stand by."

Paul surged back toward the street, firing as he went. He wanted out of that alley. As he reached the opening, he looked across toward Kata. The pile of bodies in front of her alley was taller now, but the wave of foot soldiers had not slackened. They pressed their attack.

Navarro was going all in.

A loud ripping noise drew Paul's eyes skyward in time to see half a dozen missiles streak over the village in the direction of the approaching QRF.

"Dragon Three!" Paul transmitted. "Incoming mis—"

Paul's voice seized and his knees buckled as he was hit by a terrible last gasp as Dragons Two, Four, and Six disintegrated.

Kata screamed into her helmet and her vision blurred as Buford and Talon Four incinerated.

Paul realized then how fucked they were.

Navarro obviously had a sophisticated anti-aircraft capability, and he had held it back until the most disruptive moment.

At first, Paul thought they were Rapiers. But he quickly realized these missiles were smaller. Faster moving. More of a kinetic munition than an explosive one.

Paul's mind raced as he shot enemy. It looked like the missiles were the type that required guidance. That meant something in the village. Something that could detect and designate targets. Navarro must have gone shopping with the Chinese again.

Two huge explosions erupted from the buildings around Kata and Magellan. The three-story buildings shuddered and fragmented as they fell.

Kata's three soldierbots were knocked down by the explosions and engulfed in a massive dust cloud that surged into the street and engulfed Reynolds and the converging enemy troops.

They had been in the village for only a few minutes and had lost four aircraft, a beta, five XPs, and dozens of soldierbots, and now Kata and Magellan were trapped under two buildings.

They had walked into a trap.

Paul was enraged.

He went berserk.

Paul lunged out of his alley toward Kata and Magellan. He put his suit in sprint mode and activated his bayonet. It unsheathed from his battle suit's right forearm, and he decapitated an exoskeletoned enemy. The four soldierbots running with Paul extended their bayonets also.

Paul forgot the situational display as they slashed across the street. He forgot two biped tanks were headed their way. He didn't hear Top on the radio. He went into a killing frenzy.

He was shooting.

Throwing grenades.

Bayoneting.

He used everything he had to cut through them.

Reynolds fought toward him from the north. They converged on Kata's alley as the dwindling wolf pack of three got to their feet, bayonets extended and weapons blazing.

Paul was just meters from the alley when one of the tanks stepped into the square.

"Kata!" Paul yelled into his radio. "Do you copy?"

Reynolds impaled a battle-suited enemy and lifted him over his head. He flung the bloody and inert armored body at a group of attacking soldiers. They flinched at the sight before Reynolds cut them down with minigun fire.

"Outlaw Zero Six!" Top said over the radio. "Dragon Three is still airborne. We've got an exfil plan. Sending you coordinates. Need you all to start moving south immediately."

"Negative," Paul said. "Not without them."

"Captain Owens!" Top said over the radio. "Need you to start moving now so you can put distance between you and the tanks. We'll figure out a way to get them."

"No, goddamn it!" Paul shouted. "They're trapped!"

"Captain Owens!" Top yelled. Paul could hear the urgency in her voice. "It's over, sir! Get out of there!"

An explosion interrupted their argument, tearing Reynolds to pieces and destroying two soldierbots. Shrapnel ripped Paul's right shoulder open and knocked him off of his feet as bits of Reynolds whizzed by.

Paul flailed through the air for an instant before his suit's gyros calculated a solution. He landed on his feet and spun to see the tank running at him from the northern end of the square, closing the distance, smoke drifting out of its main cannon.

It was a big one. And fast.

The tank aimed its minigun at Paul.

Paul tried to evade, but his suit was damaged and sluggish.

The tank's minigun spat armor-piercing rounds at him.

Paul braced for their impact.

The last soldierbot dove in front of Paul, absorbing the rounds.

By the time the soldierbot landed in sparking pieces on the ground, Paul had raised his left arm. He fired his last missile at the tank. It struck the heavily armored tank impotently but kicked up enough dirt and smoke to obscure Paul for an instant.

He turned toward the smoldering pile of rubble to find Kata.

But instead of running toward it, Paul's suit discharged all its electromagnetic smoke grenades.

A large, sensor-obscuring cloud of chaff and smoke engulfed Paul and then filled the square as he yelled into his radio, "Goddamn it, Top! You fucking better not!"

"I'm sorry, sir," Top responded. "I recommend you relax."

"No!" Paul yelled. But it was too late. He had just become a passenger. His suit turned and ran at max speed. The speed and violence of the maneuver and sprint knocked the breath out of Paul and wrenched his wounded shoulder.

All battle suits had an emergency escape mode. The suits were programmed to discharge their e-smoke grenades and then egress along the most tactically advantageous route at the highest possible speed the occupant could survive.

For the occupant, it felt like a car accident.

The tactical operations center had the ability to put suits into emergency escape mode remotely. Once you did that, a suit could then only be controlled from the TOC.

Paul's battle suit carried him out of the square and southward. The rest of the surviving team members were close behind him, as well as the dozen soldierbots that were still operational. Fortunately, Navarro's tanks had run right into the middle of the village. It was a stupid move.

Snapshot and Chamberlain dropped a few buildings behind them with their remaining missiles hampering the enemy's pursuit.

Dragon Three, now about ten kilometers away, fired everything he had, putting down a line of indirect fire between the retreating team and the enemy. It was danger close. Two soldierbots were engulfed in the explosions and shrapnel.

But it worked. They gained some separation.

Snapshot and Chamberlain took some bad hits covering the retreat as rear guard, but they also made it out.

They met up with D3 and leapt on board. Snapshot, Chamberlain, and the remaining soldierbots leaned out of D3 and fired the last of their ammunition at the advancing enemy as the aircraft surged up and forward.

Dragon Three's engines howled and glowed red as he accelerated beyond three hundred knots while maintaining only twenty feet of altitude.

Top gave back Paul control of his battle suit.

Paul moved up to the command seat to start planning a counterattack. His shoulder was throbbing badly now, an indication that his nanobots were working hard to close the wound. He could feel the blood pooling in his armored glove, and his right side felt damp.

Magellan's POV came back on line. It was dark at first but grew lighter as the tank kicked aside debris and large chunks of the building. Soon, it was dragging Magellan from the rubble.

Paul could see from his telemetry that Magellan was unable to move his legs and none of his weapons systems were online. He was helpless.

There were over a hundred soldiers around Magellan now. They were taking turns screaming in his face and spitting on him.

Some of them bound Magellan's feet with a large metal cable. They tied his arms above his head as well. They drove the old manual car over and tied one of the cables to it. Then the tank walked over, and they tied the other end to it.

Then they pulled Magellan apart.

Magellan's lower chassis separated from his torso. The tank and the old car dragged their halves of Magellan around the square for a few laps while the soldiers cheered.

Then they found Kata.

She was unconscious when they dug her out. But she slowly came to as they dragged her toward the center of the square. Kata's POV transmitter was intermittent, so Paul only caught glimpses of the angry Navarro foot soldiers as they spit on and kicked her.

A man walked up to what was left of Magellan. Paul recognized him. It was Navarro. The hard and angular face, the sun-dried skin, the moustache, were all chiseled into Paul's memory from thousands of intelligence files.

Navarro propped up Magellan's upper torso, sneering at the broken beta and smiling like a devil as he turned and walked back toward Kata.

Navarro wanted the Americans to be able to watch.

They were all watching. Paul. The Dragons. Top, back on Outpost Devil.

"D3, I am ordering you to turn around!" Paul screamed. "Turn around now!"

But the mission was over. Every soldier was in a recall state. Dragon Three tried to ignore him.

Paul charged toward the door when he saw the foot soldiers tie Kata's upper body to the tank.

Snapshot blocked him from jumping out.

"Get the fuck out of my way!" Paul commanded.

He tried to shove past Snapshot but was stunned by pain as his wound tore open wider.

Paul shook his head clear and screamed, "You are a bunch of fucking cowards! Hold on, Kata, I'm coming!"

Paul tried to lunge out of the aircraft. He was going to jump out and run back to her.

Snapshot blocked him again, and Top disabled his suit.

Battle suits could be deactivated remotely. A precaution against battle-suit hijacking and other rare tactical situations, such as preventing suicidal actions.

Paul fell to the floor of D3.

His IHD display was still active, and he watched as they tied Kata's feet to the car.

The feed from Kata's POV flashed on and off. The transmission of her terrified screams came in and out. But Paul could make out his name.

She was begging Paul to help her.

Magellan wiggled his torso to try to avert his gaze, to disrupt the data flow, but Navarro's soldiers held him fast as Navarro got into the driver's seat of the old car.

The tank stood still as Navarro revved the car engine. Its tires threw sand and gravel, trying to get purchase to accelerate.

Kata screamed. She was not in pain yet, though. Her battle suit was holding. Then the tank lifted one leg to shift its weight back against the pull of the car.

Kata screamed louder. She felt it coming.

The tank leaned back.

Kata was pulled apart.

The car surged forward, and the tank nearly fell backward at the sudden release of tension, but caught itself, taking half a dozen steps backward. The crowd of soldiers cheered as Kata's entrails dragged across the ground behind her upper body.

Kata's POV feed flashed on a few more times. The suit had failed just above its hip actuators. A ragged flap of her lower abdomen extended beneath the armored suit. Strands of gore dragged across the dirt.

The last image transmitted from Magellan's POV was of a soldier approaching with a large weapon. Seconds later, armor-piercing high-explosive rounds tore Magellan apart.

Paul had lost too much blood to withstand Magellan's last gasp. He passed out. It was a mercy.

# Chapter Seventy-One

*0745 Hours, 16 December 2055*
*Outpost Devil*

"What the hell, First Sergeant?" General Schofield yelled over the secure videoconference. "They both went on the mission?"

"Yes, sir," Top replied, standing at attention in front of the large screen. The general sat in the center of the briefing table. General Keil sat to his right, Lieutenant Colonel Wainwright to his left.

"And now I've got a dead captain in my area of operations?"

"Yes, sir."

"And these equipment losses," Keil said, reading again the battle damage assessment. "A fucking disaster."

"Yes, sir."

"Well, I bet even your pea-sized artificial brain can do the math on this one, First Sergeant," Schofield said.

Top stayed quiet.

"I told those arrogant hotshot jigsaws that they had one fucking job!" General Schofield continued, yelling. "Don't screw up. Don't bring any heat on me while I'm trying to counter the Chinese empire's aggressive fucking adventurism in South America. Don't lose any big pieces of equipment." The general jabbed his fingers in the air, counting his points as he made them. "Don't do anything that would embarrass me. And for God's sake, I told them, nobody gets killed in fucking action!"

The general paused to catch his breath. He realized he was shouting. Keil looked down. Wainwright pretended to take notes. Schofield rubbed his eyes.

"Look, First Sergeant," the general said. "I'm real sorry about Captain Vukovic. It's a damn shame. When Captain Owens is released from the medpod, let him know that his orders are to roll it up and return to base. Your mission is over."

"Yes, sir," Top said. The general had started to get up from his seat when Top said, "Sir, if I may?"

"Go ahead, First Sergeant," he said, without sitting back down.

"I know that Captain Owens will feel strongly about this. And I do as well. The whole unit will. We still need to recover the bodies of our dead, and we'd like to go after General Navarro tonight. We have indications that he—"

"Are you out of your quantum fucking mind, First Sergeant?" General Schofield said, more bemused than angry.

"No, sir."

"Seems like you are to me," the general said, impatiently gesturing at Wainwright to get the hell out of his way. "Because I just recalled your metal asses. I am working other angles for the body recovery, and I want your whole misbegotten outfit here, behind the damn wire, on my fucking base."

The general pointed forcefully down at his feet as he halted his progress toward the edge of the screen.

"By 1800 hours tomorrow," Schofield said, pointing at the image of Top in front of him. "Between now and then, you will stand down. No more missions. Do you understand me, First Sergeant?"

"I do, sir."

"Good." The general continued toward the edge of the screen. Before he disappeared off to the side, he looked into the camera and said, "Again, First

Sergeant, please tell Owens I'm sorry about Vukovic. She was an arrogant jigsaw. But she was a good officer."

Then the screen went dead.

Top left the command hooch and walked directly to the medical bay where Paul lay healing in the medpod. Top typed in the revival command and waited.

Thirty minutes later, Paul sat in the open medpod. He rubbed his eyes as Top debriefed him.

"General Schofield has recalled us, sir," she said. "Our orders are to stand down and report back to Stalwart by 1800 hours. Also, the general wants you to know that he is really sorry about Captain Vukovic and they are working other channels for body recovery."

"You woke me up for this?" Paul asked his first sergeant in an angry voice. They had not yet discussed the failed raid, and Top overriding Paul's suit. But each knew there would be a reckoning.

"Yes, sir," Top said. "And to tell you that there are indications that Navarro is going back to the same village tonight. The intel suggests that the villagers had been evacuated from the town in preparation for the ambush. That's why there were none around during the fight. This morning, they were allowed to return. Obviously, the damage to their town was extensive. Navarro is going to thank them for their patriotic sacrifice, and intercepts say that the Chinese are going to fund reconstruction. It is going to be a big moment for Navarro."

Paul stood up from the medpod. He swooned. Top reached out to steady him.

"Help me get to the planning hooch," Paul said.

"Have you learned anything about Navarro's new anti-aircraft capability?" Paul asked minutes later as he stood over the mapping table, steadying himself on a chair. As he talked, Chief changed his bandage and inserted an IV. "Our first concern is surviving on the way in."

"Yes, sir," Top said. "We analyzed the spectrum emissions captured during last night's failed mission and were able to identify the threat as a kind of mobile Argus system."

"A mobile Argus what?" Paul asked.

"It is a super observer," Top explained. "It is hypersensitive across the electromagnetic spectrum and can detect everything from radar altimeter emissions to weapons-targeting systems to radio transmissions. Any emission at all can be targeted and destroyed down to altitudes as low as fifty feet. It also has its own radar and laser designators, to home in on targets once it detects them. It is a new system, only in the field for about six months. Intelligence has given it the code name Argus, after the many-eyed Greek god."

"How nice," Paul said.

"The fact that it is mobile means that we should assume it goes wherever Navarro goes."

"Yeah," Paul said, looking at his bandaged shoulder. Blood oozed from the unhealed wound. He had not spent enough time in the medpod. "The other factor is that General Schofield will probably be keeping some kind of eye on us. We're going to have to go in with everything off. That means every emitter on every system."

"We will be nearly blind," Top said.

"And nearly invisible," Paul responded. "Neither Navarro and his Argus nor Schofield and his forces will be able to track us."

"World War I style," Top said.

"That's right," Paul said, smiling wearily at his first sergeant. "So, let's assume we make it in," Paul continued, his smile vanishing. "How about troop strength? Find anything to indicate how many soldiers Navarro will have with him?"

"Nothing, sir," Top said.

Paul nodded, weighing the lack of intelligence against his remaining combat power. He had three betas, three QC-10s, ten operational soldierbots, and no extension platforms.

"I suppose we'll have to take that as a positive indication," Paul said.

"Yes, sir," Top said. "The more soldiers he had in tow, the more likely we would have gotten an intel hit."

"Doesn't matter anyway," Paul said.

"No, sir," Top agreed. "It does not."

The mission was simple. Go in and kill them. Paul and his first sergeant spent no time planning exfil or recovery. They didn't care about what happened after. They were going to deliver justice.

"Have you spoken with Colonel Filson yet, sir?" Top asked Paul. "He has tried to hail you on the satcom several times."

Paul shook his head.

"Not yet," he said. "Let's do that when we get back, OK?"

The first sergeant nodded. "Roger that, sir."

Later, as the sun set, Paul's last O.A.T favors confirmed that Navarro had arrived at the village.

"Let's go," Paul said to Top. "I want wheels up in five."

Paul struggled into his battle suit as Top went to round up Snapshot and Chamberlain. The last three operational QC-10s began their preflight checks.

Chief ran up to Paul as he walked toward the aircraft.

"Sir!" Chief called. "Captain Owens!"

"What is it, Chief?" Paul asked as he stopped and turned around.

Chief stood in front of him, a minigun in his arms, ammunition belts crisscrossing his shoulders, a bayonet on his hip.

"Top said it was up to you," Chief said, shifting on his feet as Paul sized him up.

"This one is probably not going to go very well, Chief," Paul said.

"All the more reason I should go, sir."

"You're not part of the neural network," Paul said, shaking his head.

"But I am part of this unit," Chief responded, jamming the butt of the minigun into the ground.

Paul nodded.

"Ride with Snapshot," he said, turning back toward the aircraft. "Do exactly what he says."

"Yes, sir!" Chief said, hoisting the minigun. He ran to the trail aircraft, where Snapshot was watching soldierbots mount up.

They took off in the direction of Schofield's base to throw off any potential observers. That made it look like they were starting the pullout early.

Several miles north of the outpost, though, the aircraft dropped down below the peaks of the Andes and into the shadows. They followed the canyons just fifty feet above the craggy terrain to avoid detection. The aircraft had turned off all their emitters, even their radar altimeters, so they flew with only passive visual references and inertial navigation data. It was challenging and made for a bumpy and tilting flight.

They leveled out over the valley floor and streaked toward the target.

This time, though, they didn't insert kilometers away and walk it in.

Facing an unknown number of enemy troops and probably a Chinese tank or two, Paul wanted to maximize their advantage of surprise. He wanted to shock them, keep them off-balance, and kill them. If there were too many to achieve that, so be it.

Two of the QC-10s flew over the square at a hundred knots.

Foot soldiers and civilians ran in all directions.

The three betas jumped out of the shrieking aircraft.

Snapshot and Chamberlain struck the walls of the municipal building in the village center. They crashed through and started killing enemy soldiers inside.

Top landed outside, digging a crater in the dirt in front of the building. She quickly got busy killing Navarro's soldiers as well.

As chaos overtook the village, Talon Six broke off of the flight of three. She banked hard to her left at rooftop level and decelerated.

"It's too hot for me to stop and land," she said. "I'll tell you when to jump."

"Roger that," Chief answered.

"Get ready," she said to Chief as she approached a rooftop to her front. T6 lunged left and right as tracer rounds sought her out.

"I'm ready," Chief answered as he struggled not to fall out of the door.

"Go! Go! Go!" Talon Six yelled as the roof passed under her nose.

Chief leapt out of the aircraft.

He tumbled across the roof, coming to a stop a few feet from the edge.

"You set yet, Chief?" Snapshot called on the radio.

"Roger that," Chief answered, standing up and getting his bearings.

He turned to face the high-caliber tracer rounds erupting from around the village square. Two of Navarro's big biped tanks were trying to get a bead on the attacking aircraft. Their tracer rounds sprayed through the moonless sky like drunken green fire hoses.

"Then get busy," Snapshot said. "If it is shooting and it is not us, kill it."

"Roger that," Chief answered, raising the weapon to his shoulder.

The flashes popped like muted fireworks in Paul's mind. He focused on them, making certain no civilians were killed. This was a revenge mission. Not a murder spree.

Paul stayed on Dragon Two during the fight. He had forgone more medpod treatments to make this mission happen and was not yet fully healed. His mobility was still hindered.

He still got into the fight, though.

Even over the village, with the slaughter begun, Paul did not allow the aircraft to turn on any of their targeting systems. Knowing if they did so, the Argus would have a better chance of taking them out. They would also pop up on Schofield's detection network, and Paul didn't want that either.

So, Paul used the trick Colonel Filson had taught him and Kata seemingly a million years ago, back on the Fort Bragg range. He drew an X on the Dragon canopy with a grease pencil and used it as an aiming reference.

The other two aircraft flew in tight formation on either side of Dragon Two, as if welded to each of her wings. Paul used the grease-pencil reference to walk their rocket fire into each of the tanks. In less than two minutes, the tanks were destroyed.

Paul then strafed a number of other vehicles, hoping to get lucky and take out Argus components.

As they flew back and forth above the village, Paul had Dragon Two repeat on her loudspeaker, "We are here for General Navarro. Turn him over immediately, and we will cease our attack!"

On the ground, the betas led the wolf pack through the village, searching for Navarro and killing any soldiers that resisted.

Within ten minutes, Paul got the call over the radio: "We have Navarro in custody."

Once they had Navarro, it was over. His soldiers stopped fighting. They dropped their weapons and looked nervously at the dark sky.

Dragon Two landed so that Paul could get out.

"Dragon Flight," Paul said before walking away, "get back in the air. Make it seem like a whole squadron is overhead and let me know of any inbound."

"Roger that, sir," Dragon Two said as they leapt back into the sky.

"Top," Paul transmitted on his radio. "Search the prisoners to ID those on the list."

"Roger that, sir," Top responded. "We already have two."

"Bring them to the village center," Paul said. "I will meet you there."

Before launching, Paul had Chief go through all of the POV footage from the failed raid the day before. They had facial-recognition data for every soldier that had been involved in the murders of Magellan and Kata.

Fifteen minutes later, Paul stabilized himself against Top as the last of the soldiers on the list was identified and brought to the village center. Three had been killed in the fighting. Paul had their bodies dragged to the feet of the eight living prisoners.

The eight, including Navarro, stood in a line under the guard of the Chief's minigun.

Paul walked to the captive group, unholstered his pistol, and shot the first one in the head.

Two tried to run. Paul shot them in the back of the head.

The remaining terrified men fell to their knees, begging.

"Sir, what are you doing?" Top asked Paul.

"For Kata," Paul mumbled. "Magellan and the rest."

"Sir, I don't think—" she tried to say. But Paul cut her off.

"At ease, Top," he said. "This is my call. This is what we came here to do."

Paul stopped at Navarro.

The old general glared at Paul. Paul holstered his pistol and turned back to Top.

"Do we have their bodies yet?"

"Yes, sir," Top said. "They are loaded on Dragon Three."

"Good," Paul said, fighting dizziness. He looked at the old car. It still had the bloodstained cable tied to it.

Paul walked to the old car and looked inside.

The keys were still in it.

Paul got out of his battle suit. Blood was running from his shoulder down his arm, dripping off of his fingers.

"What are you doing, sir?" Top asked him. "You need to get back into your battle suit."

"In a minute, Top," Paul said.

Paul eased himself into the car. He winced as he closed the door. The pain in his shoulder was getting bad. He had not taken any pain meds that whole day to stay as sharp as possible for the mission.

The old vehicle coughed to life. Paul drove it over and parked in front of Navarro. He left the engine running.

Navarro was shaking now. The general recognized death when he saw it. He prepared himself for Paul's rage, but he said nothing.

Paul pulled himself slowly out of the car.

Paul tied the cable around the general's chest, under his arms, making sure it was uncomfortably tight.

The rest of the Ōkami kept their weapons trained on the mass of foot soldiers. The prisoners' eyes widened as they realized what was about to happen to their general.

Paul stepped back when he was done fastening the cable. He pulled his pistol out and pointed it at Navarro's head.

"Lay down," Paul ordered.

Navarro was frozen in fear.

"On the ground!" Paul yelled, striking him in the face with the pistol.

Navarro stumbled to the ground. Blood flowed from his mouth. Paul tied the general's feet with another cable he had found nearby.

Navarro begged now. Pleaded.

When Paul was done, he stood up slowly. Paul swooned. He almost fell over, but Top stepped to his side and steadied him.

"What are you doing, sir?" she asked him.

"For Kata," Paul said. He pushed himself away from his first sergeant, walked to the municipal building, and tied the other end of the cable to one of its large columns.

Paul then walked back to the car, past his first sergeant as she asked again, "Sir, what are you doing?"

"For Magellan," Paul said as he got into the car.

Paul started it up. He revved the engine to make sure it was good and warm and then popped it into gear.

"Sir!" his first sergeant yelled. "Don't do this!"

"Paul inched forward, dragging Navarro through the dirt until the cables were tight. He put the car in neutral and gunned the engine again. He wanted Navarro to be terrified. Like Kata was.

The old gasoline engine roared.

Most of Navarro's soldiers looked away.

Paul cried out in anguish, thinking of Kata and Magellan. And all of the Ōkami that had fallen. His voice was lost in the snarl of the roaring engine.

Paul reached up to put the car in gear.

A single gunshot rang out, surprising Paul.

He looked in the rearview mirror and saw Top standing over Navarro.

Paul turned off the car. He got out slowly, the arm of his flight suit now soaked with blood. His vision blurry. He walked over to Top, who reached out with her hand to steady him.

In her other hand, she held her pistol. Smoke drifted from its barrel. Paul looked at the general. His body was limp. His head in bloody pieces from the antipersonnel round.

"I'm sorry, sir," Top said. "What you were doing did not seem right in my gut."

Paul looked at Top but didn't answer. His strength was fading.

"We're done now, sir," she said. "Let's go."

The other two aircraft landed, and the team loaded up.

"Put me on D2," Paul said to Top in a nearly inaudible whisper.

Paul stared at Kata's body bag on the flight back to Devil until he passed out.

# Chapter Seventy-Two

Paul woke up a day later in the medpod. He opened the pod's clamshell top and climbed out. He was unsteady and had to brace himself with a hand on the wall. When the room stopped spinning, he saw Colonel Filson sitting in a chair on the other side of the pod.

The colonel's face was clouded.

"Listen, Paul," Filson said. "We don't have a lot of time—"

"Sir," Paul interrupted him. "Kata is dead."

"I know, son," he answered, raising his hand to shut Paul up. "I know. I need you to get dressed and on the bird quickly."

Paul realized he was naked. He stepped over to the side table where someone had laid out a flight suit. He pulled it on, wincing at the pain in his arm and shoulder. He needed a few more days in the pod.

Paul zipped up and turned to face Filson.

"OK," the colonel said. "Let's—"

"When did you get here, sir?" Paul interrupted him again.

"I came as soon as I heard about Kata," he said. "I had just landed at Stalwart when we heard about the massacre. I convinced the general to let—"

"Massacre?" Paul asked.

They were interrupted by the sound of multiple aircraft over Devil. The medical hooch shook as an aircraft flew low over it.

"What the hell?" Paul shouted as he moved for the door.

The colonel caught him by the arm. "Goddamn it, Paul," he yelled over the roar. "That's what I'm trying to tell you. It's Schofield. They're here for you."

"What?"

Paul shoved past the colonel and opened the door. Wind ripped through the medical hooch as the door flew open and sand bit into Paul's eyes.

The colonel grabbed him by the flight suit, between the shoulders.

Paul jerked free.

"Damn it, Paul!" he heard the colonel yell before being enveloped by the noise and flying sand.

The sand hammered Paul's eyes. He struggled to see. A large military gunship hovered over the medical hooch, its forward weapons turret trained on him. The rotor wash knocked Paul off-balance, and he fell to the ground.

Paul tumbled for a few meters before strong composite hands jerked him to his feet.

It was Top.

Paul held a hand up to shield his eyes from the flying sand and surveyed the assaulting force. There were at least eight aircraft in the air. Maybe eight already on the ground as well.

A handful of soldiers in exoskeletons exited one of the aircraft on the ground. They were over a hundred meters away, but Paul recognized one of them. It was Lieutenant Colonel Thurman.

A civilian male talked to Thurman. The civilian looked familiar to Paul, but he was too far away to recognize.

As the group conferred under the stubby wing of the aircraft, more armed soldiers spilled out of the its aft ramp. But they were not exo battalion soldiers. They were wearing a different and darker armor, almost black. Their weapons and equipment were also different, not standard issue. Something was wrong. But Paul's head was too fuzzy to pinpoint it.

The dark-suited commandos fanned out. There were dozens of them. Paul was confused.

The civilian turned and pointed at Paul. Thurman nodded. He and the other exoskeletoned soldiers started walking toward Paul and Top.

"What's going on, sir?" Top said to him in whisper mode.

"I don't know," Paul said. "But I'm sure it's fine," he lied.

Colonel Filson walked over to them and steadied himself against the gale-force winds on the first sergeant's other arm. He turned and looked at the hovering gunship and gestured forcefully. His combination of middle finger and direction pointing would have been hilarious had menace not been so thick in the air.

But Filson got the message across, and the aircraft hovered backward, away from the medical hooch. The sand dropped out of the air as the rotor wash slackened and they were able to speak.

"I think we are under arrest, Top," Paul said.

"I think you are right, sir," she said.

"I've been trying to tell you," Filson said, stepping around to face Paul and Top. His back was to the approaching soldiers.

"Schofield sent the exo battalion to bring you in. I convinced him to let me come along. Your mission last night was a global headline this morning, Paul. Caused a real shit storm."

"Who are the ninja-looking assholes?" Paul asked the colonel, pointing at one of the dark-armored soldiers moving to flank them.

"Malloy's paramilitary contractors," Filson said, nearly spitting.

Paul looked back at the civilian. He remembered him now. It was Pruden. He worked for Determined End States. Paul thought he remembered Pruden saying that a Malloy somebody was his boss.

Thurman stepped in front of Paul and the colonel. Two staff sergeants, each armed with suit-mounted minigun systems, stood on either side of the lieutenant colonel. Both aimed their weapons at Top. Thurman's right hand rested on his pistol. All three of them seemed nervous and twitchy to Paul.

"Captain Owens," Thurman said. "We're here to take you back to Stalwart."

Filson turned around and faced Thurman.

Six of the dark-armored paramilitaries jogged up and surrounded them. Another large group was running out to the parked QC-10s. Paul tried to keep track of them, but he could feel himself sagging into Top. His time in the medpod had helped, but he was still weak.

"OK, Thurman," Colonel Filson said as he gave them a calm-down gesture with his hands. "Like I said, this is going to go quietly. Just like I promised. How about we ease up on the weapons."

Lieutenant Colonel Thurman waited half a tick before giving his men a quick nod and taking his hand off of his pistol. The two staff sergeants lowered their miniguns but continued to stare at Top.

Paul noted that the paramilitaries did not lower their weapons. He looked back at the aircraft. Pruden stood under one of the wings, talking into his phone. He looked agitated.

"We understand that you secured Captain Vukovic's remains last night?" Thurman asked.

"That's right," Paul said.

"Where are they now?"

"In the cooler in the medical hooch." Paul pointed at the shipping container behind him.

The lieutenant colonel looked over Paul's shoulder, then spoke into his radio. A pair of soldiers, not wearing exoskeletons, ran by and entered the medical hooch.

Thurman looked back at Paul and said, "Look, Owens. I don't want to make a big deal out of this. I'm assuming Colonel Filson briefed you. We've got orders to bring you back to Stalwart to face charges."

"Charges?"

"This is what I was trying to tell you, Paul," the colonel said, turning his back to the exo soldiers and stepping in close so that Paul could hear him over the hovering gun copter and other aircraft.

"I don't understand," Paul said.

"The mission they took you on…" He glanced at Top. "It went too far, son. You let them murder those men."

"The mission they—?"

"Let's go, Colonel!" Thurman yelled, interrupting.

"Now you listen to me!" Filson's face was red with anger as he turned from Paul to look at Thurman.

"No, sir," Thurman said, stepping forward with the flanking staff sergeants, whose miniguns were back up, trained on Top and Paul. "You're not in my chain of command. Now get out of the way and stop interfering with my mission."

Thurman reached out and shoved the colonel to the side. He took a step closer to Paul and drew his pistol.

"Captain Owens," he growled. "We can do this the easy way, or we can do it the real easy way."

Paul raised his hands to show he preferred it easy.

Top mirrored Paul's actions, raising her hands, as did Chamberlain, who approached from behind Paul.

"Is everything OK, sir?" Chamberlain asked.

"Whoa!" one of the paramilitaries yelled at Chamberlain, aiming his large-caliber weapon at the beta.

One of Thurman's staff sergeants swept his minigun to the left to cover Chamberlain.

Thurman said something into his radio and then gestured at Top and Chamberlain. "You two step back over there."

Six more paramilitaries jogged up, weapons drawn, completing the encirclement.

"All right, goddamn it!" Filson said, stepping back into the middle of the tense group. "Everybody fucking calm down!"

"I warned you, Colonel," Thurman said.

"If you'll give me sixty seconds," Filson answered, "I will save you a lot of trouble."

Thurman's face was cloaked in disgust. But he nodded slightly and then made a show of looking where his watch would have been on his wrist.

Filson turned back to Paul. Paul could see the concern on the colonel's face. It scared him.

"Listen to me, Paul. Go with them. I'll meet you back at Stalwart."

"Sir, I'm confused. What is going on?"

"We'll discuss everything back at Stalwart."

"What about them?" Paul asked, gesturing at Top and Chamberlain, who had stepped several feet back and were standing together in a ready position, heads tracking multiple targets.

"Malloy's paramilitaries are here to take custody of them," Filson said. "They are being recalled."

Paul started to shake his head.

"Listen to me, Paul!" Filson yelled. "Look around. You have zero leverage here. Don't make things worse. Go with Thurman. I will take care of them," Filson said, pointing at the Ōkami betas.

Paul looked at Thurman, then at the black-suited paramilitaries, then at Pruden, who was now walking toward them. Paul had a bad feeling but didn't have a choice.

"OK," Paul said. "OK, I'll go."

"Just in time," Thurman said with menace. He waved Paul over.

Paul stepped toward them, expecting the tension to ratchet down after his surrender.

But it did not.

One of the staff sergeants shifted his weight on his feet, minigun still covering the Ōkami.

Paul turned to look at Top and Chamberlain. As fuzzy as he was, Top was still able to get through to him on whisper mode.

"This doesn't seem right, sir," she said. "What do you want me to do?"

Paul glanced at the colonel. He did not seem unduly alarmed. "Nothing," Paul whispered back to Top. "Do what they say. I'll figure things out when I get in front of General Schofield. Follow Colonel Filson's lead."

"Roger that, sir," she said.

Lieutenant Colonel Thurman grabbed Paul roughly by his bad arm.

"Shit, sir," Paul said, reflexively trying to jerk free. But Thurman's armored hand held fast.

"Let's go, Captain," Thurman said. They started walking toward the aircraft that was idling on the ground a hundred meters away. Pruden was halfway to them now, still talking on his phone.

Thurman turned his head away from Paul and spoke into his radio.

Paul looked back over his opposite shoulder. Filson was yelling at the staff sergeants. Top and Chamberlain had been separated from the colonel. A dozen paramilitaries stood between them and Filson, bearing down on them with heavy weaponry.

Past them, Paul saw a dozen dark commandos marching Snapshot, Chief, and ten soldierbots, at gunpoint, toward Filson's group.

Farther away, Malloy's paramilitaries ran around the QC-10s. They jumped in and out of the Dragons and Talons, doing something Paul couldn't quite figure out.

Another pair of paramilitaries jogged past. They nodded at Thurman.

Pruden was off his phone now, walking toward Colonel Filson.

Paul started to feel the pieces clicking into place.

He looked back at the colonel and the Ōkami. One of the staff sergeants had drawn a pistol on Filson and was waving him to the side, his minigun still trained on the Ōkami.

Paul looked back toward his first sergeant. Malloy's paramilitaries shoved Snapshot and Chief toward Top. The ten soldierbots marched obediently into the captive group.

The paramilitaries were now lined up in front of the Ōkami, who stood in a tight bunch.

Paul tried to jerk away from Thurman.

The lieutenant colonel dragged him forward.

Paul tried to reach Top on whisper mode. But his head was too fuzzy.

Pruden was only a about ten meters away now, walking toward the colonel. His face was tight with stress. He looked at Paul for an instant, and then looked away.

"Pruden!" Paul yelled as they passed each other. "What the hell is going on?"

Pruden looked away from Paul, refusing to make eye contact.

Paul looked back. Paramilitaries were running away from the QC-10s. Filson was being restrained by one of the staff sergeants. The line of black armored soldiers was raising their weapons. Top turned in Paul's direction.

Pruden, approaching Filson, looked back at Paul, then looked down at his feet.

"No!" Paul yelled.

"At ease, Captain," Thurman said dismissively, squeezing his arm harder.

Paul looked back again.

There was no doubt.

It was a firing squad.

Paul glanced at Thurman. His helmet was open, his face exposed.

Paul had one shot.

He leaned forward, stretching as hard as he could. He winced at the pain in his arm as his wound burst open but managed to get a handful of sand.

He used the lieutenant colonel's grip to slingshot his body up and slung the sand into Thurman's eyes, letting the motion conclude in the hardest punch he could muster.

Paul felt Thurman's nose break beneath his knuckles.

The lieutenant colonel threw Paul to the ground reflexively. Howling in rage and pain, he retracted his armored gloves and pawed at his eyes with his bare hands.

Thurman's face was red and pinched in an angry, narrow-eyed grimace as he turned back to face Paul. He managed to yell, "Goddamn it, Owens! You're only making shit worse!"

But he was yelling at Paul's back. Paul was sprinting back to his soldiers.

Top looked at Paul.

She cocked her head to one side.

"What?" Paul heard her say in whisper mode.

Fire and sand engulfed the first sergeant and the rest of the Ōkami as Malloy's commandos opened up with every weapon they had. Armor-piercing high-explosive rounds ravaged the Ōkami. Sparks and fire jumped across them as pieces of their bodies were blown off.

Filson screamed and pinwheeled his arms against the staff sergeant holding him. The sergeant was smarter than Thurman, though, and his activated helmet protected him from the colonel's blows.

Pruden, hand to his forehead, stared at his feet.

Explosions erupted from the flight line as charges detonated inside of the Dragons and Talons. Flames engulfed the dying aircraft.

Paul, screaming as he ran, heard the sound of rending ceramic and metal over the din of the circling aircraft. He thought he saw Top for an instant, standing against the impacts.

Then she fell.

Paul was slammed to the ground and passed out under the weight of the worst last gasp yet.

# Chapter Seventy-Three

*1912 Hours, 17 December 2055*
*Forward Operating Base Stalwart*

P aul woke up hours later. He lay on a cot in a small cinder-block room. He was in bad shape.

His head was pounding, and his shoulder wound, ripped open at during his struggle with Lieutenant Colonel Thurman, was bleeding. Fresh bruises told him they had not handled him with much care when he was unconscious.

Paul sat up. Blood pooled on the cot where his shoulder had been. It soaked through the nylon and dripped to the floor.

Paul stared at the wall and listened to drops of blood impact the floor. He had no sense of time when General Schofield walked in, holding a tray of food.

The general placed the food on the end of the cot and walked back to the door. He turned and faced Paul.

The two officers stared at each other.

"You're going back to Bragg in a few hours," Schofield said.

Paul looked at the floor.

"Is Colonel Filson around?" Paul asked, not looking up.

"No. He left on a transport back to the States as soon as we got him patched up."

"Was he wounded?"

"He broke two fingers punching an exo's helmeted head," the general said. "Then he sustained third-degree burns and cuts to his arms, chest, and face when he dove into the pile of destroyed equipment."

The general chuckled dismissively. "He was ugly to start with. If he survives, he's going to be even worse."

"Soldiers," Paul said.

"What?"

"They were soldiers. Not equipment."

"Oh," Schofield said. "Soldiers. Right." He shook his head.

"Why did you kill them?"

"Wasn't my call," the general said with an indifferent shrug. "Those things were the property of Determined End States, a big AI weapons company owned by Fiona Malloy. Your sweetheart robots were just on loan to the colonel's Special Development Activity. When they went haywire, it was Fiona Malloy's decision to destroy them in place. She offered to do it with her own paramilitaries. And I'm glad she did. Saved my men a lot of hassle."

Paul blinked several times as the name Fiona Malloy burned into his brain.

The general crossed his arms, studying Paul.

"It's not your fault, son," Schofield said without anger. "All the crap they jam into your jigsawed head. The Centaur program has always given me the creeps…" His voice trailed off as he searched for an answer. He shook his head in weariness and revulsion. "That's the only way I can explain what you let happen," he concluded.

"I didn't let anything happen," Paul said. "I was the—"

"It's on video, Owens!" Schofield interrupted him.

"What?"

"There was a reporter there. Got the whole thing." He saw the puzzled look on Paul's face and pulled out his phone. "Couple hours after you left that village, this was picked up by the media. Went viral. Globally."

He handed Paul his phone.

Paul pressed play.

It started off chaotically, panning back and forth in a village as gunfire erupted around the camera. Paul recognized it as the night they'd struck General Navarro. Same village. Same terrified foot soldiers. The cameraman was among Navarro's forces. Orders were barked from off camera, and there were shrieks of pain as men were killed. Every few seconds, the camera would jerk to the sky, trying to catch a glimpse of the streaking QC-10s above as they rained bullets and rockets down on the disorganized rabble of soldiers. Paul smiled, satisfied by the pandemonium. They had achieved total surprise.

The view cut abruptly to that of a beta. Chamberlain, Paul thought, rounded a corner, minigun blazing. Then another shot of Top firing at an unseen target with one hand while swatting away exo-wearing foot soldiers with her other arm. Her blows sent the men flying out of frame.

Another abrupt cut. The Ōkami were lining up men against the wall. Then a view of betas firing their weapons. Then a pile of dead men.

"Wait a minute," Paul mumbled.

The pile of corpses was made up of the men Paul had executed.

The video kept running.

A view of Navarro, taken from a distance by a person in a crowd. But Paul could see Navarro was whimpering now. He recognized the moment. He was about to pull Navarro apart as the general had done to Kata. But instead, the video showed Navarro begging, and then cut to Top shooting him in the head as he lay on the ground. The video did not show Paul tying him up or getting into the car.

Just Top executing him.

General Schofield took his phone back and said, "It finally happened. An autonomous machine made the decision to kill a human. Many humans. And you did nothing while your precious robot soldiers committed murder. Navarro was no saint. But we don't get to just execute the folks we don't like. And we certainly don't let robots execute humans they don't like."

Paul's head was spinning. For an instant, he doubted his memory. Then he started to get angry. Paul looked at General Schofield, but words did not come.

"You were supposed to be the leader out there, Owens," Schofield said, rolling his eyes in disgust. "That's what they told me. But the truth is, I never expected Centaurs to be capable of that. You and your tin cans set back the American effort in this region for decades. And have brought shame on your military and your country. You're going back to Bragg to be court-martialed. If it were up to me, you'd face a firing squad." The general opened the door to leave.

"Eat your meat loaf. You're going to need your strength."

# Chapter Seventy-Four

*0712 Hours, 5 January 2056*
*Italy*

"There she is!" Eugene said, standing up from his seat at breakfast on the patio.

"Morning," Fiona mumbled. She walked out onto the patio under the pergola and took a seat next to Eugene.

Eugene scowled. Wearing only jeans and a black T-shirt, she was underdressed for the chilly winter morning. He shook his head and walked inside, returning moments later with a warm blanket and thick socks.

He handed them to Fiona. As she wrapped herself and put the socks on, Eugene poured her a cup of coffee without asking, preparing it as she liked it. One raw sugar.

"You look a million times better," he said, pushing the cup of coffee in front of her and taking his seat.

Fiona nodded and took a sip of coffee. "It's amazing what sleep can do for a body," she said. "That's the first I really slept in about a week. First time I slept through the night in at least a year."

"Through the day," Eugene said, pouring himself more coffee.

"Pardon?" Fiona said.

"You slept through the day," he said. "And then through the night."

Fiona put her coffee down and looked at her watch.

"What day is it?" she asked.

"Wednesday."

"Don't bullshit me."

Eugene looked at her across his coffee cup. He let her try to do the math for a moment.

"You got here late Monday, Fi," he said, putting his coffee down. "Drunk."

He handed her the basket of croissants.

"And babbling," Eugene added.

Fiona looked at him.

Eugene stared back.

"I was not drunk," she said, grabbing a croissant and tearing it open. "And I was not babbling."

She spread butter on one half of her croissant before taking a large bite. Eugene stared at her while sipping from his coffee.

"I was exhausted," she continued after swallowing.

"Is it true?" Eugene asked. "Is what you told me true?"

"Yes," she said. "The lien on Mio Posto is paid off. One hundred percent. You own it free and clear."

Fiona leaned back in her chair with her coffee. "Let's never do that again, brother," she said.

A relieved smile took over Eugene's face. He shook his head and exhaled.

"I was so scared you were going to tell me you were just drunk," he said. "I'm so sorry, Fi. But I thought for sure you were lying."

"Why?" she asked.

"You have never shown up in the middle of the night like that before."

"I've shown up in the middle of the night plenty of times," she said.

"Not looking like absolute hell and on the verge of tears," Eugene said, eyes wide in emphasis. "Let's face it. That is not Fiona Malloy behavior."

"Lack of sleep will do that to you," she said.

"No," Eugene said. "That wasn't it."

Fiona looked at Eugene, waiting for him to continue. But he looked away from her, out past the grounds of Mio Posto, at the rust-colored hills.

"What do you mean?" she asked him.

"It wasn't lack of sleep," Eugene answered, still staring into the distance, recalling two nights ago when Fiona showed up at Mio Posto with no prior warning. "You looked haunted, Fi. You looked guilty."

Fiona's face darkened, and she looked down at her hands.

"But you know what, Fi?" Eugene said.

Fiona did not look up.

"We don't ever have to talk about it," he said. "And you looked fucking great on TV."

The two weeks before Fiona arrived at Mio Posto had been the longest, hardest part of the longest, hardest year of Fiona's life. And the final day had been the worst of it.

After it was all over, she'd sat alone in her office. Pruden had left the day before, during the press conference.

She was wearing the same clothes from the press conference the previous day, and she knew she needed to sleep. But she could not find the motivation to get out of her chair.

The knock on the door startled her.

She looked at her watch. Too early for the nightly cleaning crew.

Fiona got up and walked toward the door.

It pushed open before she got to it.

Robert Malloy II walked in.

"Hello, Roberta," he said.

"What are you doing here?" she asked.

"That was not the celebratory greeting I expected," he said, walking past her into her large office. "Not at all," he said, looking around. "And this is not the celebration I expected to find either. Where is everyone?"

"This is my office," she said. "The company office is in Virginia."

"Ah yes," her grandfather said. "Near the customer. Of course. Very good."

He looked around some more, his eyes falling on Pruden's empty desk.

"Your partner, then," he said. "At the very least, you and he should be celebrating."

"He quit yesterday," Fiona said. "Packed his things and left while I was on TV."

"Oh dear," her grandfather said. "And not so much as a goodbye note?"

"Didn't need it," Fiona said. "Nothing left to say."

Malloy looked at Pruden's desk. "Should I be concerned about his departure?" he asked before locking his gaze back on Fiona. "Does it constitute a risk?"

"No," Fiona lied.

Malloy stared at his granddaughter.

Fiona was now used to his awkward silences. She walked past him back to her desk.

"I thought the press junket was handled well," he said, walking slowly toward her desk. "But don't ever do another one. Ever. Do you understand?"

"This one was unavoidable, Grandfather," she said. She grabbed her briefcase and started packing up her desk.

"Look at me, Roberta," he said.

She stopped packing and looked at him.

"No more," he said. "Do you understand?"

"Yes."

Fiona had objected to the presser, and her grandfather knew it. But the military had insisted. When she realized it was part of the Pentagon's effort to distance themselves from the Ōkami, Dr. Musashi's architecture, and the massacre in South America, she went along with it.

Anything to keep the deal moving.

She'd sat in the Bloomberg studio with the CEO of Spitting Metal. After the CEO announced that they had just been selected to provide the entire US military with its next generation of fighting robots on an accelerated schedule, Fiona was asked to say a few words.

"I'm very excited and proud of Spitting Metal," she'd said. "Their architecture is superior to that of any technology solution that has been fielded to date. The

Spitting Metal ability to put robots forward into combat zones while keeping the officers that command them in specially designed, high-tech command-and-control pods safely positioned in bunkers here in the States is a huge leap forward. It guarantees that humans stay in control, complies with all aspects of the Tokyo Accords, and gives commanders highly flexible, low-risk capabilities to fight and win our wars. The accelerated procurement means we can assist with the effort to roll back China in South America. And that is something we are honored to do."

Talking points complete, Fiona had smiled and cast her gaze down to her shoes.

"I mean, I'm no Sun Tzu," Spitting Metal's CEO had added, "but why put the flesh, blood, and brain downrange if we don't have to, right?"

"Learn from me," her grandfather said, snapping Fiona back to the present. "The more your face is out there, the more people will peck at you. The more they will find."

Fiona nodded and went back to stuffing her briefcase. She was suddenly dying for a shower.

"What have you learned about their next steps?" her grandfather asked her. "With the court-martial, I mean."

"They've classified the whole process as top secret," she said, not looking up.

"Good," her grandfather said.

"Limited testimony. No press. Sealed records. The works," she continued, voice sounding more grim with every word. "The captain will take the fall. Probably twenty years before he gets out."

Robert Malloy II nodded. He put his hands in his pockets and cleared his throat.

"I am going to say something to you now that I must admit I never thought I would ever have to say," her grandfather said, stepping closer to her desk.

It was an odd windup from him. She looked up.

"I am impressed, Roberta," he said, the thinnest trace of a smile on his face. "Truly."

Fiona was dumbstruck. She stood motionless.

"The disastrous mission was good," he said, nodding slowly. "It likely would have been enough. But the massacre, Roberta. The massacre was inspired."

"I had nothing to do with that," Fiona said, mostly to herself.

"Because the massacre made them urgent. It made them needy," he continued.

"I had nothing to do with that," she said, louder.

"It made them move quickly," he said. "And you know better than anyone how hard it is to get the government to move quickly."

"I had nothing to do with that!" she yelled. "The only thing that I—"

"No!" her grandfather shouted, slamming his fist on her desk and startling Fiona into silence.

His glare gradually slackened, and the thin smile surfaced again.

"No details," he said. "Those are yours to bear. I have more than enough of my own secrets."

Fiona stared at her desk where her grandfather's fist had struck. She regained control of her breathing but did not look up at him.

"This conversation took a turn I did not intend," her grandfather said. "You've impressed me, Roberta. I stopped by for the sole purpose of telling you that."

"Mio Posto," she blurted out, still staring at her desk.

"What about it?" he asked.

"It's free and clear now?"

"That was the deal, was it not?" he said.

"Answer my question, please."

"Mio Posto is free and clear," her grandfather said. "I will have my attorney send you the paperwork in the morning."

"Thank you." Fiona nodded.

Her grandfather started to leave but hesitated. He turned back and looked at Fiona. She stared down at her desk in grief.

"Roberta," he said. "You are a defense industry titan now. You must bear the words of the Duke of Wellington in mind."

Fiona put her hands on her hips and looked at her grandfather.

"Nothing except a battle lost can be half so melancholy as a battle won."

Robert Malloy II turned and left.

Fiona stood behind her desk, trembling, after the door pulled shut.

She was horrified.

Horrified at how good it felt to hear she had impressed her grandfather. For him to actually say it to her himself. In person.

She looked at her half-packed briefcase and then ran out of her office.

An hour later, her charter took off from Teterboro on its way to Italy.

"What is it, Fi?" Eugene asked her.

Fiona blinked. She looked across the table at him, steam rising from the coffe cup in her hands.

"What?"

"You just went so far away," he said, reaching for her hand. "Are you OK?"

She let him take it and squeezed.

"Yeah," she said. "Like I said, I haven't slept much this year."

She pulled her hand back and sat up straight, running her fingers through her hair.

"Well, I hope you can stay and rest a while," he said, offering her more coffee.

She gestured yes.

"A few days," she said as he poured. "End of the week, maybe. Then I'll have to get back."

"Will you be on TV again, gorgeous?" he asked her.

"No more TV," she said. "Ever."

# Chapter Seventy-Five

*1815 Hours, 11 January 2061*
*Company Launch Facility, Cape Canaveral*

"**P**risoner Owens!" the launch facility guard called over the intercom. "You've got a visitor downstairs."

Paul lifted his head off his pillow and cursed. The Company's prelaunch quarantine facility had a visitor's area on the first level that enabled no-contact interactions. It all complied with Company prelaunch protocols, but not with Paul's desires to be left alone.

He was so close to the solitude of his belt-and-back voyage that human interactions were more irritating than they had ever been. He was scheduled to launch in the morning and, after a cycle aboard the American high lunar orbit terminal facility, would board the *Odysseus*. Then, in less than a month, he would finally be underway.

But he had to get through the next ten hours on Earth.

"What now?" Paul mumbled to himself as he walked down the hall to the guard desk. "I'm Owens," he said to the man behind the desk.

"You got a visitor," the guard said without looking up.

"I don't want any visitors," Paul said.

The guard looked up.

"Well, then, why the hell is he here?" he asked.

"I have no idea," Paul said. "Who is it?"

The guard looked down at the ledger as Paul hoped it was not Colonel Filson.

The colonel had been trying to get in touch with Paul since the court-martial. Paul had not let it happen. He refused at every turn, whether he was in pretrial confinement, prison, or training for his belt-and-back. He would not accept visits or read anything the old man sent him.

Paul had even snapped at the Geek, the person he owed so much to at this point, when the topic came up. They were meeting in Paul's prison cell, strategizing how to get Paul into the Fly It Off program.

"You know," the Geek started, "Filson really wants to talk to you."

"I know," Paul said. "But I don't want to talk to him. I can't."

"Why not, Paul?" the Geek asked. "What would it hurt? You wouldn't believe what the old man is like now. He's so…vulnerable. It's kind of sad."

"I don't want to fucking talk to him, Wallace!" Paul said. "I wouldn't expect a fucking REMF to understand!"

The Geek nodded and smiled.

"I'm sorry," Paul said.

"It's all right, Paul," the Geek said. "It's none of my business. I shouldn't meddle."

"I'm just so—" Paul started to say. But he choked up.

"Paul," the Geek said, putting his hand on Paul's shoulder. "Forget I mentioned it. Please. It's OK."

"It's a doctor," the guard said, jerking Paul back into the moment. "Dr. Mu… Mu-something."

"Musashi," Paul said.

"Yeah," the guard said with a smile. "That's it. Musashi. He's downstairs in the no-contact visitation room."

"I don't want to see him," Paul said. "My file was supposed to be marked 'No Visitors.'"

"It is," the guard said. "The old dude just showed up."

"Fine," Paul said. "I'm going back to my room."

Paul turned and started back down the hallway.

"What?" the guard said, standing up. "What do I tell the old doc?"

"Tell him to go away," Paul said.

An hour later, the guard knocked on Paul's door.

"The old doc left," the guard said. "But only after I promised to give you this."

The guard handed Paul a paper grocery bag and went back to his desk.

In the bag, Paul found a leather-bound book, an English-to-Japanese dictionary, and a blank leather-bound journal.

Paul flipped through the pages of the book. It was in Japanese.

An envelope fell out of the book and dropped to the floor. It was addressed to him in the doctor's handwriting.

Paul stood motionless, staring at the envelope on the floor and debating his next move.

*Fuck it,* Paul thought, reaching down to grab the envelope. *The stubborn old doc came all this way, after all.*

Paul opened the envelope and pulled out the letter.

---

*Dear Paul,*

*I hope you will find peace on your journey. The past is not what we wish it was. Nor is the present. Nor are we.*

*Still, all we can do is our best.*

*When I heard about this text, I knew that you must have it. It is called Utsu. Which means "avenge." It was written by a masterless samurai sometime around the year 1500, when the clan fighting in Japan was at its worst, and the life of a soldier was at its hardest.*

*The text was only recently discovered. It has not been translated into English yet.*

*I have read it.*

*I believe it has a message for you.*

*I had it printed and bound for you. I thought that it might help you pass the time.*

*I wish you all the very best in your next chapter.*

*Your friend,*

*Dr. Musashi*

# Chapter Seventy-Six

*Utsu Book One*

*Circa 1510*

*Translated from the Japanese*

The river carried me far.

I washed up on its rocky bank a mile away sometime after the moon had risen. The next morning, I was found by a kind farmer who hid me in his barn and nursed me back to health, though I cursed him for doing so.

When I was strong enough, I thanked the farmer and walked to the closest village.

I needed a katana to commit seppuku, but I had no money. So, I determined that I would steal one. My failure and dishonor were so black, common thievery would leave no mark.

Before setting to my task, though, I asked passersby what they knew of the recent battle between Clans Hayato and Shingen.

They regaled me with tales they had heard. Hayato withstood the Shingen siege for months. Hayato himself suffered a great loss when his only son and the leader of the Elite Guard was slain by Hiroaki and his one hundred bandits. It was only through the great wisdom of Lords Shingen and Hayato that disaster and more bloodshed was averted. Why, they asked, should two great houses bleed themselves to death? Samurai must be mastered, and war is too important to be left to the generals.

The bloodthirsty Hiroaki and his one hundred bandits were thankfully destroyed, and wiser heads prevailed.

Peace was made.

There was much talk of the marriage between Hayato's only daughter and Shingen's son, uniting the two clans that had been at war for over a century. Tales of conquests by the Shingen-Hayato alliance were spoken of everywhere and written about in every paper. It seemed that none of the other clans could resist their advance. There was talk of the dawn of a new shogunate.

Despondent and awash in lies, I went to the village crossroads and sat by the well to wait for a victim. I hoped to find an elderly man carrying the katana from his youth who I could ambush. Once I had his blade, I would leave the village, walk into woods where no one would find me, and disembowel myself.

With no second in attendance, it would be almost all that I deserved.

There were also many posters proclaiming all graduates and associates of School Hiroaki outlaws and wanted men. Rewards had been placed on our heads.

It was dizzying. I alternated between rage, confusion, and sadness.

No matter. I planned to be dead that evening.

I did pull the hood of my kimono over my head, though. I wanted to remain free to kill myself, after all.

I waited all day, but a suitable victim did not pass by.

As the sun set, three young rōnin walked into the village square. They stopped to drink at the well. The each wore both a katana and a shorter wakizashi. But, weak as I was, I would be no match for one of them. Much less three.

Stealing their blades was not possible.

Nonetheless, I sized them up from the shadows. Perhaps if they dozed off or otherwise lowered their guard. As I did, the tallest of them left the well and walked across the street to the inn.

I listened to the other two as they drank from the well.

"This is the tenth village we have stopped in with no luck," I overheard one say. "Perhaps we have gone too far?"

"Or perhaps we have not gone far enough," said the other.

"You're right. Who knows how far the river swept him along?"

"Or maybe he drowned?"

"No. I do not think so. No body was ever found."

"Perhaps it was," the fellow said. "But they did not recognize that it was the body of Manji Saito."

I froze at the mention of my name.

When it became clear that they were paying me no notice, I stood up slowly. When I was sure that they had not noticed, I turned to go.

As I turned, I came face-to-face with the tall rōnin as he came back from the inn.

"It's you!" he said to me. "It's him!" he shouted to his comrades. "Right here! It's him!"

They approached me slowly, from three different directions.

I was done.

I had no weapon.

I was in no shape to fight.

But I was determined to exact a price for my capture. I threw off my kimono and assumed a ready stance.

"Very well, traitors," I said. "Draw your katanas and come at me. I will show you what Hiroaki Ashikaga taught me!"

"Shhh!" the tall one said, raising his finger to his mouth. "Don't say that name!"

None of them drew his sword.

"It is against the law to speak of him," another said. "And we graduates of the school have been deemed outlaws."

"We must stick together," said the third. "In secrecy."

I was confused. My wounds, fatigue, and sadness were a heavy fog encircling my mind.

They could see my confusion. The tall one stepped closer. I flinched at his movement.

He gestured with his palms down. "It's OK," he said. "We mean you no harm. We were sent to find you."

"Find me?" I stammered.

"You are Manji Saito, are you not?" he asked, taking another step closer.

My own name made me tremble. I was heartbroken and bewildered at its mention and all that had happened.

"Only survivor of the Battle of the Covered Bridge?" he said to me, almost in a whisper, as he put his hand on my shoulder. "Student of School Hiroaki? And friend of Hiroaki Ashikaga himself?"

"How do you know this?" I asked.

"Many know, Manji," he said in a low and respectful tone of voice.

The three of them smiled and then quickly blanked their expressions.

"We were sent to find you," the tall one said.

"By whom?" I asked.

"There are many of us," one of them said.

"All seek revenge for Hiroaki and our comrades," said the third.

"The time of being pawns to lords, shoguns, money, and politics is over," the tall one said.

"And you must lead us."

# Chapter Seventy-Seven

P aul walked under the flagpole on their compound on Fort Bragg. The sun was setting behind him, and his shadow stretched to his front, far beyond his footsteps. It was early summer, and the Carolina evening was comfortable and breezy. The smell of roasting deer grew stronger as Paul walked forward. Chief had been at it for a few hours, and it smelled close to ready.

Paul heard the voices of his soldiers ribbing each other and talking about the toils of the day. He heard Kata also, laughing loudest of all.

The fire came into view as Paul rounded the corner of Filson's command building. A large deer rotated slowly on a spit.

Chief tended to the cooking animal in a grease-stained white apron over his olive-drab T-shirt and cutoff camouflage shorts. Stainless-steel tongs hung out of one cargo pocket, a large, dirty rag out of the other. Chief's biceps bulged under the T-shirt, as did his gut. Spotting Paul, he gestured at his sizzling handiwork and smiled with just-like-you-taught-me pride.

Paul held both thumbs up in approval as he walked toward the group.

Stuntman stood in front of the crowded wooden table, foot on an ammo crate, gesturing dramatically to describe his actions on the range that day. His wavy golden-blond hair and thick moustache were totally out of regulation and made Paul chuckle. Stuntman whipped one hand through the air to get his point across as he held a beer in the other without spilling a drop.

Mia rolled her eyes at him, her lithe body leaning back against the table, short brown hair pulled back. She never believed the braggart.

Dragon One and Magellan sat next to each other, arms crossed, regarding Stuntman with bored skepticism. D1 wore his trademark Ray-Bans and, despite the warmth of the summer evening, his leather flight jacket. His short black hair was gelled into a perfect spiky flattop, and his silver dog tags swung in front of his chest. Paul shook his head at the sweat-drenching D1's white T-shirt. No one loved flying or being a pilot more than D1. But Paul thought D1 loved *looking* like a pilot even more. He'd seen D1 wearing that damn leather jacket in August on Fort Benning in Georgia.

Magellan jotted notes in his small black notebook. Paul didn't have to read them to know they were full of random observations and tactical thoughts. He was always surprised by that kid's brain. But Paul learned not to let the glasses and relatively slight build fool him; Magellan was deadly on the battlefield.

D1 spotted Paul first.

"Evening, sir," D1 said to Paul, giving him a jaunty salute with one finger. "Beer?"

"Yes," Paul said. "Please."

D1 reached over and yanked a beer from the large bucket of ice at his feet.

"Long day, wasn't it, sir?" Magellan said.

"It surely was," Paul said, taking the beer from D1.

"What took you so long?" Kata said, standing up from her seat at the end of the table.

"Got hung up, is all," Paul said, opening the beer.

"Well," Kata said, walking over to Paul and holding her beer out to him. They knocked the cans together. "Better late than never, partner," she said.

They each took a large swallow of beer.

"The colonel is here," Kata added. "Said he had to go grab something. Not sure what. But he should be back soon."

"He's here?" Paul asked, startled. "Really?"

"Yeah," Kata said, puzzled by his surprise. "Why wouldn't he be?"

Paul nodded. He knew it was a good question. But he was overcome by the ache of familiarity and couldn't think straight.

"Sir, you made it!" Top called out as she rounded the corner.

Paul turned to see his first sergeant walking toward him in a black utility tank top and olive-green cargo pants. Her pants and boots were covered in mud, and she carried a large cooler.

Over six feet tall with broad shoulders, Top had the build of a professional basketball player. Her sandy-blond hair was pulled back into a thick braided ponytail that betrayed her Norse bloodline, as did the runic shield knot tattoos that covered the length of her arms.

She handed the cooler to D1.

"This thing is heavy," D1 said. "What's in it?"

"Vegetables," Top said.

"Thank God," Magellan said.

"Last time we did Chief's meat-only dinner, you guys nearly destroyed the latrines," Top said.

"That is the truth," Kata said, giving Paul a knowing glance.

"Well, I'm not having that again," Top said.

Top looked around the table, pointing at each soldier in turn as she said, "Everyone will eat their veggies this time!"

Grumbles ran through the table, but no one dared argue.

Top looked at D1 and said, "Would you mind taking a break from your posing and taking them over to Chief?"

"Roger that," D1 said, popping up from his seat and walking toward the fire with the cooler.

"Sir, your seat is over there at the head of the table," Top said to Paul, pointing.

Kata walked around to the other end, where she had been sitting.

Paul stepped behind his chair and looked around the table. All twelve of Alpha and Bravo Companies' leadership were there. Kata talked intently to her first sergeant at the other end of the table. Reynolds and Chamberlain argued with D3 and Mia about something stupid.

Emotion welled within Paul.

"Take one and pass them around," Chief said, stepping up to the table with an armful of plates.

He returned a minute later with a large coffee can full of forks, spoons, and knives and placed it in the middle of the table, along with a pile of napkins.

"We're ready, sir," Chief said to Paul. "I'm going to serve it all up at the fire when you give the word."

Chief gestured over his shoulder. The deer now hung on the edge of the fire, while the vegetables grilled on a large metal grate positioned over the flames. The aromas wandered over on the breeze. They smelled wonderful.

"At ease!" Top said.

Conversation at the table ceased.

"The floor is yours, sir," Top said with a smile, standing next to Paul.

All heads swung to look at him.

Paul fidgeted. He wanted to say how sorry he was. How heartbroken. But it didn't seem like the right time. He was frozen by emotion.

"Sir?" Top said. "Don't you want to say something to us?"

Paul opened his mouth, but he could not speak.

"Sir?" Top said, putting her strong hand on his shoulder.

Paul looked at Kata. Her smile had faded.

D1 crossed his arms in disappointment.

Chamberlain shook his head.

"Sir?" Top said again, this time shaking Paul's shoulder. "I need you to say something."

Paul struggled to focus on Top, but her face was fuzzy now.

She shook him again. "Sir!" she said in a loud voice. "Sir, I need you to say something."

The fire vanished, and night fell in an instant. Paul was freezing. It was dark and he couldn't see the table or anyone at it.

Top shook him again.

"Sir," she said. "Focus on my voice. Can you hear me? I need you to say something."

Paul opened his eyes.

He was floating in the *Odysseus*'s amputated bridge. It was cold. He could see his breath.

A large robot held him by the shoulders.

He blinked in disbelief.

It was a shorter version of Top. There was no advanced ceramic-composite armor and accompanying iridescence. She was all metal. But she was identical in features and slender but powerful proportions.

He knew it was her.

"There you are," she said in a familiar voice. "Can you hear me, sir?"

Paul's eyes widened as he tried to comprehend.

The void loomed behind his first sergeant.

Paul looked around to confirm for himself again that he was on the bridge. He spotted Althea floating a few arm lengths away, wrapped in blankets. She was motionless and her eyes were closed. Two soldierbots like the one in front of him held on to her.

The last thing Paul remembered was the tug engines giving out and weightlessness returning to the bridge. They'd wrapped themselves in blankets to share body warmth.

After a few cycles, it had been clear that Althea was not coming out of rest mode. Paul had kissed her on the forehead and bound himself to her with a few power cords before taking another hit of hibernation drugs and falling asleep for the last time.

But that was a long time ago, it seemed.

He looked at Top and then back to Althea with concern.

He tried to speak, but his voice croaked.

"She is fine," Top said. "She is in a deep rest-mode setting. We will be able to revive her aboard the ship."

Paul blinked. His eyes darted around.

"Here," Top said, holding a squeeze bottle in front of Paul's face. "Take a sip of water."

He opened his mouth, and she gave him a squirt of water.

It helped.

"I don't understand," he said.

"I know," she said. "But you will."

"How long?" Paul asked, his voice cracking again.

Top gave him another squirt of water as she said, "I don't know. But the mission clock over there says it's the six hundred and eleventh cycle. When did you cut loose from the *Odysseus*?"

"I'm not sure," Paul said. "Maybe four twenty? It's fuzzy."

"That sounds about right," Top said. "We detected a large explosion around then. Had us worried. Especially when the *Odysseus* didn't show at the rendezvous. We started a search pattern but had to be careful. We're supposed to be a lost ship, after all, and we're trying to stay that way."

Top started to unfold the blankets around Paul.

"It's a miracle we found you," she continued. "But whoever put you on this course knew what they were doing. You're right between where we were supposed to link up with the *Odysseus* and where we are going. Nonetheless, we were shocked to find this"—Top looked around the bridge and then back to Paul—"whatever you call this thing you are traveling in."

"But how are you here?" Paul asked, confusion and anxiety gripping him.

"The *Perseus*," she said, while waving an arm to beckon one of the other soldierbots.

"No," Paul said. "I mean, how are you alive?"

The other soldierbot handed Top a pressure suit. She opened it as Paul's anxiety increased.

"The maintenance boss," Paul said as the thought raced into his head. "The navigator. They were working for you? How did you…"

Top gently took the last blanket away from Paul's naked body. "Get into this pressure suit, please, sir," she said, pulling one of his legs into the suit, then the other.

"The maintenance boss and the navigator!" Paul yelled. Confusion started to suffocate him. Nothing made sense. Panic surged. "How did they know?"

He kicked his legs free of the pressure suit and pushed away from the first sergeant.

Paul floated away from her, his back toward the large window.

"Tell me what the hell is going on!" he yelled.

The other two soldierbots looked at Top, who was gesturing at Paul with her palms down, trying to exude calm.

"I will explain it all, sir," Top said in a reassuring voice. "But first I want to get both of you transferred to the *Perseus*. You've been drifting on this freezing wreck for too long. We'll get you warmed up and fed and flush the hibernation drugs out of your system. They are contributing to your agitation."

"You'll tell me now!" Paul shouted. He had drifted across the bridge, his back now against the large window. His naked body glowed pale against the black void.

Top regarded Paul for a moment and then said, "OK, but I don't have all the details."

Paul waited for her to speak, oblivious to the cold.

"Colonel Filson saved my memory sphere when he dove into the broken and dying pile of us," she began. "Somehow he got the sphere to Dr. Musashi, who got it smuggled on board the *Perseus*. The doctor used every trick, connection and bribe he could to get specifications, code, and other supporting Ōkami systems hacked into the *Perseus*'s factory so it could rebuild us on the way to the belt.

"We had just taken over the *Perseus* and were executing our plan when Dr. Musashi learned you were joining the crew of the *Odysseus*. He set in motion a scheme for us to rendezvous with the *Odysseus* so that we could get you back. I can only guess that it was the maintenance boss and the navigator you are talking about. The Doctor must have bent them somehow to our purpose."

"Why?" Paul asked in whisper.

"The doctor realized that he..." Top paused. "That we," she continued, "had been betrayed by Fiona Malloy. And that, at the age of ninety-two, he did not have long enough to protect and avenge his own. He entrusted that to you."

"But—but why?" Paul stammered again.

"Because you are our leader. He trusted you," she said. "He believed in you. We all do."

"But I failed," he whispered. "Do you remember what happened?"

Top nodded but said nothing.

"I'm so sorry…" Paul said.

"It's OK, Paul," she said. "I am much more interested in our next chapter."

# ACKNOWLEDGEMENTS

I started *Spirit of the Bayonet* with the simple goal of writing an engaging science fiction story. After wrestling with the semi-autobiographical material of my first book, I was excited to immerse myself in the genre I have loved since learning to read. As I got into it, though, I found myself wading into ideas that I've been thinking about for a while now: Ethical questions raised by military applications of artificial intelligence. The accelerating change in military life, culture, tactics, and service caused by technology. The ever-present, never-virtuous military-industrial complex. And that fundamental essence of military service that never, ever, ever changes.

Not allowing all that to drown the (hopefully) engaging science fiction story was a challenge. To the extent I have succeeded, it is because of my trusted and faithful band of beta readers. No indie writer has a better crew, period. Kirby Andrews, David Weinstein, Ted Miller, Jennifer and Dan Ruiz, Adam Parrish, Kevin Virgil, James Aiken, Anna Russ, Jean Russ, Mike Russ, Morgan Watson, and Russ Watson. Their encouragement, feedback, and tough love were invaluable and made *Spirit of the Bayonet* a better book. The remaining faults and shortcomings of the novel are entirely my own.

Finally, and always, I am grateful for my wife, Anna. This was her second time through my process. She didn't waver. She never does. I am so lucky.

*Ted Russ - December 2019*

# ABOUT THE AUTHOR

Ted Russ is a novelist, executive and entrepreneur that lives in the mountains with his wife, Anna, and their dog, Henry. In a prior life, he served as an army officer after graduating from West Point. He left the military after nine years of service in 2000 with experience as a special operations helicopter pilot and a philosophy degree. Possessing no marketable skills, he went back to school and got an MBA and now balances writing with his business career. *Spirit of the Bayonet* is book one of the *Ōkami Forward Trilogy* and his second novel.

If you want to know when book two of the *Ōkami Forward Trilogy* will come out, please visit his website at www.tedruss.com.

CPSIA information can be obtained
at www.ICGtesting.com
Printed in the USA
LVHW090255040920
665004LV00002B/18/J